THE JUDGE AT SAINT JANE'S

A gripping cozy murder mystery full of twists

LIS HOWELL

Suzy Spencer Book 4

Joffe Books, London
www.joffebooks.com

First published in Great Britain in 2022

This book is a work of fiction. Names, characters, businesses, organizations, places and events are either the product of the author's imagination or are used fictitiously. Any resemblance to actual persons, living or dead, events or locales is entirely coincidental. The spelling used is British English except where fidelity to the author's rendering of accent or dialect supersedes this.

Cover art by Dee Dee Book Covers

ISBN: 978-1-80405-207-5

For Arthur

AUTHOR'S NOTE

St Jane de Chantal
Patron saint of those separated from their children.

Born at Dijon, France, 28 January 1572; died at the Visitation Convent, Moulins, France, 13 December 1641.

Jane was well educated and from a noble French family. In 1592, she married the Baron Christophe de Rabutin-Chantal. Their marriage was happy and they had four children, though the baron wasn't faithful and his financial affairs were a mess. Jane took over the management of his estates and turned them around.

Her husband was killed in a hunting accident when she was 28, and she was forced to go and live with her father-in-law, who was a bully. He threatened to disinherit her children if she didn't run his estates for him. He must have seen the success she had made of her husband's properties. She lived a wretched life with him for seven years.

In 1604, while living in her father-in-law's household, Jane met the new Bishop of Geneva, Francis de Sales, and a friendship and collaboration ensued. Later they founded a religious order for women too weak, old or poor for the traditional religious life. Jane founded eighty-six houses of the

Visitation by the time of her death in 1641. She was beatified in 1751 and canonized in 1767. Her feast day varies but can be celebrated on 12 or 21 August.

CHAPTER ONE

And Deborah, a prophetess . . . she judged Israel at that time.
Judges 4:4

Deborah Arbiter paused to get her breath back after climbing up the ladder and out onto the roof. It was a glorious autumn evening. The sun was dipping down to the west in a silver-gilt ball. She gasped at how far she could see. She had lived in this country house for most of her life, but she had never been up on the roof.

Tarnfield Hill House, now the St Jane's Hostel for women, was at the head of the Tarn Valley, screened by a large fir plantation. It could only be reached by a single-track lane through the trees.

On the roof of the house you could see over the fir trees. Deborah felt growing confidence and peered around. She saw where the single-track lane became a bridle path cutting east over the fells towards Hadrian's Wall. Tarnfield village could be clearly seen below in the valley. To the west, the town of Norbridge was just a haze. Beyond, in the far distance, Deborah thought she could make out the thin silver rim of the Solway Firth.

Immediately beneath the house to the right she could see the top of Deborah's Tree — a large, healthy old chestnut with a wooden seat around its trunk, where she would sit with the women who now lived in her family home. There were six of them, and there was room for a seventh. She had been expecting someone from London who hadn't arrived, but Deborah had kept the room free for her. That was her prerogative as director. She had started this small hostel nearly forty years ago, when independent refuges for women were being set up all over Britain.

She breathed in the heady air and felt as well as she ever had in her life, though she'd celebrated her seventieth birthday only a few months earlier. No dizzy spells for a while, and the intoxicating air on the roof filled her with optimism. She was Deborah Arbiter, nicknamed 'The Judge' after Deborah in the Bible: activist, philanthropist and founder of St Jane's Hostel. A local legend.

Well, that was all very gratifying. But now she needed to find what she'd come for. She had a good head for heights, but this was risky. St Jane's roof was flat on top, like on many large Georgian houses. It sloped away gently to a stuccoed parapet around the building. Deborah thought it would be quite easy to edge down, feet first.

She could see that the ledge behind the parapet was wet and blocked with leaves. But that wasn't her problem today. With relief, she spotted what she had been looking for. The last of the sun picked up its metallic sheen. If she were careful, she would be able to retrieve it and scramble back up, and no one would ever be any the wiser. Slowly, she edged down.

But when her feet touched the parapet, it suddenly gave way, and the ground rushed up at her. Her head cracked on the masonry, and she was dead before her body had landed. The woman who found her screamed until she vomited; the others heard and came running. The sound of weeping and wailing echoed through the last of the golden autumn day.

* * *

At the same time, almost three hundred miles away, Euston Station in London was predictably busy. It was the Friday before the October school break. Suzy Spencer just missed tripping over someone's wheelie bag and going headlong. She looked up at the departures board. It told her that the train north to Cumbria was being 'prepared'. Unlike her. She was laden with bulging bags. She felt a flurry of panic — where was her ticket? Of course, the one on her phone would do. But she had a horrible feeling the phone might be flat — she'd left in such a hurry from the North London Academy of Journalism.

She had been working there as a visiting lecturer, aka human sacrifice, for a week. She had escaped as soon as possible after finishing a module called 'Practical Television Production'. She wasn't a lecturer, she was a freelance TV producer, but she always accepted any job which came along. This one had cropped up when a former TV colleague, now a professor, had called her with a plea disguised as an opportunity.

'It would be great experience for you, Suzy. I need someone to stand in for me, teaching a hands-on course, for a week in October. I've just been asked to give a paper at a conference in Naples that week. It's on emojis in communication. It should get a good response to the use of the colon.'

A gut reaction? But Suzy bit back the joke. Her ex-colleague wasn't famous for his sense of humour. She murmured, 'Fascinating.'

'Absolutely. You see how I can't miss this chance to give my paper.'

'So why ask me to stand in for you? Isn't there a proper academic available?'

'I want a working TV producer to do this — it's so much more meaningful for the students.' He went on: 'You could explain how programmes are developed, with your gift for blue-sky thinking.'

What blue sky? It wasn't Suzy who would be swanning round the Mediterranean. But she had just won an award for successfully transforming a daytime TV show from a tacky confession series into something quirkier. Maybe it was that which had made him think of her.

'And you'll find it very stimulating being with students. They'll love the fact you got a BATV award for *Living Lies*. A reality show! Who'd have thought it!'

Suzy put his rudeness down to envy, then took a deep breath and said yes. It might be interesting and would fit with a break between her contracts. Plus, a job was a job when you were freelance.

But now the work was done, and she was on her way home. She checked the departure board again. Not long to go. She always loved being in London. But she loved leaving it more. Home was a village called Tarnfield, near Norbridge in Cumbria, where the train on the way to Scotland would stop in around four hours' time. She shut her eyes and thought of the solid, double-fronted stone-built house called the Briars, which she shared with her husband Robert Clark.

When Suzy and Robert had met, she had been a broadcast journalist and a single mum, stuck in the village. Her first husband had decamped to Newcastle after their first wet winter in the country. Robert, on the other hand, was a childless widower who had lived in Tarnfield for years. He was ten years older than Suzy, and she had initially thought him dull and conventional.

But they had become the village 'odd couple', and they were happy together; though with Suzy's two children, now young adults, life had never been easy. Or cheap. Music and art courses, sports, driving lessons and, of course, trips, all cost money. Suzy paid, but Robert always helped. And he didn't seem to mind as the kids took over the house. They used up all the space in the small old-fashioned garage with their junk: bikes, skateboards, skis and snowboards. Suzy had tried to get them to clear it out so they could actually park the car there, but her daughter Molly had said snippily, 'Robert says it's okay. You couldn't get the car through those narrow doors anyway.' Suzy had met Robert when she drove into his fence, which caused Molly a lot of condescending amusement. Suzy's daughter was making a big issue out of learning to drive but the idea of Molly at the wheel filled Suzy with dread.

And on top of that, now Molly wanted to turn one of the attic rooms of the Briars into an art studio, which meant decorating and rewiring. More expense. At least Suzy's son Jake, now in his early twenties, was more independent, living in Durham, where he was doing a postgraduate course. Molly was in the lower sixth form at Norbridge High and still at home. But both kids thought of the Briars as the base camp for ever-increasing mounds of their stuff.

'Do you really want to try lecturing?' Robert had asked her. 'It's not as easy as it looks and there's a lot of admin . . .'

'I could give it a go.'

Suzy said nothing about the money being handy to pay for Molly's next school trip. She added, 'And it would give me a chance to stay with Rachel in London for a week.' Rachel was Suzy's best friend, a real urbanite, who thought Suzy was insane to live more than five minutes' stroll from an artisan coffee shop.

But now the lecturing job was over, Suzy could make up for being away so much, and she and Robert could spend time together. She wasn't due back at work on *Living Lies* for another week. Robert was a senior lecturer on the prestigious English Literature course at the University of Mid Cumbria in Norbridge, and it was 'reading week'. As for Suzy, all she had left to do was mark the students' assignments. Somewhere in the North London Academy of Journalism's academic management system there were twenty-five essays to assess on the new government report about the regulation of social media. It gave Suzy a headache just thinking about it.

She put that to the back of her mind. They would have a blissful week in Tarnfield — the glorious autumn colours, the first log fires, tidying the garden and planting some more bulbs, popping out to the pub for supper, reading, even doing a bit of flower arranging in the beautiful village church. Well, it would probably rain, and there was a crack in the Briars' chimney stack to see to. But it was home, and where she wanted to be. And Robert was the person she wanted to be with.

'Oops. Sorree.' Another wheelie bag lurched over Suzy's foot. She saw that the train was boarding. A wave of purposeful travellers was surging towards the platform and the ticket checkers. She did a quick check of her own: her overnight bag, the huge handbag which kept slipping off her shoulder, a tote bag of assorted stuff and the little backpack with, hopefully, her wallet, phone and car keys: all there. Phew.

And then her phone started ringing with that loud insistent ringtone which she'd been meaning to change for months. At least the battery wasn't flat. The ringtone reached a horrible climax. Suzy smiled pityingly, as if it belonged to someone else, and kept on going.

She was the last to arrive in the carriage. Of course, someone was sitting in her reserved seat. Suzy sighed. 'Excuse me, I'm sorry about this, but that's my seat.'

The pierced goth, with black eyes, blue mouth, and a cleavage she could park her broomstick in, stared at Suzy blankly, and then said, 'What?'

'That's my seat. Look, it says reserved, Euston to Norbridge.' Suzy's legs were aching. She had been standing for most of the day. 'There are other seats down there.'

'Why don't you take one, then?'

'Because I booked the table.'

The goth girl mumbled. 'I got here first. Why should I have to move?'

Because you didn't book a seat? Suzy thought, but there was no point in making a scene. She waited and smiled brightly. After a few seconds, the girl sighed noisily and got up. She grabbed her greasy burger box and reached up for her bag, showing a rough tattoo of barbed wire round her wrist. She pushed past the elderly man in the aisle seat, then elbowed Suzy out of the way before shambling off down the carriage.

Suzy settled into her window seat, plugged in her laptop on the table, and waited for the train to start. She loved travelling north at dusk, through Lancashire and the Lakeland fells. In Norbridge her Golf would be waiting in the long-term car park, and it was only fifteen minutes' drive to Tarnfield. Robert would be there as promised, with a fire burning, a bottle of wine opened and a cozy late supper. He had promised to cook — another family joke. A takeaway from the Star of Bengal again; he called it his signature dish. Suzy smiled. She loved cooking but was happy to share his sense of humour and a tikka masala from Tarnfield's only fast-food outlet.

The Victorian houses of Camden topped the steep cutting as if on the edge of a cliff as the train slowly moved out of London. This was near the area where she had been staying for the week. Her friend Rachel was also a television producer who now worked on political programmes. It had been great to see Rache, although the week had turned out to be busy, with needy students clamouring for Suzy's attention well into the evenings.

And Suzy had also been hoping to spend some time with another Islington contact, but Ellie Fox hadn't replied to her emails. That was a shame. Suzy would have loved to see Ellie again. They had met on a skiing holiday earlier in the year. Suzy had been drawn to Ellie's sense of humour and her excitement about a new stage in her life. She remembered Ellie's cheerfulness, her wide grin and her curly brown hair, which shook when she laughed. But you couldn't keep up with everyone.

Suzy yawned. She ought to log on, of course, but she suddenly felt exhausted. She shut her eyes. Then the maddening ringtone started again, and she scrabbled for the phone. It was Robert on voicemail. When she heard his message, her heart sank. 'Suzy, there's a bit of a parish crisis. I'll tell you about it later, but it looks like I'll be out till late. I'm so sorry, my love . . .'

* * *

In Tarnfield, Robert Clark had been sharing an early drink with Alan Robie, the other churchwarden. Alan had walked over to the Briars, which meant he could have his routine G&T. He was clearly agitated and asked for a double. Alan's voice still had the loud, cut-glass timbre of the country squire he would have liked to be, but he was a former solicitor. He had inherited his aunt's picturesque cottage in Tarnfield and moved there with his new partner Stevie Nesbit about a decade before. In the last few years Alan had gradually 'come out'. Not that his sexuality was a surprise to anyone in Tarnfield, although his new role as the local gay rights campaigner had been unexpected. But they should have known. Alan undertook everything he did with total commitment.

Stevie had been an actor before meeting Alan and had languished resentfully in the village for a few years. But recently he'd landed a part in a TV soap and was doing very well. After a difficult time, Alan and Stevie had settled down companionably.

And this was causing the latest parish crisis.

'I've put poor Linda in a terrible position,' Alan boomed, as he always did when embarrassed.

'Poor Linda' was the Reverend Linda Finch, who was the parish priest at All Saints, Tarnfield. She was much loved and had a growing congregation. There was a relaxed, accepting atmosphere in the church. So, when Alan had decided it was time for him and Stevie to exchange vows, he was sure Linda as vicar would find a way for All Saints to be involved. All Saints was a huge part of Alan's life. But it had given Linda a bit of a headache.

Robert sympathized. The official line of the Church of England was that marriage meant, by definition, the union between a man and a woman. So gay weddings were off the agenda.

Robert could see the logic of that, although it seemed hard on someone like Alan, who was in a more loving relationship than in many heterosexual church marriages. As with everything — when you knew the people involved you felt differently about the rules. But on a celebratory level, the Reverend Linda Finch had found a compromise which suited

Alan and Stevie very well. The Church acknowledged civil partnerships, and accepted that some people felt 'called' to be in loving same-sex relationships. So Alan and Stevie would have a civil partnership ceremony in Norbridge and then come to All Saints for personal prayers. Not a blessing — the Church was clear on that. But prayers were acceptable, and would be just for the two of them, followed by a party in the church hall for everyone from the village.

Then the plan had hit the buffers. The new Archdeacon of Workhaven had objected to Alan's party and had made his feelings clear in pretty brutal terms.

Alan boomed once more: 'This new archdeacon, the Venerable James Bentley, told Linda that her plan is gay marriage by another name and said it was out of order. But it's completely in line with the Church's policy. Anyone can hire the church hall and the prayers are a private matter. But he's so categorical! I even get the feeling he thinks I shouldn't be churchwarden!'

That would be a shame, thought Robert. Alan was diligent and dedicated, and people weren't queuing up to be on the Parochial Church Council of All Saints. He asked, 'But the Venerable James Bentley isn't the boss. That's the Bishop of Norbridge. So what can he do to Linda, our vicar?'

'Nothing, on the face of it. But James Bentley is the sort of person who throws his weight around.'

'And how did he find out about the party?'

Alan squirmed. 'Actually, I told him. I met him at that North Cumbria Council drinks do for local influencers last week. He seemed a good sort of chap, a bit macho, but in a rock star way, and I never thought he would be so narrow-minded. I didn't expect him to turn on Linda!'

'He must have been very forthright to upset her. She can usually cope with anything.'

'Yes, but he's one of these people with totally uncompromising views. And he's downright rude. He thinks he's God's gift. He calls himself the "Ven Jim"! And he rides a motorbike!'

Robert smothered a smile. 'So, what do you want to do about it?'

'I did have a bit of a brainwave. I think we should get Deborah Arbiter on the case.'

'Deborah's amazing, but she's got a lot on her plate. How would you involve her?'

'Well she's got a fantastic reputation, running that hostel for victims of domestic abuse, using her own money. She's a staunch Anglican and they don't call her the Judge for nothing. She could whip up support for Linda. Deborah's going to be at a civic lunch for community activists tomorrow. I could lobby her then. I've also taken the liberty of asking Linda to meet us at the vicarage this evening to talk through the whole situation.'

'This evening isn't great for me, Alan. Suzy's coming back from London.'

'But Suzy would be the first person to understand how urgent this is! Linda's very upset. She's actually talking about leaving Tarnfield. What would we do without her? We can't let her go over something like this. I need you on board, Robert.'

For the first time Robert felt genuinely worried. This was a crisis, not a storm in a chalice. They couldn't afford to lose Linda Finch as their vicar. 'Okay,' he said, 'I'll come with you. I'll drive.'

'Good man! I think we need to talk to Linda, make an evening of it, talk her round about leaving us. I'll pop home and get changed. I said we'd be at the vicarage at six thirty, sharp.'

'I'll pick you up at six twenty, then.' Robert said.

Which was just when Suzy's train would be speeding through Lancashire on its way north, Robert thought sadly. She would be coming home to an empty house and a parish crisis. Just what she didn't need.

CHAPTER TWO

Oh my Lord, if the Lord be with us, why then is all this befallen us?
Judges 6:13

On the train, Suzy woke suddenly, her mouth open and dry and her neck cricked. They were leaving Preston. She was glad she had woken in time to glimpse Morecambe Bay as twilight turned to night. The crowds on the train had thinned out a little — and the goth girl was nowhere to be seen. Suzy groped for the water bottle in her giant handbag; she felt better after a few sips. But she was exhausted. The week in London had proved that she was doing too much, though it had been good to stay with Rachel.

'Let's have supper out a couple of times,' Rachel had said. 'I want to know all about the latest, north of the Wall . . .' It was their in-joke.

Suzy retorted, 'Well *Game of Thrones* is better than Game of Zones.' Her friend lived in Zone One on the London Underground. Rachel said, 'Very funny. Remember to bring your own Oyster card for the Tube. We can hit the town. It will do you good.'

But in the event, they hadn't seen much of each other, which was a real shame because it was the second time in six months that their plans had been ruined. In the spring, Suzy had managed to arrange an evening at Rachel's before a news shift, but it had been spoiled when the air ambulance, a bright-red helicopter, had landed on the park behind Rachel's Islington loft apartment. They had watched it hover and come down, and then seen a stretcher being put on board. It was hard to have a gossip while that was going on. Suzy had left for work shortly afterwards, and their sociable evening had been abandoned.

As she sat on the train, Suzy ran her hand through her spiky, blonde-tipped hair, now with touches of grey. It was a mess. She hadn't had time for the hairdresser's — she had been so busy. Too busy. She needed to review her life.

Mentally she listed all the things she had been doing. Her main earner by a mile was *Living Lies,* which would go into production in another week's time in Manchester. As the executive producer, Suzy's routine was steady — four weeks based in Manchester for intense prepping, then a few weeks filming, and then the editing period. The show now ran for twenty-six weeks a year, in two thirteen-week seasons. The production company needed her, she was good at her job, and her role was relatively secure, thanks to winning the BATV. But of course it couldn't last forever. Sometimes she worried about what she would do when it came to an end.

So what else did she want to do? Something local and community-based would be good. Deborah Arbiter at St Jane's Hostel for women, at Tarnfield Hill, had approached her about communications work for them. Like many people in the area, Suzy found Deborah impressive. It would be interesting and worthwhile. She would say yes to that.

But what should she say no to? She would never try lecturing again. Leave that to Robert. Next for the chop was being the 'go-to person' for a media consultancy. The money was peanuts and the job too much hassle. She'd done it to 'build her profile', but the only thing her profile needed was a nose job. And there would be no more one-off production gigs or news shifts, which brought in added money but meant exhausting commuting or overnight stays.

And the travel writing would have to go. For the last few years Suzy hadn't had a holiday, but she had done reviews for a friend's website. She had taken the kids, which made good stills for the site, and it gave them discounted breaks. But Robert wouldn't come — he said he added nothing to the cute pictures and got in the way of her work. She missed him while they were away.

And, to be honest, the holidays were sometimes more trouble than they were worth. Like the one where she had met Ellie Fox. It had been a skiing trip earlier that year, in the French Alps. When Suzy had tentatively suggested it, the kids had jumped at it, even though Suzy feared her son Jake would be too old for a family holiday. But he and his sister Molly had had a brilliant time, teaming up with other young people in the new purpose-built chalet.

For Suzy it had been dire from the start. There had been heavy snow every day, making her feel cold and scared — what if there was an avalanche? Skiing, which she had loved before the children were born, felt very different twenty-five years later. And the night before they were due to fly home, drifting snow had blocked the flue from the chalet's heating system. They were all evacuated because of the danger of carbon monoxide poisoning and sent to the chalet's basement. The *pompiers* and paramedics had swarmed all over the place, but the guests couldn't go back to their rooms till morning.

Suzy had found herself wrapped in a duvet, sitting on a pallet, surrounded by a week's supply of vegetables. She had started talking to Ellie, one of the other guests, who was there on her own. They had bonded quickly in the crisis.

'This is a crazy adventure. I love skiing,' Ellie had said. 'I had to get away from London and I got a last-minute holiday here. I've had a brilliant time, even with this mess. But now I have to go back to Islington.' Ellie had pulled a face.

'Really?' said Suzy 'Whereabouts? My best friend lives there.'

Ellie worked in insurance and lived on the Barnford Estate, a block of flats near to Rachel's converted loft. But she wasn't looking forward to going back. When she went home, Ellie was determined to break off with her lover of five years. After a couple of increasingly surreal hours swapping life stories, Ellie had confided to Suzy that her relationship was seriously difficult. She had begun to realize she was being controlled and used, and she hinted that she suspected her lover of some sort of dubious business dealings. She had to escape and was determined to do it. She had booked the skiing holiday alone and made the first steps in a final break. Ellie had wanted to talk; but looking back, Suzy was hazy about the conversation — she'd begun to have a bad headache. She had eventually nodded off as Ellie talked. Then the reps had come bustling in, getting them back to their rooms to pack before they left for the airport.

Suzy hadn't heard from Ellie again, but the week before going to work at the Academy of Journalism, she had sent Ellie a couple of tentative emails suggesting they should meet while Suzy was in London. But Ellie hadn't replied. Which was a shame, as meeting Ellie had been good. But overall, for Suzy, the skiing trip had been a bad experience and the carbon monoxide was the last straw. Whether it was the stress or the whiff of the gas, by the time they had got back to the UK the next day Suzy felt as though mountain ogres had been beating anvils in her head.

So there would be no more travel journalism. She had a lot to keep her happy at home.

The train laboured through the narrow gorge below Shap Fell. It grew darker.

* * *

In Tarnfield, Robert backed his car onto the track outside the Briars, where Suzy had crashed her car into his fence and his life years before. He had been a widower when they had met, and he had been lonely, despite his busy life. His first wife had been a powerhouse in Tarnfield, a mainstay of the village, but she'd had a nervous energy, an echo of her past. Robert liked tradition, but from his own experience he knew that sticking to a rigid moral code could cause misery. He had no trouble accepting that things change, and, despite his quiet manner, he could be forceful when needed. He had always supported Alan Robie where others had raised their eyebrows, or even their voices, at the thought of a gay churchwarden. Now, though, Alan was accepted as a crucial member of the church council.

Alan was waiting for Robert on the doorstep, ready to go to the vicarage. 'Stevie's not here tonight; he's on the set till tomorrow,' Alan said as he got into the car.

'How does he feel about all this?'

'I haven't mentioned it yet. But he's used to homophobia. More than I am, truth be told. The new archdeacon's attitude has really shocked me.'

Robert understood how hurt Alan felt. Not only was it vital that the Reverend Linda Finch stayed in Tarnfield, but it was also important that they tackled Archdeacon Bentley — about his manner if not his views. Even if it ruined the start of Robert's precious week with Suzy. She had been working away far more this year, and it had started to worry him. He was aware of how frustrated Alan's partner Stevie Nesbit had become with village life, until he landed the acting job in Leeds. Did Suzy feel the same, now the children were older? Is that why she grabbed every shift in the big city she could?

He and Suzy needed to talk, but now it would have to wait until tomorrow. He did a neat three-point turn onto the main road. It was a short drive to the vicarage. He saw flashing lights cut through the twilight towards them, as two police cars and an ambulance raced towards Tarnfield Hill.

'I wonder what that's about?' he said to Alan.

'Could be something up at St Jane's. But never mind that, Robert. What are we going to say to Linda?'

* * *

Suzy was home by nine thirty. She parked on the track outside the Briars. Molly was staying over with a friend in Norbridge for the weekend; the house was in darkness. Suzy got out and stood for a moment in the lane. It was cold now, with a hint of winter. There was a slight tang of woodsmoke on the air, the smell she always associated with Cumbria.

The peace was fractured by her stupid ringtone. It had rung several times when she was driving. Probably another message from Robert. The signal could be erratic on the train. She would answer it when she was in the house, where the kitchen would be cozy; she could sit there and relax with a glass of wine, by herself. Or not quite by herself: Flowerbabe, Molly's aging and crabby cat, named after a once favourite doll, commandeered the cozy spot in front of the range. Suzy gathered up all her baggage, struggled up the path, opened the front door and put on the light.

The house was just the wrong side of room temperature. She dropped her bags and walked through to warmth of the kitchen. It was a striking room, but it seemed a little grimy and old-fashioned after Rachel's state-of-the-art cooking lab in N1. Two glasses had had been left on the draining board along with a plate. Robert's jacket had gone, but his scruffy tweed cap, which Suzy hated, was still hanging on the peg by the back door.

There was a bottle of red wine opened on the table, a packet of cheese straws (Robert's idea of canapés) and a note: '6pm Friday. Have gone with Alan to the vicarage. Back as soon as I can. Tried phoning again, but the train must have been in the hills . . . Have a drink! See you soon. Rx.'

The stupid ringtone pealed, and she took it. Voicemail. It would be Robert.

But it wasn't. 'Suzy, it's Joanne Butcher. The administrator at St Jane's Hostel at Tarnfield Hill.' There was a pause which gave Suzy long enough to think, *This sounds bad.* There had been a catch in Joanne Butcher's voice.

'Please phone me, Suzy. Deborah Arbiter has had a terrible accident. She fell from the roof of the hostel. She's dead.

The police have gone now. I'm ringing you because we're worried about the press, and I know Deborah talked to you about communications work. Can you call me back? You're the only person I know who can help us with this.'

Suzy felt cold to her bones. Deborah Arbiter was a local celebrity, with a big following and a great reputation. Suzy took a deep breath and pressed call-back. The administrator answered straight away. Her voice was distressed but crisp.

Joanne Butcher told Suzy that Deborah had gone up to the roof of the hostel without telling anyone, while the residents had been having their usual Friday meeting. One of the women had been outside and had seen Deborah fall. She had screamed; the others had come out and run over to the chestnut tree, which dominated the grounds where Deborah had landed. They had called the ambulance and the police.

Suzy said, 'That is terrible, Joanne. Ghastly. I'm so sorry.'

'Yes. We're devastated.'

'But why did she go up to the roof?'

'She'd been worried about a leak. The roofer came on Wednesday to look at it and left the ladder in place while he finished another job in Tarnfield. He was due back here on Monday to do the work. He says he warned Deborah against going up there to look, but you know what she was like. She must have slipped down, and the parapet couldn't hold her and collapsed.'

'People are going to ask questions about this. There'll be a lot of local interest.'

'Which is why we need you, Suzy. We're going to have to put out a statement. We need to get the tone right. Deborah had a high profile round here, but she was controversial, as you know. There will be some people who think she got what she deserved, climbing onto a roof at her age.'

Too true, Suzy thought. Deborah Arbiter was a feminist; not everyone's cup of tea by any means. People might say she was overconfident and reckless. The local press would be all over this.

Suzy said, 'I'll do everything I can to help. The hostel is off the beaten track and I doubt the police will have put out a statement yet. It will probably be tomorrow before you need to worry about journalists. Just sit tight and refuse to comment if anyone calls. I'll come over first thing.'

Suzy needed to gather her thoughts. She was starting to feel the shivers of shock herself. She made some coffee, and while waiting for Robert to come home she googled everything she could find about Deborah Arbiter. Locally at least, this would be a big story.

* * *

Robert came back at around eleven. He had taken the vicar, Linda Finch, to St Jane's when they had heard the news about Deborah. The hostel had a close relationship with the church, and Linda was their chaplain. When he came home, he and Suzy sat in the Briars kitchen, nursing glasses of whisky. After talking about Deborah's death, Robert went through the events of his evening.

'Things were going pear-shaped even before we heard about the accident at the hostel. Alan came round here this afternoon in a real state. We went to see Linda because she's had a big row with the new Archdeacon of Workhaven.'

'Really? I can't imagine the vicar having a row with anyone.'

'It was about the plans for Alan and Stevie's party. Alan was daft enough to tell the archdeacon how accommodating Linda had been, but it backfired. Alan desperately wants some sort of church element in his celebration. Linda has worked on a compromise, but it's taken the diplomatic skills of a UN ambassador.'

'Linda is so good at that.'

'Exactly. But the new archdeacon seems seriously homophobic and is badmouthing Linda. That's why Alan and I went round to the vicarage. But we'd only been there about half an hour when Joanne Butcher called from St

Jane's with the news about Deborah's death. That trumped everything. I took Linda up there, but she didn't want to drive. She'd had a drink with Alan. Fortunately I'd stayed on the tonic.'

Suzy and Robert sat in silence for a minute before going up to bed. Deborah's death had put their world out of kilter. Robert soon slept, but Suzy was restless, her mind careering. Her troubled dreams featured red ambulance helicopters and skiing runs. And the woman she had met while skiing, Ellie, talking of fear in a chalet basement. Where had that thought come from? When Suzy woke in the night, for some reason she couldn't get Ellie out of her mind. But it was Deborah who had fallen to her death . . . not Ellie. Why was Suzy connecting the two?

Suzy felt worse than when she had gone to bed. She managed to get back to sleep, but only for a few hours.

* * *

At St Jane's the next morning, overtired but buzzing, Suzy sat in the office, a large, bright room with a full-length window looking out onto the drive. It had two desks with workstations, a sofa, easy chairs and a coffee table, plus a heavy Edwardian sideboard with a scratched surface which had presumably been side-lined to the office. Everything else about St Jane's was light and elegant.

Joanne Butcher said, 'It was good of your husband to drive Linda Finch here last night. She's a wonderful chaplain, so sensitive with the residents. Of course, after the shock, they mainly wanted to know if the hostel would have to shut.'

Joanne was in her late fifties, Suzy guessed, and had a drawn-looking, anxious face, though she looked slim and fit, almost muscular, in her fitted active wear.

'And will it close?' Suzy asked.

'There's no reason to think so. We have a decent board of trustees. Deborah's irreplaceable, of course, but she always said she would leave us well off, with an emergency fund.

And the charity owns all the property outright. Plus we have money from renting out the cottages.'

'The cottages?'

'Yes. There are two cottages around the back, outside the main wall. Our handyman, Geoff Black, and his wife live in one, and we have a tenant in the other, an American man who pays more than the going rate for the peace and quiet.'

'Doesn't it upset the residents, to have men around?'

'They rarely see them. Geoff is in his early seventies, but still very fit. He's been here for years. He was fully vetted by Deborah. The American has only been here a few months but he has impeccable references. He's researching his family history and wants seclusion to work. The cottages are completely separate from the hostel on the other side of the perimeter wall, which is security-alarmed. And it's not easy to let property out here. We're glad to have the money.'

'But who will run the place now? Deborah was such an icon. The local press will want to know how you'll carry on.'

Joanne pursed her thin lips. 'I can go on managing but I'm certainly not up for the director's job myself. I don't get involved with the counselling and therapy side, except for making the appointments. I came here first as a resident, and Deborah saw my potential as an administrator. I'm secretary to the board too, and I get a small salary. And a room. That's all I want.'

'They're lucky to have you.'

'That's kind of you. I can cope with most things, Suzy, but not with the press.'

Deborah's death had been the lead story on the local radio's eight o'clock breakfast news, a short, stark item from the police. Suzy thought the immediate media feeding frenzy might peak with the Saturday bulletins, but interest was bound to grow. And there would be an inquest. They needed to think ahead.

'For today, we need to draft a short statement and maybe do some interviews. Later, we'll need to write an up-to-date life of Deborah and be prepared for requests for an obituary and features about her. Who's chairman of the hostel's board of trustees?'

Joanne paused. 'It used to be the old Archdeacon of Workhaven. We all thought that the new archdeacon would take over. But he had some issues with Deborah.' *Ah*, thought Suzy. This would be the same archdeacon who was causing difficulties for the Tarnfield vicar, Linda Finch. The Venerable James Bentley.

Joanne said, 'So we have an acting chair. It's the area dean.'

Suzy nodded. She knew the area dean, Neil Clifford. He was a good man. Then she paused, but she had to ask the next question.

'You are sure, aren't you Joanne, that this was an accident? If the police have any suspicions, we need to be ahead of the game.'

'It most definitely was. Deborah would never have taken her own life. And she would never let St Jane's get unwelcome attention. Also, she seemed very happy. Things were going well. She'd mentioned that we would soon have a lot to celebrate. Although I did tell the police she'd been suffering from dizzy spells.'

'Dizzy spells?'

'Yes. She thought it might be something to do with low blood pressure. She was going to go to the surgery this week.'

'Could the dizziness have made her fall?'

'Possibly. It wasn't serious. But worth mentioning.'

'Or could somebody have pushed her, and then sneaked down?'

'Not without us seeing. Anyone from outside would need to be buzzed in by me. Then they would have had to come down from the roof through the house, and out of the front or back door, both of which are in view from the chestnut tree. I can account for everyone. We don't have any domestic staff wandering about. Deborah liked to run the place like a commune.'

Then Joanne looked at her watch. 'Look, Suzy, I must get on. I've got the residents to think about. Most of us haven't slept much and there's a lot of tension after the police questioning. Not to mention delayed shock and grief. I'm trying to get in touch with the therapists we use for counselling. And the GP again.'

'Okay, Joanne. I'll start with writing this press statement. Just one other thing . . .'

'I'll do whatever I can to help, Suzy.'

'Could I meet the residents? It's hard to communicate a sense of the place if I don't know who it is that you're helping. I appreciate the need for security. But could you trust me?'

Joanne looked uncomfortable. 'I'll ask them. But I'm warning you that some of our residents have a very dim view of journalists.'

Who doesn't? Suzy thought. This job was going to be tougher than she had anticipated. And she wondered how the press really would react. Joanne seemed certain this was an accident. But a seventy-year-old woman prowling around on a roof to inspect a leak didn't sound like the responsible behaviour of the person they called the Judge. There was something odd about this, Suzy thought.

She wouldn't be the only journalist asking questions.

CHAPTER THREE

Her wise ladies answered her, yea, she returned answer to herself.
Judges 5:29

At the same time, Robert was at the vicarage renewing the conversation with the vicar. Deborah's death was a tragedy which had stunned them, but they still had another major crisis with Archdeacon James Bentley. As Alan Robie had said, Jim Bentley seemed determined to make his mark, forcefully. In the Church hierarchy, the archdeacon came under the Bishop of Norbridge, though every archdeacon had their own patch. So the bishop was Bentley's boss, but the Ven Jim was influential. And although he was new to the job, his forthrightness gave him clout.

On the other hand, the vicar of Tarnfield, Linda Finch, had a much more nuanced approach. She was a small, dark-haired woman with a slight Cumbrian accent and an unobtrusive manner. A widow herself before being ordained, her own tragedy had strengthened rather than undermined her faith, so parishioners — and others — going through difficult times found her a great support. She was kind, hard-working and down to earth.

It was unsettling to see Linda so unhappy. She was sitting with her coffee going cold, looking into space. She turned slowly back to Robert. 'Of course, I should be thinking about all those poor people who are so upset about Deborah, not my own problems. But I keep remembering things Archdeacon Bentley said about Alan's party.'

'How angry was he?'

'Oh, outraged. He's from the evangelical wing of the Church. Usually they're good people, but they can be a bit uncompromising about matters of sex. Why they worry about it so much, I don't know. Jim Bentley can't see that I'm just doing my best for Alan, out of love. And realism. We depend on Alan.'

'Can't we just ignore Bentley?'

'Not really.' Linda sighed. 'He's on the patronage board of All Saints.'

'Really? The board which appoints the vicar? That makes him quite significant. Why him?'

'Well, it goes back to the Arbiters, who were big benefactors.'

'The Arbiters?' Robert was surprised.

'Yes. You know that they were very wealthy and important, and big supporters of All Saints. But they were also very evangelical. They insisted on having the Archdeacon of Workhaven on the recruiting panel for Tarnfield vicars. Workhaven has always been a bustling working-class port, and their archdeacons are traditionally evangelical, from the Low Church wing.' She sighed.

The Arbiters had fingers in every Tarnfield pie, Robert thought. He was good on local history. He knew the family had made a fortune in mining the haematite ore from Tarnfield Fell in the nineteenth century. They were incomers, who developed the mines and exported the ore from the industrial port of Workhaven. With their newfound wealth they had become bigwigs in the local church and had bought the country house at Tarnfield Hill from local gentry. The house was lovely and in an amazing setting. From the roof the panorama would be stunning. On a day like yesterday, he could see why Deborah had been tempted to go up there for a look through the skylight. But not out onto the roof. That was crazy.

Now, like Linda, he was in danger of staring into space, which would get them nowhere. Better get back to the point. 'It would be a disaster for us if you left All Saints, Linda.'

'The Venerable Jim Bentley doesn't seem to think so. He's not the sort of person to let things go. I imagine I'll be under scrutiny with every funeral and baptism from now on.'

'He might make your life uncomfortable, but he can't fire you. You have tenure. The Parochial Church Council trusts you completely. And surely the Bishop of Norbridge wouldn't want you to go? I know you get on well with her. This isn't the time to consider leaving us. We need you. You're our parish priest, Linda.'

Linda Finch looked at him for a moment, and then shook her head as if to clear it. 'Yes of course. I've been so blindsided by Bentley that I've stopped thinking straight. But you're right. Whichever way this plays out, Alan and Stevie are my parishioners and need my support. They're having a civil partnership ceremony in Norbridge in December. That means the world to Alan, and I must acknowledge that.'

'Can't you work around it? Do something that even Bentley can't object to?'

'Maybe. They could have the ceremony in Norbridge, and then have the party a few days later. I could pray for them privately in church at another date. There's no way that would look remotely like a gay marriage.'

'That sounds good. Alan might be disappointed, but he'd understand. And I'm sure Stevie won't mind. Mention "village people" to Stevie, and he doesn't think of Tarnfield.'

The vicar laughed for the first time in a while. 'Good thinking. I'll speak to Alan at church tomorrow; then, seeing that the archdeacon brought up the issue, I'll write to him telling him what we're going to do. I'll copy the email to the

Bishop of Norbridge herself. Maybe things aren't as bad as they look. Thanks Robert.'

* * *

At St Jane's Hostel, Joanne came back to the office to see how Suzy was getting on with the press inquiries about Deborah's death.

Suzy told her: 'I've already done a phone interview with Radio Cumbria and talked to the *Mid Cumbria Times* for their website. I checked our official statement with your acting chair, Neil Clifford the area dean. We need to email it to anyone and everyone. But we need some images for websites and TV . . .'

Joanne clicked on publicity pictures of Deborah on the office PC. The most recent showed her with thick dark hair, without a trace of grey, neatly pulled back into a glossy bun. It had been taken five or six years earlier when Deborah was in her mid-sixties, and she looked every inch the mature, shrewd woman that she was. She was wearing a dark suit and a plain, dark-purple silk blouse. An earlier one showed her with fuller, curlier hair, wearing a lilac shirt dress. In another picture Deborah was wearing court shoes, a bright indigo top and a short leather skirt, with a chunky pink-and-purple necklace. She looked smart and original, with luxuriant locks and a full-lipped smile.

'She never wore make-up, except for a pale lipstick. Very high-end. And she never put on weight. She could even take sugar in her coffee! And there's this photo as well,' said Joanne. 'It's a print. She kept it even though it was just a snap. You can see why . . .'

Suzy looked at the much-fingered old photo with its curly edges, which Joanne took out of a yellowing envelope. Deborah was sitting under the tree in the grounds looking thoughtful. Her arm was draped gracefully over the back of the bench beneath the branches. She had a purple pashmina on, like a shawl. Her black hair was loose and long, and around her head was a thin band of cloth, hippy style. Suzy guessed the snap came from the eighties, when Deborah had started the hostel.

'Gosh yes,' said Suzy. 'She certainly liked purple, didn't she?'

'Her favourite colour. I think she was posing like that for a bit of fun! Deborah had quite a sense of humour and didn't take herself too seriously . . .'

'Well, she does look just like an Old Testament prophet. Deborah from the Book of Judges!'

'Yes. And Arbiter means "judge", doesn't it? It's a Jewish-American name originally. Deborah certainly has that look. Her forebears came to England from the States in the nineteenth century, keen on prospecting and mining. It's the opposite route across the Atlantic to most emigrant stories!' Joanne spoke easily and knowledgeably. She had obviously known a great deal about her charismatic boss. *She must be devastated by Deborah's death*, thought Suzy, but she was still holding everything together.

'Maybe that explains Deborah's interest in the Old Testament judge who shared her name.'

'Well, she was very keen on the comparison. And of course, our Deborah had been an up-and-coming lawyer in London before she started the hostel. It was some clever Norbridge journalist who called her "The Judge" back in the eighties.' Joanne suddenly looked worried. 'Oh . . . talking of journalists, they won't come out here in person, will they?'

'No, I don't think so.' The local press had shown respect for the hostel, promising to keep quiet about its exact location, and to work through Suzy. The nationals would be a different matter, but Suzy thought this might go under their radar. No need to alarm Joanne, who looked paler and more strained than earlier. Keeping the residents calm was clearly stressful.

There was a knock on the office door; Joanne looked surprised. 'Yes?'

A young woman, hair in a caterer's net, wearing a large shapeless overall, said in a flat grumpy voice, 'I thought you might like some coffee.' She seemed surprised at herself.

'Thank you, Chelsea, that's very considerate of you.'

'That's all right.' The girl sniffed. 'That coffee machine of yours is an effin' antique, though. Talk about past it!' Her manner was confrontational for no reason, like a bad habit.

Suzy waited for her to leave. 'I thought you said you didn't have any staff?'

'We didn't until last night when Chelsea arrived. I'd finally persuaded Deborah to take on someone to help with the more routine catering. I didn't want to spoil the commune atmosphere, but there were times when things didn't get done. You can imagine.'

Suzy nodded sympathetically. Deborah might not have noticed mundane things like grease and dust in the kitchen, but Joanne was tougher on the practical side of things.

'And we could provide a young woman with a room and board and give her an opportunity. Chelsea came to us from Stoke on Trent, after we advertised online through a special website. She was a runaway who ended up in a hostel there, but she'd done a catering course. She looked a sight when she turned up, but I had a word with her, and she took it quite well. It was awful for her, arriving in the middle of all this. What a time to start. Poor girl.'

There was something familiar about the girl's face and manner, Suzy thought. But she couldn't put her finger on it.

* * *

Across the grounds, the handsome Texan who rented one of the two cottages next to St Jane's Hostel looked out of his bedroom window. Between the cottages and the hostel to the right was a high brick wall. In front of the cottages on the steep downward slope there was a thick plantation of fir trees. Typical of your British landowner, he thought, to build labourers' cottages in one of the most glorious parts of the county and then cut off the view. But Jarrold McHugh was taller than the average nineteenth-century British labourer, and if he stood up straight and stretched, looking out of his front bedroom window with his binoculars, he could see beyond the firs to the village of Tarnfield.

The cottages must have been cramped for the large families of those days, and the amenities basic. Outside there was still an obsolete 'netty', as the estate agent had called the toilet in the yard. But Jarrold guessed those labourers would have been grateful for any accommodation. He had often wondered about the British working class who had stayed behind, when more adventurous pioneers like his forebears had gone west. Jarrold McHugh was fiercely proud of his American upbringing.

Yet there had always been this pull towards England which he'd tried to fight. He'd visited London many times before. But now, here he was in the depths of the north, which was new for him — in a chocolate-box stone-built country cottage.

He'd come to look at the place one beautiful day in the spring. Geoff Black, handyman to the hostel, had been working in his front garden, digging aggressively, but when Geoff stood up, Jarrold realized the man was older than he looked.

'Hi there!' Jarrold had said. He pointed at the 'To Let' sign. 'So, who does this real estate belong to? And why all this security? It's like the National Trust meets Alcatraz.' He'd said 'National Trust' with an exaggerated upper-class English accent, which made Geoff Black smile. But immediately afterwards Geoff's face went blank.

Eventually Geoff said dourly, 'The big house is the hostel. St Jane's.'

'Oh yeah? What sort of hostel?'

'Why don't you call the letting agents if you're interested?' Geoff had said shortly.

'I think I'll do just that.' Jarrold didn't mention that he'd already started the process to rent the cottage. It was perfect for him, off the beaten track but in exactly the right location. Jarrold had no desire to become part of anything. If anyone asked, he was happy to tell them he was here investigating his family history, taking it as seriously as a paid job, and needing to conserve his time and space.

But to save himself from getting stale, he wanted to have at least one other recreational interest apart from his work. He had picked music. Jarrold was a singer, a good tenor with musical knowledge and expertise. He was highly intelligent, and he did everything thoroughly and well. His plan was to work in the cottage in the morning, then walk the fells in the afternoon. He was deeply into fitness. But he needed something more. At Rice University in Houston he'd been in the chamber choir, and once he'd even had the opportunity to sing in England on a cathedral tour, but he'd been a student with attitude and had turned down the chance.

But now, with his usual single-mindedness, once he'd arrived in Cumbria he had started to look for a music course online. He'd done some shape-note singing back in the States and was interested in folk singing. But he had the church and classical interest too. He'd found an outreach course at the University of Mid Cumbria: *Folk music and its links to part songs, church music and madrigals. A fascinating insight with practical exercises and online singing. Video. Tutor: Dr Paula Stovey.*

He had liked the idea of practical exercises with Dr Paula, who looked pretty fit herself from her biography and pictures. He didn't want to get involved in a face-to-face choir, but Paula's online course fitted the bill. Just bonkers British enough to amuse him. He could keep his face in a soft-focused wide shot and opt out if the course made him feel too exposed. And he wanted some distraction from the job in hand, as long as he was in control.

Jarrold supposed his growing friendship with Dr Stovey came into that category. A distraction. Funny how women fell for him, but there was the nagging suspicion that she was special, not the usual pushover. She was seriously good looking, cool and independent. More of a challenge. He liked that.

And he didn't want to be a total recluse. He also wanted to be friendly enough to suss out his nearest neighbours. Once his tenancy was sorted out, he'd gone back and banged on Geoff Black's door. His wife had looked at Jarrold suspiciously. 'Can I help you?'

He'd given one of his rare smiles and it had the usual effect. He saw her melt and tentatively smile back.

'Yeah. I'm renting the cottage next door from next week. Are you guys around? I thought if we were going to be neighbours it would be good to say hi.'

Moira Black had called a bad-tempered Geoff and they had sat in the garden with a cup of tea. Jarrold had explained that he'd made money in IT in the States but had taken a break and come to Britain to research his family. An ancestor had been called Arbiter. It was originally an American name, he told them, but it was obscure, and he wanted to dig into it.

Moira had said, 'Well, you should introduce yourself to Deborah Arbiter. She's the last one around here.'

'Hey, I guess if she's going to be my landlady I ought to reach out to her.'

The look on Geoff Black's face said, *Reach out? Your hand might get bitten.* But the handyman said nothing.

Now, this Saturday morning, Jarrold moved away from his window. He had seen the police cars and the ambulance the evening before and kept away. After a while, he had called Mrs Butcher at the hostel, and she had told him the news. Deborah Arbiter was dead.

He went downstairs, turned to his Apple Mac and clicked on 'The Arbiter Files'. The light from the screen lit up the curtained room.

* * *

At the big house, Joanne was back in the office with Suzy. 'I've got the GP here again, and two counsellors. They're seeing the residents now.' She paused. 'Maybe after lunch you could meet the women if they agree. Especially if you're going to be here a lot.'

Am I? Suzy thought. 'Okay. But I'd like some fresh air. Would it be a problem if I walked round the grounds?'

'I think I'd better come with you,' Joanne said. 'It might upset the women if they see a stranger wandering about. Some of them have been frightened for their lives. They're paranoid about publicity. They don't know you and they might think you're from the tabloids. Or the police.'

Suzy followed Joanne through the kitchen. Deborah Arbiter certainly hadn't been short of funds. The kitchen was large, light, modern and well appointed. The coffee machine was the oldest thing on view, but it was the best brand. Chelsea the new domestic must have been impressed, Suzy thought. Perhaps that was why she had to find something to criticize.

The hostel was at the top of a steep track, but the high wall which went all the way around made a clear separation between the grounds and the rise of Tarnfield Fell behind. The immediate area around the house was gravelled and free of foliage or outbuildings. 'No sheds or bushes where anyone could lurk,' Joanne said.

The security had been very carefully thought through. Outside the imposing front door, steps dropped down to the gravelled drive, and there was one large rose-bed in front of the house. The drive then split a lush lawn and curved down to the big wrought-iron gates, in line of sight from the hostel doors.

On either side of the gates, on the inside of the original red-brick wall, there was an impenetrable hawthorn hedge along the wall's length, about two feet deep. There was a discreet alarm system along the top of the wall. And in the unlikely event of anyone getting over, they would land in the hedge.

'Who does the gardens?'

'Geoff Black. I told you about him earlier. He and his wife Moira live in one of the cottages.'

‘Was he here yesterday?’

‘No. They’re away this weekend visiting their daughter and grandkids. He’s often away. He works down south sometimes. He does stuff for a couple of builders.’

‘Where are the cottages?’

‘They’re outside the perimeter wall at the back of the grounds, towards the right. You can just see the roofs over there. There’s a little old door through the wall, but it’s got a keypad now, and you need a code.’

‘So how do legitimate visitors get in?’

‘You can only get into the hostel through the security gates at the end of the drive; you need to either have the code or phone through to the house. It’s quite difficult to find the place if you don’t know it. Satnav doesn’t work terribly well at this end of the valley, and it’s single-track to the main road, so cars can’t come and go quickly.’

‘The security is amazing. Deborah spared no expense, did she?’

‘She was very generous, and she knew that the residents needed to feel totally safe. The women here are survivors of some awful things. The hostel was Deborah’s life, and the residents were her family.’

To the right side of the house, with a bench around it, was a large chestnut tree. Deborah’s Tree. In the Old Testament, the Judge, Deborah, had sat under a tree to give her verdicts. As Joanne had explained, in the eighties a smart local journalist had used a picture of Deborah sitting under the tree and called her ‘The Judge’ from the Bible. Not everyone would get the reference, but Deborah was thrilled.

As they walked back up to the house, Suzy pointed to a small but open arch, grotto-like and made of stone, on the other side of the chestnut tree. In it was a statue.

‘And is that St Jane?’

‘Yes, it certainly is.’ Joanne pursed her lips. ‘Deborah put the statue here, discreetly, for people to come to, privately, for prayer or contemplation. But everyone can see it, we have no secret nooks or crannies here. People think St

Jane's is a made-up name, but she really existed and lived in the French Alps. Deborah loved that part of the world. She didn't often have holidays but every two or three years she would go to Savoy.'

For a second Suzy felt as if someone had walked over her grave. Shivery and anxious. It must be overtiredness and too much of Chelsea's coffee. Just when she had been dreaming of that terrible French skiing holiday and that weird night in the chalet basement with Ellie. Something was tugging at the back of her mind . . . but she was muddling dreams and reality.

She pulled herself back to planet earth. Joanne was talking about how Deborah had found the statue of the saint languishing in a French antique shop. It was one of those local stories everybody in Tarnfield knew, including Suzy. Apparently, the hostel had originally been called just that — 'The Hostel'. But when she found the statue, Deborah saw it as a portent and changed the name.

Suzy looked at the saint. She seemed to be smiling. She looked middle-aged, plump and friendly. Dressed in a black nun's habit, she was holding a sacred heart.

Joanne gazed at St Jane. 'Deborah brought that statue back from France in a van. It cost a fortune. It used to have rather a beautiful silver halo with a lovely motto, but it must have worked loose and come away in September's storms. The wind would have blown right through the little arch. It must have rolled away somewhere. But we can't find it. Deborah was upset about that.'

'The weather was really violent then, I remember.'

'Yes, it was the same storms that led to the leak on the roof.'

'And caused the crack in our chimney breast at the Briars. I can see how it might have damaged the statue. How do the women feel about the saint's name for the hostel? It sounds a bit religious. Do they have to be churchgoers?'

'Not necessarily. But most have church connections. They're usually referred by clergy. You see, Suzy, our hostel is different from most refuges.'

'In what way?'

'Our residents are older women who've made the incredibly brave move to get away, after decades of abuse. When our residents hear about St Jane, they get the connection. St Jane was like Deborah. She founded a convent for women who were too old or poor or sick to get into the popular religious orders. She's also the patron saint of women separated from their children.'

Joanne stopped abruptly. Suzy got the impression that chatting was not what Joanne did. The administrator was under enormous pressure, and Deborah had been her close friend. Perhaps she needed to keep going; if she stopped, she might collapse.

And they had the residents to meet later. That would be tense for everyone.

Suzy followed Joanne, striding back to the house.

CHAPTER FOUR

The highways were unoccupied, and the travellers walked through byways.
Judges 5:6

At the same time, Robert left the Reverend Linda Finch and the vicarage to stroll home to the Briars. It was a pleasant walk, although the verges beside the road sometimes disappeared. You had to tuck yourself into the hedge if a car or tractor came along.

He thought about his conversation with Linda, and how he had come to take the peaceful and welcoming atmosphere of All Saints Church for granted. What Robert loved about the Church of England at its best was its tolerance, perhaps an outdated virtue. But he knew that few of his friends could relate to his affection for Anglicanism. He was grateful that Suzy gave his faith the benefit of the doubt. When he had asked her why she went to church with him, she had said that we could all do with a bit of forgiveness.

Ahead, the fells to the east of the village unfolded in sage- and olive-green waves until they crumbled into soft sandstone and then hard granite outcrops. Down here in the Tarn Valley, the landscape was still lush with autumn leaves on the trees. The beck was full, and he could hear it rushing alongside the road, carrying away with it the end of the summer: the mud, leaves and twigs that it would later deposit when it met the River Eden.

But the morning sunshine had taken on a metallic quality which Robert knew meant rain and the end of the few days of glorious weather. A thin layer of cloud was coming in from the Irish Sea. Suzy was still up at the hostel. But she would be home by five o'clock at the latest and they'd arranged to go out that evening to the pub. Molly was staying with her friends, and it would be good for Suzy not to have to cook.

He thought again, uneasily, about how often Suzy had been away that year. The disastrous skiing holiday, then the night at Rachel's in the spring, disrupted by the air ambulance — Suzy had told him all about that. Then numerous trips to London or Manchester. And the week away at the Academy of Journalism. He could hardly keep up. He realized he hadn't asked her anything about her lecturing, or about Rachel, whom he liked a lot, or whether Suzy had managed to contact the other woman she had wanted to see in Islington — Ellie, was it?

But surely an evening with just the two of them, at the Plough, with its log fires and private corners, would help put things back in perspective. It usually just took an hour or two for them to catch up and get back on track.

Robert wasn't concentrating when the Harley Davidson came roaring around the corner at a crazy angle and forced him to leap into the hedge.

* * *

Joanne led Suzy through the front door of the hostel into the large blue-and-gold-painted hall. It was bright and airy, with an imposing wooden staircase and pictures in gilt frames on the walls. But what struck Suzy most was the reproduction of a famous painting which caught the morning light.

'Ah, you're looking at our most controversial picture.' Joanne smiled. 'Not everyone appreciates it. I'm afraid the new archdeacon, Jim Bentley, was rather horrified.'

The subject was Jael, a woman from the Deborah story in the Book of Judges in the Bible. She was about to murder the army general Sisera, the enemy of Israel, who was asleep in her tent. Jael held the tent peg she would use to pierce the side of Sisera's head. *Yuk*, Suzy thought. But the painting had a luminescent beauty, and in this picture Jael's act of violence was yet to come.

'Mmm . . . It's by Artemisia Gentileschi, isn't it? One of the few famous women painters.' Suzy peered at the picture. 'You don't actually see the tent peg going into his temple in this one. I think this sort of painting is part of a tradition. There are some gruesome baroque pictures of women.'

'Oh, I don't know anything about art, except what Deborah told me,' Joanne said, 'but I do know this one is by a woman, and it's ruffled a few feathers round here. Anyway, you'll want some lunch. If you go back into the office, I'll get Chelsea to bring you a sandwich.'

'Yes, fine. It's kind of you to offer.'

Joanne smiled, and it changed her face. 'I've asked the residents if they're happy to meet you this afternoon. One or two have already been on Twitter, with anonymous profiles, to say nice things about Deborah, but most avoid any contact with the outside world.'

'So the residents have phones?'

'Oh yes, of course. But visitors' phones are banned.'

Suzy went back into the office and looked at the books on the shelves. There was a *Life of St Jane Frances de Chantal* with a picture on the cover which looked very like the sensible saint in the garden — plus a halo of light, not the silvery one with the motto which Joanne had described. There were a couple of histories of Cumbria and the Norbridge area, numerous academic books on politics, domestic abuse and psychology, and a few tired-looking much-thumbed volumes on mines, quarries and metals — that would be the Arbiter heritage, Suzy thought. On another shelf was a whole set of hefty books about the Old Testament. The Deborah of St Jane's had certainly taken the connection with her namesake seriously.

Suzy sat down at the desk to wait till she was summoned. It would be interesting to meet the residents. She was aware of them, out of sight but indicated by the rustle of clothing or the feeling that a foot had just whisked out of the way.

Then the office door opened to the very solid form of Chelsea holding a tray. The young woman looked shifty, truculent and worried all at the same time. And she definitely looked familiar. But where had Suzy seen her before?

'Cheddar and tomato on wholemeal,' the girl intoned.

'Thanks, Chelsea. That looks great.'

The girl put the tray on the desk and the overall slipped away from her wrist to reveal a tattoo. At the same moment, her eyes caught Suzy's. Suzy's eyes opened wide in response; Chelsea grimaced and dropped her glance.

Joanne had followed Chelsea into the room and was already commenting on how well Chelsea was coping with the kitchen. Chelsea's chest was heaving, and she didn't move.

'Yes. Thank you so much, Chelsea.' Suzy smiled at the girl. 'It's a terrible time to arrive here, but you'll be a huge support to Joanne.'

The girl's face relaxed and slackened into blankness. 'Ta,' she said. Then she turned round and was gone.

'Poor soul,' said Joanne. 'This place should have been a refuge for her too. But now, with all this terrible business . . . She seems a bit uncouth, but she's had a tough life. I hope she settles in.'

I hope so too, thought Suzy. Because the expression on the girl's stricken face had been out of all proportion to their short but unpleasant meeting on the train the night before. Why was the goth girl so frightened?

Suzy was still eating her sandwich when a motorbike roared up the drive to St Jane's, churning up the gravel.

Joanne hurried down the steps and waited while the rider took off his crash helmet, shaking out his grey ponytail.

'Archdeacon,' Joanne said edgily. 'How nice of you to come over.'

'Yes. I want a word with you. Let's go inside.'

* * *

The Venerable Jim Bentley was a big man. From the office window which looked out on to the drive, Suzy watched him stride towards to the front door. Joanne called from behind him, 'Archdeacon, please . . . Go straight into the office. The hostel is a man-free zone.'

'I know, I know. And it's *Ven Jim*.' He swerved into the office, all leathers and metal, with a clerical collar showing above his studded jacket. 'I'm the Archdeacon of Workhaven. Who are you?' he said bluntly to Suzy, who was trapped by his bulk behind the desk.

She stood up awkwardly. 'Hi. I'm Suzy Spencer. I . . .'

'Ah yes. Now I realize who you are. The self-styled spokesman for the hostel. You were on Radio Cumbria this morning. I'd be interested to know who authorized you?'

Suzy felt the hostility pouring from him. He was sweating profusely. 'Joanne asked me to help. Deborah had contacted me about taking on a comms role here. So I came over . . .'

'Well, you overstepped the mark.'

Suzy stared back at him. After a five-second standoff, she smiled and said, 'Fine. I'm off, then. Radio Cumbria want another live two-way for the evening bulletin before the sports show. You need to access an ISDN line. The *Mid Cumbria Times* want some more pictures of Deborah, which you'll have to select and scan and send. And a stringer for the *Mail* has been on. That's a tricky one, but I'll leave it up to you.' She started to unplug her laptop.

'Okay, okay. Whoa,' said the archdeacon. 'I can see we have problems here. Now you've set off the press, you'd better finish what you've started. But I'd like to know why you didn't contact me.'

Suzy said. 'Why should I? I understand there's no chair of the board currently. So I spoke to the acting chair, Neil Clifford. He agreed the wording of the press release which I sent to every trustee, including you. He also suggested that I handle the interviews. But I'm very happy to leave you to it.'

Instead of replying, the archdeacon turned on Joanne. 'And who do you think you're reporting to?'

Joanne said, 'It's in the press release Suzy sent you, Archdeacon. Haven't you seen it?'

'I don't get a chance to check up on everything in my inbox . . .'

'The press release clearly says Joanne is reporting to Neil Clifford, who's coming over later. But in the meantime, she is trying to deal with six distraught women, and I am trying to deal with the press. That is, if you want me to get on with it.'

The archdeacon had the courtesy to lower his voice. But he was still officious. 'So what time is Neil coming?'

I'm not your PA, Suzy thought. 'Why don't you call and ask him yourself? On your mobile, from outside of course.'

Joanne added, 'Suzy's right. It really would be better for us if you made your phone calls from the drive and waited somewhere else. The residents are still very shaken. We have a meeting with them now and we need to reassure them.'

The archdeacon paused as if deciding what tack to take. He looked from Joanne to Suzy. Suddenly he went for a boyish smile. 'Okay, okay. *Mea culpa.* I can see things are under control here, ladies. Great stuff! Hey, I know I tend to rush in where angels fear to tread, but we can't all be angels. I ought to be the next chair of the board, but I accept that hasn't happened yet. Deborah and I had a few details to sort out. Anyway, I'll pop outside and make those calls. The signal's better there anyway.'

The room seemed twice as big when he had gone. Suzy heard him call loudly from the hallway, 'I see you've still got that ghastly picture up there. Jael and Sisera. Nasty thing. I did mention it. Of course, Deborah took no notice of me. What a woman!' He laughed heartily, but it wasn't funny.

Joanne said quietly, 'I'm sorry, Suzy. I should have realized he would think he was in charge where the press was concerned. Awful man. Deborah wasn't keen on him. With any luck, Neil Clifford will put him back in his box. Why don't you come with me now and talk to the residents? I'll deal with Archdeacon Jim Bentley.'

Joanne led Suzy across the hall into the lounge. It was a lovely room decorated in very pale lemon with white details. The furniture was minimal and well-spaced, but the chairs were deep and cozy.

'Years ago that sideboard in our office used to be in here with two heavy metal ornaments on it. Something to do with the Arbiter history. But Deborah got rid of them. It was important to her that the hostel looked stylish. She was always having the décor freshened up.'

As if to prove her point, Joanne took Suzy through the lounge and into the dining room. It was beautifully done in pale turquoise with gilt paint picking out reliefs of garlanded fruit and flowers on the panels. Suzy was surprised to see that the table was a huge mahogany affair. The cutlery and crockery were elaborate. Suzy had expected something more utilitarian, but she supposed it made sense to use the Arbiter china and family silver. She didn't envy Chelsea the washing up and polishing.

It was also odd that she took in these details before seeing the six women. They were sitting around the large central table, but she found she couldn't look at them. Even to think about it seemed intrusive. Joanne pulled out a chair for Suzy but remained standing herself. After a moment, Suzy sensed that two of the women seemed to be leaning forwards. One of them, a tall, stately woman with black braided hair and a beautiful but watchful face, looked her in the eye. The other was tiny, blonde and fidgety, dressed like a teenager but in her fifties at least. She wore tight skinny jeans and a faux-leather biker jacket with a big fake-fur collar. Her glance raked over Suzy suspiciously. The other women all seemed to be leaning back, towards the panels and friezes of the walls.

'This is Suzy,' said Joanne. 'She's been dealing with the press for us. Suzy, just so you know, most people here would prefer to be anonymous. So Adelina is our spokesperson.'

The woman who had given Suzy the eye slowly nodded at her.

'I don't know why we're doing this,' the little blonde edgy woman interrupted sharply. 'The press are all pigs.' She seemed to pulse with nervous energy. Her streaked hair was scraped on top of her head in a scrunchy, showing ears with rows of hoops and studs. 'We all know who did it, anyway.'

'We're not sure about that, Leila,' Adelina said firmly. She turned from the other woman and looked at Suzy. 'But we do wonder why the hostel needs to respond to press enquiries.'

'Fair question.' Suzy answered. 'But the hostel benefits financially from some local support, and it's arguable that the public have a right to know what's happening. And there was a lot of affection for Deborah beyond these walls.'

Leila, the edgy woman, snapped: 'That's rubbish about the money. We all know that the dosh comes from Deborah's trust.'

'Yes, most of it does,' said Suzy, who had found time to look at the accounts in the hostel's annual report. 'But there are some local grants. And there's the association with the Church.'

It would have been inappropriate to mention that the women had all been referred by Church organizations or individual clergy. Suzy had been interested in Deborah's method of allocating places at St Jane's. Which reminded her to ask Joanne later about the one place which hadn't been taken. Joanne had quietly withdrawn, leaving Suzy to it. Suzy felt grateful and pleased that the administrator seemed to trust her.

Adelina went on, apologetic but insistent. 'Can you tell us which press have been asking. No one here is local, but we're all worried we might be traced.'

'One stringer for a national paper has been in contact, but I haven't called her back. Locally, of course, this story won't go away, so it was important to tackle regional press enquiries today. Often a quick PR response can stop speculation about a story growing.'

'You do realize,' Adelina said softly, 'that what you call a story could be life or death to us?'

This was going to be difficult. Suzy knew that it would be impossible to provide complete reassurance. But for the next half hour she tried to answer everything as honestly and openly as she could. It was only then, looking at the emotion working in Adelina's face, that Suzy even began to understand. The hostel really was a haven, not unlike the original convent of St Jane. But now it had been pulled ruthlessly back into the real world. No wonder most of the women wanted to merge with the walls.

Suzy felt drained herself. Joanne came back to get her, but as she turned to follow the administrator out of the dining room Adelina called, 'Suzy?'

'Yes?'

'We've all talked about this. We all agree that this was totally out of character for Deborah.'

Suzy was aware of the other women nodding and a faint susurration around the room.

'What makes you say that?' Suzy asked.

'We knew her. She was everything to us. Lawyer, counsellor, therapist, confidante . . . judge. We loved her. And she loved us. She would never have done something dangerous which would expose us like this. But the police won't listen to us. No one does.'

Joanne had turned to come back into the room. She said firmly, 'It was just a terrible accident, Adelina.'

'Was it?' Adelina replied.

'No!' snapped the edgy Leila. 'You should be talking to Geoff Black. He hated Deborah. He pushed her off that roof. I know.'

CHAPTER FIVE

Why abodest though among the sheepfolds, to hear the bleatings of the flocks?
Judges 5:16

The Texan, Jarrold McHugh, looked with surprise at Geoff Black's pickup, parked outside Geoff's garage next door to his cottage. Jarrold had thought the Blacks were away for the weekend. The Saturday morning weather was just right for a walk on the fells — not hot and bright like the day before, but with the usual grey-blue milkiness he now associated with autumn in Tarnfield. As it was a weekend, he wanted a walk that was easy and recreational. He had packed his stuff in his backpack, less kit than usual. But he had remembered to include a book on local history.

He left the cottage on foot, double locking the door, and set off up the lane, which dwindled to a bridle path with a thick tuft of vegetation running down the middle. It had once been a much more significant route, going up to the Arbiter mines.

In the few months he had lived here, Jarrold had seen only half a dozen vehicles come this way. He strode off to the left of the track, up a sheep path through the gorse, and before long he was up on Tarn Fell. The remains of the Arbiter mines still cut into the hills, but they were covered now by more than a century of growth. The last Arbiter mine had closed in 1910. But the family had made more money since then, despite two world wars and the Great Depression. Deborah Arbiter had been a very rich woman.

Jarrold had done a lot of work finding out just how rich, before he came to Cumbria.

Reaching the ridge, he got out his flask of coffee and his energy bar. Below him was a palette of greens, metallic glints, brown rocks and grey sky. He had to admit it was getting to him. He'd had no idea that Britain could be so vast and empty. Then, despite himself, he looked at his phone. There was no signal here, but he could re-read his old texts.

They confirmed that in the evening he would be meeting Dr Paula Stovey, the leader of his online music course. She was a Scarlett Johansson lookalike, though taller and slenderer. She had a taut, fit body, but a surprisingly soft and sensual face. They had met several times for walks on the fells. Last time she had come back to the cottage, and they had talked until the small hours. He knew he was taking a risk in seeing her, but it was exciting and he couldn't resist.

And their relationship was at a critical point. It would be safe, he thought, to take Paula to the Plough Inn in Tarnfield that evening. It was in the *Good Beer Guide*, and he wanted to try traditional English ale. The pubs he had been in before were in London and he had drunk lager. He fancied the idea of a country inn, but so far he'd avoided going there. But Paula would think it odd if he didn't suggest going out somewhere soon. She was driving her car over to his place again, so she might park and stay overnight. He felt pleasurable anticipation. It had been a long time . . .

He would leave the next move up to her, but he felt he had done the groundwork. They could walk to the village and back — it was only a couple of miles. They were both quite fit, so it would be an easy walk to them. No one in the village would recognize him and they certainly wouldn't know her. And anyway, it didn't matter as much now. He still had to be careful, but the main job was done.

He pulled the local history book out of his backpack and began to read about the Arbiters. But he soon lost interest and went back to striding over the empty terrain, looking for miles towards Hadrian's Wall.

* * *

Late on Saturday afternoon Stevie Nesbit drove his new Mini Cooper convertible up to the door of Church Cottage. He had to admit that it was good to be back. Life with Alan was going well. All those years ago, when they had met at the Edinburgh Festival, Stevie knew he had been a jaded failure at thirty-five, too old for pretty-boy roles but too pretty for anything with more depth. Alan Robie had been a sort of sugar-daddy figure, and for some years their relationship had been rocky.

Stevie had tried to be content with life in Tarnfield. He had orchestrated interesting rows with Alan, followed by dramatic reconciliation scenes. But nothing had made him happy. And after sniping at them for years, he had missed the company of his friends too much.

In fairness to Alan, the older man had tried too. They had regularly gone down to Manchester to revel in the gay scene there, which wasn't Alan's thing at all. And all Stevie had really wanted was for them to build an extension to the cottage, so that his friends could come and stay and admire his good fortune. But in the early days Alan didn't want anyone in the village to know for sure that they were a couple. *Discretion*, he called it, but Stevie said it was ridiculous. *As if!*

And Alan had also refused point blank to extend Church Cottage because that would mean getting rid of the orchard. The row over the orchard, and the deathly trouble in the village that followed, had shown Stevie that there was a limit to how much Alan would give in to him, even though he was the love of the older man's life. Until then Stevie had thought that Alan was too desperate to keep him happy, and that knowledge had led to a sort of contempt. But he discovered a steely element to his partner which he hadn't appreciated. So, their relationship had survived, and Stevie had tried even harder to settle in Tarnfield, but it had been tough.

Then Alan had done something remarkable. He had set himself up as Stevie's agent and started bombarding the drama production companies based in the north with his lover's CV. He had paid for a glitzy photo shoot and a new wardrobe. He'd found Stevie a drama coach and a life coach. He made it his job to relaunch him as an actor. Stevie was presented to casting directors as someone who could portray a handsome has-been washed up at forty, with an interesting touch of bitterness, gay or straight. Perfect for your minor villain or disillusioned sidekick. It had worked.

And it had come at a time when the big content providers were starting to think about more rural British scenarios: Northumbria, Morecambe Bay, Aberystwyth. Stevie could do Yorkshire and Lancashire accents with ease, Ulster at a pinch. Welsh was more specialized. But as he was originally Scottish, a brogue came naturally.

He had landed a bit part in a detective series set in Berwick-upon-Tweed, and afterwards the offers had come in. The best thing about it was that Stevie was actually very good. 'I'm not surprised, darling,' Alan had said when he read a review one Monday morning mentioning Stevie as a 'not-so-slight character with a twist in the curl of his cherubic lips'.

A month later he had arranged for Stevie to audition for the part of a cynical Scottish office manager at a health centre in *The Medicine.* It was a new soap set in an inner city, where gentrification and urban deprivation struggled to come to terms with each other. It was a success. Now Stevie was often recognized in the street, and it was rumoured the series would soon be available on Netflix too.

Life was excellent. Of course, the civil partnership was more important to Alan than to Stevie, especially as Alan wanted to have some sort of religious thing as well. Stevie was okay with that, but he wasn't as committed to the church, although he adored the Reverend Linda Finch and regularly told her that she should have her own podcast. And he liked going to All Saints with Alan because it always turned a few heads.

After parking at the front of Church Cottage, Stevie took his suit hanger out of the back of the car and grabbed his Louis Vuitton bag. He looked up and saw Alan in the front doorway. Alan had his usual evening glass of gin and tonic in his hand, raising it to Stevie as he walked up the path.

'Good to see you,' Alan called.

'You too. Great to see my agent looking so relaxed.'

'Well, another series has been commissioned. What is there not to like?' They kissed briefly. Stevie left his bags in the hall and followed Alan down to the living room, which opened on to a small westward-facing patio in the garden, with views of the fells behind. It had been one of Alan's early concessions to a social life. The evening was going to be glorious, once the sun had dropped below a line of cloud. Even as they stood there, the last rays suddenly burst over the garden and found them.

'It's good to be home,' Stevie said. But just to show that he wasn't being sentimental he rolled his eyes and added, in an exaggeration of the voice he used for *The Medicine*, 'but home isnae where the hearrt is. The hearrt is in that ice box, for a transplant!'

Alan laughed. 'Let's sit out here for a minute.' Stevie shivered but sat down.

After a pause, Alan asked, 'Did you get my message about Deborah Arbiter?'

'Yes. Terrible.' Stevie picked up the drink Alan had ready for him.

'She should have been at the diversity lunch today at the Town Hall. It was the only thing anyone talked about.'

'I can imagine. It's such a careless way to die. Not what you would expect.'

'Well, she was game for anything.'

'I suppose. Seems odd, though.'

'Mmm, maybe.' Alan paused. 'And there's also a bit of an issue about our civil partnership which I didn't go into when I called you.'

For a moment Stevie wondered if for some reason it was off and was surprised by how much the thought bothered him.

When Alan finished explaining, Stevie sat and thought about it, rolling his glass in his hand. Alan offered him a top-up, and Stevie nodded absently. One day in the future he would love to have a big church wedding and could see himself in a beautifully cut morning suit walking down the aisle on Alan's arm. But, so far, the Church hierarchy wasn't having any of that, which contributed to Stevie's alienation. On the other hand, the thought of some old archdeacon having a go at the Reverend Linda Finch infuriated and engaged him.

'What do you think Linda will do?'

'Robert went to see her again this morning. He called me this afternoon to say she has an idea . . .'

'An idea that means the party can still go ahead?'

'Oh yes. Linda is determined to find a way, whatever the archdeacon says.'

'Especially,' said Stevie with a wry smile from the now famous lips, 'if we invite all the cast from *The Medicine*. And post it on YouTube!'

* * *

That evening, getting ready to go out, Suzy and Robert finally had time to talk. There was so much to discuss. Suzy told him about the strange coincidence of meeting Chelsea, the goth from the train, now a domestic worker at St Jane's Hostel.

'The train was packed. She was in my seat. The display said the seat was booked to Norbridge. Maybe she didn't understand about booking. Or maybe she thought that as she was going to Norbridge she'd be safe in that seat if no one came to take it. But then I turned up.'

'And you're sure it was the same girl?'

'Absolutely sure. I may be tired and overworked Rob, but I'm not delusional. I also met Alan's angry archdeacon today.'

'And what did you make of him?'

'He was over-the-top aggressive. All that macho stuff. As our vicar, Linda should stand up to him.'

'I think she will. She may compromise a little, but not give in.'

They strolled under an umbrella in the soft rain, through the gathering dark to the lights of the Plough on Tarnfield village green. In the pub they made their way towards their regular table. It was unusually busy. Robert did a quick scan of the place to see if there was anyone they knew. The last thing he wanted was to get caught up with other people. He and Suzy needed to talk.

To his annoyance he saw the irrepressible Scott Jermyn propping up the bar and giving the regulars the benefit of his views on Deborah. Scott broke off when he noticed them.

'Robert!' Scott hailed him loudly.

'Who's that?' Suzy asked.

'It's Scott Jermyn. He's bought Tarnfield House on the Green. He's a sort of investment adviser from London, but with an interest in local quarries. Allegedly doing some work for Deborah. Rolling in money. Look, let's just say hello and then we can move to our table.'

Scott Jermyn was yet another large man dominating his space, Suzy thought, but whereas Archdeacon Bentley had been broad and solid, Scott Jermyn was thin, with a shaved head. He was very tall, his slim build emphasized by a too-tightly fitted jacket and narrow trousers. To Suzy he looked rather snakelike as he leaned forward. He signalled vigorously for Robert to join him.

Fine, Suzy thought, *so I don't exist*. After a brief introduction, when Jermyn hardly even nodded in Suzy's direction, he insisted on buying them both a drink, assuming to Suzy's irritation that she wanted a sweet white wine, and then focused his attention entirely on Robert.

He segued neatly from an analysis of Deborah's character ('amazing but scary') into a repeated attempt to persuade Robert to invest in some sort of venture. He had a braying laugh, usually at his own remarks. Being squeezed to one side, Suzy could hardly hear what he said, but he obviously thought he was being very witty. The Plough was busy; Scott Jermyn was taking up valuable space at the bar with a small group of hangers-on. Robert finally extricated himself and they made their way to their table.

Robert said, 'Sorry about that. He's new to the neighbourhood. When he moved in you were away somewhere, and I made an effort to be pleasant. But he's a bit insistent and he keeps trying to get me to invest in a quarrying company.'

'Well he didn't invest any time in me . . .'

'He's what they used to call a man's man. Divorced I think — he's on his own now. Made a lot of money in the City and moved up here to be a country gent. He had some dealings with Deborah though, so he's holding court tonight!'

'Really? He doesn't seem her type at all. Not that I would really know. There are so many different versions of Deborah. All variations on a theme: a strong independent woman. The residents at the hostel loved her . . .' She remembered Adelina, their spokeswoman, and her questioning eyes, and for a minute Suzy was lost in thought.

'Come back to me, Suzy! You look worried.'

'I am, to tell you the truth.' Suzy paused. 'Rob, d'you think Deborah's death might not have been an accident? Would she really take that sort of risk? She was called the Judge. People acknowledged that she was wise as well as forceful.'

'But if it wasn't accidental, how did she die? Don't overthink it. Everyone else thinks it was an accident. Leave it be.' Robert knew he sounded tetchy. But he didn't want to talk about Deborah's death. This was their time to talk about their own lives.

Suzy was surprised, but all she said was, 'Okay. Maybe you're right.'

They ordered food and Suzy tried in vain to relax. They chatted about her son Jake's job plans and her daughter Molly's demand for driving lessons; then, unusually for them, the conversation dried up. Suzy really did want to talk about Deborah's death. She needed Robert's good sense and valued his opinion. But Robert wanted to avoid it. He knew that if Suzy got embroiled in a suspicious death at the hostel, he would lose her for the week. A day or two was all right, but he wanted her to himself for a while before she went back to work on *Living Lies* in Manchester. They could go walking on the fells, with fresh air, scenery and the proper perspective. Or just stay at home. There was the proper perspective there too.

Suddenly Suzy felt exhausted. 'I'm so tired, Rob. It's been a long day. And I know you'll think I'm mad, but it's not just Deborah who's on my mind. I can't stop thinking about Ellie Fox, the woman I met on that skiing holiday in France back in February. I tried to contact her in Islington but there was no reply. There's something which has been nagging at me all day . . . something we talked about which I can't really remember. For some reason Deborah's death has brought it all back . . .'

'Oh Suzy, please don't start again. Maybe this Ellie person has just moved on. And what on earth can she have to do with Deborah Arbiter? You're bringing London into everything. Can't you just enjoy being back in Tarnfield?'

'But I can't suddenly switch off.'

'Well, you seem more interested in being anywhere else than here with me.'

'That's not true, Rob.' Suzy leaned back in her chair. 'I was looking forward to coming home. But there's something about Ellie tugging at the back of my mind. I can't help it.'

'Okay. Maybe I'm getting a bit heavy. Let's change the subject. We should talk about some practical stuff . . .'

There was a silence between them. Then Robert said, 'For a start, that crack in the chimney stack looks worse. We'll have to get it dealt with.' He sighed.

Oh dear, Suzy thought, *Robert must be worried about all this expense on the house. And there's Molly campaigning for that art studio in the attic as well . . .*

'Well, if we need a roofer, Rob, there's the chap who was going to do the work at St Jane's. He seems to be well thought of. Yes, we do need to get it done before it deteriorates.' She sighed too.

Oh dear, Robert thought. *Suzy sounds so jaded. The old house must have been really shown up by Rachel's smart apartment in London.*

The food at the Plough was lovely, but the atmosphere between them was flat, and they both knew they were at odds. There was none of their usual laughter. Then Suzy became aware that Robert was looking over her shoulder.

'What is it, Rob?'

'Well oddly enough I'm sure I've just seen someone I know, from the university. But I can't think why she would be here. I must be imagining things.'

Suzy turned around, as a tall, lithe, tanned blonde woman looking like a film star swayed past from the ladies', not seeing them. Suzy said, half-jokingly — but only half — 'And you accuse me of being distracted! While you're ogling that stunning woman. I thought you said we should be enjoying our evening together. Perhaps you're getting bored with me!' Suzy was aware that she felt flabby and dowdy. Overwork was doing her no good.

'Don't say that, Suzy. That's ridiculous.' Robert was stung and alarmed. He wondered if it was projection, and she was the one bored with him, provincial old Robert Clark.

Then they both self-consciously re-booted the atmosphere. Later, they chatted lightly as they walked home, talking blandly about other things — books, films, village gossip. Anything but Deborah's death or Suzy's strange memories of Ellie Fox in the skiing chalet. On the surface, things were back to normal. But the sparkle was missing. And Suzy wanted it back.

CHAPTER SIX

When any man doth come and inquire of thee, and say, 'Is there any man here?', that thou shalt say, 'No'.
Judges 4:20

On Sunday morning Suzy overslept; she and Robert drove separately to All Saints Church. Linda the vicar led prayers for the residents at St Jane's and for everyone coping with the shock of Deborah Arbiter's death. People clustered around afterwards, talking about the tragedy.

Robert was collared by Alan Robie, who wanted him to stay behind to discuss Linda's new suggestions for the civil partnership party. Alan was keen to share Stevie's idea of inviting the stars of *The Medicine* to the 'do' in the church hall. He thought it could also be a way of raising much-needed funds for repairing All Saints' roof. They could have the party as planned but ask guests for donations to the roof fund, rather than gifts. Linda Finch was enthusiastic.

Suzy drove home. She had grabbed any old clothes before leaving for the service, covering them with her puffer jacket. All Saints catered for all sorts, and there were weirder outfits than hers in the congregation. But she felt tired and messy. She would have liked a little bit of time to pamper herself. Maybe that afternoon she could soak in the bath and do her roots.

But not yet. She still had to mark those wretched assignments from the North London Academy of Journalism on the regulation of social media and the new report to government. It had been compiled by a Lord Warsbrook of Whinsea, a powerful lawyer. The deadline for the students to upload their work had been ten o'clock on Friday night. Suzy needed a code to access them, but the email with the code had never arrived. She sighed. If she'd had the code, she could have made a start. She wasn't looking forward to the marking and, frankly, she thought Lord Warsbrook's report was a bit thin.

She let herself into the Briars, tripped over Flowerbabe the cat, took a coffee and something to nibble (bad, she knew) and went upstairs to the spare bedroom she and Robert used as an office. She logged on. Still no code from the academy. Irritating.

Even more irritating was the sudden urgent knocking at the door. She hurried downstairs again and opened it.

'Oh. Hello.'

It was the long thin man from the pub. He smiled broadly but was clearly disappointed. 'Hey. Is Robert in?' He had a sort of Estuary twang, reminiscent of the yuppie style of the nineties. It sounded affected.

'No, sorry, Robert's still at the church. Can I help?' Not that she wanted to. He'd clearly forgotten meeting her. Suzy knew what he saw. She was small, unkempt, slightly harassed, wearing one of Robert's old plaid shirts over jeans, with tatty hair. This was doing nothing for her self-esteem.

The man said ingratiatingly, as if to a child, 'I've got these new colourful prospectuses I mentioned to Robert last night. About a little investment possibility. Can I leave them for him to look at?' His eyes slid past her, focusing on the interior of the house, which clearly intrigued him more than she did.

Nettled by his manner, Suzy replied, 'Or why don't you show the brochures to me?'

'You?' He looked at her as if the pet dog had spoken.

'Yes, me. Robert's wife. Come in.' She wasn't sure why she was doing this, but she resented his assumptions. Why shouldn't she look at his wretched brochures? Did he think Robert made all the decisions?

'Oh, all right, thanks.' He followed her with big strides down the hall into the Briars' warm kitchen.

'I've got coffee. It's not the freshest but it's hot. And have a brownie — home-made.' She had the biscuit tin open on the table. Molly had made the brownies, but she didn't tell him that.

'Oh very nice.' The man gave her a leering grin. Then he actually looked her up and down. He snaffled a brownie, sat down and wound his long legs round each other, stretching across the kitchen floor.

'This is a very nice room, I must say!' He was obviously taking in the collection of copper pans inherited from Robert's first wife, and the big range, the original flagged floor and the huge wooden dresser. Yes, Suzy thought. It *is* nice. At least as nice as Rachel's cooking lab in London N1. I must have been mad to think it looked dingy.

He went on: 'Well, you probably know that I've bought Tarnfield House on the Green. Name's Scott Jermyn.'

She said, 'Jermyn? Like the street? Off St James's?'

He looked startled. 'That's right,' he said. 'How do you know that?'

'I work in London from time to time. I was there all last week.'

'Really?' He seemed surprised. Suzy silently passed him a steaming coffee mug. He seemed to be reconsidering and relaxed, unwinding in a reptilian way. 'Well, well,' he said. 'Fancy that! You and me should see more of each other! There aren't many guys who know the Smoke around here. I moved about six months ago and snapped up that pile on the Green.' He clicked his fingers. 'I was looking for a house in the sticks that I could do up, somewhere a bit classy. It's costing me an arm and a leg. But at least it ain't London prices. What were you doing down there, then?'

'I was lecturing.' She had a feeling that wouldn't impress him enough. 'But usually I'm a producer on a TV show, *Living Lies*.'

'Oh wow.' Scott perked up. '*Living Lies*. I don't watch telly myself, but I've heard of that one. Well, well. That's a turn up . . .'

'I don't see why. Someone's got to do it.'

'But you don't look like a TV producer.'

I'm too ordinary, am I? Suzy thought. 'Actually I've just won a BATV award. We haven't met before because I'm usually away working.' Why was she talking like this? She felt an uncomfortable need to show off, perhaps because of his shameless confidence.

He grinned, chewing visibly. 'These are nice. Maybe you should be on *The Great British Bake Off* too!' and then guffawed at his own stupid remark with his mouth full of brownie. She couldn't bring herself to tell him the baking was Molly's.

She made a show of looking through his brochures. 'Thanks for these. They're beautiful. But look, I don't want to mislead you. I really don't think we're in a position to invest.'

'Not now maybe. But you should think about it. Things are changing in little old North Cumbria. There used to be dozens of mines round here, and quarries for all sorts of stone. It's a geological smorgasbord out there. The portions might be small but the menu's varied.' He grinned. 'These quarrying companies are quite bijou and they're digging up specialist stone for the building that's going on all over the north. And metalwork too. Genuine local materials. Limestone, sandstone, slate, ironwork, copper, bronze, all lovely stuff that's in demand now. Have a look . . .'

Suzy found herself transfixed by the pictures, with their rich glossy finish and the pages of warm stone or shiny metal.

'You see?' Scott Jermyn said with an air of triumph. 'It gets to you, doesn't it? Don't deny it. It's fab stuff and it's a growth industry. A chance for you and hubby to invest on a small but key scale. The board of DecorMetal are looking to give an opportunity to a discreet, local, discerning body of investors.'

'I don't think we'll be taking it up,' said Suzy. 'We're really not into that sort of thing.' But at the same time, she glanced down involuntarily at the original flagstones which formed their kitchen floor.

Scott followed her glance instantly. 'Lovely stone, but have you got underfloor heating? Do you know that DecorMetal will dig them up for you, put in the electric element — or water pipes if you prefer — and then re-lay your flags exactly — exactly, mind — as they were before?'

'Well, thank you, but it's usually warm enough because of the range.'

'But wait until the day that packs up! It looks in good nick now, but you never know the minute. DecorMetal are developing a sister company, DecorScran, which specializes in fitting Cumbrian country kitchens. In fact . . .'

'Stop now!' Suzy almost shouted. 'We won't be investing!'

'But what about hubby? What would he say? You're not one of those harpies who wear the trousers, are you?' He sniggered. Suzy was speechless.

'I tell you what,' Jermyn ploughed on, oblivious. 'Why don't you and old Robert come over to Tarnfield House this week and have a look at what I've been doing there with my refurb? I've gone back to its Georgian roots. It will knock you out.'

Suzy was about to refuse. But then again, Tarnfield House had been a big, decaying, depressing place. Any refurbishment worth showing off must be interesting.

Scott Jermyn almost sniffed her hesitation. 'Drinks and nibbles? Wednesday, six p.m.? How about it, babe? And you can tell me all about the TV business,' he said with a final flourish, as if offering her a bouquet.

'Yes, well, I don't know. I'll have to check with Rob . . .'

'I bet you can persuade him.' He winked. 'I'd better be going. But I'm going to assume we have a date for Wednesday. What's your first name by the way, Mrs Clark? I don't think I caught it.'

'It's Suzy but my surname isn't Clark—'

He cut across her: 'Suzy! Cute. Well, Suzy. I'd better love you and leave you. You can keep the brochures.'

He uncoiled himself from the chair and ducked his head, though it wasn't necessary, going out through the kitchen door. Suzy followed him. She had a horrible feeling that if she didn't see him off the premises, he would spring out of a cupboard later, still talking about stone floors. He strode down the hall and opened the front door for himself. She kept going behind him.

He turned round in the path in front of his BMW and looked back appraisingly at the house. 'This is a lovely property,' he said. 'Mind you, you've got a nasty crack in your chimney stack.'

'Yes, we know,' said Suzy.

'You need to do something about that before the weather gets much worse. Tell you what, I'll ask my roofer to come over and take a look this afternoon. He's called Lee. He might need the work now that job at the hostel is cancelled.' He didn't wait for a reply. He waved without looking back as he set off jauntily up the lane to where he had parked his car, full of his own bonhomie.

When Robert came back ten minutes later Suzy was still at the kitchen table looking at the pictures of green slate, dressed sandstone and copper-tipped railings.

'What's that?'

'Your mate Scott turned up with a prospectus. He seems to think we'll find the money to invest in bespoke quarrying.'

'Blimey.' Robert paused on his way towards the clothes hooks by the back door and smiled. 'Well, he's certainly a trier.'

'He's invited us over for drinks on Wednesday. He's a real jack-the-lad. He seems to be into property as well.'

'I'm sorry you got stuck with him.'

Suzy brushed off the troubling thought that she had somehow been bested by Scott Jermyn. 'Oh, he was amusing really. All salesmen are like that, I suppose. He was a bit patronizing, but I must say I'd like to see what he's done to Tarnfield House. And when he found out we had London in common, he almost started to treat me as a human being!'

Robert turned away from her and put his cloth cap on its peg. 'London again,' he said quietly. But Suzy was banging around washing up the coffee mugs.

'He said he'd send a roofer around this afternoon,' she called over. 'He spotted the crack in the chimney stack.'

'Well, we'd better get on with it. I hope his roofer won't be too expensive.'

Suzy turned away back to the sink. If Robert was worried about the money, perhaps she ought to take on more production work rather than less. There were always last-minute calls for freelance news producers over the Christmas holidays. She sighed, and the sound hung in the air.

Whatever she says, Robert thought, *she's fed up with the Briars and the endless work it takes. She's thinking about somewhere more interesting, like Rachel's loft apartment. How long before she tells me she wants a place of her own, in London or Manchester? I couldn't bear it if she said she needed a bolthole somewhere else.*

Suzy left the kitchen without speaking and he heard her stamping upstairs. He sighed and took his folder containing the Parochial Church Council documents from the dresser. The Arbiters, as he had remarked, had fingers in every pie in Tarnfield. But he wanted to know just how deep those fingers went.

* * *

At the same time, a few miles to the east, Jarrold McHugh was still in bed, but he could hear Paula Stovey, his music teacher, downstairs making the coffee. He liked the feeling that she was there, though he had been careful to lock the front room where he kept all his research. Their intimacy couldn't stretch that far — yet. The effects of lazy morning lovemaking and a long Sunday lie-in were starting to wear off. He sensed that she wanted to talk about the future. Women always did, in his experience.

Paula came into the bedroom with two coffees, and some croissants she had picked up the day before from Tarnfield's bakery. She was wearing one of his sweatshirts and a tiny pair of knickers which were different from the night before. So she had meant to stay . . .

'I suppose that was a bit of a give-away,' she laughed. 'I mean, bringing breakfast obviously meant I'd be here overnight.'

'Yeah. And the cute new underpants. I don't think you'd make a secret agent.'

'I don't play games, that's true. So, what's next, Jarrold?'

'Yeah. Right. I should go back to Texas for Christmas as planned, but there are a couple of things to tie up here.' He frowned.

'Like what?'

Jarrold sensed she was used to having her questions answered pronto, so he just watched as she ate her croissant, and waited. He would never be rushed by a woman. He studied her even harder, till she looked away.

Paula looked back at him, willing him to speak. God, he was good looking. It was true that there was a lot she didn't know about him, but his detachment was compelling, and she found herself striving to please him. It was a new feeling for her.

Paula had never been married but she'd had a series of relationships, all of which had been very grown-up and been ended amicably — by her. But Jarrold had got under her skin. He was tall, fit and handsome, with lovely dark red hair and a warm smile, which you saw so rarely it had special value. And he was genuinely perceptive about music. Paula's other relationships had been practical and rational. She was a modern woman, with no desire to have children — yet. She controlled her own life. She indulged in organized, predictable sexual friendships with men ordered from the internet who ticked all the boxes. This was her first random, unexpected love affair since her teens. The thought suddenly shocked her. Yes, it *was* a love affair in all its madness. Not what she did at all.

She remembered with almost painful tenderness the moment this friendship had become different. One glorious summer day on the hills Jarrold had opened up to her, just once. He had told her about his background, and it had made her heart bleed for him. His father was an academic scientist now working for a big company in Austin, Texas. But his mother had deserted them when he was tiny. It had caused him a lot of pain. He had been happy enough, but he had always missed her, till loss turned to bitterness and anger. He had rejected her side of the family completely and wanted to relate only to his father, with a passionate intensity which had recently turned to a study of his paternal family history. He had traced his paternal grandparents, great grandparents and great-great grandparents, and found that one of them was called Arbiter and born in the UK. Arbiter was an unusual name, and he had decided to find out more, and also see some countryside. So here he was.

He had been in IT in the States, he told her, and made a lot of money. So he could afford this career break.

'I'm not sure what will happen next,' Jarrold said.

'But you're definitely going home? I'll miss you a lot if you do, though I could cope. But if you're thinking of staying, I'd like to know.'

'I'm not sure. Look, Paula, I don't like being quizzed. We've had one wonderful night together, but you need to give me some time. No more questions, please.'

Paula paused. She had nothing to lose by being patient, although she had a sense of being dismissed, which annoyed her. Though conversely that also made her feel more insecure and needy. She should walk away. But she couldn't.

'Okay.' She got up from sitting on the bed and looked out of the window. She had pulled the curtains slightly apart to look out at the weather, which wasn't promising. No hill walks today.

Then a movement caught her eye. She quickly let the curtain drop back into place.

'I'm not trying to change the subject,' she said in a different tone of voice, 'but that creepy neighbour of yours is out there packing stuff into his truck. I thought you said that he was away this weekend.'

'Geoff Black? Yes, I thought so too,' said Jarrold. 'But he's not creepy. Just grumpy and a bit secretive.'

'You can talk!' Paula could tease him a bit, but she knew better than to push her luck. 'Okay. Move over and let me back into bed. I need to lick up those crumbs!'

* * *

Outside, Geoff Black glanced up at his neighbour's bedroom window. He thought he'd seen the curtains twitch, but he must have been imagining it because he was so on edge. He watched but there was no more movement. The American was usually out on the hills by this time at the weekend. Geoff planned to freewheel the truck out of the cottage's front garden and down the single-track road until it disappeared into the pines, when he could start the engine. It was a pity about the pickup being on view outside the cottage, but only the American would have seen it. Geoff was under pressure to deliver, but, thank goodness, now she was dead, there was no chance of Deborah nosing around. And no one suspected him.

Geoff got in the truck and breathed a sigh of relief.

CHAPTER SEVEN

Ask counsel, we pray thee, of God, that we may know whether our way which we go shall be prosperous.
Judges 18:5

'Geoff Black was away on Friday and all weekend,' Joanne said irritably to Adelina, who had taken the role on as the residents' spokeswoman and asked to see Joanne in the hostel office in private.

'Are you sure? Geoff Black never really liked Deborah. We could all see that. Leila insists that he did it. He could have come in through the back door, gone up the stairs to the attic and pushed her.'

'That's not what happened. We'd have seen him when he came down. Anyway I've told you: the Blacks were away.'

'What about the American man?'

'That's madness, Adelina. He's a perfectly nice young man who's studying his family history.'

'It's a funny place to be doing that, isn't it? Out here in the middle of nowhere. And nice young men can be misleading. We all know that.'

'This one is fine. I saw his references myself. And I interviewed him before letting him have the tenancy agreement.

Deborah was very happy with him. You don't have to see him and there's no way he could get in here.'

'But we all think that Deborah must have been pushed.'

Joanne said crossly, 'I don't know why I'm even having this conversation with you. Why on earth would Geoff Black or the American want to harm Deborah? She fell. It was an accident. Lee the roofer said that the parapet was made of brickwork over two hundred years old, with a plaster fascia. Stucco they call it. The brickwork had dried out in several places. The mortar would have gone, and the plaster couldn't hold any weight. There are other places where you can see the same problem, but Deborah went through at the weakest spot. Lee told her not to go up there.'

'What about Lee the roofer then? He could have come back and followed her on to the roof.'

'Oh yes? Having left his not inconspicuous van parked in the woods? And walked in here with no one noticing? How would he have got through the gates? Anyway, he was at the big house on the Green in Tarnfield all day Friday, with other people. Builders and roofers were working like crazy until late to make the most of the good weather. I know because I had to call him to tell him the police wanted to interview him. Honestly, Adelina, let's stop this. It's madness.'

'But you must admit Joanne, it wasn't like Deborah.'

'A lot of things Deborah did weren't like Deborah. I still find it hard to believe that she didn't tell me she was going on the roof. Of course I would have tried to stop her, but she wouldn't have taken any notice.' Joanne frowned. One little question nagged at her. Deborah always told her what she was doing and where she was going, even if she didn't always share all the details. Maybe this time she just didn't want an argument, not that she ever lost. Joanne said tetchily, 'We must stop agonising over this, Adelina. It's going nowhere.'

Adelina shrugged. 'True. The police will treat anything we say as victims' paranoia.'

'Survivors, Adelina.'

'You can change the word, but not the meaning. No one is going to believe us, whatever you call us.'

'So just let it go. It's winding the residents up. Look at Leila. She's a bag of nerves. Never off her phone. But I'm not Deborah's replacement. I'm an administrator, not a therapist.'

'And there's no one like Deborah. Who's going to take over?'

'That's not a problem just yet,' Joanne said firmly. 'The board will get a new director in the fullness of time, and I'll keep the practical side going. We have no money worries. If Deborah was as good as her word, we can afford all the staff we need. Counsellors, lawyers . . . anything.'

'Then maybe you can start by getting rid of Geoff Black and getting a decent handyman. Or woman. He should have been looking after that roof and not letting it get into that state. He's never been Deborah's greatest fan. Leila might be right. He could have pushed her.'

'For goodness' sake, stop going round saying things like that. You've no evidence. Just let it be.'

* * *

Suzy and Robert ate Sunday lunch, but he was preoccupied. Finally, Suzy said, 'You're very quiet. I saw you reading at all that Parochial Church Council stuff. What were you looking for?'

'I was going back over lots of complicated property issues. It throws up some interesting things.'

'Such as?'

'Well, the All Saints church hall was built in the early twentieth century with strings attached, and guess who paid for it?

'Who?'

'The Arbiters. But there were a few stipulations. For example, the church hall shouldn't be hired out for activities inconsistent with the beliefs of the Church of England . . .'

'Like a gay partnership party?'

'Exactly.'

'But that's nuts, Robert. Times have totally changed. The Arbiters probably didn't agree with indoor loos for the working classes! And anyway, there have been loads of secular events there. There's a yoga class. And Tai Chi. The Arbiters wouldn't approve of that. And the Muslims used the church hall for an Eid celebration last year when it was too wet to use the village green.' There were three or four Muslim families in the wider neighbourhood, and no one had objected when they had used the church hall as a one off. It was thought of as the village hall really, and that was the job it did.

'Of course, in practice, these days we wouldn't dream of invoking this sort of clause. But if Archdeacon Bentley gets hold of this deeds document . . . I'm going to ring the vicar and see if she's free to talk this afternoon. I gather she's doing a service at the hostel, but hopefully she'll be back around three o'clock.'

'But what about Scott Jermyn's roofer? Remember? He's coming this afternoon.'

'Can't you deal with him, Suzy? It doesn't matter about the money. If the guy can sort it out, we'll just pay what it takes.'

Money again, Suzy thought. But Robert was in too much of a hurry to talk about it. He grabbed his jacket and the cloth cap she hated.

'See you later,' he said. 'Good luck with the roofer.'

'Okay,' Suzy said to his back. He hadn't kissed her goodbye. Normally she wouldn't have noticed but today she did. Robert went out into the gloomy weather.

She went up to the office and logged on. Still no code from the Academy of Journalism, so she couldn't start marking the students' essays on the Warsbrook report. Instead, she decided to declutter the bedroom. That would be a massive task, and dusty. There would be dark clouds everywhere that afternoon.

* * *

Lee Lewis drove up to the Briars in his silver van with the bright blue letters saying 'Roofs, gutters, balconies, extensions — if you have problems *LEE'VE IT TO LEE*.'

He'd been a roofer, like his father before him, since leaving school in Newcastle twenty years before, but he'd built up his dad's business and had slowly moved westwards to take in Cumbrian villages. He specialized in traditional buildings. The people who owned older houses these days were usually well off and were interested in keeping the style of the property, but with state-of-the-art comfort. And Lee had a friendly, open manner and was scrupulously fair when it came to value for money. He was also ingenious and often thought of interesting ways to make things work. He prided himself on being a bit more creative than your average roofer.

He'd told everyone that he'd been chuffed to get work at the hostel, and he sincerely hoped that once the shock of Deborah's death had worn off, Joanne Butcher would invite him back to repair the parapet.

But as his wife Mandy had said, he was obviously gutted about Deborah. 'She was amazing,' he'd said to the lads in the Plough on Saturday night. 'At first I thought she might be tricky. One of these know-all hinnies.' His mates had nodded sympathetically — they'd all had customers like that.

Lee went on: 'But ya know what, lads? Deborah was a good 'un. Prepared to pay top dollar for top graft and keen to get it done. I did the gutters for her, during the storms. Then the leak started over the attic bedrooms, and she got me back to have a look at that. I'd done a bit of smart thinking about that ledge behind the parapet. That was the cause of the trouble. It was a real mess. I saw how the rubbish had piled up over the years, and I was right, it covered a big hole. Howay, sorry about the craic. It's the shock.'

Lee was always very chatty but on Saturday night he'd seemed almost garrulous. He took a swig from his pint and Mandy had taken the opportunity, while his mouth was engaged with his beer, to put her hand on his arm and calm him down. Mandy was small and blonde with a pretty face and hair in bunches. 'Don't get worked up, pet,' she'd said softly. 'Accidents happen.'

Lee had gulped and started again. 'Try telling the coppers that. They gave me the real third degree. But I told them! I made Deborah agree not to go up there till I could get back and fix it. I didna think she would do what she liked!' He took another swig, finished his pint and shook his head. 'I thought the police might get me for leaving ladders there, but there was no one living on that top floor, so there was absolutely no danger. I think they were trying to pin some sort of negligence on me, but it wouldn't stick.'

'C'mon, marra, forget it now,' one of his mates had said. 'Have another.'

At that moment, Mr Jermyn ('Call me Scott, old son') had come into the Plough. Lee had been working on the roof at Scott's house on Friday, but that job was finished now. Scott bought Lee a whisky and said, 'Don't worry, fella. There'll be other work. Just let me put out some feelers.'

And Scott had been as good as his word. That had been last night and already, the next day, Scott Jermyn had found him a new job.

* * *

Lee got out of his van and gave the Briars a professional appraisal. He placed it accurately as a late-nineteenth-century stone-built house, with brick chimneys on each side, probably built for a superior sort of tradesman like a blacksmith or wheelwright. A brick porch had been added later, and he wondered shrewdly if the roof had been raised at some point, to give the house more presence, perhaps as the owner got richer. But the crack up the chimney stack was nasty.

He knocked at the door. 'Mrs Clark? Have I got that right?' Best to err on the safe side.

'Thanks for asking. But my name's Suzy Spencer.' Suzy smiled at him. 'Robert Clark's my husband.'

'Ms Spencer. Great. I'm Lee the roofer. Leave it to Lee!'

He grinned, but not like Scott Jermyn. And Suzy liked his voice with its Tyneside burr. 'Oh yes,' she said. 'I can see the logo on your van. The job's about our chimney stack. If you stand here, you can see the crack in it.'

Lee stood back and squinted upwards. 'Nasty. Have you noticed any interior damage? Damp stains in the attic rooms, maybe?'

Suzy shook her head. She felt rather ashamed of not having inspected the attic for a while. She was trying not to get exercised about Molly demanding a room up there for her art studio.

'Okay, bonny lass.' Lee grinned reassuringly. 'Well, I'll get the ladder out straight away and have a look. It might not be as big a job as you think. I can do a bit of smart thinking about how to put it right from the outside. I don't want to disturb you, so I'll knock at the front door when I'm done.'

'That's very considerate. I'm in the middle of doing some pretty serious clearing out.' Unlike Scott Jermyn, Lee hadn't looked her up and down, but Suzy felt aware of the dust on her face and in her hair, the result of crawling under the bed for the first time in months.

Lee said cheerfully, 'No problem. My rates are in line with what you'll find on *GetYourRoofer*. There's Scott Jermyn for a referee — Tarnfield House. And of course I did some work for poor Deborah. Lovely lady. A belta! You should know that I'm free this week because I was booked in to do her roof tomorrow. That's off now, of course . . .' He looked away and winced. Suzy felt sorry for him.

'It must have been a shock.'

'You can say that again. But my wife says I've been going on about it too much. I was gutted though. Absolutely gutted.'

'Yes, it was a terrible accident. Well, give me a shout when you're done looking at the chimney.'

No sexist nonsense about checking with the man of the house. He seemed a nice enough bloke, Suzy thought. She went back up to the office and checked him out online.

His website was surprisingly impressive. He would do, she thought, and she liked the idea of him working outside and not coming in the house.

Then she went back to sorting out all the old boxes which had been in a crate under the bed. There was all sorts of rubbish there. And some things which were quite precious but hard to place. On a whim she took out a jewellery box which had belonged to Robert's first wife.

Suzy hadn't opened the jewellery box for years. She looked at the small collection of valuables. One was a thick, heavy, silvery-looking ring. Suzy wondered what it was made of — white gold? Or platinum? It wasn't the sort of thing Suzy would ever wear but she wondered if Molly might like it. Molly was starting to show signs of having some taste, though they were heavily camouflaged. She would ask Robert. It was a shame to have these things just lying under the bed.

And she vowed to deal with the boxes on top of the wardrobe too before Robert came home. Perhaps tonight they really ought to clear the air, she thought. She really loved the Briars, but if it was getting too much for Robert, she would live anywhere with him. Perhaps she needed to tell him that. Or if money was a problem, they could make savings. The most important thing was for them to talk, in the old easy way. She pulled a feather duster over the wardrobe top and the dust sank down and settled, coating the bedroom. Clearing the air was easier said than done.

* * *

Jarrold McHugh watched Paula back her Honda Civic out of the space beside the cottage. She waved to him cheerfully as she drove away. They had spent the remainder of Sunday reading the online papers, talking about all sorts of things, and then eating the late Sunday lunch he had prepared. They had said no more about the future, and he knew he was keeping her guessing.

But she was an intelligent woman who made a big deal out of self-reliance. If she had fallen for him, it was hardly his fault. He wondered if he'd be able to get her to curb that independence . . . it was an exciting thought.

And next week things would come to a head. Then he could decide what to do about Paula.

CHAPTER EIGHT

There shall they rehearse the righteous acts of the Lord, even the righteous acts toward the inhabitants of his villages . . .
Judges 5:11

Late on Sunday afternoon, Geoff Black picked up Moira from the train at Tarnfield Junction. She'd been staying with their daughter Tracey. He accelerated out of the tiny car park, revved up his pickup's engine and said little until they were on the road to the village.

'Everything all right in Hardcastle?'

'Yes, thanks Geoff. Did you get that extra job done at home?'

'Yes.' Geoff was brusque. To Moira's surprise he pulled over into a layby and stopped the truck. She saw him take a deep breath and she knew trouble was coming.

'There's something you should know. Deborah's dead.'

'What?'

'You heard.'

Briefly and in blunt terms he told his wife about Deborah's accident. Moira had already had an emotionally draining weekend. She started to cry until she saw him looking at her with contempt. Then she blew her nose and said, 'Sorry Geoff, it's just the shock. Oh poor Deborah.'

Geoff sniffed eloquently. Moira turned to him. 'Whatever you thought of her, Geoff, it's an awful thing to happen. Why didn't you phone me? I might have heard it on the radio or seen it online or anywhere, and that would have been awful.'

'Tracey doesn't have Radio Cumbria on, and you're hardly an internet whizz-kid. I needed to talk to you properly. Not on the phone where Tracey could overhear you.'

Moira recognized Geoff's bull-headed manner, which brought back unpleasant memories. He'd been a squaddie before they married, and sometimes he still had that passive-aggressive manner of some men of his age from the ranks. He hunched over the steering wheel and looked straight ahead.

Moira tensed. They had been married for forty years, but she couldn't say it had been happy. Geoff had never laid a finger on her, or so much as broken a teacup in anger. But his cold, silent sulks were hard to bear. She had married him because she was 'used goods' — there were few secrets which weren't ferreted out in Hardcastle, and most men who approached Moira thought she was an easy lay, so she had created a hard shell around herself to fend them off.

Geoff had been the only one who seemed prepared to commit. He'd been good looking in a rugged way, and very fit and strong. After coming out of the army he'd become an odd job man, a fixer, a bit of a loner. He lived in his own world of little enterprises. Moira still never knew when he'd be called away on a job. He usually did a few hours a week for St Jane's, but he often disappeared, for weekends or longer, doing his own thing; building work, helping at pheasant shoots, lending a hand on jobs down south — there had been quite a few of those.

Those were the terms on which they'd married. He was getting on a bit and doing her a favour. She got the security, and he got regular sex and his washing done.

He wasn't a bad provider. He took opportunities when they came up, and he made a good enough living. They'd got a deal on the cottage with Deborah and had been through all the vetting. Moira knew Geoff disliked the Judge, but she had to hand it to him: he rarely let it show. Like in the early days, when Deborah turned up with that wretched model of a saint, which they treated like the Venus of whatsit. But Moira knew that on some visceral level Geoff found the whole idea of the hostel distasteful.

Geoff said tersely, 'You need to listen to me, Moira, and do exactly what I tell you.' This was unusually straight. Geoff was more inclined to say nothing and leave his wife in suspense, wondering what it was she had said or done to annoy him. But this time it was as if he had prepared a speech. 'If anyone asks, say I drove you to Hardcastle as planned. And stayed. No need to mention the train.'

'What are you talking about, Geoff?'

'Don't interrupt. Tell the police that I drove you over there on Friday night and stayed with you and Tracey and the grandkids. Don't say I dropped you at the Junction and came back home.' He shook his head in vexation. 'Or tell them what you like Moira. You'll think of something. You're good at keeping secrets.'

She felt her breath coming quicker. But she said nothing.

Geoff went on, 'We'll say no more about what you've been up to, if you keep your trap shut about me. Everyone thinks I was away. If the American says he saw my truck outside the cottage, I'll think of something. But if you ask me, he's up to no good as well, so I doubt he'll mention it. The most important thing is that no one knows I was here this weekend. Keep it like that.'

'All right,' she said. What did he mean by the American being up to no good *as well*? As well as who? Geoff?

Geoff started the truck again and pulled out into the main road. The conversation was over, and Moira was left in a minefield. If she made the wrong move, there could be an explosion. 'I think we'll have fish fingers for tea,' she said.

'Something easy.' It was the right tactic. Geoff's big neck relaxed.

As he drove, he thought about what had happened on Friday. First the phone call in the morning asking where the first consignment was, in no uncertain terms. Geoff had been slow getting it ready because the American had been hanging around more than usual. Then there were his efforts to get hold of the boss man. He'd needed to have the pickup handy and so had no time to drive Moira to Hardcastle and back. So he'd taken her to the train at Tarnfield Junction, driven back and left the truck in the woods, then arranged the meet, transferring the stuff from his truck. No one at the hostel had seen him, not that they'd necessarily be looking out, but you could never tell with that Joanne Butcher woman.

He'd been sorting the next consignment in the garage when he'd turned round and seen Deborah. She'd given gave him a hell of a shock.

'Hello Geoff. I thought you were away this weekend. What is it you've got there?'

'Just some materials.'

'Really? Looks like quite a lot of material to me!' she said archly.

Geoff didn't want to think about the incident any more, but it was going round in his head like a camshaft. He'd felt for a while that Deborah was paying him more attention, but not in a good way. Deborah only came up to the cottages once in a blue moon, and it struck him that she must have been prowling around, thinking he was in Hardcastle. What a snooty cow she was, with that knowing look. He bet that she'd wanted to know what he had in the garage, and thought she'd have a look-see while he and Moira were both away at the same time, which wasn't often. For all he knew, Deborah might have a key.

She'd laughed, raised one eyebrow and walked back to the track. He'd followed her, just to make sure she'd gone. But she'd been getting under his skin for the last few weeks. He'd told the boss. It wasn't like him to be spooked, but there was something about Deborah's manner, almost amused, waiting for him to blunder and give himself away, which frightened him. She needed sorting out.

Later he'd heard the ambulance and the police. If they'd come to his door, he would have told the truth, that he hadn't gone away. But it was much better if they thought he'd been in Hardcastle with Moira. He'd parked the truck squarely in front of the garage. If anyone thought of looking in there, they would have to ask him first.

But the police had come and gone without calling at the cottage. He'd stayed all night in the dark, hoping no one had seen him. And he'd lain low all weekend — except when he needed to make the delivery. Geoff felt much better knowing Deborah wouldn't appear again to check out what he was doing. He was deeply relieved that she was dead. And deserved to be.

* * *

Later on Sunday afternoon, Suzy lay in the bath and tried not to think about the new stain on the ceiling. Hopefully it was caused by the chimney crack and would magically vanish when Lee fixed it. *Lee've it to Lee.* Quite a good slogan in a terrible way.

Both Lee and Scott were new to Tarnfield. The village was changing.

When Suzy had arrived in Tarnfield the village had been dominated by families who had lived there for decades and had a stranglehold on local commerce. They were still around. But there were more newcomers now. Remote working, the attractions of sanitized country living, more property owners in the population — all this had contributed. Now the village had a new bakery, plus the Star of Bengal takeaway run by the Hossein family, a bigger convenience store and a nail parlour. In a way, Suzy missed the links with previous generations, but there was no doubt Tarnfield was more open now.

She sometimes forgot how lonely she had been until she met Robert and moved into the Briars. The happiest time of her life had been spent in this old house, watching the children grow in confidence and seeing how Robert loved them.

Suzy sat up with a splash. Idiot. She had been daydreaming too long in the bath. She knew it had been a mistake to lie there with her hair streaking kit on, but it was so restful. Her plan had been to get dried, put on some body cream, rinse out her hair, condition it and then use the super-straighteners she had found neglected under the bed to turn her hair into a sleek bob of glistening highlights. But if she didn't get a move on, she would look like Worzel Gummidge.

She had hardly started her beauty routine when she heard Robert come back, and other voices.

'Hi Suzy!' Robert called up the stairs. 'I've got Stevie and Alan with me. Where are the crisps?'

'In the bread bin.'

'Where?'

'The bread bin . . .' *Don't ask*, she thought, remembering she had just dumped them there after their last big shop.

'Okay. Stevie's brought some fizz. No reason — just to cheer us up after a fraught afternoon. Get down here as soon as you can.'

Just when I was hoping to have a good go at my toenails as well, Suzy thought. And she needed to get the streaking cap off. She liked Alan and Stevie, but an evening alone with Robert would have been good. On the other hand, the visitors might lighten the atmosphere.

'Coming!' she called cheerily, towelling hurriedly and applying the hairdryer to her unconditioned mop. Then she tried to cram herself into her newest jeans. They were tight; a bit of muffin welled over the waistband. She found herself thinking she was glad she hadn't been wearing them when Scott Jermyn came round — or Lee Lewis for that matter. But what was she thinking of? Trying to look good?

Fat chance, literally. She glanced in the mirror. The highlight kit had been a disaster. Good job Alan and Stevie were only interested in her brain, though these days that felt as frizzled as her hair. She really needed to relax. Maybe Stevie's bottle of champagne was just the thing. She abandoned the jeans for her jogging bottoms and slipper bootees and went downstairs.

'Wow, crazy hair-do, Suzy,' Stevie giggled. 'Bit wild for Tarnfield! You're branching out. Literally!'

Suzy laughed. 'Maybe I should.'

Robert turned away.

* * *

Later in bed, feeling as if the room was slowly pulsating, Suzy snuggled up to Robert, but he was fast asleep. She knew that she wouldn't be able to sleep and took another swig from the glass of water by the bed. It had been a fun evening in many ways, but it had soon split into Stevie and Suzy talking about TV gossip, and Alan and Robert talking about church events.

The headlines were that the Reverend Linda Finch had received an email back from the Bishop of Norbridge almost immediately after her new suggestion for Alan and Stevie's civil partnership party, and the bishop had summoned the key players to come to her office the next day. The topic was the controversy whipped up by the archdeacon.

'The Ven Jim!' scoffed Stevie. 'He's trying too hard.'

'He's an odd person,' Suzy had said. 'Really aggressive. He only backed down over the press coverage of Deborah's death because he was out of his comfort zone. Who's been asked to the meeting?'

'Only one churchwarden, to keep numbers under control, allegedly.' Alan's laugh had been rather forced. 'That means Robert, for obvious reasons. Linda as vicar. And Neil, the area dean.'

'Why the urgency?' Suzy had asked.

'I think,' Robert had said slowly, 'that there are issues raised about the use of the church hall. Fortunately there seem to be plenty of recent precedents for using the hall in ways which would have been taboo in 1906 when it was built.'

'But the archdeacon's bound to argue that they were infringements.' said Alan.

'Oh get real!' Stevie was in high good humour. 'No one in their right mind would want to stop a party in a little village church hall, with half of the cast of one of the most successful TV drama series in attendance. Even Winston is coming.'

Winston Harris, actor and singer, was the unbelievably handsome star of *The Medicine*. Stevie had waited for Suzy to pick her jaw up from the floor, and said, 'He's actually quite keen on the church himself. Rather up the candle, as they say in theological circles.' He sniggered.

'You mean a bit High Church?'

'That's right. Bells and smells. You know, if I ask nicely, he might stay over and have a part in the Sunday service. Winston singing! All Saints would be packed! Imagine what it would do on Instagram! What a coup for Linda. Winston would raise the roof — in fact, he'd probably raise the money to have it completely repaired. Of course he's a 'friend of Dorothy' too, but very discreet. We just won't let the Ven Jim in on that secret.'

That was when it had turned into a conversation of two halves, with Suzy and Stevie digging up more and more outrageous media gossip as they drank the champagne, and Alan and Robert discussing tactics for the following day. When it was time for another bottle, Robert had found one under the stairs and Suzy discovered some home-made wraps in the bottom of the freezer, so they had kept going with an impromptu supper.

Now, in bed with her head spinning, Suzy remembered another bit of the conversation. She had been moaning to Stevie about freelancing. She had found herself gabbling away about how hard she'd been working.

'I even tried teaching at the North London Academy of Journalism last week. It was awful. And now I've got to mark twenty-five essays. I can't get out of it and I'm still waiting for an email with a code for me to use to access them. I can't think why it hasn't arrived.' She was being so boring. But Stevie started to nod sagely.

'Aha,' he'd said. 'I've had a similar problem myself. Did you use your *Living Lies* email address for the academy?'

'Yes. I thought that helped with my credentials.'

'But I assume you get everything from the *Living Lies* address diverted to your main personal email? I do that. Everything that comes to my *Medicine* email gets sent on to my Gmail. Saves me using two accounts, even though *The Medicine* insist we have an account with them.'

'Yes. I do exactly the same with the *Living Lies* account.'

'Well, you might not have spotted this — a lot of us didn't — but earlier this year some companies ramped up their email security. They're more ruthless now at filtering. And they don't send everything on. You probably check your personal email spam all the time . . .'

'Yes, of course, just in case . . .'

'Well, you need to go back to your *Living Lies* account and check the junk there too. There isn't much that doesn't get through, but some of the weirder one-off email addresses get blocked. Don't rely on everything being re-sent to your personal account like it used to.' He took a bite out of his wrap, chewed for a moment, and asked, 'Have you looked in that spam folder?'

'It's a chilli tortilla actually. Is my cooking that bad?' They had both fallen about in tipsy laughter.

But now, unable to sleep, Suzy slipped out of bed and went into the office. Maybe the code sent by the academy really was sitting in the junk in her *Living Lies* email account. She logged on. Yes, Stevie had been right. There were several minor one-off unopened emails there. She sorted them in alphabetical order. Hooray, there was the code to access the marking, sent by Eliza Jones, the course officer at the academy.

And underneath it was another email which caused Suzy's head to throb and her mouth to dry. It was a message from Ellie Fox. Dated months earlier.

CHAPTER NINE

Now therefore up by night, thou and the people that is with thee.
Judges 9:32

Suzy's was not the only lighted window in the valley that night. But the pale oblongs of electric light which dotted the sleeping village were outshone by a moon like a large beaten pewter plate above the fells.

Geoff Black woke, went to the bathroom and got into his black keks and fleece. He tutted when he saw the moon through the thin washed-out curtains that Moira used in their bedroom. Though Geoff liked that thriftiness about Moira. She wasn't so bad. In the old days she'd had strong, dark good looks and he had admired her bloody-mindedness in holding her head up, despite the small-town censure. Now though, at night when he turned over and his bony knees collided with her solid legs, he felt a wave of disgust. Moira was like a sack of potatoes. But he knew he could rely on her total loyalty.

It was a pain about the moon, but it was unavoidable. It reminded him of the big round shiny halo on that stupid statue of St Jane that he'd had to erect in that pile of stones at the hostel. Ridiculous thing. But Deborah always got what she wanted. He felt a tremor of concern, then grabbed his boots. The problem was over. Deborah was dead.

He pattered in his stockinged feet down the stairs.

* * *

Moira lay on her side wide awake and motionless. She didn't want an earful. A little bit later she heard the truck freewheel down the track, Geoff's preferred way of leaving. Where was he going? Best not to think about it.

* * *

At Tarnfield House on the village green, moonlight kept Scott Jermyn awake. He uncurled his long thin legs in his boxer shorts and loped over to the window. He had no curtains up yet — they were taking months to be made. He peered out over the Green, towards All Saints Church and the pretty Georgian villas on the other side. It was weirdly still and quiet, making him hold his breath. It was also very bright. *I'm a city boy*, he thought for the millionth time. *This is new for me.*

Best to get under his top-quality duvet in its Egyptian cotton cover. He padded back to bed and thought about his life in Tarnfield. The house was coming along great. He had made progress, and the comforts of his former life in the Smoke were not too far out of reach. He liked going to the pub and holding court. He had enjoyed meeting little Suzy whatsit, who was feisty enough to amuse him. He could see that old Robert was attractive in an old-school way, but all that churchy stuff could hardly be a turn-on for a TV producer like Suzy.

Now there was his impromptu drinks party on Wednesday to look forward to. Maybe that old queen Alan would turn out, and he could even ask the secretary from the hostel. He'd met Joanne when he'd been having dealings with Deborah. Poor Deborah. She came over as just the sort of woman who would try poking around where she'd been told not to. Fancy her going up, alone, onto the roof . . .

That reminded him of Lee the roofer, shattered by Deborah's death and terrified of being blamed. Lee was a bit of a rough diamond. It might be risky to invite him to the party, but his wife Mandy was quite tasty, not as common as Lee, although that funny hairstyle with the bunches on the side of her head was a bit juvenile. She worked in the big chemist store in Norbridge, and people always liked talking about drugs, even the over-the-counter sort. Scott sniggered. On the other hand, though, he wasn't too thrilled at the thought of Lee's garish van being parked outside Tarnfield House on party night, especially now he'd got rid of the skip. Better suggest a taxi. He'd pay.

Somewhere in the distance Scott heard the noise of a truck pulling up. It was hardly more than a soft purr. All the same . . . he uncurled himself and went to the window again.

* * *

At the Briars, Suzy read the email from Ellie Fox in her *Living Lies* spam folder, for what seemed like the hundredth time. She must have given Ellie her work email account because she'd been impressed by Suzy's job.

> *Hi,*
>
> *So great to have met you in the chalet from hell! What an exciting job you have! I hope you got home safely. I didn't have any carbon monoxide effects — did you?*
>
> *I'm so glad we talked. I don't tell people about the mess I'm in with J. It's too humiliating. But I'm so glad I told you.*
>
> *Anyway, as predicted J went berserk over me having a holiday. It's been terrible since I've been back, but I'm determined to make the break, whatever J threatens. And there's a coincidence I didn't mention at the time because I had to think about it. But I've checked out the woman at the hostel you told me about. I might contact her, but I'd like*

your advice. Call me! Here's my phone number . . . It was wonderful to meet you, and let's talk!

Ellie Fox

Suzy felt sick. Ellie's email address was Ell.foxylady@hotmail.com — the kind of address sure to be destined for the spam folder. Suzy checked her spam over again in case Ellie had changed her email address or the name she used. But this was the only message from Ellie, back in the spring.

Yet Suzy had emailed Ellie twice, only a fortnight ago before she went to stay in Islington, with no answer. Why? Where was Ellie now? Had something happened to her?

Suzy re-read the old email yet again. Ellie said she felt threatened and wanted to talk. If only Suzy had got this first email, she would have responded at once.

Suzy tried until her head ached to remember the conversation in the basement of the chalet. She had felt nauseous as the hours wore on. She had blamed it on the coffee and the stress. But now she wondered whether the carbon monoxide had affected her. She had no memory of mentioning St Jane's Hostel to Ellie, but it had obviously been one of the things they had talked about. That explained why Ellie had been nagging at the back of her mind since she came home to Tarnfield. The Savoy saint must have started that thread in the conversation. Suzy must have talked with enthusiasm about Deborah and the Alpine connection, and in the email, Ellie said she was thinking of contacting the hostel. Did Ellie want a place in St Jane's? Suzy just couldn't remember. The whole night in the chalet basement had the quality of a nightmare. And now the silence from Ellie was sinister, and Suzy felt guilty and worried.

She thought she would go and wake Robert. She could talk to him, and together they would sort out all these threads of dream and reality. But he was fast asleep. To be fair, he had his own worries — problems with the parish and money concerns about the house.

Suddenly Suzy stood up from the desk. She would cope with this on her own and not bother Robert. He had made it clear he didn't want to talk about Deborah's death. Fussing about Ellie on top would irritate him even more. She left her desk and went to the bathroom. She had a pee, washed her hands and drank some more water. She looked at her reflection in the mirror. She didn't look like a wild-eyed mad woman. Her own sane, usually perky face looked back at her. A bit haggard, but normal.

And she suddenly thought — the simplest thing was to text Ellie. Now. She could do that straight away because Ellie had sent her phone number. Suzy went back to the spare bedroom-cum-office and picked up her mobile.

Hi Ellie,

I'm so sorry not to have answered your email. It went into my spam folder. I emailed you a fortnight ago but with no luck. Now I have your number so I can text.

How are you?

Suzy

She pressed 'send'. If Ellie hadn't replied within a day or two, Suzy would try to find her. But how could she do that?

For a start, she could call her best friend Rachel in London in the morning. There were a quarter of a million people in Islington. But Ellie lived on Rachel's doorstep. Suzy's best friend would be bound to know someone, who would in turn know someone, who would know of a local woman called Ellie on the Barnford Estate across the road. Rache wouldn't mind nosing around — in fact, she'd probably enjoy it.

Suzy could also check with Joanne Butcher at St Jane's. Would Joanne tell her if anyone called Ellie had made enquiries about the hostel? Would that be a breach of confidentiality? Possibly. But surely Joanne would want to help and would know Suzy could be trusted.

And Suzy could call her old friend Ro Watson, a police community support officer, and ask how to go about tracing someone who might have gone off the radar between

Islington and Tarnfield. That is, if Ellie really was trying to get to the hostel. If something awful had happened to Ellie, Ro just might be able to find out. And wasn't there something called a Missing Person's Register? Ellie couldn't disappear without anyone noticing.

Or then again, maybe Suzy was just being melodramatic. Maybe Ellie wasn't interested in replying to her. It had been months since they were in contact, after all, and Ellie might feel let down by Suzy not replying to her first email, however good the reason was. She would talk to Ro, who was always very down to earth, and might help her put it into perspective.

She felt better. Maybe it was good that Robert was distracted by problems at the church, so she would have time to get on with locating Ellie. Of course, Molly would be home later that day after her weekend away — yes, it was now Monday — but her daughter was seventeen and doing her own teenage thing.

Suzy took a deep breath. She would find Ellie and stay in touch this time. Then Suzy went back to bed and cuddled into Robert's warm back. But he didn't wake.

Somewhere in the village she thought she heard a truck starting up and moving off. But the sound faded away as she drifted into a troubled sleep.

CHAPTER TEN

And she dwelt under the palm tree of Deborah between Ramah and Bethel in mount Ephraim: and the children of Israel came up to her for judgment.
Judges 4:5

On Monday morning, Suzy arrived at St Jane's Hostel before nine. Before setting out, she had called Rachel, her friend in Islington.

Rachel had sounded harassed. 'What time d'you call this? I'm trying to get out. I've got an outside broadcast in Berkshire. There's a by-election coming up in case you didn't know . . . But why should you? You've practically declared independence up there . . .'

'That's Scotland, Rachel.'

'Practically the same. Hills. Rain. Wellies.'

'That's outrageous. Try putting that comment on Twitter and see how many followers you lose! To be serious for a minute, could you find out about somebody for me? That woman I met on holiday. The one who lives on the Barnford Estate. The one I tried to contact last week. Ellie Fox. You remember?'

Rachel had sighed melodramatically and made grumbling noises, but Suzy knew that she wouldn't be able to resist. Yes, all right, she would try to help, and get back to Suzy as soon as she could. But it would be the next day at the earliest. She was big mates with the secretary of the Barnford Tenants Association. But it might take a drink at the local gastropub, with triple-cooked chips in sea salt and turmeric, to get her pal chatting freely about everyone in the flats.

'Thanks. You're amazing Rachel.'

'I know. You owe me a bottle of designer gin. Frogspawn, sage and quinoa flowers, please.'

'Mmm, sounds sooo North London.'

Suzy put the Ellie situation to the back of her mind and set off for Tarnfield Hill. She took with her to the hostel the printouts of the weekend's media coverage of Deborah's death. There was also a new list of requests. Radio Cumbria wanted a much longer tribute piece for later in the week, the *Mid Cumbria Times* likewise, and one of the Northumbria papers was also interested in a feature.

At the hostel, she worked for an hour without saying much, but when it came to the tribute piece, she wondered what questions the local radio journalist would ask. If Suzy were doing the interview herself, the first thing she'd want to know would be why a woman like Deborah might open a hostel in the first place.

From the straightforward CV on the hostel computer, Suzy knew that Deborah had been to boarding school in Windermere, then gone to Oxford at the early age of seventeen. Deborah had been a high flyer. She had then qualified as a barrister and worked in chambers in London before coming home when her father died, when she had turned all her energy towards running St Jane's. It made sense. But it also seemed too pat. Why would a rising-star barrister give it up and turn to charity work? Religious fervour, maybe?

Chelsea brought her and Joanne some coffee, and Suzy looked up and rubbed her temples. She had a slight headache. Her article for the *Mid Cumbria Times* seemed lifeless. She said to Joanne, 'I'm bothered about this feature I'm writing on Deborah. I'm churning out a list of facts, but it's got no life. No insight. Do you know why Deborah wanted to start this hostel?'

'Everyone wonders about that,' Joanne said. 'People think she must have been a survivor herself, but she hadn't suffered from abuse or the loss of a child. She was just one hundred per cent committed to helping other women.'

'Did she have any significant relationships?'

'No.' Joanne paused. 'I wouldn't like you to print this, but I really don't think she was interested in sex. She wasn't a lesbian. And she never referred to any men in her life. She had no desire to have children. I think she was asexual, and ahead of her time in coming to terms with it. And having no sex-drive doesn't mean you lack love or understanding. She was wonderful with the residents.'

Suzy thought for a while about what Joanne had said. It fitted with Deborah's objective, forensic work on behalf of the women in St Jane's, sorting out their problems and offering her judgment in the widest sense, free of relationships of her own. The residents all had difficulties, naturally. It was a hostel for older women with nowhere to go, who had lost their children.

But interestingly, none of those criteria fitted with Ellie Fox. She had a home and a job, she had no children, and she was much younger than the average resident at St Jane's. So why had she been attracted to this hostel? Just because Suzy had mentioned it and she liked the sound of Deborah? Unlikely.

'Joanne, I know you shouldn't talk about the residents, but I'm wondering about someone who never became one! If I mention a name, could you check it for me? It's someone who might have made enquiries. She was someone I met months ago, and I'm worried about her. Her name was Ellie.'

Joanne thought for a moment. 'I can't see that would do any harm.'

Suzy waited while Joanne clicked about on the hostel PC. 'Here we are. As you know, we're one resident short. Deborah was talking to a possibility back in the spring.

Unfortunately, we haven't got Deborah's notes. I can't think where they are . . . She was very careful to check out anyone who wanted to come, you know. She kept a lot of background information. It's shame I can't find her papers anywhere.' Joanne tapped away. 'Anyway, we never heard from this one after last May. I just have a name. I suppose she might go by Ellie. Yes, Eleanor Fox.'

Suzy had grabbed hold of the desk and closed her eyes. 'Do you mind if I go outside, Joanne? I need to make a personal call.'

* * *

Detective Sergeant Jed Jackson had his own office in Workhaven. This was largely thanks to the fact that Workhaven CID was housed in a Victorian building with a lot of small, odd-shaped partitions.

He looked at the screen. It had happened again. Two more catalytic converters nicked from cars over Sunday night. One was from the Indian family, the Hosseins, who owned the takeaway in Tarnfield — their old Prius would be a cinch for these thieves — and one was at Pelliter, further up the coast.

He felt it was a particularly mean theft. The catalytic converter was attached to the car's exhaust system to reduce pollution, but it could be sawn off and stolen. Losing the catalytic converter led to people in rural areas being stranded for days until new converters could be fitted.

Thieves wanted the precious metals in the converters. Even a tiny amount of platinum or rhodium was valuable. The thieves were operating once or twice a week throughout the area, and Jed knew from liaising with other forces that it wouldn't just be catalytic converters they were after but any metals — lead particularly. There had been a spate of thefts of lead from church roofs in Cumbria, Lancashire and the North East, and a few metal statues and plaques had also disappeared.

He looked up to see PCSO Ro Watson hovering outside his door. They had been colleagues for years and were friends in a downbeat way. They had met when they were involved in the nasty murder of a local schoolteacher. Jed was a keen Christian and Ro, a firm agnostic, had found him sanctimonious at first. But in the end, they got on well.

Ro was an unusual person. She was sharp and committed, and had weathered a few crises in her own life, like bringing up her son alone. He had cerebral palsy. He was now at university studying computer science in Edinburgh. But Ro had never wanted to progress from being a police community support officer.

'Hi,' Ro said, putting her head around his door. 'What gives?'

'Two more catalytic converters gone. But there's something more to it, I think.'

'What's making you so worried?'

'Well, usually these gangs move in on a neighbourhood, blitz it and then buzz off to whatever rural crimes their gangmasters choose next — massive fly-tipping or butchering farm animals. But this has been week after week for a while now. I think they're local. Building up supplies for some reason. Maybe a commission. There's something about it . . .'

'*By the pricking of my thumbs, something wicked this way comes*,' Ro quoted the witch in *Macbeth* with a grin. 'Your instinct is usually right, Jed. Though I've heard nothing about it on my grapevine. But of course I'm just plastic police, so not into metal.' 'Plastic police' was a label that had been given to PCSOs when they were instituted. It had once made Ro angry, but now she quite liked the term. Plastic had a bad press these days. But though Ro was into ecology she thought plastic had its uses. It was resilient, easy to maintain, impossible to get rid of and unfashionable. Like her. Ro had never subscribed to popular opinion.

After a pause, she said to Jed, 'Have you got any news on the inquest on Deborah Arbiter?'

'Yep. Unless anything new turns up it will be a fortnight on Wednesday. We've got a provisional slot. Our colleagues took Deborah's computer on Friday night, but I've heard on the QT that it's squeaky clean, from what they've seen so far. She'd lost her phone, but according to her administrator she only used it for calls and texts.'

'No notes or indicative emails?'

'No. Remarkably little. Her assistant told us she'd booked a doctor's appointment to talk about dizzy spells, which checks out. It seems clear that she'd gone onto the roof, against advice, and slipped and fell through some damaged masonry. So the boss has asked the coroner to go ahead.'

'No thumb pricking on this one then, Jed?'

'Well . . . I don't know. I've heard some murmurings. But I'm sure that the Norbridge uniform who were there on Friday night didn't miss anything.'

'Fair enough. It's just that Suzy Spencer called me . . .'

Jed nodded. He knew Suzy and Robert from way back, though they hadn't been in touch for a while. Suzy was a close friend of Ro's. They had been at university together.

Ro said, 'I've hardly spoken to Suzy for months. She's never around these days. But she's taken on the press communications role for the hostel.'

'And what did she want?'

'To trace a friend of hers who was supposed to turn up there as a resident. Probably nothing to do with anything. But I took the opportunity to ask her about Deborah's death. Going on the roof was an uncharacteristically daft thing for Deborah to do, apparently. Unless she'd decided on suicide.'

'Maybe we should pop over there just to put our minds at rest. Tomorrow?'

Ro nodded. 'Thumbs pricking now?'

'Maybe. But we don't want to have to delay the inquest unless absolutely necessary.'

'Sure. Mind you, Suzy has good instincts too. We might find something wicked *has* come this way. You go to church, Jed. Maybe you should start praying.'

'I never stop,' he said.

* * *

After calling Ro Watson, Suzy went back into the hostel and spent a few minutes in the loo washing her hands and face. As Ro had said, the fact that Ellie hadn't turned up at St Jane's didn't necessarily mean anything.

Joanne had told Suzy that unless someone was in immediate crisis, Deborah made sure the women who came to the hostel were genuine and needy. In Ellie's case, she seemed to have started the process, but then Ellie had gone silent. That sometimes happened. When it did, Deborah accepted that the potential resident may have gone back to her abuser or been coerced. The accommodation was under Deborah's control, so she didn't necessarily race to fill the room. The situation could chop and change for the woman involved. The room was still there for Ellie, months later.

After another sandwich lunch, made by Chelsea — who appeared with a tray resplendent with tray-cloth and china — Suzy asked Joanne if she could have a walk around the grounds without a minder. The residents knew her now. She wanted to be by herself and to think. It wasn't a particularly nice day, but the wind had dropped. There had still been no reply to her text to Ellie. Suzy had checked her phone every fifteen minutes that day.

She went out of the front door and strolled down the driveway. A path led off to the left towards the wall. There was the old door in the Georgian brickwork, with a keypad needing a code to get out. On impulse, Suzy tried the same code as for the front gates; the door eased open and closed behind her. There was no keypad on the outer wall. No one from outside could get in. Suzy would have to walk round, back to the main gates, on the single-track road.

She found herself where the road became a bridle path on the way up to Tarn Fell, after it passed the two cottages. When she looked back towards the cottages, she could see someone who must be Geoff Black the handyman shifting boxes around outside his garage. He spotted her, scowled and disappeared inside.

As Suzy got her bearings, she saw a tall, attractive young man wheel a bike out of the nearer garden shed. He saw her and called out, 'Hi. You okay? You lost?' She realized how out of place she looked, in her jeans, fleece top and puffer jacket, without a rucksack or hiking paraphernalia. People didn't just turn up for a walk in this terrain. They needed kit.

'No, I'm fine. Just having a look around.'

He said nothing but stared at her with a furrowed forehead. She was struck by how handsome he was. He had auburn hair and large brown eyes. His bike helmet hung on the handlebars, and he was wearing tight thigh-length shorts and a T-shirt despite the October chill. There were panniers on either side of the rear wheel, full of stuff. Usually men in Lycra repelled Suzy, but he casually raised an eyebrow, and she smiled back. She felt she owed him an explanation.

'I'm just having a stroll and a break. I'm acting as press officer at the hostel,' she said. 'You'll know all about Deborah's death. It's caused a lot of local interest.'

'Yep, I can understand that, for sure,' said the man, with a pleasant, understated American lilt. *Of course*, Suzy thought, *the family historian.*

'See you later,' she said, and turned to walk down to the main gates.

'Have a good one,' he replied.

Jarrold McHugh looked after her and wondered if this stranger in the mix was something that he should be worried about. He wondered why she was wandering around unaccompanied. A complication was not what he needed. He frowned.

CHAPTER ELEVEN

At her feet he bowed, he fell, he lay down: at her feet he bowed, he fell: where he bowed, there he fell down dead.
Judges 5:27

Robert had gulped a quick cup of tea and eaten some toast before leaving the Briars shortly after Suzy that morning. He was driving over to Norbridge for the bishop's meeting about Alan and Stevie's party in the church hall. He wasn't sure how it would go, and he wasn't looking forward to it. He wondered if Archdeacon Bentley would be there. He had yet to meet him.

Robert had known all sorts and conditions of men, to quote the prayer book, despite living in a quiet village in a far northern corner of England. He knew of several marriages which were far from conventional under the surface — his own with his first wife for a start. In his view sexual morality was relative: it featured rarely in the Gospels, and when it did it was often a matter of compassion rather than compulsion. In Robert's own lifetime he had seen many changes to what were once thought of as immutable moral rules. Now many couples didn't marry at all. Good parents no longer thrashed their children, and being a single parent was seen as a brave thing, not a disgrace. Wives no longer promised to obey — that seemed absurd now. The idea of Suzy as an obedient wife made him smile. In any case they had always managed to agree.

Until now. He thought of the feverish way Suzy had been chatting to Stevie the night before, about the media world. What was that joke about her branching out? More indication that she wanted to move to the big city? And he was aware that she had been up in the night, on her computer. What was that about?

He'd reached the car park in Norbridge where he usually parked when visiting the diocesan headquarters. Norbridge had a beautiful abbey which functioned as a cathedral. The monks had gone from Norbridge even before the Reformation, seen off by pagan border raiders and the harsh climate. The building never failed to impress him; he found it beautiful, though it lacked the tracery of Gothic architecture. It made a dramatic centrepiece to Norbridge. This is a lovely place to live, he thought, and Tarnfield is one of the nicest villages in the north of the county. We should be happy here. On a whim he took out his phone and texted Suzy.

> *Suzy, so sorry things have been fraught since you came home. Let's try and talk tonight. I know Molly wants that room in the attic for her art. We must discuss. Much love, Rxx*

He met Linda on the steps of Church House. He needed to say something to her before the meeting.

'Linda, I don't think we should mention that Stevie has invited the cast of *The Medicine* to the party. Alan thinks it will be a big fundraiser for the church roof — and that's a great idea. But we don't want the Bishop of Norbridge to feel pressurized.'

Linda's reply was drowned by the noise of a motorbike roaring into the drive. 'Oh dear,' she said when the racket had died down, 'I didn't know he was going to be here.'

* * *

Suzy didn't see Robert's text until after lunch. She had gone back to the hostel, worked on the tribute to Deborah and checked out more enquiries. Condolences were now coming in from women's groups nationally as the news spread. And some were raising questions about how this could possibly have happened.

Then she reviewed Robert's message a couple of times, trying to read between the lines. Obviously, he had a problem with Molly wanting that attic room. What did he mean, '*We must discuss*'? She knew what he was going to say — the Briars' upkeep was costing too much, just as a base for the kids. Robert did a lot of the maintenance, but he was now in his early sixties — he was fit and well, but how long would that last?

Suzy suddenly felt tired. It had been a long night, with the hope of a text from Ellie keeping her awake. She decided that if Joanne had no more need of her at the hostel, she would go home as soon as possible after lunch. She was still hoping Ellie would text her back, and if she did they had a lot of catching up to do. And she also needed to crack on with marking the students' essays on the wretched Warsbrook Enquiry. Funnily enough, there had been a piece about the report in *Broadcast* magazine online that day. There was an imposing picture of Lord Warsbrook. He looked every inch the urbane, successful metropolitan lawyer. He was an expert in regulation, she read.

Joanne said, 'Will you be back tomorrow? There are still so many enquiries and there's going to be more around the inquest. And the funeral, whenever that will be. There'll be press interest in that.'

'Okay, if you think I could be of help.' Suzy sighed. The work for St Jane's was piling up.

For a change, Suzy went out through the main hall rather than the kitchen, stopping to look at the Jael and Sisera picture. The killer's face had a calm, almost transcendent quality as she prepared to plunge the tent peg into Sisera's temple. Suzy stared at it for a while; then she was aware that someone had passed behind her and gone out through the big front door.

Suzy followed and started to walk around the house to where she had parked her car.

'Suzy . . .' Adelina, the residents' spokesperson, was under the chestnut tree, where Deborah used to sit. Suzy walked over to her.

'I saw you admiring our picture,' Adelina said. She was truly beautiful, tall with a full figure. She had a heart-shaped face, deep, dark eyes, and a sensual mouth. But close up, Suzy noticed the tiny criss-cross lines around her face and an ugly scar on her neck. It was hard to tell how old she was; probably older than she looked.

Suzy said, 'I was just wondering how the residents feel about a violent painting like that.'

'It's a message from Deborah to other people, not us.'

'So what was the message?'

'"*Until this tyranny be over-past.*" Psalm 57. But I didn't call you over to talk about the picture. You remember Leila?'

'The thin blonde woman? A bit edgy . . . ?'

'Yes, that's her. She's convinced Geoff Black pushed Deborah off the roof.' Adelina paused. 'And Leila has been uptight for a while. She'd had a lot of tree time from Deborah lately.'

'Tree time?'

'Deborah would talk to us individually, under the tree. Even in winter. It was where she gave her judgments. But Deborah was obviously worried about Leila. Leila has been so twitchy this last month. Ever since the storms. Never off her phone, out here where she could be sure of a signal. And of not being overheard. And she's worse now Deborah is dead. But Leila won't talk to any of us about it.'

'Okay, so what has this got to do with me?'

'You're working in Deborah's office. She had notes on all of us. You could find those notes and see why Deborah was so concerned about Leila.'

'Deborah's PC is with the police.'

'What about her phone?'

'Joanne says she lost it, but she didn't use it much anyway.'

'Then she must have hard copies of the notes. You should be able to find them.'

'That's Joanne's province, Adelina. I can't go poking around in her filing cabinets. If she says there are no notes from Deborah to be found, there are no notes.'

'But you're a journalist. Can't you find *something* in the office?'

'I'm not that sort of journalist. I mainly work on *Living Lies*, a daytime TV show. It's entertainment, not investigation.'

'But living lies is what we've all done here. And you're someone who needs to know the truth, aren't you?' Adelina got up from the bench in one flowing movement. Then she patted Suzy on the arm, and Suzy felt the warmth of the other woman's hand.

'Try to find out about Leila. I know you want to.' Adelina said. She gave a gentle half-smile, turned and walked slowly and calmly back to the house.

* * *

As Suzy drove home, she felt increasing resentment. She had enough to think about without Leila. The police had Deborah's computer, and if there was anything on it worth finding, they would have found it. But maybe Adelina had a point about the notes. Joanne had said that Deborah was well known for keeping detailed information. But where was that information now?

When she got home, the flashy *LEE'VE IT TO LEE* van was parked outside. Suzy had completely forgotten about the roofer starting work that day. As she got out of the car, Lee was coming down his ladder and smiling.

'Well, bonny lass, I've had a shufti and made good temporarily. If it pours tonight, you won't get any more rain in. Your brickwork needs pointing, but I can get to it from the ladder and patch it up. Should be finished by Wednesday.

I've got a contract here for you to sign . . . but you can pay me online. I'm good with computers. I do as much as I can electronically.' So he was efficient, as well as prompt and cheerful.

The rain that had threatened all day was starting now, cold little spikes blown down from the fells.

'You'd better bring the papers inside,' Suzy said. 'Would you like a cup of tea?'

Lee grinned; he had an infectious smile. 'That would be fantastic. It's a bit parky now. Ta very much. Wow, what a lovely old house this is.' His Tyneside accent was more pronounced with his enthusiasm.

'Yes, isn't it?' Suzy led the way into the kitchen and put the kettle on the range. Lee spread the papers on the table. He drank his tea while she read them through properly and signed them. He grabbed a brownie, which reminded her of Scott Jermyn. 'So you've been working at Tarnfield House?'

'Correct. That's a crackin' place. Very elegant. But not cozy like this. I love this kitchen — and your pans!'

'To be honest I never use them, but they look great don't they!'

'Real copper. They must be worth a bob or two! Bet they weigh a ton. Haddaway, man. You'd sprain your wrist if you tried serving spuds from one of them!' He went on: 'By the way, we'll see you and your husband at Tarnfield House on Wednesday. Mandy and me will be there. Mr Jermyn mentioned that you and Mr Clark had been invited to the party.'

Aargh. Scott Jermyn's invitation. A party seemed inappropriate that week, but Scott Jermyn hardly seemed the sensitive type. If everyone else was going, she and Robert should too.

Lee said kindly, 'You know, I think I've outstayed my welcome, bonny lass. You haven't even taken your coat off. That tea was much appreciated. I'll be off now because this rain is coming on heavy. I'd say see you tomorrow, but maybe I won't, as I'll be up a ladder and you'll be down here. You don't have to worry about me. I'll just get on with it.'

'Thanks Lee.' Suzy watched him leave. She didn't feel the same need to see him off the premises as she had with Scott Jermyn. At the front door Lee turned and waved. He was a small, stocky, rather good-looking man with an open face and a pleasant manner. She had worked briefly on a programme called *Geordies in Space* a few years before. Lee might remember that; if so, they would have something to chat about at Scott's party. A night out at Tarnfield House, even with Scott Jermyn, would be a break from the guilt and worry about Ellie and all the wretched responsibility at the hostel.

Her phone rang — it was Molly, caught in the rain at the bus stop on the main road. 'I'll come and get you, sweetheart,' Suzy said. She still hadn't taken her coat off. But it was good to be wanted, although Molly would probably start another rant about why she needed driving lessons. I won't even listen, Suzy thought. Tonight I'll make spag bol and we can have a lovely family supper, and then Rob and I can straighten things out. He seems terribly stressed and not at all himself. It must be worry about the house. If he really wants to give up the Briars of course I'll go, but I hope he doesn't.

Her phone rang again. Robert's strained voice said, 'Hi Suzy, it's me. I'm in A&E at Norbridge General . . .'

CHAPTER TWELVE

The earth trembled, and the heavens dropped, the clouds also dropped water.
Judges 5:4

The meeting Robert had been to at the Bishop of Norbridge's office that morning had started badly. Archdeacon Jim Bentley was already seated at the table when Linda Finch and Robert entered. Jim Bentley had nodded briefly in their direction and fingered a heavy chain round his neck. The area dean, Neil Clifford, the old friend of Robert's who was also the acting chair of St Jane's Hostel, was there too. But he was keeping very quiet.

The Bishop of Norbridge was a slight woman with a plain cross under a simple dog collar. She began by expressing her sadness at the death of Deborah Arbiter, and neatly went on to explain the patronage system in the Church of England. In the nineteenth century, organizations could buy seats on the patronage boards which recruited parish priests. One significant organization in the North of England was the Rural Reformation Association, which was supported by the Arbiters. The RRA in Victorian times was about converting the working classes from godlessness in the dark northern industrial towns. But now, it seemed to represent the more uncompromising form of Christianity. Or at least it did in the shape of Archdeacon Bentley!

'That's right,' the Ven Jim had said, unnecessarily loudly. 'I'm a proud member of the RRA, which adheres strictly to biblical principles.'

'Don't we all,' the Bishop of Norbridge said calmly. 'But the Rural Reformation Association is rather more fundamentalist than many of us. Until recently it's not been very active, but in the last twenty years it's become very much more influential, with the growth in evangelism.'

The Ven Jim had nodded, without false modesty. 'Quite right. I can take it from here, Bishop. When I got this job six months ago, the RRA nominated me, and I was grateful, and the relationship developed. I had a few issues after coming to Workhaven and the RRA became my guiding light.'

'I'm not sure even the RRA would approve of some of your more forthright pronouncements, Jim,' the bishop had said. 'The Church, including the RRA, does advocate listening to people with different views . . .'

'But not if they're wrong!' Jim Bentley's voice had risen a few decibels. 'I'm not sure we should listen to arguments about homosexual churchwardens and gay marriage.'

'That's not fair, Jim,' said the Reverend Linda Finch.

'How would you describe it then?' Bentley said aggressively.

Robert had replied, 'Alan Robie, our churchwarden, and his partner are having a civil partnership ceremony in Norbridge. And then a party in the church hall. This isn't a gay marriage, Jim. It's a loving attempt to include two genuine Christians who worship at All Saints Church and who have something to celebrate. And it doesn't break any rules or guidelines.'

'It's in flagrant disregard of Leviticus 20:13.'

'The Book of Leviticus also says you shouldn't eat rabbit. Or pork. It's full of detailed rules about sacrifices which I'm sure the RRA wouldn't want to enforce.'

Linda had added, 'Not to mention women with their period being confined to a separate dwelling. Would you enforce that too, Jim?'

Archdeacon Jim had harrumphed, looked embarrassed for a nanosecond, and then launched into a diatribe about the Anglican Church's commitment to marriage. Much of what he said would have resonated with many people, but not the aggressive way in which he said it.

'We understand where you're coming from, Jim,' Robert had said. 'But if you read the Church's guidelines, they try desperately to understand what it's like for people who genuinely believe that God is calling them by a different route. Remember the Ash Wednesday prayer: "Almighty and everlasting God, who hatest nothing that thou hast made . . ."'

For a minute the Ven Jim looked nonplussed. Robert desperately wanted to try and find some sort of compromise. He asked, rather tentatively, 'Can't we think of the word "marriage" as a description, rather than a definition?'

The bishop had smiled at Robert. 'That's an interesting idea, Robert, but something for a future discussion. You might think about that, Jim.' She paused, and then went on: 'Linda, I've read your email about the plans for a party for Alan Robie and his partner, and completely separate private prayers. This new plan couldn't lead to the sort of misunderstanding which so distressed Jim. I think you should go ahead.'

'That's an outrage!' the archdeacon had raised his voice even more. 'The Arbiter family funded the church hall in Tarnfield. They'd be appalled. The deeds to the building say it should be used for activities approved by the Church of England. No truly evangelical priest would let his church hall be used in this way.'

'I'd check your pronouns if I were you, Jim,' the bishop had said tersely.

'But isn't that a case in point?' Robert had said. 'The definition of a priest used to be that it was a man. A woman was a priestess. Or an author was a man and the feminine was an authoress. No one says that now. Those definitions have changed, some just by usage and some after great discussion. It happens.'

'But some things are absolutes,' Jim Bentley had said, and banged his fist on the table.

'That's enough, Jim,' said the bishop. 'It's quite clear, anyway, that what we are talking about here is not a marriage but a celebration of a loving civil partnership in a church hall. The Church is quite explicit about us being able to pray for such relationships in a positive way. You are making an enormous fuss, Jim, about something which is quite acceptable. I'm not sure the RRA would support you, either. But where we agree is that you believe in authority. Now respect mine. I'm ending the meeting. Give my regards to Alan and Stevie, Linda. Thanks so much everyone.'

The archdeacon had left first, moving angrily out of the room. The bishop had got up and calmly poured herself more coffee. No one added anything more, except to say goodbye. Linda had looked shaken but clearly relieved, though Robert had felt subdued. The acrimony had distressed him. But it seemed unwise to start a post-mortem on the meeting while they were still in the grounds of Church House.

'I'll follow you back at to the vicarage, Linda,' Robert had suggested as they got into their separate cars. They would have a lot to talk about. Linda had seemed more upbeat when they left — from being physically bowed, she had regained some stature and her habitual pleasant smile.

Robert followed her as they left the car park behind Church House and made for the gates on the drive. He was driving behind Linda when a Harley Davidson came hurtling out of the car park and swerved, unseeing, in front of her Nissan Leaf. Linda had braked so forcibly that her car skidded on the gravel and bumped the stone gatepost. Robert had pulled up just an inch behind her. Now Robert waited in A&E while the vicar was being checked over for whiplash. He re-organized his week in his head. This was not going to be good for him and Suzy.

* * *

Suzy said goodbye to Robert and ended the phone call. For a moment she put her head in her hands. But then she had to go out and pick up Molly.

Her daughter was standing at the bus stop on the main road, drenched in the persistent rain. She was wearing laced-up ankle boots, shocking pink tights, a tiny tartan kilt and a black pea-jacket. Her fingers were encrusted with chunky rings and her arms jingled with bangles. She would have looked quite good if she hadn't been freezing cold and soaked to the skin.

'Where've you *been*, Mum? I've been waiting *hours*.'

'Get in and try not to drip everywhere. Why didn't you get the bus into the village?'

'I missed it. There's only one an hour from Norbridge but there are four an hour that go along the bypass. I didn't think it would be *so* difficult for you to come and pick me up. Of course, if I could drive . . .'

'Sorry — it's just that Robert's at the hospital. The vicar has had a minor road accident and Robert is with her. Linda's going to be out of action for the rest of the week.'

'That's a shame.' But Molly's dismissive tone really meant: *What's that to do with me?*

'Robert's going to have to take on a lot of the church stuff this week.'

'What?'

'I said, Robert is going to be pretty busy this week. So we won't be seeing much of him.'

'Oh no. I can't believe it!' Molly sounded blighted. 'That means he won't be able to take me out for driving practice tomorrow. That's *so unfair*. Robert promised me he'd take me, now I've got my provisional licence.'

'You've what?'

'Got my provisional licence. Robert told me to apply for it. He said he'd give me some off-road practice to get me started.'

'Oh, did he?' Suzy squinted so she could see the road ahead, but also because she was furious. She didn't want

Molly driving. Not yet. She had been racked by anxiety when her son Jake had started driving. He had needed three goes to pass his test. Even then he had been lucky.

'Well,' Molly said, 'it'll just have to be you that takes me. But you won't be as good. You're too impatient.'

'I beg your pardon. I am not!' Suzy recognized the trap just after she fell into it. If she argued that she was just as patient as Robert she would have to take Molly driving to prove it, and she didn't want to do that.

'Well, okay then, Mum. If you think you can do it, we can go out tomorrow.'

'Molly that's not what I said . . .'

'Oh don't tell me,' Molly said snippily. 'You're working tomorrow. Is it London or Manchester? You're *never* at home. All my friends' parents are giving them driving lessons and at least they're around.'

'I go to work, Molly, so you can have holidays and expensive trips, and art materials and . . .'

'There's no point having art materials if I've nowhere to use them. Robert says . . .'

'I don't care what Robert says!' Suzy lost her temper and her voice rose. 'You should stop asking him for things. He's not your father.'

'And what about Dad? When did you last see him? You never talk to him, so why should I?'

They had arrived at the Briars. Molly wrenched open the car door and stormed out, boots squelching and skirt sticking to her thighs. Suzy followed her into the house and to the kitchen, where they always ended up. Molly nudged the cat out of the way, peeled off her soaking jacket and flung it over the towel rail at the front of the range. Within seconds she was gently steaming — or at least smelling of warm polyester.

Suzy was relieved Molly hadn't stomped off to her bedroom, but she suspected it was only because she was too wet to face going upstairs into the chill. Suzy said nothing but bustled over the kettle.

'What's for tea?' Molly asked suddenly.

'Spaghetti bolognese.'

'Oh *no*. Mum, where have you been? No, don't answer that. I don't want to hear about the posh places you go to. You should have remembered I'm a vegan now. Robert made vegan all last week.'

'He did?' Suzy felt a rush of shame. While she'd been in Islington eating at gastropubs, Robert had been cooking plant food for her daughter. He must have been working on his catering skills.

She went up to the bundle of angry, smelly, wet man-made fibres and embraced it. Well, at least if Molly's clothes were made from chemicals, they were vegan, she supposed. And though she hardly responded, Molly didn't flinch or move away.

'Get into your onesie, Molls, and I'll make veggie pasta instead. Then maybe we can watch something on telly. Not *Living Lies*, I promise.'

'Okay.' It was petulant but better than nothing. 'And can we plan where I'm going to drive tomorrow?'

Defeated, Suzy nodded. Finally she took off her coat, over an hour after arriving home.

* * *

Still waiting in A&E, Robert took a call from Neil Clifford. 'I'm sorry that meeting this morning was so vituperative,' Neil said. 'How's Linda? We're all quite upset about that bump. I'm sure Archdeacon Bentley didn't mean to carve her up . . .'

'No, I don't think he did,' said Robert. 'I got the impression he was just driving angrily. Bentley seems to be a very angry man altogether.'

'But that's what I wanted to tell you. Like he hinted, Bentley seems to have had some sort of crisis just after getting the job.'

'Ah. Something to do with his past?'

'I'm not sure. I know the bishop thinks that he needs a spiritual director at the very least, and possibly counselling. In many ways his views are understandable, though I personally disagree with him. But his bullying manner and lack of empathy are a problem. Bentley used to be a very good clergyman back in London. He was fast-tracked to this archdeacon position and he's ideal for the job — his energy is colossal and he's great with young people. Or was. But something happened to him after he came to Workhaven earlier this year.'

'Perhaps the power went to his head?'

'Maybe. I just wanted to tell you that the bishop knows something needs to be done.'

'Yes. Sooner rather than later.' Robert dreaded to think what the Ven Jim would make of Stevie's gang of thespians, boogying the night away in the church hall at the civil partnership party.

On the phone from the hospital, Robert had told Suzy he wouldn't be back till late and that the rest of his week was in chaos. She had been silent for a moment, and then had said, 'That's okay, Rob. It's disappointing, but we'll cope.' Suzy never made the most of a crisis.

But there was still something wrong between them. When this week was over, they would talk it all out. He just needed to get through the next few days.

* * *

In Tarnfield, Suzy and Molly had supper and watched an old episode of *Call the Midwife*. Then they had a good catch-up about everyone they knew. Molly seemed glad to have her mum to herself and talked more openly than usual, especially about her current closest friend.

'She's decided to identify as a lesbian,' Molly said with careful casualness. 'But she doesn't really fancy girls. Don't laugh, Mum. It's disrespectful.'

'Sorry sweetheart. But presumably she doesn't fancy boys?'

'No, of course not, if she's a lesbian.'

'Maybe she doesn't fancy anybody. It's not mandatory, you know.' Suzy thought of Deborah Arbiter. How many people were asexual? What did it really mean?

'Who do you fancy these days?' she said daringly to Molly.

Molly blushed and looked a bit embarrassed. She had never shown much interest in dating, but recently she had been out more often and worn even weirder clothes. Molly was a late developer. 'Oh, I quite like Rafi Hossein. You know, his mum and dad own the Star of Bengal takeaway.'

Suzy did indeed know Rafi Hossein and his brother Jamel. The Hossein boys were very bright and intense, both determined to become medics. Rafi was the younger one, with jet-black hair cut bizarrely short on one side and in a huge cow's lick on the other. He had dark eyes plus a painfully bony body and a soft adolescent face which had yet to grow to accommodate his bushy, deep-black eyebrows. Trust Molly to fancy the most exotic boy in the district.

Molly said, 'I came home with him on the bus today. His dad couldn't pick him up because their car's been vandalized. The catalytic converter was nicked.'

'The *what*?'

'The catalytic converter. It reduces the toxic emissions from the engine.' Molly sounded very knowledgeable. 'Rafi's mum says there's a gang round here pinching the converters because they contain precious metals. It's the platinum and rhodium they're after, but all metal is at a premium.'

Suzy was impressed by Molly's knowledge. Her daughter went on: 'Anyway, Rafi will have his own wheels soon. His brother's got a car. It's an old banger he got from a farmer. A Subaru pickup. It's got bull bars. It's not been moved since Jamel went to uni in September. It doesn't start. But Rafi's going to tinker with it . . .'

Suzy smiled at the old-fashioned phrase. Then, as always, the worry bells rang . . . 'Has Rafi passed his test? Be careful if he suggests taking you out in it.'

Molly shrugged. 'Yeah, yeah. Message received.' She yawned. 'That was a nice tea, Mum. Better than Robert's, actually. He just bought those vegan ready meals. I was only having a go at you. It pissed me off that you were away so much.'

'Don't swear, Molly. And I go to work for all of us.'

Molly raised her eyebrow in a surprisingly sophisticated way and said nothing, which was even more sophisticated. Then she announced, 'I'm going to do my coursework tomorrow morning, and then we should go over to the old industrial estate and try some driving in the afternoon.' It was a statement, not a request. Suzy nodded, cornered. At least Molly wasn't wanting to get straight onto the dual carriageway to Newcastle.

'I'll wash up, sweetheart. You go up and have an early night.'

Molly smiled and, surprisingly, gave her mother a big hug. Suzy reflected that Molly had seemed much younger that evening. She worried that Molly was immature for her age. She wondered if it came of being the baby of the family, with her brother Jake being so much older. Maybe the return to peevish adolescent behaviour was some sort of reaction to Suzy's absences. Then Suzy remembered poor Chelsea at the hostel, working miles from home, with complete strangers. The same age as Molly. Why would a teenage girl want that job?

As Suzy was washing up and stacking the dishwasher, the relaxed state she had been in with her daughter receded and she became wide awake. There had still been no text from Ellie, and Suzy was beginning to think there never would be. She was impatient to hear from Rachel, hoping her friend in Islington had traced Ellie somehow, but it wouldn't be tonight. She also felt guilty about her reaction to Adelina up at the hostel that afternoon. Was Adelina's request so unreasonable? Would it be possible to find out more about Leila and her phone calls without upsetting Joanne?

And what was really going on with Chelsea, allegedly from Stoke on Trent, but travelling on the train from London?

So many complications. But it was inevitable that the hostel would be a Pandora's box of nightmare stories. What had Adelina said? *We've all been living lies here.*

Suzy sat down at her keyboard.

CHAPTER THIRTEEN

And her husband arose, and went after her, to speak friendly unto her, and to bring her again.
Judges 19:3

Suzy heard Robert come in at about half past ten. He put his head round the office door.

'How's the vicar?' she asked.

'Linda's fine. She needs to rest for a few days. She's on medication and will have exercises to do but the whiplash will slowly get better. I've spent the evening trying to contact people and rearrange things. It's amazing how much Linda does. What have you been up to?'

'Rearranging Molly's driving practice for a start. Why did you encourage her?'

'She's a force of nature. Like her mother. What's that you're looking up?' He saw over her shoulder that she was googling divorce lawyers. 'Is it that bad?' Suddenly they both started to laugh.

'Very funny. I'm trying to find out more about Deborah Arbiter, if you must know. Most women barristers in the seventies and eighties seemed to specialize in family and divorce. But not her.'

'The Arbiters again! In that case I'm going to bed.' Robert said. Their laughter left him feeling lighter. 'Don't stay up too late, Suzy. And listen, whatever happens, let's go out for a walk later in the week. We haven't really talked since you came home and there are things . . .'

'Yes, I know. Let's promise each other some personal time on Friday.'

'Ah. On Friday I've got to stand in for Linda at meetings. Saturday?'

'I've got to give Molly a lift to Norbridge for her art class.'

'Saturday night. The Plough. This time without Scott Jermyn butting in.'

'It's a deal.' Suzy smiled. 'We can celebrate the chimney stack repairs.'

'Truly romantic, Suzy. I'll leave you to your googling. Come to bed soon.'

Suzy wasn't sure about that. She was itching to call Rachel, as much for a chat as anything, but her friend wouldn't have anything to tell her yet about Ellie. If she had, she would have been in touch. Meanwhile, Suzy had looked up women's refuges and found that there were numerous small charities all over Britain, many started thirty or forty years before. St Jane's website made clear that the hostel was a small independent organization which, unlike most others, catered especially for middle-aged and older women. It had close ties with the Church of England. Reference was made to St Jane of Annecy and how she had been a patron of old and poor women, and those separated from their children. For security reasons no one other than Deborah and each trustee was listed on the website. No mention of Joanne Butcher.

Suzy clicked again on Deborah's official CV. It named the chambers where she had been a young lawyer in London. It no longer existed. But when you googled it another woman's name popped up. Her professional contact details were listed on LinkedIn.

On an impulse, Suzy rattled off an email to her asking if there was any way she could fill in some of the details about

Deborah Arbiter's early career. Suzy left her phone number, without much hope. But it was worth a try.

* * *

Chelsea lay in her lovely clean bed with its floral duvet cover and matching pillows, and let the panic swirl around her. At some point, she knew, the truth was going to come out; then they would probably pack her off on the train back to London. Chelsea had recognized Joanne's sort as soon as she had arrived. A manager. Efficient. Unsentimental. Okay, on Friday Joanne had been too busy to ask for Chelsea's paperwork, but she had made it clear she would get round to that later in the week. Chelsea was dreading it.

In the meantime, there was no doubt they needed Chelsea. No one had felt like cooking after the tragedy. Chelsea had been in charge. But it had taken a long time to clear the unfamiliar kitchen after the big communal Sunday lunch. The residents had slowly melted away. She had worked hard that day, making meals, washing up, taking teas and coffees around, getting water and stuff for that vicar woman. Then she had sat at the back of the communion service and drunk in the words. Lovely stuff. But a loving father? Dream on.

Later, left on her own, in the room to one side of the kitchen, Chelsea had seen Joanne in a dark anorak and skin-tight black leggings, leaving by the kitchen door. Joanne had walked towards the car park outside. But instead of getting into the car, she went around it and down the path which led to the door in the wall. Chelsea had followed her. Joanne had keyed in a code and gone through the door, and before it swung back Chelsea saw that she was meeting someone. Joanne bent forwards to embrace a man.

Chelsea had run back to the house. In the hostels she had called home, her experiences included a suicide, a homicidal attack and numerous dramatic meltdowns. If anyone had told her that there would be more drama here than in

Brixton or Hackney, she would have laughed in their face. Yet here there had been a fatality and now this mystery, in three days.

Chelsea thought as clearly as she could about her situation and listed the risks to herself. Number one, she was in danger of Joanne evicting her from the hostel when she found out the truth. Number two, Suzy knew that Chelsea was hiding something. Number three, what was Suzy going to do about it? It was effin' bad luck that Chelsea had run into Suzy on the train from London when she should have been coming from Stoke on Trent!

Or maybe it wasn't. Suzy hadn't shopped her when she'd had the chance. She seemed decent. And she might be interested in what Joanne was up to. Maybe there was some sort of leverage there . . .

After all, what Chelsea was doing wasn't so awful, was it? Not like pushing someone off a roof.

* * *

Moira Black was still up. Geoff had gone off that day on another of his trips and would be away for a few nights, thank goodness. That had given Moira time to think.

Deborah was dead and now Moira could grieve. With Geoff around, that had been impossible. He always dominated proceedings. Once in a while he let her take the lead, but she always paid for it with his sulks and silences. Like with the cottage.

All those years ago, when Moira Black had heard that Deborah Arbiter was back in Tarnfield, Moira had arranged to see her. Moira had heard that Deborah was running a home for women on the run from their husbands, and who'd had their children taken away. The popular view in Hardcastle was that they probably deserved it, but Moira knew differently: her child had been taken away from her. And now there was another baby on the way. She and Geoff were living with Moira's parents in a two-bedroomed terraced house and

Moira was desperate for a home of their own. She knew there was a cottage to rent at Tarnhill House, and that Geoff had a lot to offer as a handyman.

When she met Deborah, the Judge understood. By the eighties, openly having a baby when you weren't married was not uncommon, but it had been totally different in 1965 when it happened to Moira. Moira's family had been fiercely respectable. It made Moira bitter to think what a terrible crime it had been to get pregnant then, and to have no chance of marriage.

The baby's father had been a local lad whom Moira had known since childhood. As soon they knew for certain that she was expecting, he'd told everyone that Moira had led him on, saying she was on the pill. It was nonsense, of course. Unmarried girls couldn't get the pill in Hardcastle or anywhere else for that matter, but everyone accepted the explanation. He played the victim. And in the eyes of most people in the town, the lass was usually to blame, trying to trap a husband. Any excuse would see the lad let off scot-free.

Moira was sent to a mother-and-baby home in the North East, and when her daughter was born the child was adopted by a second cousin whom Moira hardly knew. The cousin moved south, and the child was never heard of again. In those days you never spoke of such a thing. The baby was gone. Respectability was restored. You were totally dependent on your parents and lucky not be thrown out on the street like girls in the nineteenth century. It was as if the pregnancy had never been.

But of course everyone in Hardcastle knew.

Moira had soldiered on, working for the grocers in the town. At first, people sniggered or snubbed her. Then, as time went on, attitudes changed. But Moira couldn't bring herself to 'go with the flow', try the drugs, listen to the music, chill with her contemporaries in the seventies.

It was ten years later when Geoff had come along, and he had been better than nothing. Geoff didn't mind Moira's past, it made her more acquiescent, but he made it clear that he didn't want her to have anything to do with her illegitimate daughter. What was done was done and there was no point in upsetting the applecart.

When she told Deborah her story, the Judge had given her verdict, succinctly, sitting under the tree in the garden.

'You were so unlucky, Moira. It happened at the wrong time. A decade either way and things would have been totally different. Ten years earlier and the father would have been marched to the altar. But it was the swinging sixties, and he took advantage of that to get out of his responsibilities. Ten years later, no one would have cared about you being an unmarried mother. What happened to the baby's father?'

'Nothing much. He married someone else.' Moira had shrugged, but she still remembered with resentment his big white wedding and his golden-haired children.

'And your baby girl was best forgotten. I see. How awful. You deserve some luck, Moira. You and Geoff are welcome to the cottage. At a discount.'

Moira had closed her eyes in relief. Deborah had said, 'And if you ever want to find out what happened to your first child, I'll help you.'

'Oh no! I couldn't. Geoff would go mad. And we're going to have one of our own now.'

'Well if you ever change your mind . . .'

Since then Moira had often thought wistfully about what Deborah had said. It was a coincidence when her second daughter, Tracey, had gone to live in Hardcastle, but it meant Moira walked those streets again, and memories came back.

And a year ago, for the first time in over fifty years, Moira had spoken to her lost baby's father. He had stopped her in the market square. She didn't recognize him. He had cancer, he said. It had made him think. He and his wife had divorced a long time ago, and his children didn't bother with him much.

'Did you ever know what happened to the bairn? Our bairn . . .' he'd asked, pathetically, wiping his eye, whether from tears or just the wateriness of age. 'I've not got long,' he'd said. 'If you ever find out . . .'

She'd wanted to say, *Serves you right you old bugger. I hope you rot in hell, and if you're regretting what you did, then good, you need to suffer.* But instead she'd heard herself saying, 'I've always wondered. I could make enquiries. My husband wouldn't like it, but he needn't know. I'll try. Don't beat yourself up, Billy. We all had to survive. We were victims of the times.'

'You're a good 'un, Moi,' he'd said. 'I made a big mistake.' He had pressed her hand and then shambled on, leaning on his stick.

Later, Moira had told Deborah, and together they had started trying to trace Moira's lost child. Of course, Moira hid this from Geoff. The last thing she wanted was rants and sulks. She was getting better able to weather Geoff's form of control, but he was still a force to be reckoned with.

'It will all work out. St Jane will work her magic,' Deborah had said, and smiled that wide forgiving smile which always made everything seem all right. But this time Deborah had been wrong. They'd got so far, but then there had been silence.

And now Deborah was dead. Life was a bleak business.

Moira went back to her empty bed and sleep finally came.

CHAPTER FOURTEEN

Why are ye come unto me now when ye are in distress?
Judges 11:7

On Tuesday, Suzy woke up feeling a bit better. Still no text from Ellie, but hopefully Rachel would get back to her with news from the Barnford Estate. Suzy needed to get through the day doing other things — the dreaded hour of driving practice with Molly, for instance. How on earth had she got stuck with that?

Robert was already dressed. He had to cope with a meeting with Diocesan Human Resources in Norbridge about new health and safety rules, deputising for the vicar, who was still suffering from whiplash. Suzy had a quick breakfast and set out herself. The day was crisp and clear with high clouds.

She had hardly parked her car behind the hostel before Joanne came out of the kitchen door to meet her. 'Thank goodness you're here. The Workhaven police are coming again this afternoon. The inquest is scheduled for two weeks' time, with luck. But I'm worried because now they're saying they want to go over things once more.'

'I thought the police were satisfied about everything?'

'DS Jackson said that they were ninety-nine per cent sure the inquest could go ahead but wanted to make one more check. There's been some stupid gossip about it not being an accident. He's bringing one of those PCSOs with him . . .'

'Ro Watson?'

'Yes, that's right. She's a link with the Workhaven social workers. A few of our residents have them. At least she'll be good with the residents.'

Suzy followed Joanne back into the office and plugged in her laptop. For the first half hour she went through the latest enquiries and answered the phone. After a while Joanne announced she was going upstairs to try and sort out Deborah's clothes. At eleven o'clock there was still some sun outside, so Suzy locked the office and went out through the kitchen, using the keypad. A few minutes later, leaning on the windowsill with her coffee, she heard a noise and turned to see Chelsea standing there. The girl's wide pale face was impassive, but she didn't move.

'Are you okay, Chelsea?'

'I'm not Chelsea,' the girl said.

Suzy very carefully refrained from turning her head in surprise.

'Oh,' she said neutrally. After a minute she heard the girl snuffling.

Suzy said, 'So that's why you were on the train from London? You didn't come from Stoke on Trent?' This time Suzy turned round fully and put her mug carefully on the windowsill. The girl nodded.

'Don't worry,' Suzy went on. 'No one's around to listen. Joanne is upstairs sorting out Deborah's stuff. You'd better tell me what happened.'

'Well, Chelsea was my mate. Sort of. She's a bit of a dork. She got this job. It was advertised online on a special website. Her social worker helped her. But then she changed her mind because she met this boy.'

'So you took her place?'

'Yeah. I met Chelsea in London. She'd run away from home, but she went back to Stoke. We stayed friends on Facebook. Anyway she got the job here and didn't want it. But I did. I really wanted to come here.'

'It must be hard answering to the wrong name. What's your real name?'

The girl shrugged. 'Who cares. For the last year it's been 'hey you' anyway.'

'So why are you telling me this?'

'Because I'm not thick. At some point Joanne will twig and chuck me out. The paperwork won't fit. Joanne hasn't had time yet to ask for it. But she will. And then she'll get rid of me. I was going to tell the woman in charge. I swear I was. Deborah. She sounded lovely. But Joanne's different. Harder.'

'Joanne seems to like you well enough.'

'Yeah. Until she finds out I've lied. But there's something else. Joanne's up to something. I saw her on Sunday night going through that gate and meeting a man.'

'What?' For the first time in this sorry tale Suzy was genuinely surprised.

'If Joanne tries to get rid of me, I've got something on her. Now you know too. Meeting a fella on the sly won't go down well here. Joanne could keep me on if she wanted to. I've got a National Insurance number and I've worked before — a bit in a shop. Retail clothing.' She added with an air of pride, 'Goth fashion.'

Suzy tried not to smile. 'But why shouldn't Joanne keep you on? Why don't you just tell her that the real Chelsea was unreliable and asked you to swap with her? That would be the truth, wouldn't it?'

'Well . . . I s'pose.'

'And Joanne would've been badly let down if no one had turned up. You did her a favour, really.'

'Oh . . . yeah. I hadn't thought of it like that.'

'When's your day off?'

'Today. Tuesday. But I'll stay here and clean. It needs it.' She sounded more confident now. 'And then I'm off Friday afternoon.'

'You can come to my house on Friday for tea if you like.'

'Oh. Well. Okay, ta,' she said. 'Ta very much. I just wanted to tell someone. And to make sure you wouldn't shop me.'

'No. I certainly won't.'

The girl actually smiled, then turned and trundled surprisingly quickly back to the kitchen.

* * *

At the same time, in a different kitchen, Scott Jermyn was having coffee from his state-of-the-art espresso capsule machine, leaning on the island, and thinking about his party plans for the next day. He had employed four servers from an agency in Norbridge to come out and do the catering. He was hoping to have about a dozen guests.

There were Robert and Suzy Clark, Lee and Mandy Lewis, and to his surprise Joanne Butcher had said yes. So had Alan Robie from Church Cottage and his famous little friend Stevie, the Hosseins from the Star of Bengal takeaway which he patronized a lot, and the two smart-arsed professional couples from the elegant Georgian villas across the green. He was learning fast about the dynamics of north country living. You had to be inclusive rather than exclusive or you'd find yourself with no friends at all. Unless you were landed gentry, you couldn't be too choosey.

Which left him with the problem of the Blacks. He had used Geoff Black quite a lot when he'd arrived in Tarnfield. But Geoff had made a few blunders lately. Far from being on his guest list, Geoff was a worry . . .

Scott's thoughts moved on. On a whim, he thought about inviting someone else. It was a bit risky, but it would be interesting. He smiled and picked up his mobile. He had the number. He left a message for the Texan, Jarrold McHugh.

* * *

Suzy left the hostel after lunch. There was still no text from Ellie and no message from Rachel in Islington. Taking Molly driving would distract her.

It certainly did. After ten minutes Suzy could only think about surviving. Molly's excited attempt to start the Golf led to three kangaroo-style stalls; then she chugged off around the old industrial estate still used by Tarnfield kids for their first off-road driving attempts.

It was obvious that steering was going to be the first problem. Molly managed to head straight for a pothole, just miss a dry-stone wall, career round to the left and pull off a dramatic emergency stop in the middle of the concrete roadway. It wasn't helped by the arrival of another learner driver.

'Hey. That's a kid from year twelve!' Molly said excitedly as she restarted the car, lurching forward.

'No!' Suzy yelled, grabbing the handbrake. The car pulled dramatically to the right and then stalled again. 'Molly you can't just drive up to people to say hi. You need to keep a wide berth! Think about stopping distances!'

'I know, okay?' said Molly tetchily, starting up again and steering dramatically in the opposite direction. After forty minutes she had managed to drive in a straight line and to understand the gears, in theory anyway. But Suzy felt completely shaken up. When they changed places to go back to the Briars, Molly was pink and elated but Suzy was a pale shaky wreck.

'D'you think I'll pass first time?'

'Molly! You are light years away from taking a test. And you've got to stop treating this like some sort of fairground ride. You could kill someone.'

Molly pouted. 'You're *sooo* negative. It's not that hard, for goodness' sake.'

Suzy felt her head pounding. 'I'm not negative. I want you to understand how serious this is.'

'In the States and Canada everyone drives automatics. Maybe we need one. Then I'd be ok.'

'Don't be ridiculous. And in the States and Canada they've got long straight roads. Here, there could be a tractor round every corner.'

Suzy had a stress pain burning through her left eyebrow. The afternoon's driving practice had convinced her that Molly should be kept away from the roads until she was at least forty-five. Suzy squinted as they approached the junction where the old industrial estate ended in a forlorn collection of derelict garages.

'Watch out, Mum!' Molly suddenly screamed, and Suzy did her own emergency stop. A pickup had shot out, too fast, from between two low brick-built workshops. 'You weren't looking!' yelled Molly triumphantly.

After that, Suzy drove home at thirty miles an hour and made for the wine bottle as soon as they were inside. Molly went straight up to her bedroom, to show off to her friends on social media about her first driving lesson. Suzy found she was still shaking.

And still nothing from Ellie. But there was a very brief text from Rachel, just saying 'call me'. Suzy caught her breath.

She took her wine glass and went into the living room, out of Molly's way. She wanted to sit down somewhere comfortable and listen carefully to what Rachel had to say. She knew it was going to be something tricky. Otherwise, Rachel would have texted 'good news' or 'mission accomplished'.

She called Rachel's number and knew from the moment her friend said, 'Hi' in a strained, flat voice that she was going to hear something awful.

'Hi, Rache. You're back from the OB?'

'Yeah. I could have had an overnight, but I came home in the small hours. I'm off today but I couldn't sleep, so I got hold of my friend from the Barnford Estate.' Rachel paused.

'Get on with it, Rache. I can tell it's not going to be good.'

'No.' Suzy heard Rachel breathing in. 'I'm really sorry, Suzy, but your friend Ellie's dead.'

Suzy knew that on some level she had expected this, but she heard herself make a little mewing sound of shock. 'What happened to her?'

'You remember the air ambulance that night in the spring?'

'Yeah.' How come all this sounded like something she had already known? Was it shock giving her déjà vu? Or some deeper sort of intuition?

'I told you then that someone from the Barnford Estate had died. Suicide, people were saying. I saw it on my phone. Don't you remember?'

'No! Not the details. I was so busy. I was going out to do a shift at the news channel. I didn't have time to think. I sort of parked it. How did you find out it was Ellie?'

'It wasn't hard. It was big news around here. There were headlines in the *Herald*.' This was the free paper pushed through doors in West Islington every Friday. 'I remembered it from the time,' Rachel said. 'To be honest, I already thought that was who it might be when you called yesterday morning. But I needed to be sure. Now remind me how you knew her . . .'

'I met Ellie on holiday, and I must have told her about St Jane's Hostel in Tarnfield, though I don't really remember. She was having terrible trouble with a man. She actually applied to come here. But she never made it.'

'That's tragic. My friend in the Tenants' Association said her death was a terrible shock. She was a lovely girl. She'd been skiing and seemed so well and happy when she came home.'

The mewing noise came again, louder.

'But there's nothing you could have done, Suzy. She's been dead for months and it's all over with now. It's a shame you didn't keep in touch, but you couldn't have done anything more to help. She was just a person you met on holiday. Someone you gave a tip to, about a hostel. An acquaintance is all.'

If only I'd gone round to see her that evening, Suzy felt herself howling inside. But she hadn't known Ellie's address. 'Rachel, I found this old email from her. She'd written to me, but I didn't get it because it went into my spam folder. Ellie was scared of someone, Rache. Did your friend tell you that?'

'Sort of. She had "man trouble", the sister had said. Her sister did all the awful admin and identifying stuff, according to my mate.'

'How did she die?'

'Don't you remember? She threw herself off the building. I told you at the time someone had fallen from the roof. She climbed over the balcony rail. She had one of the flats with a mansard roof going out onto a little bit of roof garden . . . Suzy are you still there?'

Suzy had gone cold and quiet. After a few seconds she said, 'Yes, I'm still here. I'd forgotten about the roof. Or maybe it was tugging at my mind.' She thought of her recurrent memory of the red air ambulance, a memory that had come back with full force once she had heard of Deborah's death. Falling from a roof. 'You're absolutely sure it was Ellie?'

'Yes, absolutely. What is it, Suzy?'

'It's just that this is the second one. The second death falling from a roof. The other one was the woman who runs the hostel here. St Jane's. The hostel Ellie wanted to come to. The director was Deborah Arbiter. I told you, she was killed falling from a roof on Friday.'

'That's a bit of a coincidence.'

There was a long silence. Suzy said quietly, 'A coincidence? Two women dying like that? One is unquestionably suicide, and one is unquestionably an accident. But what if we start asking questions?'

'Suzy don't. It *must* be a coincidence.'

'Not necessarily. The women's hostel is the link. I made the connection for Ellie. She told me in person *and* in an email that she was scared of someone. Whose name began with the initial J. If I'd got back to her maybe I could have helped her . . .'

'But you did help her, didn't you? You told her about the hostel. Think straight Suzy. You met Ellie and told her about St Jane's. She squirrels away the info. Things get worse, she thinks of going to the hostel, but she was depressed and frightened and then she kills herself. There must have been a huge underlying issue. You couldn't have done more.'

'And then the founder of the hostel dies the same way? I can hear the doubt in your voice, Rache. You're trying to talk sense, but if it's a coincidence, it's a very big one.'

Rachel was silent. Then she said, 'So, if it's not a coincidence, Suzy, what is it?'

'I don't know.'

'I know the way your mind works, Suze. You think Ellie's lover might have killed her. Or pressured her to kill herself. And then he came to Cumbria to get his revenge on the woman called Deborah who was going to take her from him — and killed her the same way.'

'Is that so stupid?'

'Yes. Think about it Suzy. How would someone who killed Ellie even know she was planning to go to a hostel in Cumbria of all places? Has it occurred to you that the only link between these two women is you? I think you're wrong. It's probably all nonsense. But if there's even the scintilla of a suggestion that someone is going round pushing opinionated women off roofs, you're obviously in the queue. Be careful, Suzy.'

CHAPTER FIFTEEN

Come, and I will show thee the man whom thou seekest.
Judges 4:22

'Mum . . .'

Suzy was still sitting looking at her phone when Molly put her head round the door.

'Mum, is it all right if I go to Rafi's for supper? His mum's got a new dish for the Star of Bengal to try.'

'Lovely.' Suzy heard her own voice from a distance. 'What are you going to eat, sweetheart?'

'Chicken Tarnfield biryani.'

'Is that vegan chicken?'

'Not funny, mum. You can be so *inflexible*. This is a new cultural experience.'

'Of course, sweetie. Give Rafi's mum my regards. Don't walk home on your own. Call me to pick you up if you need me.'

'But you've already had a big glass of plonk! What use are you?' Molly thrust her arms into the air dramatically. She'd always been good at turning indignation into performance art.

'Molls, if Rafi's parents can't give you a lift because their car's been vandalized, I'll call you a taxi. Or Robert might be back in time to pick you up. But I don't want you walking along the main road and down the track by yourself. Do you understand, Molly? And get home before ten o'clock. And keep your phone on . . .'

'What's rattled your cage, mum? I mean, *risk averse* or what?'

Suzy looked at her daughter with a feeling of pain. Life was so fragile and so easily derailed. Molly was all talk now, but what if one day, like Ellie, she had nothing left but the ultimate act of self-harm? Suzy jumped up and hugged her daughter.

'Oh, for flip's sake, Mum,' Molly twisted away. 'See you later.'

When she had gone, Suzy leaned back in her armchair and massaged her forehead. Her wine tasted metallic. She picked up her phone and rang Ro Watson, her PCSO friend. It went to voicemail, and Suzy left a message: *'Hi Ro. I've had a bad shock. Could you come over? Robert's out and I need a drink. Correction, another drink. If you join me, you could stay the night here. Or get a cab home. Sorry to sound so needy — but I am.'*

She went upstairs. It seemed easier to think clearly and logically in the back bedroom office. She jotted down a few notes, as if she were working on a story. What were the facts? Suzy was nervous now, of false memory. What had Ellie actually said on that weird night in the chalet?

First, she had definitely mentioned a difficult relationship with someone whose name began with J. She had said she had made a big decision to book herself a last-minute skiing holiday without saying anything. She had pumped herself up to make a break with J when she got home and was determined to do it. Was she *so* downtrodden, terrified or undermined that she would say all that and then commit suicide? Surely coerced and bullied people didn't go skiing by themselves.

Secondly, Ellie had applied to come to St Jane's. But why? There were dozens of women's refuges in London, and Ellie had the wrong profile for St Jane's. For a minute Suzy wished she could do what Adelina had suggested and get into Deborah's computer. If what Joanne said was true, Deborah kept notes on possible residents for the hostel and everything about Ellie's case would be there.

But where were those notes?

Thirdly, there was no doubt that Ellie had died after falling over a balcony rail, from the top floor of a block of flats. And months later the woman who had offered her a lifeline, Deborah Arbiter, had also fallen from a roof. There was surely a link between their deaths — there had to be. How often did people fall off roofs? Had the killer been successful once, and decided to try the same method again? Who would ever make the connection?

Only me, thought Suzy.

She heard the knock at the door and went down to meet Ro, still in her PCSO uniform.

'I came straight here,' Ro said. 'My God, you're as white as a sheet, Suzy. Tell me all about it.'

They sat in the kitchen. Ro listened intently and didn't dismiss what Suzy suggested — at least, not at first. 'But Suzy, Deborah wasn't pushed. The police have established that. Anyone who pushed her would have had to scramble back up the roof, get down through the skylight and come back through the house. St Jane's only has two doors, front and back, except for the French windows in the lounge, which are locked for the winter. Both doors are visible from the tree where Deborah's body landed and where the women all crowded round.'

'But they would have been looking at the body . . .'

'Not all six of them, all the time. One was being sick, anyway, and looking away. They didn't see anyone come out of the house. St Jane's is totally exposed, which is one of the reasons it works well as a hostel. No undergrowth to lurk in. Jed and I went over it step by step this afternoon.'

'But say the killer waited in the attic?'

'I don't think so. The women eventually went back inside and milled about, making tea and consoling each other. They would have seen the killer come downstairs. Later the hostel was swarming with police and paramedics. The killer, if there was one waiting upstairs, would have been found. They went all over the building.'

Suzy shrugged. That was all true. Ro went on in a more conciliatory voice: 'I think it might be easier in London to kill someone that way. The attacker could chuck a person over the balcony railing and then get down the stairs and out of the back of a big block of flats while everyone's flapping over the body at the front. But the Met will have thought of that. Jed's got a mate there he was on a course with. I'll ask him to check it out. If your friend Ellie killed herself, Deborah's accident must be just a coincidence.'

'But could we at least talk about other possibilities?'

'Such as, your friend Ellie was murdered and then the same person, intent on revenge, did the same to Deborah months later? But why would he wait?' Ro's eyes narrowed as she thought. 'Or do you really think it's possible that the delay was caused while the killer established a new identity up here? Should we be asking how many secretly coercive controlling men from London have appeared in Tarnfield in the last six months?'

'Yes! Exactly!'

'That sounds mad, Suzy. But go on, tell me. Who've you got in mind?'

'There are quite a few possibilities! There's one horrible man, Scott Jermyn, who's turned up in Tarnfield lately, from London. He was doing some work for Deborah, though we don't know what. And there's another newcomer who's an American. He could have come via London. And there's an older guy, the hostel handyman, who works down south sometimes, though he's really a longshot. And for that matter there's a new roofer, though he's a Geordie with no southern connections. And there's even a new Archdeacon of Workhaven, who's a nightmare, and has just come up from London . . .'

'You are joking.'

'Yeah, a bit. But seriously, if anyone gives me the creeps, it's Scott.'

'Okay, let's talk about it. But first you need to eat. Let's get a takeaway. Does the Star of Bengal deliver?'

'Usually. But their car has been vandalized.'

'Oh yeah, the catalytic-converter thing. Okay, you phone them, and I'll drive over there. What do you fancy?'

'The chicken Tarnfield biryani is good, or so I hear.'

'Right, I'll pick it up. I'll be back as soon as I can.'

* * *

That morning, Robert had sat through another diocesan crisis meeting about thefts from church roofs. It was depressing. All the robbed churches had been looking for cheaper insurance and had been attacked before they got the Tagpaint protection required by the insurance companies. Tagpaint coated the metal so it could be identified by the police. It was a real deterrent.

Although it was reading week, Robert had a meeting with a postgrad student scheduled in the afternoon. He decided to pop into the university at lunchtime. He would pick up a sandwich from the café. Joining the queue for the till, he saw the unmistakeable head-turning shape of Paula Stovey from the music department ahead of him. The woman Suzy had accused him of 'ogling' in the Plough.

He liked Paula. But her sort of athletic glossiness didn't attract him. At first he'd been inclined to steer clear of her muscular glamour and Nordic good looks, assuming she would be cool and rather conceited. Then they had worked together on an academic committee 'revisiting extenuating circumstance guidelines in the marking of assignments'. They had shared some discreet smiles about a few of the scenarios up for discussion; Robert had liked Paula's common sense and admired her confidence in dealing with academic management. And he'd been delighted when she'd won an award for innovative teaching online. Dr Paula Stovey was a rising star.

'Paula! How are you?' He thought she looked more strained than usual, but still super-fit.

'Oh, I'm okay, Robert. Finding this term a bit exhausting, I must say.'

'I hope you're getting out and about though. Didn't I see you last weekend? In the Plough at Tarnfield? I didn't think that was your stamping ground.'

She looked slightly shaken. 'Oh, yes. Lovely old pub, isn't it?' There was a long silence while she looked around distractedly for the napkins. It was odd to see Paula anything other than completely self-possessed. Robert nodded. If Paula didn't want to discuss why she was in the Plough, that was fine by him. But if he explained his presence there, perhaps she'd reciprocate.

He said casually, 'I live in Tarnfield. An old house called the Briars. My wife and I were at the Plough for an evening out. Of course, the place was packed. I think half the village was there, talking about Deborah Arbiter's death. You'll have heard about that, of course . . .'

Paula stopped, sandwich in hand. He had the impression she wanted to talk, despite her silence. She could easily have rushed off. She looked white around her eyes and her mouth was tightly drawn. Without speaking, they both moved to sit down at one of the tiny tables in the café. 'Yes, Deborah's death. That was an awful accident,' she said. 'But I only found out about it yesterday.'

Paula couldn't stop wondering why Jarrold hadn't mentioned Deborah's death to her on Saturday when they went to the Plough. She thought about the buzz in the pub, and how he had kept her away from any general conversation. Being private was one thing. But not mentioning Deborah's death was either insensitive or sinister. Why hadn't he wanted her to know? Since the weekend, Paula had done a lot of thinking, most of it anxious and confused.

She went on: 'I've been googling Deborah Arbiter. She was a remarkable woman. Such a local hero. I'd heard of her before, through the women's rights network. And now there's quite a bit about her on the internet, and the local radio.'

'Yes. My wife is doing the communications work for St Jane's Hostel. There's been a lot of interest.'

'Is that because it was such a stupid way to die? What does your wife think? Does she know why Deborah went up there?'

Robert paused. Paula had an uncharacteristic pleading look as if she wanted reassurance, but he found he couldn't give it. 'Well, Suzy says people are asking questions about it, especially at the hostel. What do you think?'

Paula looked stricken. 'I'm involved in a couple of local women's groups. They're not happy.' She looked away, then looked down. 'And I'm seeing someone from Tarnfield,' she added quickly.

Robert was startled. He thought he knew everyone in the village. There was no one he could imagine being the stunning Paula Stovey's lover.

He waited. She went on: 'He's an American. He's over here tracing his family history. One of the Arbiters was his grandparent. Or great-grandparent or something. He doesn't talk about it much and I'm not into genealogy myself.'

Ah . . . The handsome American in the cottage next door to St Jane's. Robert recalled Suzy mentioning him. Paula's words tailed off. There was an uncomfortable silence, but Paula looked down at her unopened sandwich and didn't move.

Robert aimed to say something neutral. 'Great. So how did you meet?'

Paula waited, as if wondering whether to go on, and then said, 'We met online. But not dating. He was on my folksong outreach course. Don't laugh. He's extremely good at music. Then we met up for real and had some great walks. And conversations about politics, and the environment, and songs, of course. He could be very funny. He joked about the Middle East madrigal — you know, falafel, falafel . . .'

Robert looked blank. Paula said patiently, 'He meant *falalah, falalah, la*. The refrain in lots of early English polyphonic songs.'

Robert still looked blank. Paula said, 'Well, I'm sorry it means nothing to you, but it did to people on the course, and Jarrold made them laugh. Lightened it up.'

'So he's sociable?'

She pulled an odd face. 'No, actually, not at all. It's odd really. He's completely charming with people, yet paranoid about getting too close.'

'Well, he certainly lives out of the way up at Tarnfield Hill.'

'Yes.' She stopped again. 'But then on Saturday he said we should go to the pub. He'd never been to a country pub before and really wanted to try out the Plough. I was delighted. I thought it was great, like the beginning of going public, you know? But we didn't speak to another soul in there. And he never said anything to me about Deborah's death, although he *must* have known, because there would have been police and ambulances all over Tarnfield Hill on Friday night.'

It sounded disturbing to Robert. He felt a jab of anxiety for Paula. She looked as if she might start to cry.

She went on, 'Maybe he thought I would never find out about Deborah's accident. Shows how little he knows about Cumbria. Maybe he was just protecting me from something unpleasant?' She looked hopefully at Robert. But Robert didn't see it that way. Why would the American shield Paula from the death of a woman she didn't know? A bizarre thought occurred to him: maybe, given the Arbiter connection, the American was somehow involved in Deborah's death? Did he want to head Paula off before she got suspicious?

'It doesn't sound as if your romance is making you very happy,' he said gently.

'I've never been so mixed up in my life. Some days I really think this might be the one. Sounds ridiculous, doesn't it, but that's how it feels. And then on other days I think he doesn't care at all. It's as if he's got me on a string. I hate feeling like that but I can't stop it.'

Robert didn't know what to say. He and Paula had discussed some dramatic student circumstances, but she had never personally confided in him. Things must be serious for her to show any weakness.

'If you come to Tarnfield again, why don't you both come and see us? That would be a discreet way of going public, and Suzy would love to meet you.'

'No.' Paula was suddenly emphatic. 'That's the last thing Jarrold would want. I shouldn't have talked like this. I feel stupid and embarrassed. You're too nice, Robert, and I've let my tongue run away with me. Please don't say anything to anyone, will you? I have a meeting now, so I'd better go . . .' She leapt up and he didn't have time to answer, which was fortunate, because he couldn't have promised not to say anything to Suzy.

He wouldn't see his wife till much later that evening anyway. After his meeting with the postgrad student, he was going all the way to Lancaster, in place of Linda the vicar, for a summit meeting of northern dioceses about the thefts of metal from churches. He felt sorry for the clergy. It did seem tough, to have to be a curator of souls — and roofs and lead drainpipes as well! But he would have something to think about on the long drive. Paula's American lover sounded very questionable to Robert. He was a member of the extended Arbiter family, but he had said nothing to Paula about Deborah Arbiter's death . . . So was he investigating his family history with a venal motive? Deborah had been a very rich woman, even when her support for the hostel was factored in.

Perhaps Suzy had been right, and Deborah's death wasn't an accident at all . . .

* * *

A few hours later while Robert was in Lancaster, Suzy and Ro were finishing their Star of Bengal dinner, and Suzy felt better. They had eaten quickly and caught up on the local news. Life felt a bit more normal.

'Okay,' Ro said eventually, 'so let's get back to your theory. Who's your number-one suspect for J, guilty of the double murders of Ellie Fox and Deborah Arbiter? Two very different women, by the sound of it.'

'I know you're sceptical, Ro. But you didn't meet Ellie. I can't believe that within six weeks of our holiday she was suicidal. She was definitely scared, but she had made up her mind to stand up to this J person.'

'People's feelings can change in hours, never mind weeks. But okay, I'll indulge you. Who do you think this J was?'

'I've told you about this awful bloke called Scott Jermyn who's just bought Tarnfield House on the Green. J for Jermyn, like the street. He's from London. He's sexist and full of himself and the dates fit. But he has a sort of compelling attraction. You find yourself wanting to impress him. He's just the sort of person you could imagine taking over Ellie's life. Plus, he was doing some work for Deborah, but nobody knows what. He's deeply into quarries selling local stone. What if he suggested a new stone parapet to her, and took her up there to show her?'

'So how would he get down without being seen? We've been over this.'

'But there's a back staircase. It goes to the back door, which, as you say, is visible from Deborah's Tree, but if a car was parked by the back door, there would have been a tiny opportunity for someone to come down the stairs, sneak outside and turn sharp right behind the car, to go down the path to the door in the wall . . . of course, they'd have to know the code for the door. . . '

'We looked at that, Suzy. We asked about cars; Joanne Butcher says the hostel car was parked at the front that day. The back door was clearly visible.'

'But Joanne might have been mistaken? Or the man could have flattened himself against the wall and left while everyone was in a terrible state about finding Deborah?'

'Okay, I grant you there might, just might, be a teeny-weeny chance of that. But he'd be a very lucky killer and he certainly couldn't depend on it.' But Scott Jermyn had that sort of insouciance. Suzy thought of him airily announcing that he would send his roofer round to the Briars. No question of whether that was what she wanted. *Yuk.*

Ro sipped her wine, and then looked at her phone which had been on silent. 'I've got a voicemail.'

'Oh? You'd better listen to it.'

'Yes, it's from Jed.'

While Ro concentrated on the message, Suzy let the effect of the wine wash through her. She was very tired now and beginning to feel silly. What had seemed so likely in her own head sounded ridiculous when she expounded it to Ro.

Ro ended the call and put her phone down. 'What does Jed say?' Suzy asked.

'Quite a lot. I called him when I went out to the Indian, and he managed to get hold of his mate in the Met who checked out the Ellie case. It was quite memorable even by London standards because it stopped the traffic and was pretty horrific. It was an open verdict at the inquest, Suzy, but the word on the streets down there is suicide. She was taking serious antidepressants. A bottle of pills supposed to last three months was half empty on her bedside table. Her body was full of alcohol too.'

'So that's that?'

'Looks like it.'

'I still feel there's something wrong . . .'

'Look, Suzy, you've been on the edge of two tragedies in six months. And you've been working too hard in an industry that's all about lurid stories. I can see why you're thinking the way you are. But you've got nothing more to go on than sympathy for Ellie, respect for Deborah's common sense and a visceral dislike of this Scott Jermyn.'

'I suppose you're right.' Suddenly Suzy felt embarrassed. She should just put all this to one side. Her suspicion was the result of over-imagination. Scott Jermyn was just a City chancer. She should go to his party the next evening and have some fun. 'Thanks, Ro. You're right. It's all too far-fetched.'

'Yep. Now I'm going to call a cab. I'll pick up the car tomorrow. And you need a good night's sleep.'

After Ro had left, with hugs and kisses and bags of reassurance, Suzy went straight to bed.

* * *

Later that night, Robert crept into the bedroom, shattered after driving back from the Lancaster meeting. Suzy woke and said drowsily, 'Hi. It's good you're back.'

'Did you have a nice evening? I see you've had company.'

'Yeah. Ro's been over.'

'Discussing Deborah's death, I suppose?'

'Yes. And Ellie's. She's dead too. I was right to be worried about her. She fell from a roof as well, in London.'

Robert suddenly felt wide awake. 'Ellie did? Oh, Suzy, I'm so sorry. But that's very odd. The same as Deborah . . .'

Suzy yawned. 'Well, at least now I know what happened to Ellie. But what the hell, Rob. It's just a coincidence. She and Deborah both fell from roofs, but that's all there is to it. Coincidences happen. I've been a pain about this and I know I've irritated you. I'm sorry.'

'Don't be.' Robert kissed her forehead as she snuggled under the duvet. In the morning he would tell her all about his conversation with Paula Stovey.

Or maybe not. It was ironic that Suzy was giving up investigating at the very moment when he was starting to suspect that Deborah's death, at least, wasn't an accident. But as he looked at Suzy, with her face relaxed in sleep, he thought that perhaps he should leave her to rest and not mention it till he had more to go on. He could make some enquiries of his own. And then they could talk it over when he'd found out more.

Of course, this awful news about Ellie, the woman from Islington who Suzy had met in the Alps, might complicate things in Suzy's head. But Robert's theory had one benefit: it was very simple — Jarrold McHugh was an Arbiter heir and had killed the woman who stood between him and a fortune.

CHAPTER SIXTEEN

They . . . gathered their vineyards, and trod the grapes, and made merry, and went into the house of their god, and did eat and drink.
Judges 9.27

In Tarnfield House on Wednesday evening, Scott Jermyn looked round his new kitchen, with reconstructed Georgian-style double doors leading to the beautiful dining room, which in turn opened onto the large hall with new stone floor tiles. On the opposite side from the dining room was the drawing room, which now extended the whole depth of the house. A fire burned in the large sandstone fireplace he'd had rebuilt from a DecorMetal quarries speciality.

The dining room floor was modern Cumbrian limestone of the palest pearly grey-green — sealed and polished — exclusive and very expensive. Gleaming in the centre of the glass table was a huge platinum-coloured bowl full of seasonal flowers — massive pale-cream chrysanthemums, late white roses, spiky White Spires verbena and glorious foliage in shades of green — eucalyptus, rosemary and soft local pine.

In the dining room fireplace, also sandstone, but this time an unusual creamier type, there was a huge fern in a large brass pot filling the hearth, and above the mantelpiece he had placed a stunning Sheila Fell–style landscape in matching colours. It was all gorgeous even by Mayfair standards, he thought, but with real local sensitivity. And it would certainly promote DecorMetal products. Which was important. He needed to show the company he was doing a good job.

He was looking forward to the evening. The faces of his guests, when they saw the house, would be reward enough for the expense, and if it meant more clients, even better. He was exhilarated by the thought that he had managed to get a decent crowd of significant types together at such short notice. Okay, there was one pair he was less sure of. The Lewises were a bit downmarket — though maybe Mandy had a bit of retro style. A bobby-soxer — or a *bobby-dazzla*, as her husband the roofer would have said. And she worked in a pharmacy, which was always a talking point. Lee was a good talker too — with this bunch of invitees, mainly local householders, everyone would want to talk to Lee about their gutters or drainpipes.

He was intrigued about how his guests would cope with Deborah's death. Would they evade the subject? Or make suitable noises and then hit the booze? What would he hear? He thought they would be surprised to know that it was Deborah Arbiter who was behind his coming to Cumbria. But the locals didn't always know as much as they thought!

It was a shame, but there was no way Geoff Black and his stolid wife in her baggy clothes would have fitted in. To be honest, they would probably have both been uncomfortable anyway. They were more likely to feel at home waiting on the guests with trays and glasses, but they just didn't have the class he needed. He wondered how things were going with Geoff. But after tomorrow, the handyman wouldn't be his problem anyway.

One of the servers he had hired came into the drawing room to ask him about champagne flutes. There would be glasses of pop for everyone. Of course there were always party poopers like Robert Clark, who had already sent Scott a voice-mail apologizing because he would have to leave the party early. But he could spare Robert, now he had Suzy there. Everyone would want to talk to her about her TV award. And she could be quite easy on the eye, if she made an effort, he thought.

'There are crystal flutes in a box in the utility room,' he snapped at the woman. 'Fill 'em up to the top.' It will be far more fun if everyone's a bit pissed, he thought. Except himself. He was sticking to the elderflower once the guests arrived. But before that, something a bit more stimulating would hit the spot a lot faster than fizz. Scott sniffed and made for his en suite . . .

* * *

Suzy and Robert strolled up the lane and along towards the Green to the party. Robert had come back late from taking Linda Finch to the hospital for a check-up. The vicar was much better and would be back to normal that weekend. In fact, she was taking a Bible study class that night, in a village towards the coast. She was getting a bus there, but Robert had offered to pop over to pick her up and take her home, hence his early departure from the party.

'I've booked the Plough again for Saturday night,' he said to Suzy as they walked through the village.

'That's great.' A meal out together would be nice, but even so, it would be a tense weekend. Molly had announced that she wanted to drive herself to her art class in Norbridge on Saturday, with Suzy in the passenger seat, which was absurdly ambitious and there was going to be a row when Suzy said no. And there was also the problem of the attic room. They still hadn't discussed it, owing to Robert being out so much deputising for Linda Finch. Molly's art class would raise that issue again.

But for the moment they could forget all that. When they came to the Green, Suzy stopped and pointed to Tarnfield House. 'Wow!'

Tiny pinpricks of light were delicately traced through two bay trees in massive grey stone pots at each side of the front door, with its large, beautiful fanlight hinting at the soft gleam inside. No cars obscured the view of the house, which fronted onto the road on the opposite side of the Green from the church and the pub.

'There's no sign of the *LEE'VE IT TO LEE* van.'

'That's a shame,' Robert said. 'He's probably the only genuine article here!'

'Apart from tons of local stone and burnished metal. I bet the Georgians would be gobsmacked.'

'They wouldn't get it. They would have wanted cast iron from the Midlands, mahogany from the Indies, and Italian marble if they were wealthy enough. They'd think local stone far too rough.'

'You're very knowledgeable . . .'

'Well, local history is my hobby. I must admit it will be fascinating to see the house. Pity I'm going to have to leave early. But it should give me time to get a good nosey around. I'd like to have a look at the genuine Georgian bathrooms — joking.'

'You're almost as shameless as our horrible host!'

Robert said with a slight edge to his voice, 'But I thought you'd taken a liking to him — you know, your London connection.'

Suzy looked at Robert in astonishment. She was about to say, 'How could you possibly think that?' when one of the young professional couples from across the Green came to join them.

'Looks amazing, doesn't it?' said the woman. 'It'll do wonders for the neighbourhood.'

Robert sighed and followed Suzy and the other couple up to the front door. This sort of 'do' wasn't his scene at all. But he couldn't help being impressed by Tarnfield House, although he doubted that any Georgian would recognize its interior. It was now full of subtle lights, evenly distributed warmth and pale, colourless décor. No hint of the heavy matt colours or discomforts of the eighteenth century. It was undeniably lovely, though Robert found it too contrived. Not clinical exactly — there were far too many subtle aesthetic touches. But it was a show house.

'No little piles of elastic bands and receipts and sweet wrappers,' Suzy whispered.

'Or old hats and cloth caps.'

'And more to the point, no family pictures,' she added, as their coats were borne away by women in grey-and-black matching outfits. *Ha*, Suzy thought, *Rachel should get a look at this. No wellies in sight.* They were motioned into the dining room and adjoining kitchen. Both rooms were immaculate.

'Robert! Suzy! Welcome. This little gathering is all down to you!' Scott called to them. 'I've got a flyer here for each of my guests, itemising the rare and original stone and metalwork in each room. Just a little reminder for you to take home, about DecorMetal products. The whole place is homage to nature in Cumbria. And Georgian life, of course. They knew all about the environment, didn't they?'

Well, if you mean stripping it in the name of empire, Robert thought. He stifled a smile, but his host hadn't noticed. Scott was looking over their shoulders. 'Jarrold!' Scott yelled. 'Delighted to see you, matey. Come on in.'

Jarrold, thought Robert. *Well, well.* It had to be Paula Stovey's lover. The man he never expected to meet in person. The introverted American, who didn't want to talk to anyone local. Yet he was at Scott's party! And not with Paula . . .

Robert turned and had good, long, covert look at the young man who was taking a champagne flute from the proffered tray. There was no doubt he was stunningly good looking. No hint of the thug about him. It was hard to imagine him pushing someone off a roof. But then, what would a killer look like? And this man was certainly muscular enough.

'Who's that?' Robert asked Scott disingenuously as his host breezed past to get to the main crowd of guests, who were admiring his glass dining table and the floor beneath it.

'Oh, that's Jarrold McHugh. A Yank. He's staying at the cottage at St Jane's, next to the Blacks. Surprised, eh?' Scott sniggered. 'It's a laugh when an incomer like me can introduce you to your own neighbours!'

'And how did you meet him?'

Scott looked fazed for a moment, as if he hadn't expected this direct question. 'We met in the Plough, actually, a few weeks ago.'

Robert thought that there was something odd about this, but he couldn't put his finger on it. He looked around for Suzy. She had been carried off by the young couple from across the Green and was now talking animatedly to another pair, a short, dark, stocky man with a wide grin, and a blonde woman with hair in bunches.

Robert would join her in a minute, but he wanted to make sure he got to speak to Jarrold first. The young man looked somehow both more casual and more well-dressed than anyone else in the room. He had dark red hair, and wore neat blue chinos, a fine cashmere jumper and highly fashionable trainers. To Robert, he couldn't look less like a family history nerd who was into folksongs.

Fortunately, Jarrold was standing slightly out of things, on the quiet side of Scott's large shiny slate-topped kitchen island — no doubt another product from their host's quarrying company.

'It's all very impressive, isn't it?' Robert said to Jarrold. 'It's completely changed. I remember this house as the home of the family who owned the auction mart. The Simpsons. They lived here for two generations.'

'Okay,' Jarrold said, with a soft American accent, and nodded sagely. But he didn't follow up. Surely anyone researching family history would be interested in other local families? Robert was about to ask about Jarrold's genealogical interest when he remembered that he had only heard about the Arbiter connection from Paula. And he certainly didn't want to mention her. But Suzy had told him about the American in the cottage next to the hostel.

He said, 'I think you bumped into my wife a few days ago. She's helping with the press enquiries at the hostel. You live in the one of the cottages at Tarnfield Hill, if I'm right?'

'Correct.' The American stared over Robert's head.

'And I hear you're interested in family history? You have ancestors from Cumbria?'

'Yeah. Maybe.'

'I'm into local history as well, but you can probably tell me a thing or two. You'll have heard of the Arbiters, of course. Especially with the recent tragedy next door to you.'

'Yeah. Sad.'

Robert felt annoyed. The monosyllabic answers were verging on rudeness — unless they meant that the young man didn't know or care what Robert was talking about. Robert took a gamble: 'And the Arbiter family were such staunch Methodists. They funded quite a few local chapels.'

'Yeah. Absolutely. Say, would you excuse me? There's someone there I really need to speak to.'

The American gave Robert an artificial smile and moved away. He attached himself to a middle-aged woman in black, whom Robert could only see from the back and didn't recognize. Robert knew everyone, so that was odd. But not as odd as a man who had spent months allegedly studying Arbiter family history, thinking the Arbiters were Methodists. Anyone who had spent half an hour studying the Arbiters would know they were devout, if evangelical, Anglicans.

So Jarrold McHugh was a fraud.

Robert looked for Suzy. He wanted to grab her, take her to one side to tell her about Paula Stovey and the smooth young American who was a liar. At that moment Robert realized who the woman in black was, chatting to Jarrold. He hadn't recognized her without her gym gear. Joanne Butcher from the hostel. If the American tenant were an imposter, she ought to be told.

Suzy was deep in conversation with the blonde woman with the bunches. Robert joined them, hoping to detach her. But Suzy said excitedly, 'Rob, this is Mandy. Lee the roofer's wife. Mandy and Lee are both from Newcastle. We've just been chatting about that daft *Geordies in Space* show I worked on. Must be nearly ten years ago now. You know, where we took people out of the city to the country and gave them loads of space.'

'Yes, I remember.'

'So does Mandy! It wasn't a very good show, really. But we were just saying how tricky it can be to adapt to country living.'

'Yes.' Mandy giggled in a little-girl way, which Robert found annoying. 'In a village everyone knows what you're up to! You can't get away with much for long!'

'Too right,' Suzy laughed over her champagne glass. 'Sometimes being anonymous is a good thing!' Robert smiled but he couldn't join in. The last thing he wanted to hear was Suzy praising city life.

'I need to get away,' he said to Suzy. 'See you at home later?'

'Yes, sure,' she said, but she had already turned back to talk to Mandy before he moved off.

After briefly speaking to the other guests, Robert made his excuses and left. As he went through the hall, he looked back to see Suzy, still laughing with Lee and his wife. His discovery about Jarrold seemed to fade in significance. He had been looking forward to telling Suzy the story of Paula and the American. Okay, so his first theory was wrong. Jarrold wasn't an amateur genealogist out to inherit shedloads of money and prepared to murder to get it. But he *was* a fake. Which meant that Suzy's theory could be right. Jarrold could have murdered Ellie in London, and then turned up in Tarnfield with an elaborate cover, hired the cottage next to the hostel and planned a revenge death on Deborah. The idea would appeal to Suzy.

But now Robert wondered if she would even care. She seemed to have put her speculation about Deborah and Ellie behind her, and to be enjoying the party with gusto, just as he was getting interested in what might be murder. Without

Suzy to discuss the case with, he wasn't sure he cared that much either.

He thought the whole party had had a false tone. And there was something else . . . Oh yes. Scott said he'd met Jarrold in the Plough. But Paula had said that Jarrold had never been to the Plough before Saturday. Had Jarrold lied to Paula? Or had Scott lied to Robert? And did it matter anyway? He trudged up through the dark village in the start of a rain shower and collected the car to go and pick up the Reverend Linda Finch from her meeting.

* * *

In Tarnfield House, Scott had been waiting for someone to mention Deborah's death. There were no prizes for guessing who it would be. Lee the roofer was always going on about it just in case anyone thought he could possibly be to blame. The roofer had spotted Joanne and gone over to talk to her, looking anxious. Scott earwigged, pretending to chat to Mandy about a new tooth-whitening treatment on offer in the pharmacy where Mandy worked. Mandy was never far from her husband.

'How's things at the hostel, Joanne?' Lee asked the administrator.

'All right. But people are asking a lot of questions. Some folk are wondering why on earth Deborah would have gone up onto the roof. You told her it was unsafe, didn't you?' Joanne said.

'You know I did! I haven't the foggiest why she went up there.' Lee sounded wretched. 'After I'd scoped the damage last Wednesday, I told her I'd be back on Monday, and she shouldn't go near it. I blame myself for leaving the ladder there. I put it up on Wednesday for a look-see. I didn't need it for the work I was doing here on Thursday and Friday. It made perfect sense to leave the ladder at the hostel . . .' Lee's voice rose a little, so that people circulating near to him stopped talking for a minute and his words cut through the usual party chatter.

'Don't get worked up, pet.' Mandy moved over to her husband's side.

'Sorry,' said Lee. 'I just feel so terrible about it.'

Mandy informed the room. 'It's Deborah's death. It upsets him. She was a lovely person. I sometimes used to take the prescriptions up there from the pharmacy, for those poor women. I met Deborah a few times. Come on, sweet pea, try not to think about it. We all know it was an accident.' She put her hand lovingly on his shoulder. There was a silence in sympathy for Lee, who was shaking his head.

Scott worried for a moment that his party atmosphere was in danger of deflating.

But at that moment a loud voice boomed from the hall. 'Scott! Do forgive us! We've been over in Norbridge making arrangements for a little party of our own. Stevie and I have finalized our civil partnership for the beginning of December, and of course you're all invited to the party.' Alan Robie strode into the room, beaming. But he instantly caught the mood. 'I think,' he said sonorously, 'the whole village needs something to look forward to after Deborah's death.'

'Of course, mate,' said Scott. 'Life goes on.' A gentle chatter started to bubble up around him. There was a sense of relief. Now Deborah's death had been acknowledged, everyone could get back to enjoying themselves with more of Scott's top champagne. And delicious little nibbles.

'Ooh!' squawked one of the young women from the Green, and hiccupped. 'Too much bubbly! For a moment I thought you were him — you know, from *The Medicine* on TV!'

'Och,' said Stevie fetchingly. 'You're a very perceptive wee lassie!'

'Oh my God! I don't believe it. It *is* you! You must know Winston Harris?'

Good, thought Scott. Normal service had been resumed. And Deborah's death relegated. For now.

CHAPTER SEVENTEEN

Have they not divided the prey — to every man a damsel or two?
Judges 5:30

Half an hour later Alan was still holding the floor, discussing the machinations of the local council. With his work for the LGBT+ lobby he was party to a lot of general gossip. The guests' excitement at meeting the office manager from *The Medicine* was almost eclipsed by Alan's well-informed chitchat. They listened, fascinated, as he talked about controversial planning applications in the district, from a new hypermarket in Norbridge, to rumours of plans to start mining again in parts of Cumbria.

'Not here in North Cumbria, surely?' one of the young men from the villas on the Green asked anxiously. A proposed new coal mine had already caused massive controversy in the west.

'Very possibly,' Alan said. 'Small mines for precious metals are opening all over the place.'

'But there's no gold or anything around here,' said the other man.

'Not gold,' said Alan. 'They're after things like tungsten and lithium. Stuff needed for defence. And communications. Quite exciting.'

Jarrold McHugh had looked disconcerted and then changed the subject. He hadn't talked much all evening, though Scott was pleased he was there. He was decorative and gave the party a cosmopolitan feel. It had been a good move to invite him.

Now Jarrold changed the subject: 'Hey, er, someone was telling me about the family that used to hang out here in Tarnfield House. Who were they?'

'Oh, I can tell you all about them . . .' And Alan was off on village history. Jarrold listened politely for a few minutes, but then mooched off to talk to Joanne again.

Scott did a quick head count. Robert had left, but everyone else was still in the house and mixing well. The atmosphere was relaxed. The Hosseins from the Star of Bengal takeaway were talking recipes with one of the couples from the Georgian villas; Mandy and the other wife from across the Green were flirting pointlessly with Stevie Nesbit, though every so often Mandy looked round anxiously for her husband.

So Lee was missing, Scott thought. And Suzy Spencer. Not together upstairs, surely? Scott thought he'd better go and hunt them out. He took the curved stairs two at a time. He also paid a very quick visit to his own private en suite, for a little boost. He felt energized when he emerged, sharp as a box of knives.

He caught Suzy coming out of the master bathroom. She looked quite good, he thought. She was wearing slimline black trousers in some sort of shiny material, and a loose top which hung nicely. Over her shoulder he could see into his workroom, where he kept his PC and all his papers. There was a classy moleskin sofa in there, as well as his fantastic mountain ash desk and matching office accessories.

'Well, hello,' he said. 'Having a good time?'

'Yes, thank you,' said Suzy, rather formally. 'I'm sorry Robert had to leave.'

But she really wanted to get home herself and had been hoping to find her coat in one of the bedrooms, like at ordinary parties. No chance here, where every room was something from *Homes and Gardens*. She had managed to have a quick glance around so she could report back to Robert. The upstairs was just as tasteful as downstairs, though nothing like as finished and with far fewer original features. There would be another small fortune to be spent up here and no doubt there was an attic too. Scott must be made of money. He was still there when she turned around, and she was a little alarmed to see her route blocked by his long, sinuous body.

He said, 'And now you're here on your ownie-oh! So, hubby's at the vicar's beck and call. His master's voice! Or mistress. I'd watch out if I were you, Suzy. You never know what these people get up to under those robes. And I bet there's life in your old goat yet, eh?' Scott laughed in a nasty way.

Suzy found him more repulsive than ever. She had surreptitiously watched him during the evening, plying people with champagne. Scott was a feeder, she thought, supplying others while pretending to indulge himself, and watching while everyone else slurred their speech and said things they'd later regret.

Suddenly, Scott lunged at her, propelling her into the office. 'Hey, you look gorgeous. We could have a little bit of fun, you and me. I'm from your world, you know. The Big City. C'mon in here. This load of woolly backs won't miss us . . .'

He had his long arms round her and pinned her to the wall. Suzy saw his wet red mouth puckering and bearing down on her. His eyes were screwed up and closed. She could smell a horrible aftershave. She would have to kick him or knee him.

A man's voice shouted 'Hey!' At the sound Scott opened his eyes and slackened his lips but kept hold of her. Suzy couldn't see who it was.

'Howay man, I don't think the lass is enjoying that.'

'Oh, Lee . . . Caught me in the act, eh? I didn't know you were in here!'

'Obviously, marra. Are you okay, Suzy?'

Suzy got her balance back and pushed Scott away. He didn't fight. He disentangled his arms and just grinned at her. 'N'mind eh? Maybe another time while hubby's at choir practice? Or polishing the stained-glass windows?' He guffawed.

'I don't think so.' Suzy said.

'Ah, that's a shame,' Scott said. 'You seemed so fed up with this village, Mrs TV Producer. I love it myself. But then I'm not trapped between Mr God-botherer and the lady vicar. You can't blame me for trying to give you a good time.'

From behind Scott's head, Lee caught Suzy's glance and rolled his eyes. Scott seemed completely unfazed. Shameless.

'I need to get home,' Suzy said.

'Let's gan downstairs.' Lee took her arm and manoeuvred her past Scott, who was grinning inanely and had fallen back against the sofa.

'Are you okay, bonny lass? That must have been horrible for you,' Lee asked her on the landing, dropping her arm.

'Yes, really I am. He didn't get very far. Thanks to you.'

'Aye. What a wazzock. He'll feel terrible about it in the morning . . .'

'Or not. He probably thinks he was paying me a compliment.'

'One you could do without, pet. Mandy and me have a cab coming any minute. We'll give you a lift home.'

'That's really kind. There are just a few people I want to say goodbye to. And there's no point me making a fuss about this, Lee.'

'If you say so, bonny lass.'

She reclaimed her coat and chatted briefly to Alan and Stevie, who were leaving at the same time. She said goodbye to Joanne and arranged for another session at the hostel the next day.

Then Scott reappeared, sniffing but unabashed, the perfect host, saying goodbye and pressing his notes about stone and metalwork into the hands of his departing guests. When he came to Suzy he said archly, 'No hard feelings. Literally!' and laughed his hyena laugh. Unbelievable.

Lee and Mandy dropped Suzy off at the Briars with lots of sympathy about her brief encounter with Jermyn. Bur Suzy had been through worse and preferred just to let it go.

'He was probably off his head,' she said.

'Aye. A bit of the old nose candy.'

'Probably. Thanks so much for coming to the rescue. I'll say goodnight.'

She always loved coming home, but tonight it was an extra special relief, even though Robert was still out. She would stay awake and wait for him.

The way Scott had behaved was upsetting, but the worst thing, Suzy thought, was his insinuation that she was fed up with Tarnfield, and worse still, fed up with her husband. How on earth could she have given anyone that impression? And even worse again, had she given that impression to Robert? The time for their serious conversation had come. Suzy made some black coffee and prepared a couple of big, toasted sandwiches to make up for the so-called fancy food served by Scott Jermyn.

She heard Robert's car coming down the track and took a deep breath.

They sat in the kitchen as usual, this time with mugs of coffee and the sandwiches. Robert had had a difficult evening, driving in the drizzle to pick up Linda and bring her back to Tarnfield.

'I'm shattered by all this running around,' he said. 'I don't know how you do it, Suzy.'

'Well, I'm stopping all this extra work in London.'

'You are?'

'Rob, I think I've been giving out the wrong signals.' She told him, without drama, about Scott.

'Good God!' Robert never blasphemed. 'The total bas . . .'

'Don't say that, Rob. It's not like you. Don't be angry. I don't think he'd have gone much further. He was just slobbery and disgusting. I never felt really frightened. And fortunately Lee was in the room and distracted him.

'But how did Jermyn dare . . . ?'

'There are a lot of men who dare. I was never in any real danger there. It was easy to push him away, and if not, I could have kneed him in the groin if Lee hadn't stepped in. But what upset me most was his suggestion that I wasn't happy here with you. I am happy. Of course I am. But I've been so worried . . .'

'But Suzy, I've been worried too . . .'

'I know what you're going to say. It's been obvious since I came back. The house is too expensive and, let's face it, my kids are too demanding. They take you and the Briars for granted. They stuff the garage full of rubbish and now Molly is running a campaign to get a studio in the attic as well as having driving lessons. How long before she assumes you'll stump up for a car for her?'

'No, Suzy . . .'

'If it's getting too much Rob, I understand. I don't want to move, but I can see it might be better for you if we downsized and got a modern place in Norbridge.' To her own surprise she felt her eyes welling up. 'But I don't want to leave the Briars. It's a wonderful family home. We're so lucky. And you've been great for us. How could anyone, even a plonker like Scott, think I was unhappy here? It's my life.' Big gloopy tears bubbled out of her mouth and nose. *I look gross as well*, she thought. *I'm a mess.*

Robert gave her his big, white, old-fashioned handkerchief, and came and stood by her chair, his hand on her shoulder.

He said, 'But you're always working away. I thought you wanted to leave here.'

'Oh no, Robert. Nothing could be further from the truth.'

'So I got it completely wrong too,' he said. 'But you were talking so much about going to London and Manchester.'

'That's because I was worried about money! You've spent so much on the kids. However hard I work I can't pay you back for all you've done.' She buried her face in the hanky and moaned.

'Oh Suzy! Having you and the kids is the best thing that ever happened to me. It's my choice to spend money on them.' He paused. Robert was always truthful. 'Within reason, of course — that electric scooter was a bad idea . . .'

Suzy's muffled sobs subsided. 'I'm glad you said no to that before Jake ran someone over . . .' she said through the hanky. 'And the llamas Molly wanted.' That had been so ludicrous, she had to laugh.

'Seriously, Suzy, is this why you've been working so hard? Because you're worried about money?'

'I suppose so.'

Robert stroked her hair. 'Oh darling, I'm so sorry if I gave you the impression we were spending too much. At the weekend let's go over our finances. We're not badly off. The house is expensive but not ruinously so. And you do more than your share.'

'Oh, that's such a relief, Robert. I've probably been worrying too much. We should have had this talk on Friday night when I came home. But look what happened . . .'

'Yes. Deborah died. And I shouldn't have ended the conversation about her death when we were in the pub. Or about your concerns over your friend Ellie. I just didn't want you to become tied up and distracted with it all. But you've got good instincts and I should have listened.'

'And I still want to discuss it with you! Everyone else thinks I'm crazy. I've tried to forget about it. But I know I'm on to something. Two women I know have died falling off roofs. And they were in touch with each other. That has to mean something. Plus, there's that awful man at Tarnfield House. Maybe he was sizing me up as another victim? Rob, please let's talk. I know it's late, but how about now?'

* * *

They talked until the early hours of the morning.

'Right.' Robert had poured more coffee. 'I can see what your theory is. You think the same person, with the initial

J, pushed both Ellie and Deborah off their respective roofs. Two deaths of that kind among your circle is too much of a coincidence. You know that Ellie was in a relationship with an abuser and decided to leave him, and you think he killed her. He somehow knew she had planned to come to St Jane's, so in the fullness of time he comes to Tarnfield, ingratiates himself with Deborah and kills her too, the same way, for revenge. If that's true then the guilty party needs to be someone with London and Tarnfield connections, in the necessary time frame.'

'Yes! Exactly. Obviously, the ghastly Scott looks suspicious. He tells everyone he was doing some work for Deborah, and we all assume it's something to do with investing, maybe in his wretched quarries with the DecorMetal company. But maybe that was just a ploy to get near to her and kill her as well. His personality fits, and his background.'

'Yes. But there's someone else who fits too. Just when you were starting to give up on the murder theory, I got a lead! Your Texan tenant in the cottage is pretty suspect . . .' Robert told Suzy about Paula Stovey and her romance. 'I was dying to tell you about it tonight. I'd been wondering if Jarrold McHugh could have murdered Deborah for an inheritance if he was an Arbiter. But I found out at the party that he's pretty ignorant about his so-called ancestors.'

'How did you do that?'

'I just fed him misinformation about the Arbiters, and he fell for it. He doesn't seem to know very much about that family at all. So he's lying to Paula. And to the hostel. Could all that genealogy stuff just be a front for getting close to Deborah and killing her? On the other hand, he's from the States. How would he know Ellie?'

'But is he really Texan? Could he have lived in London for years? We don't know anything about him.'

'There are a lot of people we don't really know much about,' said Robert. 'What about the handyman? Did you say his name was Geoff? He travels all over England on various dodgy building jobs, from what you've said.

'Geoff Black? One of the women at the hostel, Leila, is certain he killed Deborah. But was he Ellie's lover? She was early forties at the most and he's seventy.'

Robert said, 'Seventy isn't that old, as I will remind you one day. And there are lots of cases of people having lovers thirty years older than themselves. Ellie might have wanted to come to St Jane's to be near him as well as to escape him — these relationships are complex.'

'Well, it's weird but possible. Geoff's pretty fit, no beer gut, he's tanned, he's got a full head of hair and he must be strong with all that labouring work. But he's not a great conversationalist from all accounts.'

'Your coercive controller doesn't have to be a silver-tongued smoothie.'

'But he would have to be attractive to Ellie. Mind you, there's no accounting for taste. And I suppose J could be J for Jeff, not G for Geoff.'

'So you can't discount him.'

'But it's no good going to DS Jackson with all this, Robert. Ro says he's certain no one could have been on that roof, pushed Deborah and made it out without being seen. And he'd laugh about the J connection — look at his own name! Jed Jackson. There are thousands of Js around.'

'Yes — Joanne for example? Was Ellie's lover a woman? Was Ellie coming to St Jane's to be with her? Or to get revenge on her? Did Deborah find out, and have to go?'

'Hardly likely! But there's another interesting point I haven't told you about — Chelsea, the domestic worker at the hostel, says she saw Joanne embracing a man on Sunday night. So in any case the lesbian theory might not wash.'

'Or it might. Joanne might be bisexual. Don't discount anyone with a North and South connection and a name beginning with J. The Hosseins' oldest boy Jamel is at university in London, and there's Archdeacon Jim Bentley, crazy as it sounds . . .'

'It *does* sound crazy, but thanks so much for saying it, Rob. Yes, it helps a lot to go over it systematically like this,

I've been feeling totally out on a limb! Ro and Rache are kind but they both think I'm completely batty. But I can't stop wondering.'

'Neither can I, to be honest. And I shouldn't have tried to stop you speculating. That's the person you are.'

Suzy smiled. 'I feel like my old self again.'

'What about my old self? Come to bed!'

CHAPTER EIGHTEEN

And Deborah said unto Barak, Up; for this is the day in which the Lord hath delivered Sisera into thine hand: is not the Lord gone out before thee?
Judges 4:1

Thursday was a beautiful day — not with the confident golden warmth of the previous week, but with a fragile, pale, duck-egg-blue sky, peppered with small clouds. The sun was constant but precious. The leaves glowed orange and crimson, hanging precariously on the spindly branches. Even a breath would send them scattering, but for now they clung on.

Suzy felt so much better. Molly was going into Norbridge for the day to meet her girlfriends for a half-term shopping session, so a driving lesson was off the agenda, thank goodness. Robert had a break from filling in for Linda Finch on parish duties and announced he would tackle the garden before the winds blew up — there was a sense that the rare beauty of the day couldn't last.

Suzy drove slowly up to the main road and along the Vale towards St Jane's. Last night she had been heady with relief that Robert understood her suspicions. But they both needed to be realistic. There might be dozens of people in Workhaven and Norbridge who resented Deborah and wouldn't mourn her death. It was Ellie and the London connection which narrowed the field.

And if both women were pushed to their deaths by the same killer, the person who killed them needed to have had easy access to Ellie's flat, and — much more difficult — to the hostel.

Presumably Scott Jermyn had visited St Jane's in the past, because of his enigmatic business meetings with Deborah. Jarrold McHugh was living nearby and could have somehow come into the grounds and gone through the back door and up the stairs. And Geoff Black was in and out, if not a lot, then frequently enough.

Other visitors were few and far between. The counsellors, social workers and GP would all need to log in with Joanne when they arrived. Suzy thought they were mostly women. But women couldn't be discounted — as Robert had suggested, Joanne herself was a remote possibility. She was very fit, but if you took the Ellie connection seriously, it would take a lot of muscle to tip a healthy woman in her forties over a balcony railing. Suzy thought of Geoff Black, heaving boxes from his garage into his truck. No shortage of muscle there. The idea that he was Ellie's lover had seemed ludicrous at first, but stranger things had happened.

Suzy reached St Jane's and keyed in the code. The big gates swung open, but only wide enough to allow a car to creep through carefully. It would be watched on the monitor in Joanne's office. Even pedestrians needed to be buzzed in. The code was changed every week according to a system devised by Deborah, which only Joanne understood. No one could get into the hostel unannounced — even on foot.

Suzy parked at the front of the house to test the security for herself. The large, shiny, black-painted door was usually open, giving a welcoming impression. But there was a strong glass inner door which was controlled by another keypad and code.

Suzy passed through the glass door. In the morning sunlight, the entrance hall was lit up and she paused to take in the atmosphere. The hall was painted turquoise blue with white woodwork and gold details. There was a pleasant smell of beeswax; the parquet floor had been mopped and then polished by Chelsea, and it shone. The paintings gave the room an air of substance and tradition, with the Gentileschi picture in the centre. A shaft of sunlight caught it, and Suzy walked up to it to have another, closer look. On the face of it, this was just another classical painting.

But Adelina had said it was about overcoming tyranny. Suzy looked closer. The murder of the enemy general, Sisera, endorsed by Deborah the Judge, was a single act of violence which ended a war. Suzy had heard of much more obvious revenge-style pictures, like the Judith and Holofernes story, where Judith severs Holofernes's head. That gruesome topic had been popular in past centuries, and was also painted by Artemisia Gentileschi. If Deborah had wanted a revenge picture by a famous woman artist on the wall, surely that would have been the one to choose?

But the Jael and Sisera story was about victory, not revenge. And it was from a story about Deborah the Judge in the Old Testament.

Joanne came out of the office looking harassed. 'Suzy, good to see you. Can you do me a favour? Can you work in the lounge for an hour? I've got Deborah's solicitor here. I'll come and find you when we've finished.'

'Sure.' Suzy went into the lounge and set up her laptop on the coffee table. She settled in to review what she had written so far in the tribute to Deborah. As a piece for the *Mid Cumbria Times* or other local papers it needed more local references, and more insight into the real Deborah. Suzy wasn't happy with her work. She was still no nearer understanding why Deborah had started the hostel, and she couldn't make the dates on Deborah's CV fit with the date of her father's death.

She hunched over her laptop, just looking up occasionally to see out of the huge French windows at the side of the house which looked down to the chestnut tree, now shedding its leaves. The rooms at the hostel were large and elegant. The lounge was full of light with views over the grounds on two sides. The furniture was arranged in small islands for three or four people to sit and have private conversations. Now it was autumn, the French windows were locked, so as Ro had said, there were only two ways in and out of the hostel, the front and back doors. The ground floor of the house had a clear, simple, large-scale layout. There was nowhere for anyone to hide.

Except, of course, for a small woman like Suzy in the lounge, hidden by the tall back of the settee. But on the day of Deborah's death, all the women had been sitting here, including Joanne. Everybody had been in sight and accounted for. One woman had gone outside because of a hot flush but she had immediately seen Deborah's body. Even Leila had been off the phone and in the lounge, eventually.

Today, though, the two women who came quietly into the lounge had no idea Suzy was there. They were already talking, and she didn't want to interrupt. But she could hear them clearly. She thought one voice belonged to Adelina.

'She could be in her room. But she wasn't at supper last night.'

'She was here yesterday afternoon. In the grounds, prowling round. On the phone as usual. She's been worse since Deborah died. Deborah knew there was something wrong.'

'Yes. But the Judge was very perceptive. We all knew that.'

The two women moved away towards the kitchen. Funny how they all used the nickname of 'the Judge' for Deborah. Suzy had thought it was just a journalist's witty comment.

Joanne put her head round the big mahogany door into the lounge and called Suzy's name.

'You can come back into the office now, Suzy. The solicitor has gone.'

Suzy unplugged her laptop and followed Joanne. In the office they sat facing each other and Joanne put her head in her hands.

'Was it a difficult meeting?' Suzy asked.

'You can say that again! I don't understand.' Joanne looked up. 'Deborah's solicitor has got her computer back from the police and brought it back here. He said there was hardly anything of interest on it. He had a hard copy of her will, so we went over it. The hostel is already provided for. It's been a charity for over thirty years. It's completely funded by the Arbiter Trust. There are no real worries. It's just that . . .'

Suzy waited. 'This is totally confidential,' said Joanne. 'But Deborah always said that if anything happened to her there was another small funding supply we could access easily and quickly, which would guarantee that we could keep up a really high level of emotional and mental health support, and at our own discretion.'

'So, no fuss about probate either?'

'Exactly. She said that while she was alive, she paid for things out of her own money, but that if she died there were funds we could use for the extras. But there's no mention of that in her will, and the solicitor has no clue about any extra funding supply. It's not the end of the world, of course. But it might mean the end of what makes St Jane's so special. We've always been able to afford all sorts of help without worrying.'

'I'm sure the solicitor will locate it. Maybe Deborah has left a letter or document somewhere?'

'Not anywhere the solicitor can see. There's nothing in his documents and nothing on the office PC. Apart from that, she didn't have any other devices, no laptop or tablet. And she'd mislaid her phone a few days before. She was always leaving it around. She wasn't very bothered. She didn't use it much, only for calls and texts and a couple of apps. The trouble is that Deborah was ingenious and had a sense of humour. She might have left a wad of money under the floorboards or in the fridge! But it's so unlike her not to tell me . . .'

'So how bad is the financial situation?'

Joanne rubbed at her eyes. 'It's not bad. Not really. In the long-term, Deborah has left us her personal fortune, which is great, but it will take a while to go through probate. So we're in a mess in the short-term if we're going to keep up the level of support the residents have been used to. We'll need more ready money.'

For the first time, Suzy saw Joanne flag. But the other woman visibly pulled herself together. 'I'll get Chelsea to make some strong coffee at eleven o'clock,' she said. 'I certainly need it.'

'Chelsea is turning out to be a bit of a godsend,' Suzy said. It struck her that a few words in the girl's favour could go a long way when her real identity was revealed. 'I could do with strong coffee myself this morning after Scott's party last night. Did you enjoy it?'

Joanne said, 'Oh yes, in a way, though it was odd to be going out to a social event so soon after the weekend's tragedy. Not that I go out very often anyway, but Scott was very helpful to Deborah — I never really understood what he was doing for her, maybe something to do with her personal investments. But I felt I should go to his "do".'

'I just wanted to see inside Tarnfield House.' Suzy laughed.

'Yes, it was amazing, wasn't it! But I prefer our stronger colours. More authentic Georgian.'

'It must have been tiring having an early meeting this morning. Do you ever get away, Joanne? You say Deborah used to get to the Alps every so often. But do you stay here all the time?'

'Oh, mostly. I did go to London earlier in the year on family business. I'll go and ask Chelsea to make a pot of coffee now, rather than waiting till eleven.' Joanne got up. 'I didn't expect the meeting with the solicitor to be so . . . well . . . awkward.'

When she went out, Suzy found herself daydreaming. So Joanne had a north–south connection too. And she was in London around the time when Ellie died. But if they were seriously going to suspect Joanne, then what about other outlying candidates for killer?

Suzy hadn't considered Lee the roofer. She didn't want to suspect him after he had rescued her from Scott's wandering hands. But he had undoubtedly left the ladders in place for easy access to the roof on the day of Deborah's death. But then again, he had been at Tarnfield House at the time. And he and Mandy seemed joined at the hip. And his name began with a L not a J.

And the Ven Jim? Okay, that was a crazy idea too — but he had arrived from the south in late spring, and on Saturday he had loped into the hostel with total confidence and no regard for keypads or security because Joanne had opened the door for him. The archdeacon obviously knew his way around. And he'd certainly had an agenda as far as Deborah was concerned. But a connection with Ellie was very hard to imagine. Jim began with a J though . . .

The owners of the Star of Bengal, the Hosseins, had an elder boy called Jamel. It was a pretty ludicrous suggestion, but as Robert had said, it was reading week and he could be home from university in London . . .

No, this was getting silly, Suzy thought, although all was clearly not well with the Venerable Jim Bentley. But to be realistic, Scott Jermyn at Tarnfield House was still the strongest possibility. Though Jarrold the Texan was highly suspicious. Then Suzy found her thoughts turning more to Geoff, or Jeff, Black.

Joanne came back and squinted at her computer, clicking furiously. Budgets and funding, Suzy thought. The bane of all administrators.

Suzy said, 'But you still have the rents from the cottages, don't you? As well as the money from the Arbiter Trust. Is that American chap going to stay much longer? Jarrold? He's not what I expected at all. I thought he'd be more of a sort of weedy computer nerd. But he looks as if he could stride from here to the top of Tarnfield Fell without drawing breath! And walk twice around the Arbiter mines on the way. I wonder what he's really up to . . .'

It had been a bit of a fishing trip to see Joanne's reaction. The other woman stopped scrabbling around with her mouse. She looked over her screen at Suzy.

'What on earth are you suggesting?' Joanne said sharply.

Then there was the usual clumsy noise at the door made by Chelsea trying to open it with her hips, making a sort of knocking noise with her elbow, and manoeuvring her large Edwardian butler's tray. 'Coffee,' she said unnecessarily, 'and flapjacks' and put the tray down on the scratched sideboard. Joanne said 'Thank you' in a cold voice, and Chelsea, sensing an atmosphere, scurried out.

Joanne was still looking at Suzy but had recovered her composure. Without speaking, she got up and poured herself a coffee. She didn't offer one to Suzy. Then Joanne took a deep breath, which seemed like the prelude to announcing something serious. Suzy felt a frisson of discomfort. What was Joanne going to say?

'I find this rather embarrassing.' Joanne paused, and Suzy waited. 'But that money for extras which we were talking about was going to pay for the communications role as well. And that role was designed to support Deborah with her increasing media appearances, which won't happen now. So really, Suzy, I don't think there's going to be a long-term communications job here.'

'Good heavens! That's not why I'm doing this!'

'But we're not even going to be able to pay you for this week.'

'There was no question of that, Joanne. This is all *pro bono* as far as I'm concerned. I had this week available anyway.'

'I really appreciate it. You know that. But I wanted to pay you something. Some sort of honorarium at least. I feel uncomfortable now I know we're going to be in slightly straitened circumstances.'

'It's okay. Really.'

'But I don't agree, Suzy. I've just had another look at the budgets, and to be honest, I think it would be best if today was your last day here.'

'Sorry?'

Joanne went on: 'I don't think we really need you anymore. Not here, every day. Of course I'd be really grateful if you finish the biography, but you can email it to me. We've covered an awful lot of ground already and I think I'll be able to manage from now on.'

'But that's not what you were saying yesterday!'

'No, but things change. I'd always intended to pay you something and now I can't.' Joanne couldn't look Suzy in the eye.

Suzy was surprised at how shocked she felt. She had thought that on a practical level she and Joanne worked well together, and that she had become a sounding board as well as a press officer. Only minutes ago, Joanne had taken Suzy into her confidence over the hostel funds. This sudden change of heart was astonishing. And hurtful.

'Joanne, I was only planning to be here for today and tomorrow anyway. I'm due back in Manchester to work on *Living Lies* on Monday. I was going to keep in touch with you by phone, and maybe just pop in one evening next week.'

'I'll certainly keep in touch, Suzy. But I'm going to have to ask you to leave the office now because I need to make some sensitive calls. I'll let you know if we need you again.'

'Now? You mean this minute?'

'Well, there's no point dragging this out.'

Stunned, Suzy stood up and unplugged her laptop. 'This is a bit sudden,' she said, 'but if there's anything else . . .'

'Of course. I'll get straight on to you.'

Suzy left the office in a daze. In the hall, the picture of Jael and Sisera was lit by the late morning sunlight, standing out from the other pictures. How very odd it all was, Suzy thought. But no point lingering. Joanne had given Suzy her marching orders in no uncertain terms. Suzy went out, got into the car and drove back in the direction of the Briars.

CHAPTER NINETEEN

Why is his chariot so long in coming? Why tarry the wheels of his chariot?
Judges 5:28

Robert liked gardening. He was aware that, really, he should have been either working on his research or doing his own marking today. The university's half-term reading week wasn't supposed to be a holiday. But he'd been putting in extra hours when Suzy was away, and he didn't feel guilty, either about taking time out helping the vicar, Linda Finch or having a break tidying up the mess that was the garden.

He looked around the big, untidy space at the back of the house and remembered when they'd had a barbecue a few years ago. The kids' father had come over, and they had all got on well. Now they saw less of him; he had yet another new girl-friend. Robert wondered if Suzy's ex might start a new family, and how Suzy and the kids would feel about that. Their father was only in his fifties, about the same age that Robert had been when he met Suzy and took on her family as his own. Molly had been six and Suzy's son Jake in his early teens. Life before them now seemed to Robert like another, remote world.

It was a huge relief that he and Suzy had talked the night before. It was ironic that it had taken Scott Jermyn's boorish behaviour to cut through their mutual misunderstanding. He felt furious when he thought about Scott pushing Suzy up against a wall, but he also realized it was best not to be provoked. He suspected that someone like Scott would enjoy her husband's discomfiture as much as Suzy's.

Robert realized he had been standing with the rake in his hand just staring at the fallen leaves. Usually when he got going in the garden he couldn't stop, ending up with an aching back. But today he couldn't concentrate. It wasn't just Scott Jermyn. He felt upset about Paula and Jarrold as well. In the light of day he felt he needed to tell Paula as soon as possible about her new lover's lies. After all, Paula had confided in him, and he knew that hadn't been easy for her. He didn't like the feeling of knowing something important to her that she didn't know. Paula wasn't the sort of person who would cope well with feeling foolish.

He went inside under the pretext of making fresh coffee and found himself picking up his mobile. He fingered it for a moment, clicked on the uni number and asked to be put through to Dr Paula Stovey. It went to voicemail, and he was momentarily stumped about what to say. 'Er . . . Hi Paula, it's Robert Clark here. How are you? I hope you don't think I'm interfering, but would it be possible for us to have a quick chat? It's about what we were talking about yesterday in the café.' Instantly there was the sound of the phone being picked up.

'Robert — I'm here. I don't usually answer outside calls unless I know who it is. What do you want to talk to me about?' She paused, as if even saying the name out loud was a breach of trust. 'Is it about . . . Jarrold?'

'Yes. Look, Paula . . . we went to a local drinks party last night. And your man was there . . .' He heard Paula breathe in sharply.

'What? Are you sure? Jarrold never has anything to do with the locals. Apart from that old handyman next door, he doesn't know anyone in Tarnfield.' He could hear the hurt and disbelief in her voice, and it made his heart turn over for her.

'Paula, it was definitely him. Jarrold McHugh. From the cottage. Tall, American, with reddish hair. Very good looking.'

'Yes. Oh my word, that's so weird.'

'It's not the only thing.' He paused and listened to her fast breathing at the other end of the call. 'You thought Jarrold was investigating his family history, and that he was a descendant of the Arbiters, didn't you?'

'Yes, of course I did. That was what he told me. Isn't he an Arbiter then?'

'I don't know what he is, Paula. But he isn't researching anything to do with local history. And certainly not the Arbiters. I asked him a question about them, and he had no idea. If he'd been the slightest bit knowledgeable, he would have given me a different answer. I feel really bad about this call, but I can't stand the thought that I know, and you don't.' Paula was gasping now, clearly shocked, and Robert began to regret his hastiness. 'Are you all right, Paula?'

'I don't know.'

'Is there someone you can talk to?'

There was a pause. 'There's only one person I want to talk to.' Paula sounded sharper now, and very angry. 'And that's Jarrold McHugh. If that's his name. Thanks Robert.' She clicked off.

It was so sudden; Robert was taken aback. What had he done? He put his phone down on the counter and stared at it. He had never set off a chain of events like this before. It just wasn't his style.

Suddenly he pulled off his wellies, jammed his feet into his shoes, grabbed his jacket and ran out to the car. He was going to drive to the university in Norbridge and make sure Paula was all right. It was a fifteen-minute journey if he was cavalier with the speed limit. There wasn't much she could do in that time.

But he was wrong. As he sped along the dual carriageway towards the campus, unknown to him, his car passed Paula's on the other side of the road. She was driving like a bat out of hell to Tarnfield Hill.

* * *

At the same time, Scott Jermyn was sipping his designer coffee and surveying his beautiful home. There was no trace of the party, and he congratulated himself on employing people to do all the clearing up. His guests had all left by nine o'clock the night before, slightly later than he'd anticipated, which showed what a good 'do' it had been.

He grinned when he thought of the episode with Suzy Spencer. She'd looked absolutely gobsmacked. He wondered for a moment what he would have done if she'd responded in kind. But that wasn't what he'd wanted. These days he always preferred the thrill of the chase to the catch, though usually it was a different type of prey. Needier. Scott always wanted increasing excitement, so he ramped up the pressure to push a partner into ever-greater displays of love. It was important to him to be the driver — oh yes. Scott was in control! And when he decided that the motor was going nowhere, he was the one who activated the ejector seat for the loser.

But today, there were other things to think about. The point of the party had been achieved, with some potential orders for DecorMetal products, keeping him well in with the company. There were big things afoot with Decor, and thanks to his role as consultant he was on the inside track. But for him, today's main issue was dealing with Geoff Black, the loose cannon. Scott had set things in motion, and now all he needed to do was wait for the call.

He thought about the night before and his visits to his en-suite bathroom. Maybe today it was time for something else to tickle his taste buds. It was a pretty, blue morning, sunny and bright, almost continental in atmosphere, with a pure sky, and red and gold colours in the trees. If he wore his thick down jacket, it wouldn't be too early to open one of the bottles of fabulous champers he still had left and drink it outside. After all, Winston Churchill used to have it for breakfast. Scott would relax in the garden on his suntrap terrace, in the last pool of warmth of the year, and get pleasantly pissed.

He told himself things were going well, and he probably had nothing really to worry about. He went outside and popped the cork.

Then his mobile rang. It was the foreman who had been overseeing the building work on Tarnfield House, Scott's local fixer. He said 'I'm sorry, Mr Jermyn. But things haven't gone according to plan . . .'

* * *

Paula drove off the bypass and into Tarnfield. She put her foot down despite the limit and sped past the row of shops, thinking with self-disgust about the excitement she had felt when buying the croissants on Saturday afternoon at the bakery. She had been so delighted that she would be breakfasting with Jarrold. It was her decision, or so she thought. Pathetic. She had been a complete idiot.

In the past she had always wondered how women could be stupid enough to get caught up with lying, controlling men, but she saw now that she had been on the edge of that sort of relationship herself. Maybe because Jarrold was American she hadn't checked him out properly or asked the sort of questions you would normally ask at the start of a relationship. She had just been swept up in it. She had once idly tried googling him, but nothing had come up and she had accepted that. Fair enough. He was having a break and a career change. Not everyone was tabulated from birth on the internet. But now, that omission seemed highly suspicious.

She drove through the village and out on the road through Tarnfield Vale, before turning on to the single-track road to the hostel. She roared past the big metal gates and round the perimeter to the cottages. She braked sharply and pulled up outside. She went quickly up to the door and pounded on the knocker. Of course Jarrold could be out on the fells, but his routine was to work in the morning.

While waiting, she thought about the cottage. On the right side of the door was the living room window, but the curtains were tightly drawn. Why was that? She had never been in there. It was where Jarrold stored his stuff, and had his main PC, he said. But that was ludicrous. How much stuff did you need for genealogy?

On reflection, she wondered why she had never asked where he did his family history. There was a computer in the kitchen. But what about books and maps, and perhaps photographs? Where were they? In the front room with the curtains closed? Why?

She was half hoping Jarrold was out when he suddenly opened the front door. His face twisted with surprise, but not delight, when he saw her.

'Hey. Paula. What are you doing here?'

'Jarrold. I want to talk to you.'

'But I'm working . . .'

'At what, exactly?'

He looked blankly at her. 'Er, the family history . . . I've got back to the eighteenth century now.'

'The Arbiters weren't here in the eighteenth century, Jarrold. Even I know that. You're not interested in family history, are you? I bet that was all rubbish about your poor broken heart and treacherous mother . . .'

'Hey! What's got into you, Paula?'

'I want some answers. What are you really doing here, Jarrold?'

'Leave it, Paula.' He reeled back, and she took the opportunity to stride into his hallway.

She heard her own voice, raised and angry. 'Don't come all little-boy-lost with me. You were lying through your teeth and laughing at my expense. I thought you were so sweet, but all you wanted was to jerk me about.' She was surprised herself that she wasn't physically frightened of him. He was only a little taller than she was and of course he would be stronger, but she could put up a good fight and she knew some clever moves.

Jarrold stared at her and paused. Then he said, 'Okay Paula. I've screwed up. Things should never have gotten this far. But what's done is done.'

'So are you an Arbiter or not?'

'Well, yeah . . . way back.'

'How way back? I bet you don't even know. You're a fraud. What's really going on in this house, Jarrold?' Paula wasn't an aggressive person, but her anger needed an outlet. 'What's so private that you can't even open your curtains?'

He had backed away from her towards the kitchen. Suddenly she turned sideways and grabbed the front room door handle. It moved under her pressure and the door swung open.

She wasn't sure what she had expected — but it wasn't this. A bloodstained lab coat hung over a chair. There were blue lights, and a flame on a Bunsen burner. The room smelt of ammonia.

Jarrold pulled her roughly by the arm back into the hall, wrenched the door handle from her hand and slammed it.

'I can explain all this, Paula. But not yet. I'm in a legal situation . . . trust me . . .'

'Trust you? You must be joking. I'm out of here, Jarrold.'

'Please Paula . . .' There was something hurt in his tone that made her pause. But that was how she'd been trapped before. He could turn her, with that hint of vulnerability. 'Paula, stay and talk to me. Listen. You mustn't mention this to anyone.' When she didn't respond, his voice hardened. 'Anyone, d'you hear? This is really important, Paula . . .'

The urgency in his voice alarmed her and she felt scared for the first time. She turned her back on him and started to run, fast, out of the house and down the little path to the car. Her speedy exit took him by surprise and he couldn't catch her. She hurled herself into the driver's seat and gunned the engine.

Unable to reach her, Jarrold turned back into the house and slammed the front door. Paula did a fast U-turn on the track and drove back the way she had come, this time even faster.

* * *

Robert was back at the Briars forty minutes after leaving it. The coffee was still hot. Paula had left the music department at the university twenty minutes earlier than his arrival, according to the security guard at reception. She must have put the phone down on Robert, taken her coat and bag, and left straight away. Robert didn't have her mobile number. He told himself she was an adult who could take care of herself, but that hadn't helped Ellie Fox or Deborah Arbiter. He wouldn't be able to relax until he had contacted her.

He was standing at the door of the Briars, looking out on to the track, when Suzy drew up. This was a surprise — he had thought she was gone for the day. She got out of the car looking fed up and annoyed.

'What's wrong Suzy?'

'I've been sacked.'

'Sorry?'

'Dumped. Given the push. Let go.'

Robert had no clue what she was talking about.

'The hostel,' she said. 'Joanne told me to go! They don't need me anymore.'

Robert was astonished. He was both surprised at the fact — and that Suzy seemed so upset. 'Well, maybe that's a blessing,' he said in a conciliatory tone.

'You may say it's a blessing, and if you'd told me on Monday that I'd be finished there by Thursday lunchtime I'd probably have been quite pleased. But I feel differently now. I'd got so involved. I feel really quite deprived. And the way Joanne did it was so abrupt, almost rude.'

'I'm so sorry, Suzy. But I've had a drama this morning too. I called Paula and told her about Jarrold and his lies.'

'Oh, Jarrold again. It's his fault I'm in this mess. I took the risk of asking Joanne about him. Oh . . .' she said, and banged her forehead with her fist.

'What?'

'I think things are becoming a bit clearer, Rob. Let's go in and sit down.'

At the kitchen table, Suzy went first. 'Joanne and I were getting on really well. She'd had the solicitor around this morning, and she confided in me that some ready funds Deborah had promised, in the event of her death, couldn't be found. Actually, a lot of material of Deborah's is missing. Notes on the residents, things like that. The hostel isn't in serious trouble, but they might have to cut back on the extras. So I jumped in and asked about the cottage rent. I made it clear I thought Jarrold was pretty suspicious.'

'And how did she take that?'

'Very coldly. You remember Chelsea telling me that Joanne had been meeting someone by the cottages? I didn't take her very seriously. I thought she might have an overactive imagination. But say that the man was Jarrold? I mean, he's the most obvious possibility, isn't he? He lives there.'

'Could be, I suppose. Joanne and Jarrold seemed very pally at Scott's party.'

'Well, if there's something going on between them it would be odd; but we're prepared to think a woman like Ellie, a successful insurance broker in Islington, might have a lover like Geoff Black, a handyman thirty years her senior. So why not Jarrold and Joanne? Joanne's hardly twenty years older than Jarrold, and very fit. And that would explain why Joanne suddenly turned on me and sacked me. She doesn't want questions about Jarrold. She was being so open with me about the money issue; then I mentioned the cottages. Chelsea brought in some coffee and Joanne must have had a few seconds to think. Then she launched into this spiel about how they couldn't pay me so I would have to go. There hadn't been a hint of that before.'

'Jarrold and Joanne. Well, there's a weird thought. From my side, since I spoke to her, Paula has disappeared, and I'm worried she might have gone to tackle Jarrold. I've been thinking about driving up to the cottages.'

'Should we go and see if she's all right?'

Robert stood up. 'I can hear a car.' No one came down the lane unless coming to the Briars. He went back through the narrow hall and opened the front door. 'We don't have to do that Suzy. Paula is here.'

CHAPTER TWENTY

Give me, I pray thee, a little water to drink, for I am thirsty.
Judges 4:19

Paula was very shaken. 'You told me you lived at the Briars,' she said to Robert. 'I needed to talk to someone, so I came straight round here. There's an old sign for 'The Briars' at the junction between the track and the main road.'

'So there is!' said Robert. 'I haven't painted it for years.'

Paula said to Suzy. 'Sorry. I plunged straight in. I'm Paula Stovey. I work with Robert. And I've been stupid enough to be having a relationship with one of your neighbours.'

Suzy nodded. 'Jarrold McHugh. I've already come across him, Paula. I can see the attraction. Come in. Coffee? Drink?'

'Just a glass of water, thanks.' Paula smiled rather queasily. But Suzy was impressed. Paula seemed direct, uncompromising and honest. In control of herself, if not the situation. She was also tall, very good looking and athletic. Not the sort of person you'd think easily deceived. But then, what sort of person was? Suzy had learned from meeting the women at the hostel that anyone could be conned.

Paula sat at the kitchen table with them. 'Apart from Jarrold's lies to me, there's something else I think people need to know. It's his front room. The one I thought was his office. Well, it's more like a lab . . .'

'A lab? Drugs?' Suzy thought of Scott and his sniffing. Maybe there was a connection between the two men.

'That could be it.' Paula laughed in a rather hollow way. '*Breaking Bad* in the Cumbrian fells. But there were bags of stones as well, with labels and a big microscope and blue lights. Plus a pestle and mortar, and a Bunsen burner flaming away. And goggles on the bench. And worst of all, a blood-stained lab coat, with burn holes. It took my breath away.'

'Sounds very like drugs to me.' Suzy said. 'Except for the stones and the bloodstains. Or maybe there's been some sort of damage to the room. An explosion of some sort. Then again, perhaps I've been watching too much TV! Had you seen this room before?'

'No. We were rowing about the way he'd treated me, lying, and I just turned and pushed the door open. He must have been working in there. There was all this stuff. It spooked me. I just wanted out.' She could still hear Jarrold calling after her. 'And he was so angry. He told me not to tell anyone . . .'

'Does he know you've come here?'

'I doubt it. He'd have needed to get his bike out to follow me. I drove away as fast as I could.'

'Does he know where you live?'

'No. The deal was that I would always visit him. He doesn't have a car. Maybe it made him feel good that I would traipse all the way here at his beck and call. He only had to say the word and I was driving like a mad thing along the dual carriageway. I've been such an idiot. And yet . . . you know sometimes he seemed rather sad.'

'Maybe that's how they get to you,' said Suzy.

Paula nodded, took another gulp of water and said, 'I suppose the next question is what I do with this information. They should be told at the hostel. They're his landlords, I suppose. You're working there, aren't you, Suzy?'

'Not anymore.' Suzy told how she had been given the push that morning. 'And the woman who is running the hostel, Joanne Butcher, seemed to get the wind up as soon as I mentioned Jarrold and the cottage. Joanne and Jarrold could well be in something together. Maybe they're manufacturing drugs in his front room.'

'He was certainly furious that I went in there.'

Robert asked, 'What would you like us to do, Paula?'

'I think we need to tell someone else. I don't know if what he's doing is illegal or not. But someone needs to know.'

Robert had been thinking. 'I don't think we can tell Joanne Butcher, in case Suzy's right and she and Jarrold are connected. We'll tell Neil Clifford, the area dean. He's a friend of mine and the acting chair of the hostel's board of trustees. If Jarrold is up to something illegal, he could deal with it.'

'Great!' Paula drank the water down in one. 'Thank you. I feel so much better now you two are on the case. The shock has made me so thirsty. I can't say I won't be devastated when it sinks in; I really thought Jarrold was special. But right now, I'm furious and feeding my rage. And I don't want to stick around Tarnfield in case Jarrold comes out to look for me on his bike.'

She pulled her hoodie on, and Robert and Suzy went with her to the car. They watched her driving up the track from the Briars to the main road.

'I think she'll be safe,' Suzy said as Paula's car disappeared. 'As long as Jarrold doesn't know where she lives. If he wants to silence her, he could go to the uni to find her, I suppose, but they do have security. Jarrold seems to be a bad lot. He's involved in something dodgy, whatever it is.'

Then Suzy thought for a moment. 'You know, I'm glad Joanne gave me the push. I thought I liked her but on reflection I *do* think she could be involved in something. She's tough. And she's been able to sideline her grief about Deborah as if she's got something else going on . . . I'd like to know what. I'm back at work next week. But I don't want to be away too much while all this is going on. Maybe I can arrange to talk to Adelina. Or get Ro to go to the hostel and ask more questions. I won't stay overnight in Manchester. I'll get the train to and from Norbridge every day. And maybe one evening you can meet me at the station, and we'll go out in town?'

'In town? Norbridge? Not exactly what you're used to these days!'

'It's the only city I really need.' They kissed, linked arms and turned to go to back to the house together.

* * *

At the same time, on the other side of the main road to the village, Jarrold McHugh pulled his bike out of the ditch behind the bushes where he had been waiting. He hadn't been able to catch up with Paula's Honda. But after he'd slammed the front door, he'd raced upstairs to the front bedroom of his cottage and grabbed his strong field glasses. It had taken only seconds to find her car with them, emerging from the other side of the fir plantation heading down the track to the main road to Tarnfield. His view was nothing like the one from the top of St Jane's, but it was pretty good. He had watched her car disappear when the main road to the village wound into a little wood another mile away, and waited for it to emerge.

But it didn't. He had waited for a few minutes till he had established that Paula's car was not on the road to the heart of Tarnfield. Then he had taken his bike and followed her trail. It hardly took him five minutes to get two miles along the road, just where the trees had shielded Paula's car from view. A track led off to the left. And there was an old sign for a house: the Briars. Jarrold took up his post in the bushes opposite the road junction. About twenty minutes later Paula came up the track in her car and turned left down the main road through the village towards the dual carriageway.

So that was where she had been. All he needed to do now was find out who lived in the Briars. And why Paula had gone there.

* * *

Robert tried calling Neil Clifford, but found he was away on a retreat until the weekend. Robert and Suzy discussed it, and felt it was better to let sleeping dogs lie for the moment. McHugh might disappear of his own accord now Paula had seen his lab, but it could be very risky to confront him. And it was in their interests not to disturb him. Whatever Jarrold was up to in the cottage, he could still be the person who had killed Ellie, and then Deborah. He could have been living in London, met Ellie and started a controlling affair, and then come up to Cumbria to tackle Deborah, the woman who had offered Ellie an escape route. Maybe both women had been a threat to a drugs operation. But the first step was to get Jarrold's landlord, which was the hostel charity now chaired by Neil Clifford, to find out exactly what was going on in that dark front room, and that would have to wait a day or two.

They talked about it over lunch. Of course there were still big question marks over Scott Jermyn and Geoff Black. But Jarrold McHugh was now a prime suspect. Investigating the other two could wait.

* * *

In the afternoon they both went back into the garden. Suzy found that the work seemed to soothe her. They had a load of bulbs to put in and it was amazing how much the garden had grown over the last few months. She stripped back mounds of foliage. She had been away far too much.

It started to get dark again around a quarter to six. And this weekend the clocks would go back an hour, and it would be dusk by five o'clock. Suzy liked this time of year. You knew where you were with it. Spring could be deceitful, and summer disappointing. But with autumn and winter you could manage your expectations.

Robert made a mug of tea late in the afternoon, and they stood round the pile of garden trimmings collected for a bonfire, feeling the first nip of possible frost. A family bonfire night wouldn't happen. She supposed Molly would want to go to a firework display with her friends, and Suzy knew they wouldn't see Jake before Christmas. But Robert suggested that they had a little bonfire themselves the next week. Maybe Chelsea might like to come. That reminded Suzy that she needed to contact Chelsea about her invitation to tea the following day. She could pick her up where the single-track road met the main road. That wouldn't be too far for the girl to walk, and it would be out of sight of Joanne at the hostel. Joanne shouldn't see them together. Far from being an asset to Chelsea, Suzy might be a problem for her, now Suzy was persona non grata at St Jane's.

She called to Robert, who was still putting in the last of the daff bulbs, and went in through the back door, kicking off her boots and hanging her coat on its familiar peg. It was good to be at home. This was the week as she had imagined it. She picked up her phone to call Chelsea. Or whatever her name was.

And then Suzy noticed a missed call and a voicemail. '*Hello,*' said a quiet female voice. '*I'm replying to your email. I don't want to give you my name, but you contacted a colleague of mine on LinkedIn. I used to work with Deborah Arbiter . . .*'

Suzy phoned her back straightaway. This was all very mysterious.

The answering voice just quietly said, 'Hello'.

Suzy said very warily, 'Thanks so much for getting back to me. It's Suzy Spencer.'

There was a pause then the woman said politely, 'My pleasure.' Then she seemed to think better of it. 'Well, no, not my pleasure at all. It's dreadful about Deborah. I googled her death after I got your message.' There was an even longer pause. 'I understand you're trying to write an obituary, but you feel you need to know more . . .' She stopped again.

Suzy stepped in carefully. 'Yes, I've got a lot of information about the wonderful work Deborah was doing over the last forty years. But I can't really see why she would throw up her career to come back to Cumbria and start a hostel for abused women. To me, that's crucial to the whole story of her life and I really want to know the answer.'

The other woman was silent for a moment. 'Okay. Perhaps we should talk about this. But I don't want to do it now, or over the phone.'

'Do you ever come to the north?'

Another long pause. 'I have clients in Manchester.'

Suzy felt a burst of excitement but kept her voice neutral. 'As a matter of fact I'm working in Manchester next week. Could we meet?'

Suzy almost heard the other woman thinking. Suzy sensed that she needed to be in control but was still holding back. 'Yes,' the woman said finally. 'The Midland Hotel? Tuesday evening at six?'

Suzy breathed out. 'I can do that.'

'Thank you. I'll be wearing a black business suit and sitting alone with some paperwork. This meeting has got to be anonymous, and totally off the record.' The woman's voice, still calm and quiet, was also crisp and authoritative.

'Okay.'

How weird. Suzy ended the call and looked out over the darkening garden at Robert digging away. She felt a rush of love for him. She was so lucky. But Deborah Arbiter, who had done so much for other women, was dead. And Ellie Fox had been denied an ordinary happy life with a man she could love and who would love her in return. Again, Suzy went over it all in her mind. There had to be something in Deborah's past which had made her want to start a hostel for victims of domestic abuse. Maybe now she would find out what that was. And there had to be some reason why Ellie had contacted Deborah for help, rather than going to another more convenient refuge. Maybe Suzy should look more into Ellie's life too. But how?

She called to Robert. From inside, in the lamp-lit kitchen, with the burnished copper pans and the dresser with the warm red-and-gold Spode plates, the night looked black. Robert came stamping in, bringing with him the tang of woodsmoke from the other houses in the valley, and the damp rich autumn smell of leaf mould, which was on his boots, his mucky gloves and even his face. He was pink with the cold and the work.

Before he had even pulled his boots off, she had told him about the enigmatic woman's call. Meeting her would mean Suzy getting home very late on Tuesday night. 'Go for it,' he said at once, without even looking up from his wellies. 'I'll meet you at the station, however late it is!'

'You don't mind?'

'Of course not!' He turned to her and held his arms open. 'That's the Suzy I love. You don't let up.'

* * *

At the hostel, Joanne Butcher sat in the office and looked out of the long Georgian window on to the drive. After Deborah's PC had been brought back that morning, Joanne had gone through it again. She knew Deborah's password.

The PC had been remarkably empty. It was deeply frustrating. Joanne was sure she knew ninety-five per cent of what Deborah did, but there were still things which baffled her. For a start, Deborah had always been totally conscientious about making and keeping plentiful notes. Where were they? And what about the extra funds? Why hadn't Deborah told her how to access them? And where was all Deborah's information on the residents, like the disturbed Leila, and Suzy Spencer's friend Ellie, the one who had never turned up. What had happened to her? And the notes on her investments and property. And her charity projects.

Joanne knew she had mishandled the situation with Suzy that morning, but she had needed to get her out of the hostel as soon as possible. Joanne couldn't answer Suzy's probing questions, and she knew silence or obfuscation would make Suzy more suspicious. Joanne usually kept a level head. But when Suzy asked about Jarrold McHugh and the Arbiter mines, Joanne had panicked. Suzy was perspicacious and dogged, and if she kept questioning, she would find out . . .

Joanne's mobile rang; she saw that the caller was Jarrold. 'Hi,' she said.

'You busy?'

'Not specially. Just thinking.'

'Listen, I've screwed up. I know I'm up against a deadline, but can I come and talk to you?'

Now Suzy had gone, there was no one around to see them together. Except maybe Chelsea, and what would she make of it? Nothing. If she or any of the residents were curious, they could be told it was an issue with the tenancy.

'Yes. Just come up through the main gates and I'll let you in. I hope this isn't a crisis, Jarrold . . .'

'Yeah, well, we can head it off. It might mean sorting some people out, but I think we can do it.'

'Okay.' Joanne sighed and put her head in her hands. They were so nearly there. Deborah's death had been a terrible thing, but Joanne couldn't afford to be sentimental at this crucial stage. If there was to be another setback, they would just have to handle it.

* * *

At Tarnfield House, the day after Scott's party, the evening sunshine had darkened, and it was autumnal and cold. Inside, the stone and metalwork still gleamed, showing off DecorMetal products, but the big house was no longer beautifully lit and had a soulless feel.

That morning Scott had polished off a whole bottle of champagne with some of the leftover canapés from the night before. He had slept fitfully in the afternoon, waiting for another call from his building foreman, who handled hiring the workmen. In the early evening Scott had ordered a takeaway from the Hosseins. Mr Hossein usually delivered personally but his car was still out of action, so Scott walked up to the main road in the dark to pick up his supper from the Star of Bengal.

He was walking back with a hot, slightly greasy bag of delicious food banging against his legs, when his mobile rang.

Thank God. At last, the call he had been waiting for. He stopped and put his bag on the pavement. 'Yeah?' he growled into the handset. 'Where've you been? I've been waiting to hear from you all day. Have you fixed things?'

'Not exactly,' said his building foreman. It was a bad sign.

'What do you mean?'

'Well, put it this way. It's fixed. But not by us. And not in the way you would have liked.'

'What are you talking about?'

As Scott was trying to hear the call, Lee Lewis's bright silver van with the fluorescent *LEE'VE IT TO LEE* slogan came speeding down the main road and braked sharply. Lee pulled into a parking bay opposite, climbed down from the cab and started waving.

'I've gotta go,' Scott said to the phone. 'I'm out and about. I'll be home in fifteen minutes. I'll call you back.'

'Hiya!' Lee shouted. 'Crackin' party last night, Scott. We enjoyed it, even with your hacky snog with little Suzy. You must've been mortal! You okay today? Wanna lift? You've got a leaky bag there, marra . . .'

Scott looked at the greasy, bright-orange puddle around his bag which had tipped over on the pavement. He had a pretty basic taste in Indian food, and he knew that vindaloo sauce wouldn't wash out of his cool skinny beige jeans very easily if he tried to carry it home.

'Okay, ta.'

'Great!' Lee laughed. 'Put that load of goo on this newspaper. You're lucky I came along. I've been working over towards Norbridge. Sudden demand. Kitchen extension roof. Zinc corrosion. Bloody rubbish, those flat roofs. Climb in, marra. I was giving Mandy a lift home, but there's room on the bench seat. Squash up, Mand.'

His wife smiled and shuffled along a bit awkwardly, so Scott could sit on the end. She handed him his seatbelt and he put his bag of food on the *Mid Cumbria Times* in the footwell. The last thing Scott wanted was company, but neither did he want curry sauce dripping all over his trousers on his walk home.

'Thanks,' he said rather ungraciously. He would need to make sure he got rid of Andy Capp and Flo, the Geordie cartoon characters, as soon as they dropped him off, so he could return that call — which had been all he needed, just when everything was going so well. What had gone wrong? He had been keen to get Geoff Black off his building work. But what did 'not in the way you would have liked' mean?

Lee drove expertly up the main road and swerved onto the track around the Green, pulling up smoothly outside Tarnfield House. 'There you go. You won't even have a chipped poppadum.'

'Ta. Much appreciated. I've got some calls to make,' Scott said, 'so I won't invite you in.'

'No sweat. Have a lovely evening, bonny lad.'

'Yes Scott,' said Mandy in her little-girl voice. 'And thanks for last night. It was belting.'

Scott climbed down and watched them drive away. Happy marriages. Boring. He went back into the house and pulled out his mobile to find out exactly what it was he should be worried about.

CHAPTER TWENTY-ONE

Then shall the people of the Lord go down to the gates.
Judges 5:13

Suzy woke on Friday morning and flexed her toes. Then she turned to look at the clock. It was nearly nine. She hadn't slept so long for ages. But that was because she didn't have to go to the hostel. When she thought about Joanne and Jarrold, she felt angry. But she and Robert had agreed there was nothing they could do about that, until Robert had told Neil Clifford about Jarrold's misuse of the cottage.

And it would be good to find out more about Deborah's early life from the mystery lawyer — but would that really help Suzy find out who had pushed two women off different roofs, three hundred miles apart? Suzy had to remind herself this all went back, not just to Deborah, but to Ellie. Ellie was the first victim of the killer and mustn't be forgotten.

But when it came to finding out more about Ellie, her investigations had stalled. There was nothing more she could do there either. She tried to put it out of her mind and think about family matters. Doing the garden and then having a drink and supper with Robert had led to a sleepy evening in front of the TV. Molly had come home at about nine o'clock, delivered safely by the mum of one of her friends. Suzy had a sense that, whatever else was going on, at least the atmosphere in the Briars was now better and she and Robert were back to normal. It was such a relief. Misunderstandings were bound to happen when she was away so much. That had to stop. This was home and where she wanted to be, and they would make the money work.

So today Suzy would have a day off, except for Chelsea coming for tea that afternoon.

Robert was already up — she remembered he had to be in Norbridge by ten for another meeting, this time specifically about the state of the All Saints Church roof, which might be the next target for metal thieves. She sighed, got out of bed and dressed. And then, with a cup of coffee she sat down to start reading the students' assignments.

About half an hour later, after Robert had gone out, she smelt bacon frying. Vegan bacon? She doubted it. She heard Molly stamping around downstairs.

The student essays were generally thoughtful and very good. The Warsbrook report had largely advised that social media shouldn't be regulated, and that was controversial. Lord Warsbrook was the man of the moment and had been featured in quite a few articles. He was a laissez-faire-style regulator and top lawyer and had started out as an expert on local authority planning applications, moving from that to regulation generally and finally specializing in media.

But most of the student essays had argued cogently that social media should be more regulated and claimed that Warsbrook favoured business over ethics. It was all more interesting to read than Suzy had expected, and she managed to get through the assignments with something like enjoyment.

In the early afternoon she drove up to where the track met the main road to pick up Chelsea, who was waiting for her. On her day off, the girl had reverted to her goth gear — tight black jeans, huge boots, a skimpy top with a tatty black parka over it and lurid make-up. Suzy wondered how Molly would react.

'Blimey, this is brill!' Chelsea said appreciatively about the Briars' kitchen. She was more relaxed, and her London accent was more pronounced. No trace of Stoke on Trent. Joanne would soon be asking questions if she hadn't already. But Chelsea confirmed that the administrator hadn't asked for her paperwork — yet.

'She's got too much going on,' Chelsea said vaguely. 'I'll tell you about it in a mo.'

Suzy led Chelsea into the Briars' sitting room. It was on the left side of the double-fronted house and had originally been two rooms — a big but rather bleak and formal front living room or 'parlour' and at the back a cold dining room — which they had knocked into one big open-plan family room after Suzy moved in. Suzy had paid for the refurbishment of the house. Robert was right — she had pulled her weight financially. She needed to remind herself of that.

She and Chelsea sat on the big sofa behind a low coffee table, looking out through the floor-to-ceiling glass doors which led outside. Putting in these patio doors had made the Briars much brighter. It was lovely, Suzy thought. How could Robert have ever thought she might want to move?

'How about a white wine spritzer?' she asked Chelsea.

'Ooh, that would be luverly!'

Suzy laughed. 'You sound like Eliza Doolittle. A real Londoner.'

'Cos that's wot I am.' Chelsea laughed. 'I try to speak proper when I'm with Joanne. Not that I've seen much of her as she's so busy. That man's back . . .'

'What? Really? The man you saw her with on Sunday?'

'Yes. I'm pretty sure it was him. He was up there in the office with her for hours yesterday, working on something. I offered to make them a coffee and got sent away with a flea in my ear. It's good news for me 'cos it's taken her mind off fings like my P45.'

'Just hold that thought,' Suzy said, 'while I get your wine. Then tell me more.' This was interesting. Could this be the proof that Joanne and Jarrold were linked in some sort of scheme? Suzy brought back a glass for Chelsea with some crisps, and a tonic water for herself because she would have to drive the girl back later.

'What does he look like, this man?' she asked casually.

'Hunky, to be honest. I can see why she fancies him. He's the one that lives in the cottage next to the handyman. She told me he was there discussing his rent or somefink. But they had their heads together when I went in. I knew it was him though. It was his build. Even in the dark on Sunday night I'd thought he was a looker, and there he was.'

It must have been the chinking of the glasses which made Molly materialize around the sofa. She jumped when she saw Chelsea, and her eyes widened. Suzy introduced them. 'I suppose you want a spritzer too?' she said.

'Deffo!' Molly wasn't encouraged to drink at home. But it was Friday. And the drink would break the ice, literally. While Suzy took her time in the kitchen, she listened. After a moment or two she could hear the two girls talking.

When she went back in, she heard Chelsea say, 'Then my mum died — cancer.' And she saw Molly's shocked face.

'That's awful,' Molly said. 'One of the girls at school lost her dad last year. Car crash. But I don't know anyone who's lost their mum. My gran died, which was sad. But she was old and it was Alzheimer's.'

'I never knew my nana,' Chelsea said, 'and my real dad cleared off when I was a baby. So I don't have anyone.'

'That's the pits,' said Molly, round-eyed.

'It gets worse. I told your mum, I'm not really Chelsea. I'm an imposter, I suppose.'

'What do you mean?' Molly was hooked.

'Well, the real Chelsea done a catering course and applied for this job. But she didn't want to come, so I swapped with her.'

'But you wanted the job very much, didn't you?' Suzy said. It had intrigued her why Chelsea had taken such a risk to work at the hostel. 'Why did it matter so much to you to come to St Jane's?'

Chelsea paused and looked at them both. 'Okay, I'll tell you why. My mum was adopted. I never met her folks. I think they were all right, but they had kids of their own after her, and she never really fitted in. Last year someone got in touch with my mum, about my real nan. Trouble was, my mum got really sick and then she died before she could follow it up.'

'That's so sad. And did you ever find out more? About your real grandmother?' Suzy asked.

'Sort of. I looked for letters or somefink, but my stepdad messed all her papers up, searching for money. But my mum told someone in the hospice that my real nan was up north. In Cumbria.'

'But Cumbria's a very big place, Chelsea,' Suzy said gently. 'Why did you come here, to Tarnfield?'

'Well, it was a bit bonkers, but when my mum was dying, she asked about the saint. St Jane. She wasn't a Catholic or anyfink, so it seemed weird at the time. They found a picture of the saint for her, in the hospice, but she was too far gone then to explain.'

Chelsea paused, then went on: 'After mum died, my stepdad chucked me out. I had no one. So I started looking at anyfink to do with this St Jane person and came across this hostel named after her. For women separated from their kids. And it was in Cumbria.'

'So you thought your nan might be here?'

'Well, it was worth a try . . .'

'So it was quite a coincidence your mate Chelsea getting this job.'

The girl looked embarrassed. 'To be honest, it weren't no coincidence. I put Chelsea up to it. I saw the advert, but they would never have taken me on. I don't have no qualifications. But Chelsea did. She'd run away from home to London but then she thought better of it and went back to Stoke. We kept in touch on social. I knew she hated her mum and dad, and I thought she might like this job.'

'So she would have been your spy here?'

'I dunno about that but I told her to apply. Honest to God, I didn't mean to swap with her. Or do identity theft or anyfink. I just thought that if she came here, she could find out for me if my nan was here. But then she met a fella and backed out. So, I said I was Chelsea, and came up here instead. I can cook. My mum taught me. She was in catering. I was going to go to catering college but then mum died.' Chelsea's voice faltered.

'So what's your real name?' said Molly, looking mesmerized.

'I'm Siobhan. But don't say it or people will find out. I don't want to be made to leave here. Even though my nan isn't here, I've got no one, anywhere. Not now my mum's dead. Nowhere to go except them homeless places. If I had to leave St Jane's I don't know what I'd do . . .' The girl's voice wavered.

'It won't come to that,' Suzy said with more confidence than she felt. After all, Joanne had exhibited a hard side which Suzy hadn't expected. If she could sack Suzy in minutes, she could certainly sack Chelsea.

'But there aren't many goths round here,' Molly said. Having a gang of friends was essential to Molly.

'Yeah, well, I'm not sure I'll be a goth forever,' Chelsea said. 'But it can get you through the dark side, you know. It's sort of worse than the worst thing. And goth people can be really kind and luverly. There's even a goth church in London. And black clothes are cheap and slimming and last for ages.'

Suzy felt a sudden fear that Molly might become a goth — then she remembered the bright pink tights. Molly liked mad colours too much.

'Pizza?' Suzy suggested.

'And another spritzer?' asked Molly hopefully. Chelsea grinned. 'You're a trier!' she said.

Suzy went to get the wine bottle and put the pizza in the oven, listening to them laughing together. One young woman with all the love and support in the world, the other with nothing.

Later, for fun, she and Molly let Chelsea paint their nails goth black, for Halloween. Molly was off to a Halloween party that weekend. The back nail polish was rather effective, Suzy thought. Molly's nails were long and almond shaped and Suzy's square and purposeful. She thought she would leave the varnish on. It would do wonders for her image with the *Living Lies* team. Maybe the programme could do something on secret goths.

Then Suzy took Chelsea back to Tarnhill. Whatever Joanne was up to with Jarrold McHugh eclipsed any minor deception by the goth. On reflection, Suzy had felt even more furious about Joanne's behaviour. Joanne had dispensed with Suzy in a perfunctory way, and all the time the administrator was deceiving them all about her relationship with the young American with his nasty little lab in the front room. Or whatever it was. Poor Paula. What a mess she'd stumbled into.

It was raining now, and very dark. Suzy leaned forward peering through the rain, windscreen wipers hardly sluicing off the water. She dropped Chelsea at the hostel gates; the girl punched in the code and ran through, disappearing into the darkness. Her silhouette was picked up by the security lights at intervals along the drive.

Suzy drove past the gates, doing a three-point turn where the track widened just above the hostel entrance and pointing the car back towards the main road. As she drew level with the gates on the way back, she saw a figure run out and flag her down. For a moment she thought it was Chelsea wanting to come back to the Briars, but this figure was slim and in running gear. When she drew level, she saw it was Joanne.

'Suzy — I saw you dropping Chelsea off. Listen. We need to talk to you. We owe you an explanation. And an apology. Can you come in? Please Suzy. I'm begging you, Suzy. *Please.*'

* * *

At the same time, inside the hostel, Adelina walked silently along the landing on the first floor. She was always unhurried and measured in her movements, but she felt anxious. One of the unspoken rules was that residents met in the lounge. Going into other people's bedrooms was discouraged. Privacy was all-important and every room could be locked.

She hadn't seen Leila since yesterday lunchtime, and Leila had missed her meals since then. Joanne had been far too preoccupied to notice. But a few seconds earlier, Adelina had seen Joanne run out of the hostel into the rain. Adelina had slipped into the office and taken the ring of pass keys from the open key safe.

She found the key for Leila's room and slipped it into the lock. She knocked and called Leila's name but there was no reply. She turned the key and pushed open the door.

Leila's room was a tip. There were clothes all over the floor and the bed was unmade. In the bathroom there were toiletries scattered about, but it was cold. Adelina softly padded round the room looking for clues. There was no case or holdall or handbag left, and no sign of any personal stuff — no purse or wallet. It looked as if Leila had made a quick decision to go and had just grabbed her things and walked away. Adelina felt a frisson of anger. She had put herself out for Leila in the past, but Leila hadn't even bothered to say goodbye.

Adelina slipped out, locked the door behind her and went downstairs. She would need to tell Joanne. She wasn't sure what the procedure would be. No one had ever walked away from St Jane's before. She went down the central staircase and saw that Joanne had come back in, but she was soaking, and with her was Suzy the press officer. Suzy was wet too, but she had her puffer jacket on. Joanne motioned Suzy into the office. Suzy followed her in, and Joanne shut the door.

Adelina reckoned that Joanne wouldn't notice the missing keys just yet. And it probably wasn't the moment to tell her that Leila had gone. There was nothing they could do about it, anyway. Adelina whispered a prayer for Leila's safety and went into the lounge to sit and think, on her own.

* * *

Suzy walked into the office with Joanne behind her. The first thing she saw was Jarrold McHugh sitting on the sofa. She stood and stared at him.

'Take off your wet coat, Suzy,' Joanne said. 'I'll take it. I'll go and strip off my own wet kit if you don't mind — I'll be five minutes. And then, like I said, we really need to talk to you.'

She left Suzy and Jarrold looking at each other. Suzy said, 'What's all this about? I don't want to be here, so it had better be good.'

He looked genuinely abashed and said in his pleasant Texan drawl, 'Hey, gee, I'm sorry we ambushed you. But when we saw your vehicle go past on the CCTV it seemed too good a chance to miss. We need to explain quite a few things to you.'

'Maybe you do.' Suzy paused. 'But I know Dr Paula Stovey. And I know you've been seeing her, and that she had a showdown with you this morning. I know you've got something weird going on in that cottage. But it's Paula who needs an explanation, not me.'

'That really is my bad,' he said. 'Paula is great. But I let her go to my head at the very time I should have been low-profile. I don't want to say any more yet. It's a pretty complicated story.'

'I bet,' said Suzy. 'Look, I'm just going to message my husband. I'd like him to come here too. If there's going to be a long explanation, I'd like Robert to hear it.'

She had half expected Jarrold to object but he said nothing, so she turned away from him and texted Robert.

'Come to the hostel asap. I'm here with Joanne and Jarrold. So far so good and seems safe but PLEASE come.'

Then the door opened; Joanne came in, and for the first time, other than at Scott's party, she wasn't wearing her skin-tight sports gear. She had on soft dark trousers and a loose sweater.

Jarrold turned to her. 'Great. You're back. Now we can tell Suzy everything, Mom.'

CHAPTER TWENTY-TWO

But he himself turned again from the quarries that were by Gilgal, and said, I have a secret errand unto thee, O king: who said, Keep silence.
Judges 3:19

Robert got Suzy's text when he stopped for petrol between Norbridge and Tarnfield; he heard the ping as he was putting the pump nozzle back in the holder. He read it, paid quickly and decided not to go home but to carry straight on the hostel.

Robert had left another message with Neil, as acting chair of St Jane's, about Jarrold's weird use of the cottage. He hadn't heard back and now he felt concerned in case Suzy had been caught in some sort of face-off with Joanne and Jarrold. He had a sudden horrible vision of Suzy being frogmarched onto the roof of the hostel by a drug-dealing murderer and his accomplice. Robert desperately wanted to get to St Jane's.

It was hard work driving, and he was tired after another local meeting about the spate of metal stealing. All sorts of metal was disappearing from the area, along with lead from church roofs. Some sort of local gang was clearly at work and there was obviously a big market for scrap, much of it stolen. It had convinced him that there was an urgency about getting the All Saints' roof properly insured. There was no option other than the expensive Tagpaint protection system, which coated the metal with traceable forensic liquid. They could also fit various lights and alarms. Robert wondered about asking Lee the roofer to do it. He seemed to be well liked. His work on the Briars' chimney stack had certainly been done quickly and efficiently, and was cheaper than Robert and Suzy had feared.

The rain was hitting the windscreen straight on. Robert almost missed the turn-off for the lane to the hostel. But just half a mile up the track, on the edge of the fir plantation, he saw a warning triangle and the lights of two parked cars, one blocking the road. A bulky figure wielding a torch came towards his car; as the beam flashed about, he saw the police sign on the car in front.

'I'll have to ask you to turn back, sir,' the police officer said.

'But I need to get up this track. What's going on here?'

'If you would just turn around sir . . .'

'I need to get to the hostel urgently. Can I go on foot?'

'I'll ask, if you can wait here, sir. Can't you phone them at the hostel?'

'The signal's weak here. And I want to get there in person. Please. I really need to get to St Jane's.'

'I'll find out for you sir. But for now, get back into your car.'

There was going to be a wait before he could get on with his journey. And he was increasingly worried about Suzy.

* * *

At St Jane's, Joanne sat down on the sofa next to Jarrold and took his hand. 'Yes, Jarrold is my son. His name is Jarrold McHugh Arbiter. A very distant relation of Deborah's, possibly, on the American side. Maybe I should start from the beginning. I can tell that you're angry, Suzy, but perhaps when you hear the whole story, you won't be.'

'Try me . . .'

Joanne took a deep breath. 'I married Jarrold's father, an American called Glen Arbiter, when I was twenty. He was a visiting academic. I went back with him to Texas. Jarrold was born a year later. But I couldn't cope with living in the States; I was too young, and it was too strange. Glen and I split up almost immediately after that. I brought my baby back to England and married again. My second husband was wonderful — for the first six months. He's dead now, and I'm glad. Drink and drugs. But he brutalised me. If you want to know what domestic abuse is really like, look at this.' Joanne pulled up her loose-fitting sweater. Thick, ugly, bloated scars erupted across Joanne's torso.

'Most of these were caused by broken bottles. I have a condition which causes keloid scars. The scar tissue balloons out and can be bigger than the injuries. That's why I wear exercise kit so much. Tight garments over a dressing help to push the tissue back.'

Suzy had never seen anything like it.

'I think my husband liked that. The scars were his artwork. At first it was just the odd smack and the bullying, but later it developed. He'd glass me and watch the tissue slowly blow out over the next few weeks. Jarrold didn't see the worst. But he saw the first stages. I'm not sure how much he remembers.'

'Not much, Mom, really.'

Joanne smiled at him and carried on: 'I always worked. That was part of the attraction for my husband, the money I made. He wasn't an intellectual like Jarrold's father. Like father, like son.' She smiled at Jarrold again, a slightly besotted smile. Understandable, Suzy thought.

'A year after my second marriage, I got in touch with Glen Arbiter, from the office, and I sent him a letter asking him to come and take his son away. We met at Jarrold's childminder and I handed my baby over. Jarrold was two. At that time I still thought I could redeem my new husband by love and understanding, especially if there wasn't a child in the way. I regret that bitterly now.'

‘And you kept in touch with Jarrold?’

‘What? When my husband found the boy had gone, he went ballistic. He had no time for Jarrold, but losing him to another man, behind his back, infuriated him. He made me pay, I can tell you. No contact was possible between me and Glen and Jarrold.’

‘And you had no more children?’

‘No. My husband took up all my energy. He lost his job because of his drinking and was with me one-to-one for almost twenty-four hours a day. I was allowed to go to work, part-time, three days a week because he needed the money, but the rest of the time he was always there. He used to meet me at lunchtime and after work. I was expected to go everywhere with him and dote on him.’

‘But couldn’t you just have walked away and gone to your own parents? Or a friend?’

‘What friends? He systematically alienated me from all my friends. Or charmed them into being on his side. My own mother worshipped the ground he walked on. Eventually I had no one. At first, I didn’t really know about refuges, and anyway, you’re always in denial. Then later I didn’t have the nerve. It takes years to have the courage to break away.’

‘And how did you do that?’

‘I went to a church near where I worked, at lunchtime. They had a communion service once a week. My husband let me go to it, because by then he thought I would never have the courage to leave him. And as he got older, he sometimes just wanted to go to the pub at midday and get drunk. Controlling someone twenty-four hours a day is tiring.’

Joanne paused. Telling the story as a narrative seemed to be exhausting her too. ‘And what happened?’ Suzy prompted.

‘One of the clergy sussed my situation, contacted Deborah for me and suggested I came here . . . and when I heard the name Arbiter it seemed like a sign. That, and St Jane being the patron saint of women separated from their children. One day I did just what you said — I left early and got the train here, just with the clothes I stood up in. It sounds simple but I was absolutely terrified. I've been at St Jane's ever since. First as a resident. Then, after I heard that my second husband had died, I stayed on as administrator. Deborah and I became very close. She encouraged me to try and find Jarrold. You see, that's what Deborah's judgments were all about.'

'Missing children?'

'Yes. She would talk us through our cases. For some women there was little or no chance of finding their family or getting them back. Deborah helped a lot of women come to terms with it. With others she did everything she could to help them find their children. Or be reconciled to them. Just like it says in the Bible, Deborah arose, a mother in Israel.'

'But couldn't you have traced Jarrold yourself? You must have had access to a computer at work?'

'And what would I have done then, while I was still with my husband? Suzy, you need to understand. When you're the victim of this degree of coercion and violence, the terror of being found out is unspeakable. It's worse than the violence when it comes. The violence is almost a relief.'

Is that how Ellie had felt? Had she been, like Joanne, in denial? But Ellie had decided to make the break . . . For a moment Suzy felt slightly ashamed. She had thought of herself as an empathetic person as she sat in the chalet basement and listened to Ellie's story. But she really had no idea of what women like Joanne and Ellie had been through. 'I'm sorry,' she said. 'Please go on.'

'Well, I was one of the lucky ones. It was easy for Deborah to trace my child and make contact, especially as they had the same surname. Deborah was some sort of distant relative. When Deborah was successful in tracing a child, she would say it was down to the saint. It was partly a joke, typical of her, and partly something she really believed. And Jarrold wouldn't have accepted me without Deborah and the Arbiter connection.'

Jarrold said, 'True. I didn't want to meet Mom. She'd dumped me as a baby, so why would I? But Deborah contacted me at the university where I worked. She was persistent and persuasive, and part of Dad's family after all! Eventually, Deborah talked me into coming to London and meeting my mother. Which I did, earlier this year.'

'But why the cottage and the secrecy?'

'Ah. That's a completely different story! Not what you would expect at all. I'll try and start at the beginning. But it's complicated. It goes back to Deborah, of course.'

'Doesn't everything?'

* * *

Down on the track through the plantation, Robert recognized one of the police who bobbed in and out of the floodlights. Robert stepped out of his car.

'Hi, Jed. DS Jackson, I mean. It's Robert Clark, Suzy's husband. I need to get up to the hostel. Suzy's there.'

'Oh, hello Robert. I didn't recognize you in all that wet-weather clobber. Yes. I suppose we can let you walk up. Pull over there, off the road. I'm going to stop all traffic going through from now on — not that there's ever much traffic up here.'

'What's happened?' Robert asked.

'It's a fatality, but that's all I can tell you. We're getting an ambulance for him now. You can tell them at the hostel that there's been an incident. They need to know the road's blocked. I need more help here at the scene before I can go up there myself.'

Robert went back and moved his car over onto the verge. Then he got out, locked it and set off on the long, wet walk to the hostel.

Another fatality. Was it a car crash? But his main concern was to get to Suzy. He turned and looked back. He saw a pickup truck parked just inside the plantation, now lit up by the police lights. But he had no time for speculating. He needed to get to the hostel as fast as he could.

* * *

At the hostel, Jarrold smiled. He was breathtakingly handsome.

'Start at the beginning — again,' said Suzy, trying hard not to be charmed by his good looks.

'Okay. Well, I'm not into family history, obviously. I thought it would be a good cover. But it wasn't.'

'Well, Robert certainly rumbled you. So, what are you?'

'I'm not a genealogist. I'm a geologist.'

'A geologist?'

'A mining geologist, to be precise.'

Ah. That was a bit of a surprise. But then again, Paula had seen stones in the front room. It figured, Suzy thought. But what was he doing, in secret, in Tarnfield?

Jarrold paused, then went on, 'You probably don't know this, but in the early eighties, Deborah's father sold the Arbiter mines for a neat sum, on the quiet, to a mining prospecting company. The Arbiter mines still belong to this company, though they changed the company name. I guess you've heard of it.' He paused, expectantly.

Suzy racked her brains. He seemed to think she should know what he was talking about. But what company did she know of that was into rocks and stones and minerals? She said uncertainly, 'You can't mean DecorMetal? Scott Jermyn's outfit?'

'Correct! Well done. Absolutely. They started in mining. Then, just after buying the Arbiter mines, they had a disaster in South Cumbria. They were mining there, and they pumped standing water full of heavy metal into the water table. It polluted the area for miles. They got a fine, changed their name to something totally different and went low-profile. But it was the same board of directors, and very slowly they made a comeback. They kept quiet and diversified into stone and scrap metal. Iron, lead, small amounts of minerals. Retooling it for decorating purposes. Or latterly, selling it on.'

'But what about the Arbiter mines?'

'For thirty years they lay dormant. But Deborah found out about six months ago that DecorMetal wanted to reopen them.'

'Why?'

'Because they've found tungsten there! Tungsten is very valuable. DecorMetal is a small concern, but one of the big international mining boys, Arctic America, is sniffing round the tungsten. There's big money in reopening the Arbiter mines, for the directors of DecorMetal.'

'Okay, I'm with you so far, just about. But where do you come in?'

'Deborah hired me to investigate what DecorMetal were up to, from a geological point of view. She had found out somehow that the company would be approaching the local council, making friends, preparing for a planning application to reopen the mines. But she suspected DecorMetal of bad practice. And she was right.'

'And you found out?'

'Yes, I found standing water in the Arbiter mines. The old shafts are full of acid sulphate. If DecorMetal reopen the shafts, the risk of pollution is very high. But in a remote area like Tarnfield Fell, they might get away with it, unlike last time. They just need to get out all the tungsten and disappear before anyone realizes that they've polluted Tarnfield Fell and the Tarn River . . .'

It was an appalling thought. The whole area could be devastated and then the polluting company could just up sticks and disappear. Even though they had a record . . .

Finally, Suzy said, 'So Deborah employed you on this secret mission to expose these environmental baddies. But why didn't you just tell Paula if your work is so altruistic? After all, you're telling me now.'

'Because I sent my report to the council tonight. I realize now I should have trusted Paula, but I'd signed a non-disclosure agreement with Deborah. Any leak about what we were doing might have reached DecorMetal and derailed the plan. Deborah might be dead but she's still the boss. She'd be very happy with my report. Wait till the councillors hear from me. I've asked to see them next week.'

'And these company directors who stand to make so much money — are they local?'

‘No. But someone very persuasive is helping them with their image in Tarnfield. Guess who?’

‘Of course. Scott Jermyn. Did he suspect you? Is that why he invited you to his party?’

‘Guess so. He called me out of the blue. But I’ve no idea how he got my number.’

Suzy thought about all this for a minute. ‘So why have you been stringing Paula Stovey along?’

‘I wasn’t stringing her along. Strategically, seeing Paula was a mistake, but I couldn’t help myself. I took a stupid risk but I fell for her. Big time. We’re two of a kind. Both hard to get. I’ve met my match and I don’t want to lose her, but I couldn’t risk her knowing what I was doing until I delivered my report to the council.’

‘Which you were on the brink of doing, yesterday?’

‘Correct. I had decided to confide in her, but she ambushed me and then stormed off yesterday from my cottage, and I couldn’t catch her. So I tracked her car till she disappeared down your lane. I asked Mom who lived at the Briars, and we decided we should tell you the truth as Paula obviously knew you. I hoped she would listen to you, even if she won’t speak to me. She won’t take my calls.’

‘I’m not surprised. But you must realize that she was pretty shocked by what she saw at the cottage. I mean, where does the bloodstained lab coat fit in?

‘That’s not blood! That’s spillage from when I was sampling some haematite from a mullock heap.’

‘A what?’

‘A mullock heap. A pile of spoil. It was red from the haematite. I was testing for calcium carbonate . . .’

’Okay, that’s enough. I believe you. I’ll call Paula for you. But I wouldn’t blame her if she just said “mullocks” . . .’

Jarrold laughed loudly, looking human and adorable, and Joanne smiled too, gazing at him in admiration.

* * *

Robert reached the hostel gates and pressed the bell. In the office where Jarrold, Suzy and Joanne were sitting, Joanne jumped up, business-like again, and looked at the screen. 'There's a man at the gates.'

Suzy peered over her shoulder. 'It looks like Robert. But where's his car?'

'He's on foot.' Joanne said. She pressed the button to open the pedestrian gate. Robert strode up the drive and Joanne and Suzy both went into the hall to let him in. He stood dripping on the tiles.

'Sorry about this unconventional arrival. The police have closed the track. There's been an incident, another fatality. In the pines.'

Suzy heard a gasp behind her. Adelina had approached silently — a quiet, calm, half-presence as always. She almost whispered, 'You need to know, Joanne, that Leila is missing. Is it her?'

CHAPTER TWENTY-THREE

She put her hand to the nail (of the tent), and her right hand to the workmen's hammer; and with the hammer she smote Sisera.
Judges 5:26

'What?' Joanne looked stunned. 'Do you mean that Leila could be dead?'

'I don't think so,' Robert said. 'I got the impression the dead person was a man. In a truck.'

Joanne said, 'Are you quite sure Leila has gone? We should go upstairs and check her room over.'

Adelina shrugged. 'Here are the keys. You can see for yourself. She's left a mess but she's not there. Looks like she just grabbed a few things and walked away. I didn't see her go.'

'Does anyone else know?'

'Not for sure. But most people realize she's missed the last two or three meals.'

Joanne turned to Robert and Suzy. 'I need to deal with this.'

The rest of them went into the lounge. Jarrold and Robert sat together and began to talk. No doubt Jarrold was telling Robert the same extraordinary story that Suzy had just heard. Suzy went and stood over by the French windows to call Jarrold's girlfriend.

'Paula,' she said to her voicemail, 'it's Suzy Spencer. We have the answers to a lot of your questions. I think Jarrold's okay, in fact more than okay. A good guy. But it's far too complicated for a phone call. Could you come over to the Briars tomorrow morning? Early, if poss. There's an explanation, although it's quite a long story and I'd rather tell you in person.'

Suzy rang off and stared out of the window. Things had taken a very unexpected turn. It was fascinating stuff. But it threatened to distract everyone even more from Ellie's death in London. Perhaps her theory had been too neat. She had surmised that Ellie had tried to leave her lover, who killed her by throwing her over a balcony. He then came to Tarnfield to take his revenge on Deborah and pushed her off a roof too. But now it seemed that Deborah had been mixed up in something different but equally dangerous. She had been about to expose a company which was set to devastate the local environment. A lot of people had a lot to lose if she were successful. Which meant that her death might have nothing at all to do with Ellie's . . .

But Ellie's and Deborah's deaths *had* to be linked. They were in contact with each other. They were killed in the same way . . . Suzy's head was too full of information. She needed time to think this all through.

The rain had stopped, and the clouds had suddenly lifted. Down in the Vale Suzy could see two cars with flashing lights making their way gingerly up the single-track road. The police, she thought, coming here, about the road accident. She would need to call Joanne to open the gates. But as she watched, the police cars went past and out of her vision. Where were they going? To the cottages? Why would they be going up there?

Joanne came back into the lounge and stood beside her. 'It's true. Leila's gone,' she said flatly. 'It's her right, of course. It happens a lot in other hostels, but no one ever wants to leave here. Or at least they didn't when Deborah was alive. And I can't understand why she didn't tell me.'

Suzy touched her on the arm. 'Leila seems to have been a mass of issues, Joanne. Maybe she'll get in touch. And explain to you.'

'I doubt it. She's very fragile. She was always one of Deborah's lost causes. I think she's probably in Newcastle or Manchester by now. Already back on the game or on drugs. Her brute of a husband used to pimp her, but she never lost interest in men despite everything. God knows what will happen to her.'

Suzy said, 'I saw two police cars come up the track just now, but they went past the gates.'

Joanne gasped. 'Towards the cottages? Oh, Suzy, do you think that Paula has told them about Jarrold's lab?'

'I don't think so. She was happy to let Robert and me deal with that. Hey, look, here's another car at the gates.'

'I'll see who it is.'

Joanne was away for a while, speaking on the intercom. Then she came back into the lounge and said, 'There's a police community support officer coming here. The one who came the other day.'

'Ro Watson? She's a friend of mine.'

Joanne nodded, and went to open the doors to Ro, who brought the colder air with her into the lounge.

Ro said, 'DS Jackson has asked me to come and tell you all what's happened. I'm afraid we've found a body in a pickup truck nearby. I don't want to shock you, but you need to know that it's someone who worked here, part-time. Geoff Black. I believe he's your handyman.'

'Geoff Black?' Joanne went pale as they looked at her. 'What? Dead? In a crash?'

'It wasn't a road accident, Joanne. I can't give you any more details.' Ro was interrupted by Chelsea coming in with drinks and biscuits. They were very welcome. Ro took a mug of coffee, distractedly. It had been cold outside on the fell track.

Ro went on: 'The road will be shut until the ambulance has gone. Then we'll open it, principally to get Robert's car off the track.' She turned to Jarrold. 'And are you the Blacks' neighbour? Mrs Black mentioned you.' Jarrold nodded. Ro said, 'I'm sure the police will want to talk to you about when you last saw Geoff Black.'

'I'll gladly stay here and wait,' said Jarrold. Suzy guessed he didn't want the police going into his cottage.

Adelina spoke softly from the back of the room. 'When did Geoff Black die?'

'We don't know for sure, but he was found by dog walkers this evening. They'd braved the rain. He'd been dead some time. Maybe since yesterday.'

Adelina turned away, looking worried. Suzy realized why. Adelina's only concern was Leila. If Leila had left the hostel in the last twenty-four hours and set off on foot down the track, she would have passed Geoff's pickup at the edge of the woods. But there was no way Adelina would mention Leila to the police.

'We should go, Robert,' Suzy said. Thanks so much for the drinks, Chelsea.'

'Yes,' said Joanne, and added surprisingly, 'You've been wonderful this week, Chelsea. I don't know what we'd have done without you.'

'And you are . . . ?' said Ro, suddenly noticing the girl, who froze.

'This is Chelsea,' Suzy said firmly. 'The new housekeeper here.' They'd had more than enough surprises about names that evening. She would fill Ro in about Chelsea later. It was important that the goth girl didn't panic.

Joanne whispered to Suzy as they were leaving. 'I'm so sorry. I should have trusted you sooner . . .'

'Don't worry, Joanne. You've been through so much stress. And forget about the press. They won't necessarily link Geoff to the hostel — and if they do, say nothing . . .'

* * *

Ro Watson had left the lounge, and Suzy caught up with her in the hall. Ro was standing transfixed, staring at the pictures on the wall with a very odd expression on her face.

'That's the famous Gentileschi picture, isn't it?' Ro was into art.

Suzy said. 'Yes. Jael and Sisera. Jael, the woman, killed Sisera, the enemy of Israel, by piercing his temple with a tent peg which she hit with a hammer. Sisera had been defeated by Deborah's army and was on the run. He took shelter with Jael. You can't see the actual deed here, but Jael's just about to plunge the tent peg in.'

'And he was asleep?'

'Yes. What is it Ro? You look really gobsmacked.'

'Look, Suzy, this is strictly confidential, but Geoff Black was killed just like that. An old-fashioned metal tent peg through his temple. While he had stopped for a nap.'

'What? Just like the Bible story?'

'Well, I'm not familiar with that. But just like the picture, that's for sure. Neat, precise. It wasn't a mad attack. Very strange . . .'

Very strange indeed. So, someone had killed Geoff by deliberately acting out the Jael story. But how many people would even know about an obscure Old Testament passage? Obscure by today's standards anyway. And even the picture was only famous to a few art lovers, usually feminists.

But the residents of the hostel saw that picture every day of their lives. Adelina might be too loyal to mention Leila to the police, Suzy thought. But they would find out that Leila had left the hostel and gone past the pickup truck where Geoff Black was asleep. Leila hated him and believed he had killed Deborah, whom she adored. And every day she had seen a picture showing the same crime which had now been perpetrated on Black. She could have learned her method that way.

It didn't look good for Leila.

* * *

The next morning was Saturday. Paula Stovey turned up at the Briars while Suzy was in her pyjamas in the kitchen having breakfast with Molly. She'd had a bad night trying to work out how Ellie and Deborah could both be involved with DecorMetal. She had no idea but clung to the theory that the women were linked by the same man. Was that Geoff Black?

Robert was still snoring after all the walking the night before.

'I'm so sorry it's early,' Paula said.

Suzy felt as if she had been dragged through a hedge backwards, but Paula was as sleek and beautiful as ever, her Nordic blonde hair pulled back into a band, and even her tracksuit looking absurdly glamourous. She said, 'I couldn't stay away. Especially after I heard on the local news this morning about the body found in the pinewoods in Tarnfield Vale. Please tell me this has nothing to do with Jarrold.'

'It hasn't. Except that it was his next-door neighbour who was found dead.'

'Not Mr Grumpy the handyman? The news just said police were investigating a body found in forestry land. Do you know what happened?'

'Look Paula, let me get dressed. Go into the living room, and when I come down, I'll tell you what happened last night.'

It took a long time to tell Paula the story. Suzy went over it chronologically. DecorMetal was originally a mining company which bought the defunct Arbiter haematite mines in the eighties, with a view to reopening them. But the same company caused a scandal when it went on to pollute acres of land, at another site miles away down in South Cumbria. They took the hit and paid a fine, changed their name and afterwards stayed quiet for thirty or more years, just dealing in stone and metal.

They had kept the Arbiter mines and were now planning to reopen them to mine for tungsten, which they had found on the site, a valuable mineral in today's comms and defence industries.

Somehow Deborah had found this out. By luck, she knew Jarrold, a highly regarded geologist, the son of Joanne, her friend and employee. She employed Jarrold to find out anything which might prevent DecorMetal getting permission to reopen the mines. But Jarrold had needed to work in secret, not least because he was trespassing on DecorMetal land. That was why he had deceived Paula, and he seemed truly sorry for that. But he had found that DecorMetal were prepared to pollute again by opening a toxic mineshaft. They could get the valuable but small deposit of tungsten out, and leave the district, before the effects of the pollution were seen.

Jarrold had all the credentials for this work. He was really Jarrold McHugh Arbiter, a distant relation of Deborah's, and this had given him the idea for his family history cover story, which only worked if no one questioned him closely. He hadn't told anyone in Tarnfield his real name, but once you knew it you could google him. Suzy had done so last night while Robert was having a hot bath and before they both collapsed into bed. Jarrold Arbiter really was a top geologist, currently on sabbatical from university in Texas. There was a picture of him, in a spotless lab coat this time.

Suzy told Paula all this, but it was Jarrold's relationship with his estranged mother that interested Paula most. 'I think you might find Joanne a bit tricky to deal with,' Suzy said. 'She thinks the sun shines out of him. Guilt, I suppose. And maybe the novelty. You'll have to tread carefully.'

Paula shook her sleek head. 'I'll call on Mr Arbiter, and he can explain to me in person. And then I'll give him a piece of my mind. His mother may give him unconditional love, but I won't.'

Suzy laughed. It was Paula's anger which convinced Suzy that Paula and Jarrold might stand a chance. They would be honest with each other from now on. And they were certainly well matched — both cool, both very good looking and both a tad arrogant about relationships. But they had both been vulnerable to each other.

Then Suzy got ready to take Molly into Norbridge. There had been enough drama in the last twenty-four hours for her. She was definitely not going to let Molly do the driving.

* * *

At the hostel that Saturday morning, Chelsea had made scones. The tragedy of Geoff Black's death meant little to her, and keeping up the home baking was important. The scones had come out beautifully — fluffy and soft but with a light golden crust. She took some to Joanne mid-morning.

Joanne said kindly, 'These are lovely, Chelsea. You've given me an idea. I've just come off the phone to Moira, Geoff's wife . . .'

'The one that lives in the cottage? Is she all right?'

'She's still up there at home. I thought she might have gone to her daughter's in Hardcastle, but her daughter has come to her. Moira's surprisingly calm. Her daughter's very upset, but at least they've got each other. Moira is insisting on staying here. So, why don't you go up to her cottage with a couple of these scones?'

Chelsea liked the idea of being kind and supportive to someone else in trouble. Poor Mrs Black, Chelsea thought — even if, from what she had heard, Geoff Black had been a bit of a pain in the bum.

When Chelsea had trotted off, Joanne put her head in her hands for a minute. DS Jed Jackson had been courteous but persistent the night before. He had asked who was living at the hostel, and reluctantly Joanne had told him. 'You should know that we now have two bedrooms free. One has been vacant for a while. The other is empty because one of the residents left suddenly. Either yesterday or the evening before. We can't be sure.' And that was how Jed had found out all about Leila . . .

* * *

At the same time, unlike the comfort of the hostel, the police station at Workhaven was stale and frowsty. Jed was working over the weekend, of course. A suspicious death meant everyone was called in, but he wasn't out on the road or at the scene. He wanted to think. Outside the window, the autumn leaves from the town's few plane trees blew across the view of Workhaven's ring road. The distant hills were a grey blur. There was a sense of activity in other offices, but Jed wanted to be alone. The post-mortem would happen that afternoon, but he thought that there was no doubt about how Geoff Black had died. A metal tent peg had been driven through his temple. Jed looked again at his computer screen. He had googled the picture of Jael and Sisera by Artemisia Gentileschi, the one that Ro had said was prominently displayed in the hall at the hostel. Jed had a copy of the Revised Standard Version of the Bible in his desk drawer. He had it open at the Book of Judges, chapter 4 verse 21.

But Jael the wife of Heber took a tent peg, and took a hammer in her hand and went softly to him and drove the peg into his temple . . .

It was such a distinctive death. Perhaps the first murder story in history with a specific and unusual murder weapon. In the story, Sisera had been exhausted after battle and had slept after a drink of milk given by Jael, his murderer. Geoff Black was certainly fast asleep when he died. He'd obviously managed to get into his pickup and had been driving home when he was overcome and pulled off the road to sleep. He would have been a sitting duck for someone passing. And Leila, the woman who had walked out of the hostel, would have passed his truck on the track. Jed had asked for fingerprints from Leila's room. The mallet which he thought had been used to smash the tent peg into Black's head had been left in the footwell of the pickup. They would try for fingerprints on that too.

But why was there a tent in Geoff's truck? Jed had asked the family liaison officer to question Moira about Geoff's handyman activities and to ask if she knew whether he ever camped out. Moira said she thought Geoff usually stayed in B&Bs or cheap hotels, but she wouldn't have been too surprised if he'd had an old tent in the truck, just in case he needed to sleep rough. After all, a bit of poaching, or even a night away from the world with a bottle of whisky might have been right up Geoff-the-loner's street.

Jed googled tent pegs. You could still get metal ones, usually with hooks or angles at the top to use for heavy-weather camping. The one in Geoff's head wasn't identical to the one in the Gentileschi picture, but it was similar. And was certainly a tent peg. If Leila had passed the truck, seen Geoff asleep and found a metal tent peg, she might have thought it was all meant to be, and that he would have to die in the way she had seen so often at the hostel.

It was very neat. And just because it was neat didn't mean that it couldn't have happened. Jed closed down his PC, and picked up his phone to call his boss in Norbridge. He had feared that his idea might be dismissed as the loony imaginings of a Bible-basher. His religion was no secret, but he didn't like to parade it. No one would be drawn to his faith if they thought it was the province of an obsessive. But this time he was sure it was relevant. Geoff Black's murder was a copycat killing. The fact that the deaths were three millennia apart didn't alter that.

CHAPTER TWENTY-FOUR

O my soul, thou hast trodden down strength.
Judges 5:21

On Saturday evening, when the shock of Geoff Black's murder had passed, Suzy and Robert went to the Plough again. It was quieter this weekend. Scott Jermyn wasn't there, thank goodness. But Lee the roofer and his wife Mandy were sitting in a corner of the bar as Robert and Suzy passed by their table.

'Hiya! Isn't it awful about yon handyman?' Lee said. He accepted Robert's offer of a pint and a lemonade for Mandy. 'We're just here for the craic about it. We'll be off soon. Mandy's driving. It's boogie-woogie night at the Ferret in Hardcastle tonight. We rarely miss, do we, Mand? Fridays or Saturdays.' They chatted for a few minutes about chimneys and roofs. When Mandy stood up to go, Suzy saw she was wearing a flared fifties-style skirt, with flat pumps. She looked cuter than ever with her hair in pigtails.

Robert and Suzy sat down together in the restaurant with their drinks and the menus. Robert said, 'I'm glad we didn't get caught chatting for too long. But I've been thinking of asking the church council to get Lee to Tagpaint our lead roof at All Saints.'

'But tonight is all about you and me, remember?'

'How could I forget? I'm all yours. Except you need to share me with the menu.'

'Robert, you practically know it off by heart!'

'But this is the winter one! We haven't seen it since last March.'

Suzy laughed, but she was pleased to see that the menu had a 'comfort food' theme with Barnsley chop, venison stew and whole plaice as the specials.

'This is great,' Suzy said. 'Something to chew over. Speaking of which, it was interesting what Ro said this afternoon.'

Ro Watson had called by the Briars earlier. 'It's all about fingerprints now,' she had said. 'If Leila's prints show up on the mallet in Geoff's truck, it could prove Jed's theory.'

'Which is?'

'That Leila was walking past, saw Geoff asleep and killed him like in the picture. We found his mallet and a couple of other tent pegs in the cab, clearly accessible in a tool bag in the foot well.'

Leila might have had the Gentileschi in her mind, Suzy thought. She could easily have picked up a tent peg and driven it through his temple, and then walked on. There would have been blood of course, but it mightn't have stained her clothes.'

'But where would she have gone?'

'If she walked to the main road it would take about an hour. Then she could thumb a quick lift to the motorway. She could be anywhere.'

'I can't see Leila being that cool about it all. But who knows?'

'Well, people are capable of the strangest things. If I hear more that I can share, I'll keep in touch.' Ro had given a mock salute, touching her PCSO cap, and left to go home.

Once they'd ordered their meal, Robert said, 'We haven't really had time to talk about ourselves. But in a way there isn't much to say now. If you had wanted us to move to

Manchester, or even London, I'd have gone. But my big fear was that you wanted to have a place to escape to by yourself.'

'That's ridiculous!'

'Well, I've been on my own quite a lot. And that can give you morose ideas.'

Suzy gave a mock groan. 'Don't try and make me feel guilty because you got the wrong end of the stick! I told you, I was away working because I was worried about all the money you've spent on us.'

'But you're my family. And it's our money, not my money. Anyway, the way I see it, we have enough to get by. I want you to know that you don't have to work like crazy on anything. Not even on *Living Lies*. Of course it's none of my business. And if you love it, that's great. But if you feel it's a bit of a treadmill, we could certainly make ends meet if you made this your last season.'

Suzy looked at him, astonished.

He went on: 'Perhaps you could find something closer to home? You've always worked, Suzy, and this last year has been manic. We could manage if you took a break.'

'A break? Me? I don't know what to say!'

'Well, think about it. It's fantastic how you've improved '*Living Lies*' and made it both popular and unusual. But why not quit while you're ahead and capitalize on your BATV award? You could do something different — still in media, but something fresh. You really are a very talented producer.'

Suzy took a large sip of her wine. 'Now I'm a very talented and deeply embarrassed producer. Let's change the subject and talk about the murder in Tarnfield Vale.'

'Fair enough. But think about what I've said.' He sipped his pint of real ale. 'OK, back to Geoff Black's death. So, Ro and DS Jackson seem convinced it was Leila who killed him.'

'But what about Ellie's death in London? Where does she fit into this scenario? I've been racking my brains . . .'

'Could Geoff Black be Ellie's murderer too? We've discussed it before.'

Suzy stopped eating. 'Yes, he might. I understand that it's all very neat if Leila killed Black in revenge for his killing Deborah. But *why* did Geoff kill Deborah? It could have been because Deborah offered Ellie a place at the hostel. Say Geoff Black was Ellie's abusive lover and killed her. He was a brooding, vengeful sort of man. He might have hated Deborah for being Ellie's lifeline and killed her in turn. It *does* add up.'

'But only to you and me, Suzy!'

'I know! And I'm worried that with all the attention being focused on Tarnfield, Ellie will go on being forgotten. She was a great person, Robert. Lively and bright and bubbling with determination to escape from her controlling lover. I know that Ro says people can become suicidal in hours, minutes even. But I really want to believe that Ellie had started to make the break and was still determined to do it.'

'Even if she were killed as a result?'

'If it was the same in terms of pain, I'd rather she was killed by someone else, than that she killed herself in fear and self-loathing.'

Robert thought about it. 'So was Geoff in London in the spring? It might be difficult to find out, with all his unofficial jobs on the side. The Black economy. Literally.'

Suzy thought for a moment. 'I'm sure the police would have the means to trace Geoff to London. It's just that we now need to wait for them to do it. We might not be right . . . and in the meantime, we might lose track of other suspects like Scott Jermyn. Or the Ven Jim. Or anyone who moved between North and South. We've sort of stalled . . .'

'But things *are* happening, Suzy. Next week Jarrold is going to meet the local council about DecorMetal. That will flush out Scott Jermyn. And aren't you meeting this mysterious former colleague of Deborah's in Manchester?'

'Yes. But I don't know what to expect from her. She's too wary by half. I need to understand Deborah better, though. I feel so much of this relates to her personality. She's so full of surprises. Like secretly campaigning against DecorMetal through Jarrold. And why did she consider Ellie for a hostel place? That's strange. Ellie wasn't an old or fragile woman. If she had lost a child, I'm sure she would have mentioned it when we had our heart-to-heart chat during my holiday from hell. Plus, she never said that anyone from the church was helping her . . . and St Jane residents usually have a clergy reference.'

'So maybe you should try to find out more about Ellie. After all, you only met her for one night in the basement of a ski chalet.'

But how could she do that? Next week, Suzy would be back at her real job. Usually she felt excited at the start of the production run. But now she felt she desperately needed more time in Tarnfield — time to find out more about Ellie and Deborah and what their connection might be. She almost regretted her return to work. Perhaps Robert was right and her enthusiasm for her job on *Living Lies* was cooling.

So was her supper. 'You haven't even looked at your food,' Robert said. 'Are you going to take a picture of it for Rachel? Isn't that what media types do?'

'Oh, get stuffed!' Suzy said affectionately.

Robert attacked his Barnsley chop. 'I intend to.'

* * *

The next morning Robert went to church, but Suzy stayed at home and finished marking the essays from the students at the North London Academy of Journalism. She began to feel suspicious of Lord Warsbrook, and his disregard of what even the students thought were the dangers of social media.

They had home-made soup at lunchtime, and Suzy decided to prepare a roast for the evening meal, in honour of winter. Molly had come home from her friend's that morning, slept for a few hours and then demanded to be taken driving again. But she and Robert were both back at about four o'clock when the sky was grey and low, an early twilight.

'How was it?' Suzy asked anxiously.

'Fantastic!' Molly was glowing. 'I got up to forty miles an hour!'

Robert looked less benign than usual. In fact Suzy thought he was rather pale, and that the super-stepdad persona was wearing a little thin. 'You'll be glad to hear that the industrial estate is still standing, but only just,' he said. 'Is there any of that Shiraz left? Or should I go straight for a Scotch?' He was recovering, sitting at the kitchen table, when there was a knock at the door.

'I'll get it!' Molly sang out joyously from upstairs, and thumped down, still high on the thrill of narrowly missing a brick garage on the old industrial estate. 'Oh — it's the police . . .'

'They've found out about your driving, Molly!' Suzy laughed as DS Jed Jackson came down the hall and into the kitchen. 'Hi Jed. Molly's been having a driving lesson with Robert. Pretty stressful all round!'

Robert raised his glass of red wine. 'Sit down, Jed. Nice to see you. I don't suppose you can have a drink on duty but I need this! By the way, thanks for letting me through the cordon at the plantation Friday night. You'll have had a busy weekend.'

'Too right. And I'll have a cup of tea if there's one in the pot. Look, I just thought I'd come and see you as I was passing. I was up at the hostel again.'

'Any news?' Suzy asked. 'I mean, anything you can tell us?'

'Well, we've found Leila's fingerprints on a mallet in Geoff Black's pickup cab.'

That was news indeed. Suzy turned from the sink, 'That sounds pretty conclusive. So you think Leila left St Jane's, walked down the track, came across Geoff asleep and attacked him? Because he killed Deborah? The same thing occurred to us . . .' She finished peeling the potatoes and joined them at the table. She poured herself a drink. The wintry afternoon was already darkening now the clocks had gone back. They would have a fire that evening.

DS Jackson seemed to have relaxed over his tea. 'That's exactly what I think, though I hadn't necessarily sussed out at first that Leila blamed Black for killing Deborah. That would certainly give Leila a motive to kill him. There's other evidence of Black's guilt too. Jarrold Arbiter told me that Black didn't go to Hardcastle last weekend. Arbiter's girlfriend, Paula Stovey, was there at his cottage too when I called in, and she confirmed she had seen Geoff last Sunday morning.'

That changed everything, Suzy thought.

She and Robert waited until Jed went on: 'I put all that to Mrs Black, and she admitted her husband had cried off from going to Hardcastle, so he was around the hostel when Deborah died. And Joanne Butcher remembers Deborah saying she was going to walk up to the cottages that Friday afternoon. So, it's made me wonder if Geoff Black came across Deborah nosing around? Maybe she saw something he didn't want her to see and he forced her back into the hostel grounds.'

'But there's no keypad on the exterior wall — they would have had to walk round to the main gates.'

'Maybe they did. But my bet is that Leila saw Black and Deborah coming back together before Leila went in for the weekly meeting. Leila was always last in because she was smoking or phoning in the grounds. And Black knew the hostel routine. He could have pushed Deborah up the stairs while the women were in the lounge, and out onto the roof. He may have had a knife or another weapon to threaten her with and keep her quiet.'

'But you rubbished my theory about someone pushing Deborah off the roof and getting out of the building.'

'I apologize. I think you were right, and that was what Black did. But only he could have done it. He was a special case unlike anyone else because he knew all about the hostel security system. He would have known all the lines of sight to avoid, anyway.'

'So you're convinced?'

'I think there's a good chance that he killed Deborah. Whether or not I can prove it is another matter. But one thing I can prove . . .'

'What?'

'There was a lot of stolen metal in Black's garage. Stuff from church roofs, copper cabling from the railways, catalytic converters, railings, artwork . . . If Deborah found him with that stuff, then he would have had a very strong motive for murdering her.'

'So Black was into the local metal thieving.'

'Yes. It all ties up very nicely. Deborah found out about the metal thefts, Black killed her, and Leila killed Black in revenge for Deborah.'

But there was something else. Suzy knew it wouldn't go down well, but she had to ask. 'And what about Ellie Fox in Islington, who also died falling off a roof? Deborah had offered her a place at the hostel. Where does Ellie's death fit in? Could Black have killed them both?'

Jed sipped his tea. Then he shook his head. 'No. There's no connection between Geoff Black and Eleanor Fox. Ellie Fox died months earlier in Islington. I did check because of what you said to Ro. But Geoff Black was laid up with a twisted ankle when Ellie Fox died. His wife remembers every hour he was at home. And if she's lying, there's the evidence from the doctor's surgery. There's no way he could have been in London. I'm sorry about your theory, Suzy, but Geoff Black didn't kill Ellie Fox.'

Okay. But someone did, Suzy thought. She poured herself another glass of wine. Far be it from her to argue with a detective. But Suzy caught Robert's eye and knew they agreed. Ellie's death couldn't be discounted just like that. Of course the plot had thickened. Deborah's role as an eco-warrior, with her one-woman fight against DecorMetal, was unexpected. But Suzy needed to stick to four key facts.

One, Ellie had been in an abusive relationship. Two, Ellie had contacted Deborah about it. Three, Ellie had died falling off a roof. Four, so had Deborah.

Their deaths had to be connected. It couldn't be a coincidence.

* * *

Over at Church Cottage, Stevie Nesbit was enjoying an old film on Talking Movies TV while sampling a new Amontillado which Alan had bought. Sherry was the new gin; he had heard it from his foodie friends on the snobby butty wagon they hired on location for *The Medicine*.

Alan had been on the phone for about forty minutes. Stevie really didn't mind. They were having a lovely relaxing day after the church service, where Alan had read the lesson in his most sonorous voice, and they'd had a takeaway ordered from the Star of Bengal, which was classy for a little local Indian food business. Stevie wasn't due back on set until Wednesday, so he could relax at home. He took another sip of the sherry. It was delicious.

Alan came in, talking as he opened the door, an annoying habit of his. Stevie sighed, turning the sound down on the film, where James Mason was on the run after a factory robbery gone wrong. Stevie had seen it before anyway. But James Mason was rather tasty. A bit like a younger version of Alan.

'. . . and so Tuesday's meeting could be explosive. We just can't let it happen, Stevie.'

'What are you on about?'

'I've just been talking to the chair of the North Cumbria Council Planning Committee. I called him because he's on the diversity sub-committee as well, and we've got this issue about trans people coming up — very delicate. I asked him if he might be around on Tuesday evening because I'm going to Norbridge that day for a meeting about PHSE in schools — personal health and sexual education . . .'

'Can you cut to the chase, Alan? I'm missing the bit in the film where James Mason falls out of the van after getting shot.'

'Well, it seems that DecorMetal company your friend Scott's always going on about . . .'

'He's not my friend.'

Alan raised a hairy but elegant eyebrow. 'All right. Well, the chair of the Planning Committee's not around on Tuesday evening because it seems that DecorMetal have arranged a dinner with some members of North Cumbria Council. They intend to put in a formal planning application to reopen the Arbiter mines. It will all come out when they do that, but they're buttering up the council first. It's an outrage. They've got to be stopped. But I've no idea how . . .'

CHAPTER TWENTY-FIVE

And it shall be, that in the morning, as soon as the sun is up, thou shalt rise early, and set upon the city.
Judges 9:33

Suzy left Tarnfield for Manchester at six o'clock on Monday morning. She had tried to get an early night on Sunday but had ended up talking to Rachel on the mobile for far too long.

She had been irritated when DS Jackson had dismissed her theory about Ellie's death. She didn't want Ellie to be remembered as a suicide, bullied and beaten down. Why had she been on that skiing holiday on her own? Why had she found the courage to contact Deborah about the hostel place? Ro was right of course. Ellie could have become depressed and suicidal after returning home from her holiday. But Suzy couldn't believe it.

And there *was* something Suzy could do for Ellie, before the woman disappeared into obscurity. Like Robert had suggested, she could find out more about her. Rachel had mentioned Ellie's sister. She would have all the details about Ellie's death. It was a big ask, but Suzy had picked up her phone and called Rachel.

'You know I'd do anything for you Suzy, but this is a bit much . . .'

'No, it's not, Rache. All you need to do is ask your friend on the Barnford Estate Residents Committee if she'll give me contact details for Ellie Fox's sister. Or if that's breach of confidentiality, she could ask the sister to contact me. Or take my call.'

'On what pretext?'

'Because I met Ellie on holiday, and she confided in me. Because I think Ellie might have been trying to get up to Cumbria and been killed in the attempt. Because her sister might like to talk to anyone who knew her. I don't know. You'll think of something.'

'You don't ask much.'

'Correct. If you don't do this, I'll think up something much worse. Going to bingo with me . . .'

'Done. I'll speak to her tomorrow.'

Suzy had smiled, turned off the phone and finally nodded off. Now, this Monday morning, she was wide awake. She took the train to Manchester. Then it was a short cab ride to the offices of the production company which made *Living Lies*.

When she had started working on the programme over ten years earlier, she had been a line producer and the show had been a fairly run-of-the-mill series about infidelity. Under Suzy, it had developed into a quirky programme about people with parallel lives. Her brainwave had been that at the start of each segment, the viewer didn't know whether the subject of the story was a saint or a sinner. At the start it had been hard to find contributors, but now there were hundreds of wannabe participants; the first two weeks of the production run consisted of sifting and interviewing. It was a process Suzy had been through many times, and she realized that this morning she felt jaded.

At lunchtime she found herself outside the CEO's office, knocked and went in. They had worked together for many years now.

'Suzy, it's great to see you back. Can you believe this is our umpteenth season?'

'Too true. Listen, Andrea, to get to the point, I know this must seem odd given the BATV, but I'm wondering if it might be time for a change . . .'

'Wow. Great minds think alike. I've been wanting to speak to you, Suzy, but you've beaten me to it. We want to talk to you about a new project. We want to branch out. We're thinking new channels, the internet, short docs, YouTube, podcasts. You know how good you are at thinking outside the box . . .'

Oh dear. Blue-sky thinking again. But Andrea was enthusing. 'We can't rely on *Living Lies* forever, Suzy. We need new ideas. How would you like to step off this production Peloton? How about a head of development role? An executive job. Working from home on the pitches, coming down here for brainstorming once a week. A two-year contract. More money. Less pressure. We need your brains. If it doesn't work out, no hard feelings on either side.'

'Sounds amazing, Andrea.'

'Well, have a think. And you know what, Suzy, soft-pedal a bit on this series. You've got a great team. Let them take the strain.'

So you can find my successor, Suzy thought. *Well, that's fine by me.* Then her thoughts immediately reverted to Ellie Fox. Now, she would have time to find out more about the woman everyone else seemed to want to forget.

Later that day Rachel called. 'You're working in Manchester, aren't you?'

'Yes.'

'Well, you're in luck. Carrie Fox, Ellie Fox's sister, doesn't live in London. She lives in a place called Altrincham.'

'Oh Rachel, you must know where Altrincham is!'

'Well, as it happens, I do. Cheshire is almost the Home Counties, and Altrincham is the Guildford of the North.'

'I wouldn't know, I haven't been to Guildford. But I have been to Altrincham. Just text me the number. If she's happy for me to speak to her, that is.'

'She's okay about it, but not ecstatic. She's a very nice woman, devastated about what happened to her sister. Call her, but go gently.'

During a lull in the afternoon Suzy called Carrie Fox's number. A pleasant voice answered. Glad to get a real person and not a voicemail, Suzy immediately launched into explaining why she was calling, which wasn't easy.

'My name's Suzy Spencer. I hope you don't mind me calling. I got your number via the secretary of the Barnford Estate Committee in London.'

'Oh, yes. I wasn't sure I would hear from you, but I said I'd be happy for you to have my number.' There was a pause. 'So this is about Eleanor?'

'Yes. I know it's a bit of a cheek me calling you, but I met Ellie on a skiing holiday earlier this year and we had a long chat. Forgive me, but I didn't know she had passed away until last week. I'd been emailing her recently but getting no reply. Tell me . . . did Ellie talk to you about her skiing holiday? Did she ever mentioned being evacuated to the chalet cellar, because of a carbon monoxide leak?'

'She didn't say much about the holiday, but she did mention that. She said the evacuation was fun in a way; she had met a very nice woman, and even the night in the cellar hadn't ruined her trip. Not that we talked much afterwards. I had thought the skiing was going to mean a big change but . . .' Carrie paused.

'She was still at the beck and call of her partner?' Suzy hazarded.

'Yes! Or so it would seem, as she ended up killing herself because of him. Obviously she told you about him. She hardly ever talked about him.'

'Well, we were in strange circumstances. We were both exhausted and a bit woozy. We must have talked all night.' *And if only I could remember more about it*, Suzy thought.

'Then you'll know that my big sister truly believed she could make a break from that man. I was overjoyed when Ellie said she was going skiing. Of course, she only told me when she was at the airport ready to take off. For the last five years she'd spent all her holiday time waiting for him to see if he could spend any time with her. She was always on edge about him.'

Suzy needed to be tactful. 'Look, I'd really like to talk to you. I'm a journalist — but don't panic, I work for TV in factual entertainment, and this is nothing to do with my job. But I'm very unhappy about Ellie's death. Could I meet you to talk? This week?'

There was a pause. 'I suppose so — to be honest, I would love to talk to anyone about Ellie. I miss her so much. I take it you're from around here?'

'I'm from Cumbria but I'm working in Manchester at the moment. Could we meet up for a drink?'

Ellie's sister hesitated, and then said, 'Why not? It's not as if I have much else to do. My sister's death has knocked me for six and I haven't really been able to get my own life back on track. I've got plenty of free time. How about Thursday evening after work?'

'Great. Where is good for you?'

'The wine bar on Goose Green in Altrincham. Not too far from the station. I'll text you the details. I still feel . . .' She stopped, and then went on in a more guarded voice. 'To be honest, it would just be nice for me to talk about her. I think my friends are all bored with it now.'

Suzy felt for her. 'Thanks. And just one more thing. Forgive me for being so blunt, but I need to ask you. D'you think your sister committed suicide?'

Carrie Fox gasped and then said in a rush, with a hard, almost angry tone, 'Do I heck as like. It was an open verdict. But you could see what they were all thinking. It's hard to pitch your instinct against their experience.'

'I'm glad you said that,' Suzy replied. 'I'm so looking forward to meeting you.'

* * *

At the same time, in Norbridge, Robert finished his class on Wilkie Collins's *The Moonstone* and its northern setting. He had arranged to meet Suzy at the station that evening after her train journey home from Manchester, and to have a drink and some supper in the town.

His class had gone well. The portrayal of the regions in classic literature had become his specialism. Often the students, bored by complex plots, archaic ethics and characters with little modern appeal, were excited by the moody landscapes in Collins. The Shivering Sands. What a horrible concept. There was quicksand on the coast north of Workhaven. And Wilkie Collins and Charles Dickens had visited West Cumbria and given a talk in the public rooms in Allonby, a beautiful and unusual seaside village.

The Moonstone was one of Robert's favourites. Planning the lecture about the mysterious gem had reminded him about the platinum ring Suzy had found, along with some other jewellery belonging to his first wife in the box under the bed. He was planning to take the pieces that afternoon to a jeweller with a longstanding family business in the town.

He logged off and unhooked his jacket and scarf. It was dark, wet and windy in Norbridge, and Suzy had said the weather wasn't much better in Manchester. She had called him to say she would be leaving early. She had added that she had something interesting to tell him. They were to meet when her train came in, and they had planned to eat at the Crown and Thistle. He was looking forward to telling her about the jewellery.

He arrived at the jeweller's just before it closed, but the elderly shop owner was pleased to see him. The jeweller looked carefully at the pieces. Two of the necklaces were quite valuable, and one was antique. But the jeweller was most interested in the chunky platinum ring. 'This is rather heavy, and worth quite a lot.' He quoted a price and Robert whistled. 'Yes, platinum has really gone up in value,' he said. 'You'll have heard about these gangs stealing catalytic converters?' Robert nodded. 'It's to get platinum. Or rhodium. They'd be quite chuffed even to get hold of a small piece like this. Metals are all the rage now.'

'So I hear,' said Robert.

'And rumour has it there's going to be a bit of a ding-dong about mining in Tarnfield again,' said the jeweller. 'They say some company is planning to try and get permission to open the old Arbiter mines.'

'Really?' said Robert. Nothing stayed a secret for long in Norbridge. He wondered if Jarrold Arbiter could really pull off a fight against DecorMetal.

'Bad idea, starting mining again,' said the jeweller. 'They'll ruin the area just for a tiny amount of metal and their own profit. Funnily enough — we were talking about platinum, weren't we? Old man Arbiter used to have two big platinum ingots on his sideboard. He got my father to value them donkeys' years ago. Worth a fortune even then.'

Robert was curious. 'But the Arbiter mines were for haematite.'

'Oh, the platinum wasn't local. The Arbiter family had their fingers in mining all over the world. Old Arbiter's uncle was packed off somewhere before the Second World War. He brought the ingots back. Ugly things, but the Arbiters used them for ornaments — conspicuous wealth, I suppose. They used to sit on the sideboard in the lounge at Tarnfield Hill. The house they now call St Jane's.'

Robert recalled the meeting in the lounge at the hostel on Friday night. There had been no sideboard and no ugly ingots. Just comfortable sofas and coffee tables.

The jeweller said, 'I suppose Deborah Arbiter must have got rid of them years ago to help fund her charity.' He unscrewed his eyeglass. 'I'll clean these pieces for you and give you a valuation certificate. Are they going to be a gift?'

'Yes. My stepdaughter. They'll go well with her pink tights and tartan mini-kilt.'

The jeweller laughed. 'You'd be surprised. They'll bring out the inner elegance in her. See you again soon, Mr Clark.'

As Robert left the shop his phone rang, and to his surprise it was the personal mobile of the Bishop of Norbridge.

'Ah, Robert,' the bishop said, 'I'm going to ask you a favour.'

* * *

In Manchester, Suzy left work unusually early. Just before she took a cab to the station, an emailed pinged into her PC. It was from the chair of the board of Living Production, the company which made *Living Lies*.

> *Hi Suzy,*
> *Gather you had a chat with A this morning and you're interested in our proposition. Just wanted to say we're all keen for you to take on the head of development role. We'll be making you a formal offer before the end of the week.*

It was great to have it in writing. It would be a relief to be off the production merry-go-round. But was she truly executive material? The new job would mean more office politics, and the stress of having to deliver on her ideas. But on the other hand, she had loads of them. And if the arrangement ended after two well-paid years, at least she would know where she was, instead of the fear, year in, year out, of *Living Lies* being cancelled.

There was something else about the email which tugged at her. It read '*a chat with A*', referring to Andrea, the CEO.

Ellie had written '*Anyway, J went absolutely berserk*' in her email. It was the same familiar style. Ellie assumed that Suzy would know exactly who J was. Ellie must have already told her the name of her lover, and she had forgotten it in the aftermath of that hazy night in the chalet. Was if Jeff? Or Jermyn? Or even Jim?

If only she could remember. What had Ellie said? But now she had a train to Norbridge to catch. She had a lot to talk about with Robert. Head of Development, eh? It sounded good. She left the building with a slight spring in her step.

* * *

Robert was at the station in Norbridge to meet her. It really was rather romantic, Suzy thought. But she knew the commute might become tedious and fraught if it went on. The train to and from Manchester every day, while they were in production, was going to be tiring.

The atmosphere in Norbridge was instantly different from Manchester. Suzy felt the cool breeze of Cumbria, wintry but fresh, coming through the station's archway entrance. The little city looked lovely in the dark evening with the lights on. Immediately outside the station were the floodlit remains of the old castle, and down the hill, sprinkled with streetlights and the warm glow of restaurants and old inns, was the main road to the Abbey. In the other direction the High Street boasted chain stores and the entrance to the university, once Norbridge College. Everything she needed was here. She felt so glad to be back after only a day away. There was just enough hint of cold rain on the breeze for them to huddle together and walk into the town centre, and then through the warm, glowing stained-glass doors of the Crown and Thistle.

Their table was ready. Suzy dumped her bags and went off to the ladies'. She felt like putting on a bit of make-up. It must be great, she thought, to be like Deborah, with thick, natural dark-brown eyelashes, and full lips even in her seventies. Deborah had been a real looker in her youth but, as Joanne had shrewdly pointed out, it hadn't been a sexy look. More a sort of cool beauty, but with the mischievous lift of one naturally dark, sculptured eyebrow. Suzy always needed the aid of a dash of eyebrow pencil and a bit of colour. Her hair was beyond help, though.

'You look great,' said Robert.

'Thanks. So do you!' He laughed but it was true. He looked less worried.

'Tell me your news,' he said. Then he rather surprisingly added, 'Then I'll tell you mine.' She told him all about the job offer from Living Production, and they became so involved in conversation that the server had to prod them to order.

'So, what sort of things do they want you to do? As head of development?'

'Oh, you know, think up new programme ideas. Like *Archdeacons Great and Small* or *The Great British Hoover Challenge*.'

'I'd watch them!'

'Oh, Robert, don't talk rubbish. You don't even know where the hoover is. So, what's your news?'

In his annoying non-journalistic way, instead of cutting to the headlines, Robert went step by step, telling her about his trip to the jeweller's. And about what the jeweller had said about the platinum ingots.

'That's funny,' Suzy said. 'I've seen that sideboard. It's in the office now. It's all scratched along the top as if something had been placed on it. Maybe that's where the ingots were.'

'Pity they've gone. They would have brought quite a packet into St Jane's.'

'Maybe Deborah sold them years ago.' Suzy stopped to try her Morecambe Bay shrimps, then added, 'By the way, remember that I have my meeting tomorrow evening with that weird woman who wants to talk about Deborah's past. So I won't be back till late. Then I'm taking a day off on Wednesday. And guess what — I'm meeting Ellie's sister on Thursday! I know I should be concentrating on my TV work, but I feel this need to go on digging. We must get to the answer, mustn't we? Who killed Ellie and Deborah . . . ?'

Then she remembered what Robert had said and felt guilty for doing all the talking. 'Sorry, what were you going to tell me?'

CHAPTER TWENTY-SIX

Comfort thine heart with a morsel of bread, and afterward go your way. And they sat down and did eat and drink both of them together.
Judges 19:5-6

Robert looked rather pleased with himself. 'Well, I hope this doesn't scupper any plans you have for Friday, but I've had a call from the Bishop of Norbridge. She wants me to go to an away day with the Rural Reformation Association.'

'The what?'

'Rural Reformation Association. The RRA. Haven't I told you about it? The Ven Jim's club of choice? It's an evangelical mission group within the Church of England. A bit fundamentalist. It goes back to the nineteenth century, when it was set up to drag the working classes out of alcohol and atheism. In fairness it did do a lot of good social work. But it has seats on lots of patronage boards for selecting vicars. Including in Tarnfield. The Ven Jim is a super-enthusiastic member. Too enthusiastic, I think.'

'Wow, sounds like a fun way to spend a Friday.'

'It's Friday night, actually. I'd be staying away.'

'Oh . . . well, you can't really ignore a summons from the Bishop of Norbridge, can you? But why has she picked you?'

'She wants me to talk to the Ven Jim. She thinks I might find out what's really troubling him. Apparently, he told her I was quite a reasonable chap. She was impressed with the way I handled that last meeting with him.'

'Robert Clark, therapist?! You're going to be unbearable now.'

'The bishop said I was calm, tactful and insightful.'

'Or perhaps you were just bored and thinking about Victorian novels.'

'No, seriously, Suzy. I'm intrigued by Jim Bentley. If I can pour oil on those troubled waters, I will. Anyway, I said yes. Jim Bentley will be there from Friday night. It's in Leeds and they've organized a supper. The bishop's got me an invite as a laity representative. I must say I'm a bit flattered. You don't mind me being the one who's away for the night, for a change, do you?'

'Nooo . . .' Suzy thought about it. But it was rather a shock. She was used to Robert working around her schedule. She said jokingly, 'But Robert, you're not going to come home and play the guitar, are you?'

'I solemnly swear that I am going to remain the middle-aged, middle-of-the-road, middle-sized, middle-class, middle-everything churchman that you love.'

'With a weird wife?'

'Oh yes. That's essential. Actually, she's the head of development for a successful, award-winning independent television production company.'

'So, if the RRA try to hijack you, call me. Say *I'm an Anglican . . . Get Me Out of Here*!'

* * *

At St Jane's, the death of Geoff Black had been unsettling to say the least. On Monday morning, Adelina had requested another session with Joanne.

Joanne had agreed in a preoccupied way. She had a lot to think about. Never mind the long term: in the here and now she was torn. She needed to do the right thing for Moira. She also needed, now there was no Geoff, to get someone in to fix the drainpipe at the back which had come adrift in the heavy rain. And she was very concerned about Leila. She didn't believe Leila had killed Geoff, whatever the police said.

But most of all she was worrying about Jarrold. She was aware that Paula had been staying with him and she felt a little jealous. Now she had her son back, she wanted to keep him to herself, which she knew was unreasonable. She told herself that if Jarrold married a fellow Texan or someone even more exotic, she might lose him again. So perhaps Dr Paula Stovey might be the best bet.

Anyway, that was all in the future. The most important thing was for Jarrold to expose DecorMetal at his meeting with the councillors the next day. This was what they had been working on for months. Joanne and her son were both fiercely single-minded. Joanne stuck at things, come what may, like in the early years of her terrible second marriage. Jarrold had the same characteristic. He had dedicated months of his life to painstakingly investigating the state of the Arbiter mines to prove they should not be reopened. The project had brought mother and son together. Deborah's death had been a tragedy which Joanne had somehow managed to mentally park while they completed their work. Deborah had invested thousands in exposing DecorMetal, and Joanne and Jarrold were going to see it through. There would be time to grieve later, but they would do so in the knowledge they had been true to Deborah's wishes.

Adelina knocked softly on the office door and came straight in. 'You coping okay?' she asked.

'Yes, of course.' Joanne sat upright.

Adelina eased herself into the other office chair. 'So, the word is that Geoff Black pushed Deborah off the roof. And that Leila knew he'd done it and killed him, using the method shown in the Bible picture.'

'Yes. Very neatly put. You've worked that out pretty smartish.'

'Oh, we hear things, you know. That policeman was nice enough, better than most, but you could tell from his questions what he was thinking. I mean, why was he asking how often we used to pass that picture? And all those questions about when Leila was last seen, and whether we thought she was strong enough to wield a mallet. But here's the thing . . .' Adelina gave one of her long and slightly infuriating pauses. Joanne waited patiently. 'Leila couldn't have done it.'

'Why not?'

'She hated the sight of blood. She used to faint. *Vasovagal syncope*, they call it. She was really glad to have had the menopause.'

'But maybe there wouldn't have been much blood, the way Geoff was killed.'

'There would have been some. And she'd've had to pierce his temple. She just wouldn't have done it. If she were going to kill him, which I doubt, she'd maybe have bashed him on the head and run for it. This method just wasn't Leila.'

'Well, you could tell the police . . .'

'There's no evidence. I could be making it up. And Leila's long gone. I just didn't want you to think she was a murderer, even though she's left us. Maybe there's some way you could tell Moira Black that it wasn't Leila, whatever the police say . . .'

Chelsea had appeared, peering through the half-open office door. At the mention of Moira's name she went rather pink, and her eyes opened wide and round, in the way she had of showing interest or surprise.

'You're talking about Mrs Black,' Chelsea said. Chelsea had been troubled by her daily visits with home baking for Moira and her daughter Tracey. She had a disturbed sort of feeling about it. She wanted to talk it over with someone, but she didn't know where to start.

'Coffee time?' she asked Joanne. 'Do you want some too?' she said to Adelina.

'Sure!' Adelina smiled her warm, gracious smile.

Chelsea grinned back. 'I'm baking shortbread today.' She scampered out, quite unlike her lumbering gait of the week before. Joanne wondered if Chelsea might have lost a few pounds. She was doing heavy work and eating healthy food. She certainly looked more alert.

'Did you ever find Deborah's notes about us?' Adelina asked Joanne suddenly.

'No . . . Of course, I wasn't specifically looking for them. They were confidential between Deborah and the residents.'

'Come on, Joanne. You would look at those notes if you'd found them. I don't blame you. It would be useful to know what Deborah was thinking about Leila, for a start.'

Before Joanne could deny it, Chelsea reappeared with the huge tray, which she put on the scratched sideboard. She seemed to be taller and held her head higher. The two other women found themselves looking at her. She was still pink and wide-eyed, and unused to being the centre of attention.

Chelsea said, 'Maybe it ain't my place, but I was just outside and heard you talking about Deborah's notes. Would she . . .' she faltered, then straightened up again. 'Would she have any notes on Mrs Black?'

'Mrs Black?' Adelina sounded surprised. 'Why would she have notes on Mrs Black?'

Joanne said quietly, 'She might have done, Adelina.'

'Why?' said Adelina. 'She wasn't a resident.'

'Not exactly. But the Blacks didn't get the cottage because of Geoff's talent as a handyman. It's in Moira's name, not Geoff's. I know because I administer the tenancies. I've always wondered about that. But as Deborah's notes are either lost or were in her head, we'll never know what she knew about the residents. Or the Blacks.'

Chelsea said 'oh' in the flat neutral voice of someone already worn down by disappointment. Then something occurred to her. 'But that's weird. Deborah was so clued up on tech. Look at that fancy digital oven. And the iPad just for recipes. Even the fridge has a touch screen on the door!'

She sniffed knowledgeably. 'If Deborah was that cool with techie stuff, she must've had an archive system. For her files.'

Joanne said rather shortly, 'That doesn't necessarily follow, Chelsea, and anyway, the police didn't find any background notes on her PC. There's nothing anywhere.' Joanne thought slightly bitterly about the missing funding. There was a lot of information which it would be good to find in Deborah's non-existent notes. She went on wearily: 'Deborah's phone went missing a few days before she died, and anyway she was too smart to do or say anything confidential on that. There are no other devices. There is just no information left behind.'

'What about a memory stick?' Chelsea said.

'Why would Deborah use one of those?' Joanne said snappily. 'She was based here. She never needed to take information away.'

'Oh, but they can be really useful if you want to keep stuff totally private!' Chelsea said, going even pinker with the stress of disagreeing with Joanne. 'We used them all the time in the hostels for the homeless. If you had a tablet or anything it would get nicked. All our phones were old or broken or the chargers got pinched. So we used the communal computer and saved stuff on a stick. You could sleep with the stick in your bra, so no one could get your stuff.'

'There's no memory stick belonging to Deborah,' Joanne said tetchily. 'I've sorted through her desk and her handbag and her room. And if a memory stick had been on her person when she fell, it would have been found.'

'Okay,' said Chelsea, and quickly made herself scarce.

* * *

Knowing when to quit, Chelsea retreated to the kitchen. It looked as though discovering anything about Mrs Black through the hostel was no-go. But then Chelsea thought — why not go to the cottage and talk to Moira Black straight up? She might end up making an absolute fool of herself, but so what? She would tread carefully. The older woman seemed to have warmed to her, and Chelsea was beginning to sense that she herself could have a nice way with people, if she tried. But she would blow it if she said the wrong thing.

On the other hand — who wouldn't want some of this delicious shortbread?

Later that night, in bed after visiting Moira Black, Chelsea couldn't sleep for excitement. Moira had said they had to be sure. Which was correct, of course. But she had said something lovely which Chelsea would never forget . . . 'Whatever we find out, you should stay on here. My instinct is that you belong with us. If there's trouble at the hostel you can live with me.'

* * *

On Tuesday morning Suzy awoke at five o'clock and was on the way to Norbridge for the six thirty train to Manchester. She was meeting the mystery colleague of Deborah's that evening at six and wanted to get in a full day's work first.

'I'll be working from home tomorrow,' she said to her senior producer, who just nodded. The team were finding some great participants for the show and the researchers and producers had new confidence, even disagreeing with Suzy when, in a moment of madness, she suggested a celebrity *Living Lies* series. It would be impossible to get celebs to admit to living lies, the researchers argued, even though so many did!

And by half past five, Suzy was ready for a break.

She took a cab to the Midland Hotel. It was easy to spot the woman she was supposed to meet. She was sitting at a small table towards the back of the bar, in a classy black business suit and white blouse with sensible shoes. Her neat head with its cropped hair was immersed in a pile of important-looking documents, and she also had an iPad on the table. She looked every inch the successful lawyer. Suzy introduced herself.

The woman smiled rather tightly and motioned with her head for Suzy to sit down. Then she said very clearly but softly, as if to emphasize every word, 'Thank you for coming. But I'm not going to tell you my name, and I don't want you to mention it. As far as I'm concerned this meeting never happened.'

This was abrupt, and even more cloak-and-dagger than Suzy expected. She felt it was slightly ridiculous.

'But I contacted you through LinkedIn . . .'

'Or you contacted a colleague of mine who contacted me. You don't know for certain who I am. And there's no evidence anyone responded to you.'

It seemed crazy, and for a moment Suzy felt annoyed. But she had protected her sources in the past and could do so again. She took her time, then nodded, and made some easy remarks about the weather to try and lessen the tension. But the woman hardly responded.

Suzy sighed. 'Okay. This is getting silly. If you want to speak in confidence, I respect that and I won't discuss this meeting with anyone. But you agreed to meet me. If you've changed your mind, you should go. There's nothing to be gained by messing me around.'

The woman smiled rather coldly and realigned her papers, as if this was all rather small beer. Suzy tried not to let her irritation show and said evenly, 'Deborah's CV reads very smoothly. She was a successful barrister, then she inherited the Cumbrian estate, left London and turned her family home into a hostel for women, associated with the church. Deborah was a devout Anglican. It all sounds right . . . I just wonder *why* Deborah started the hostel. And more importantly, the dates don't quite fit. Deborah left London *before* her father died. So even if she had been desperate to start a hostel, there would have been no point in throwing up a glittering legal career before she inherited the house.'

The woman sipped her tea. She finally gave Suzy full eye contact. 'You're right, of course. I see that you've realized it doesn't quite add up. No one has looked in detail at

Deborah's life story. But they will now. If things are going to come out, I'd rather you knew first, as you're the first person to raise it.' Suzy nodded. Now they were getting somewhere. The lawyer went on, rather pompously, 'This is difficult for me. I'll tell you what I remember. I've been worried about it for a long time. It's a small thing where I'm concerned, but it's been on my conscience.'

'So why are you so nervous? If it's just a question of a minor *mea culpa* about something in the past?'

The woman squirmed. 'Because my guilt isn't all. This story doesn't reflect very well on Tony.'

'Tony who?'

'Tony Warsbrook. Lord Warsbrook of Whinsea.'

Suzy marshalled her thoughts and tried to move the players from one context to another. *Lord Warsbrook, author of the report on social media regulation.* 'What has he got to do with this?'

'Didn't you know? Tony was at our chambers in the eighties. He ruined Deborah's career.'

CHAPTER TWENTY-SEVEN

The inhabitants of the villages ceased, they ceased in Israel, until that I Deborah arose, that I arose a mother in Israel.
Judges 5:7

Suzy gasped aloud, but she sensed that the other woman was on a roll and the conversation was about to change gear. The lawyer just needed a prod.

'You'd better explain.'

'All right. Tony's always been a high flyer, cozy with politicians and businessmen. Of course, that's why we thought he was so marvellous. The only one who came near him for talent was Deborah. Deborah and Tony were close friends, but they were also rivals. They both wanted to be judges eventually, but not everyone can succeed. It was fiercely competitive.'

'And you're saying he sabotaged her somehow?'

'Yes. Only, you must never attribute it to me.'

'Okay, okay. I've agreed that. So what happened?'

'Deborah was a bit of an environmental campaigner before her time. There was an application to reopen some mines in South Cumbria, and it caused a huge protest, almost Greenham Common style. There was a high-profile public enquiry. Deborah represented the protestors. If she had won, her career would have been made. But she lost, which was bad enough. And then Tony started telling people she had lost deliberately. Thrown it.'

'Wow! That's pretty nasty!'

'It's even worse than that. I think he caused her to lose the case by giving her bad advice.'

Now Suzy began to see why the woman had been so cagey. She was alleging something very serious, not just a ruthless rivalry. But she was still talking . . .

'Tony did a lot of work on land and property deals. He had a big network of landowners and businessmen in the shires. He knew that Deborah's father was trying to sell his defunct mines to the same company Deborah was opposing. But she had no idea what her father was doing. Deborah didn't get on with her family — we all knew that. I was Tony's junior at the time, and I knew about the Arbiter deal. I should have told her. Then at least she would have known she was conflicted. But I was under Tony's thumb.'

So Deborah was opposing the planning application at one end of the county, while her father was selling his land to the same company at the other. Very tricky. The lawyer went on, 'If the company lost the South Cumbria mining application, then they wouldn't be interested in the Arbiter deal. Mining in Cumbria would be discredited. But if Deborah lost, the Arbiter deal could go ahead. And she did lose. But I believe she only lost because of Tony giving her wrong advice. That's what makes it really evil.'

'But how could he do that?'

'Oh, he could suggest a tactic that didn't work. Or bad-mouth one of her witnesses so she withdrew them. And afterwards I think he suggested to people that Deborah threw the case deliberately to protect her family's interest. Losing a case was bad enough, but when your family would benefit from your deliberately losing it, that would be dynamite.'

'He'd have needed to have a lot of influence over her to make her take his bad advice.'

'But he did! He was the golden boy. She would have trusted him completely.'

'To the extent that she couldn't see he was deliberately misleading her?'

'Absolutely. Then once she'd lost, he could insinuate to the whole legal network that she'd thrown it to suit her family's interests. He wouldn't have had to prove a thing. No smoke without fire. Remember this was in the days when promotion for lawyers was a question of a tap on the shoulder.'

'Okay. What you're suggesting is that Tony Warsbrook ensured Deborah lost this case. Then he hinted that she'd done it deliberately, for her family's financial gain?'

'Exactly.'

'And her potential career as a judge was kyboshed?'

'Yes.

'I see.' Suzy paused for another moment to think. 'So, could we sum it up like this? Deborah was a potential star, betrayed by a conniving man, who damaged her irrevocably and used a sexist system to do her down for his own advantage?'

'Sounds a bit basic. But yes, I suppose you could put it like that.'

And if you did, Suzy thought, then Deborah's life was not totally unlike Adelina's. Or Leila's. Or Joanne's. Apart from the physical violence. She had been used and abused too. Though there was another big difference. Deborah had the means to reconstruct a world of her own, where she could put everything right. She had become a judge of sorts, after all. She was loved, valued and respected. She was probably a shoo-in for the honours list.

And then, when everything seemed wonderful, forty years later, history repeated itself, just when her life had reached its zenith. The same company she had fought and lost to, all those years ago, reappeared with a new name on Deborah's doorstep, ready to destroy everything she had worked for, all over again.

Suzy sensed that the woman was now keen to get away. She was groping for her briefcase by the side of the chair.

'And you won't quote me?' she asked again anxiously.

'No. You have my word. But one last thing. Was there ever any sexual relationship between Tony Warsbrook and Deborah?'

'No. I wondered when you would ask that. It's all anyone thinks of these days. Of course, people said Tony had tried it on with Deborah. He tried it on with everyone . . .' She realized what she had said and looked into her cup of cold tea. 'But Deborah was never interested in that side of life. She would just have brushed Tony off.'

And rejection would go down like a bucket of cold sick with the golden boy, Suzy thought. He was a ruthless competitor and sexual predator.

The woman softened. 'Please understand why I'm so on edge. Tony is a very powerful man. I've still got a few years left in my career, so I need to be careful. I know you can't publish a load of supposition. But you'll know what to do. And please, don't implicate me.'

'You need have absolutely no fear of that. In fact, as you said, I don't really know for sure who you are.'

The woman nodded, stood up, smiled briefly, picked up her briefcase and left.

* * *

On the train home Suzy thought it through. Now she knew why Deborah Arbiter had made that astonishing decision to start a women's hostel. Her career prospects had been rubbished by a man she trusted, and she had been professionally humiliated by his lies. She had gone back home — and presumably found out her father had sold his mines to the very same company she had fought. No wonder she was bitter. But then her father died, and the estate was Deborah's to do with what she wanted.

But what could Suzy do with this information? If it really was information. Suzy believed the mystery woman implicitly.

But she had no evidence. If only Deborah had complained at the time. But to whom? A colleague? The Bar Council? Suzy had no idea how that would have worked forty years ago. And Deborah had left no personal record of her past — no diary, or memoir, or letters, or press cuttings. That seemed increasingly odd. There were the publicity stills, of course, and the formal things like her CV on the hostel PC. But there was none of the usual admin clutter of a life. Apart from the fun snap of her in the garden, looking like a prophetess, there were no casual pictures, no certificates or memorabilia.

She called Robert to tell him her news, but he got in first. 'Guess what? Alan Robie's in the thick of this mining scandal with the council. He knows all about it. Jarrold has completely upstaged DecorMetal with his report. They'd need to do something called "extensive dewatering", which would take a while and cost a lot. And the cat is out of the bag now. A big local protest movement is going to start. Alan's the driving force behind that and you know he's unstoppable.'

Suzy said, 'That's good news. I suppose the amount of tungsten is just too small for it to be cost effective. I'm not necessarily against mining, but if DecorMetal are just profiteers who don't care what happens to the environment . . .'

'That was Jarrold's big point. If he, as a sole geologist, could identify the acid sulphate in one of the mineshafts, then DecorMetal must have known it was there too. But they didn't care. That means huge reputational damage for them. Not the sort of outfit an international like Arctic America would want to acquire these days. A few suits were seen leaving on the next train to Euston.'

Suzy's train stopped at Norbridge. She gathered her stuff and disembarked. So that was another piece in the Deborah jigsaw. Deborah had loathed and suspected DecorMetal since she lost against them in the eighties, and she had set out to block their new mining application for the Arbiter mines. And that activity could of course put her in danger.

And it did make one thing a little clearer. If Geoff Black couldn't have murdered Ellie, and one person murdered both

Ellie and Deborah, by the same method, then who was the guilty man? It put Scott Jermyn more than ever in the frame for Deborah's murder. Could Jermyn have murdered Ellie, then come to Cumbria as a consultant for DecorMetal, met Deborah, and had two reasons to kill her? Number one, her offering a helpline to his long-suffering girlfriend. And number two, being a danger to his business?

It looked increasingly like Jermyn was the killer. Now all Suzy had to do was find a link between him and Ellie. And maybe Ellie's sister would be able to provide it. Suzy was looking forward to meeting Carrie Fox on Thursday.

* * *

On Wednesday morning Suzy had the delicious sensation of relaxing in bed, listening to Robert and Molly rushing around the house. They'd had to get up, get dressed and get out, and she didn't. Suzy enjoyed a bath and decided to slum it in her dressing gown, mooching round to decide where to put her new home office. She would go and have a look at the attic.

She padded upstairs. The top floor was larger and airier than she remembered. Then she noticed a new stain down the wall. She went over and touched it. It was damp and fresh. Infuriating. It looked as though Lee's work on the chimney breast hadn't been as successful as they'd hoped.

Suzy found her phone and called the roofer. Luckily, he answered in person. 'Lee, sorry to bother you. Our chimney stack seems to be letting in more rainwater. Worse than before, actually. Could you come and have a look as soon as possible?'

'Nae! I dinna believe it! Haway, I tell you what I'll do for you. I'll pop over this afternoon after I've picked up Mandy from work. How's that?'

'Thanks. That's great. What time?'

'Oh, about half past five. It'll be dark, but I've got me lights and we should be able to see what's up. Might take a bit of smart thinking to fix it.'

'Okay, see you then.'

Suzy got dressed, had a long conference call with the *Living Lies* production team, and then set out for St Jane's. She hoped she'd be in time for Chelsea's delicious coffee and home baking.

Joanne practically welcomed her with open arms. 'I've had a few press enquiries about Geoff, but — as you advised — I just confirmed he was our part-time handyman, and I didn't let myself be led. And you'll have heard the wonderful news about Jarrold?'

'Yes. He's done brilliantly. Any news of Leila?'

Joanne's face fell. 'Nothing. And Adelina has another of her theories. Apparently, Leila couldn't stand the sight of blood. Not the sort of person to put a tent peg through someone's head.'

'Oh. Interesting . . .' Suzy said reflectively. If only they knew why Deborah had been so worried about Leila. Among so many other things.

'You look a bit distracted, Suzy . . .'

'Sorry, yes. After we've had a coffee and a catch-up, would you be offended if I had a look in Deborah's room?'

'But I've been through everything, and so have the police.'

'Could I just have a peek? Just to get a feel for her. I'm struggling a bit with this biography for the feature.'

Joanne shrugged. 'Okay. Go up yourself when you're ready. Here's the key. Deborah's room is the smallest. It's number five on the first floor.'

'Well, I'll have that coffee first. Has Chelsea been baking?'

Joanne smiled. 'Yes. We had shortbread yesterday. I think it might be fruitcake today.'

As if on cue, Chelsea performed the usual contortions needed to get the giant butler's tray through the office door and onto the sideboard.

'Suzy! You're back.' Chelsea grinned.

'Yes,' Suzy said. 'I am!'

Before going to look at Deborah's room, Suzy contacted the *Mid Cumbria Times*, Radio Cumbria and a couple of other platforms. They all agreed to a later deadline but in return wanted quotes on the changing theories about Deborah's death. Suzy worked hard at getting the right tone. '*The management of St Jane's Hostel welcomes the reopening of enquiries into the death of our beloved founder Deborah Arbiter*.' That would do.

* * *

Later, when Joanne and Chelsea were in the kitchen talking catering, Suzy went up the grand staircase to the first floor and let herself into Deborah's room. It was austere but bright and light. It was also the smallest bedroom, but it was on the corner, so it had two windows, one looking south over the drive and one looking west onto open country. There would be wonderful sunsets, Suzy thought. The room was painted white, and there was a simple single bed with white sheets and some purple cushions. Two pictures hung on one of the walls. One was a reproduction of Millais's *Christ in the House of His Parents*, which Suzy considered an odd choice until she thought about how the hostel cared for women whose family lives had been ruined. Perhaps in the brief halcyon days of Deborah's legal career, the chambers had been Deborah's family until Tony Warsbrook's ambition ruined it all. So she had come home to Cumbria and created a new family for herself.

The other picture was a beautiful photograph of the statue of St Jane in the hostel grounds, complete with a large silver halo inscribed with a motto. Deborah had taken it herself and signed the print.

Joanne had laid out Deborah's clothes on the bed. There were remarkably few, and they were quite formal, with purple shirts and dark trousers predominating. Her underwear was elegant and expensive, but much worn, and folded into a bag. There were a few shoes in another bag. In the bathroom there was a small range of organic toiletries, but Deborah hadn't used many cosmetics. There was a small armchair with an indigo throw. And there was a stool and a simple dressing-table-cum-desk. On top of this was an old-fashioned cut-glass tray. In it were a bottle of Deborah's distinctive perfume, a hairbrush, a jar of hair product and two lipsticks. One was the pale pearly pink Deborah favoured, but there was also a cheap-looking bright-red one. Maybe Deborah had her odd crazy moments. There was also a very small wardrobe, now completely empty.

Suzy felt guilty and rather stupid for thinking she would find something which Joanne and the police had missed. She lifted the mattress, looked under the bed and on top of the wardrobe, perching on the desk stool. She felt behind the pictures, which were professionally framed and nailed or screwed at the back and perfectly smooth. But Suzy felt she was being melodramatic. What did she expect? To find notes in the spare loo roll? Even Deborah's sense of humour wouldn't run to that . . .

She went downstairs to Chelsea's sandwich lunch and spent the rest of the afternoon checking in with the hostel board and any other worthies she felt would appreciate a personal call. This included the archdeacon. The Venerable Jim Bentley was much more pleasant than Suzy had expected, and even said, 'I understand your husband is joining us at the RRA weekend. I'll look forward to chatting to him.'

'Yes,' said Suzy, slightly taken aback. 'I'm sure it's mutual.'

After the final call, Suzy checked out with Joanne and said she would keep in touch during the week. As she was getting into her car, she saw Chelsea furtively coming out of the kitchen door. The girl looked rather pink and bright-eyed.

'Suzy, guess what?'

'What?'

'I think I've found my nan — really!'

CHAPTER TWENTY-EIGHT

For God hath given it into your hands; a place where there is no want of anything that is in the earth.
Judges 18:10

The words came rushing out of Chelsea. 'I took some scones up to Mrs Black at the cottage on Saturday. And then I took some baking every day. Mrs Black's doing okay. Tracey is staying with her.'

'Tracey?'

'Her daughter. I told you. Anyway, I went up there yesterday and Tracey said that she thought she knew me from somewhere. I felt my knees go weak. I'd been feeling the same. I'd been meaning to talk to them about it, but I couldn't find the words. So I stayed for some tea with them, and it all came out. I told them how I'd come up here to try and find my nan.'

Suzy nodded encouragingly and Chelsea kept talking. 'Well it took a while, but then Mrs Black said she'd had a daughter years ago, before she was married. The daughter would have been exactly my mum's age. She got adopted and taken down south — just like my mum!' And then the words bubbled out of Chelsea as she became more animated and excitable.

Suzy listened and tried to unpick the story. It was clear that Deborah had helped Moira locate her lost child, using her tech skills and her perseverance. Moira was one of the many girls in the sixties who had given permission for their babies to be taken away from them and put up for adoption. In Moira's case, the permission was nominal. Moira's parents had taken control and handed the baby over to relatives, Moira's second cousins, and a local Church of England Adoption Society had done the paperwork. It was well known that records at the time were patchy. The relatives had moved to London and Moira had never heard of her child again. Somehow Deborah had traced the family and the baby, then a woman in her late forties. But then the correspondence had abruptly ended.

'Until two weeks ago,' said Chelsea. 'And then the woman who adopted Moira's baby came back to Hardcastle and met up with Moira. Deborah had arranged it. But the bad news was that Moira's daughter had died a year ago. Of breast cancer. Like my mum. How many adopted women from the north died of breast cancer in London last year? Moira *must* be my nan. And Tracey must be my auntie.'

'I truly hope so, Chelsea. But you must be careful. There are a lot of coincidences but no proof . . .'

'Yes, there is. Moira's baby and my mum had the same first name, and the same birthday!' Chelsea was almost hopping in triumph.

'But even that isn't conclusive. Some names are really popular and loads of people have the same birthday.' Suzy felt bad, raining on Chelsea's parade. But she might be in for a dreadful disappointment.

Chelsea straightened up and said with conviction, 'I bet Deborah had documents which would prove it. She must have written to my mum in the first place. And my mum told people at the hospice that she wanted to find out about

St Jane's, didn't she? Why else would she say that? When the moment's right I'm going to tell Joanne. Though Moira says it would be good to be sure.'

'What about a DNA test for you and Moira?'

'We thought of that. But you really need samples from both grandparents. And it costs a bomb. But I'm sure Deborah must have got proof. If we could get hold of Deborah's notes . . .'

Suzy sighed. Another missing link, to be found in Deborah's mysterious non-existent files.

'There's nothing anywhere, Chelsea. Joanne's searched. I've searched. The police have searched.'

'But what about a memory stick?' Chelsea outlined her theory.

'There's no memory stick. I've looked everywhere and there's absolutely nothing.'

'But memory sticks come with all sorts of joke cases, you know — Coke cans, baby unicorns, that sort of stuff.'

'There were no baby unicorns in Deborah's bedroom.'

'Okay.' Chelsea was crestfallen. 'But I bet that was what she did. Deborah was totally tech savvy.'

Suzy wondered why, if Deborah was so savvy, they were all flailing around without crucial information. Or the extra funds which made St Jane's so special. There should be a device somewhere with the information on it. But there wasn't.

Suzy had to go. She promised to invite Chelsea to the Briars again, and to talk to Joanne on her behalf if there was any problem about Chelsea's job. Then she drove into the village and parked to go to the local shop. It was nearly five o'clock and a wintry darkness was falling. It had also become very cold. Suzy shivered. In the shop she bumped into one of the smart young professionals who lived on the Green.

'Have you heard?' the woman said. 'Scott Jermyn's done a bunk. Tarnfield House is all locked up and shuttered.'

'Really? Any idea where he's gone?'

'Back to London, I expect. Rather embarrassing for him, this DecorMetal company turning out to be dodgy.' So the word was out.

'It would take a lot to embarrass Scott Jermyn,' said Suzy.

But it was disturbing that he had gone. If Jermyn was J, the man who had been Ellie's lover, and the man who killed Deborah, how would they track him down now? Of all the suspects, he was the most likely. Jarrold was in the clear, and had turned out to be a good guy. Geoff Black looked as if he had been out of action with a sprained ankle when Ellie died. Other suspects were really unlikely. It *had* to be Jermyn.

She hurried to the car and drove back to the Briars. Lee's bright silver van with the blue logo was parked outside. Mandy was in the front seat. Suzy went to the passenger door and knocked on the window. Mandy seemed to be having trouble getting the window down, so Suzy opened the door. Mandy's arms were wrapped across her stomach.

'Hiya, Suzy. Sorry, I've got terrible period pains.' Mandy grimaced again. 'I just couldn't get the window down. I need some painkillers.' Mandy tensed and squirmed again, then started groping in her handbag. She lost hold of it, and it fell into the foot well.

Suzy bent to pick up Mandy's stuff. 'Here's your phone,' she said, handing Mandy a smartphone in a classy indigo-colour leather case.

'No, that's not mine,' Mandy said, shaking her head and looking devastated for a moment. But she pulled herself together and started stuffing her belongings back into her bag. 'I mean, it's not my new one. I've got an updated one. Where's it gone? Oh, here it is. This is it.' She flourished a phone in a rather lurid pink case.

Lee came round from the side of the house and stood on the passenger side of the van with Suzy. 'Eh, I don't know what to say!' He shook his head apologetically. 'I don't see anything up there on your chimney. The leak must be under the brick. The soonest I'll be able to come round is Friday evening. It'll probably take just a bit of smart thinking to fix it from the inside.' He smiled and gave Mandy an affectionate squeeze on the leg through the van door. 'Still having those cramps, pet?'

'Yes, but they'll pass.' Mandy smiled weakly.

'Well, I'd better get you home. Is that all right, Suzy? I'll see you Friday. Latish, I'm afraid. I'll bring me big torch.'

Mandy winced again. 'C'mon love,' she said. 'I need me hot water bottle!' Lee walked around, climbed into the driver's seat, and they moved off, with Mandy smiling and waving through the window. Suzy wondered about Mandy's cramps. They seemed severe. Perhaps she had a gynae problem. Suzy had wondered before why Lee and Mandy were childless. Maybe they were happy enough, just with each other. Or maybe there was a physical reason, which they had learned to live with. It seemed such a shame if they wanted children and couldn't have them. They were such obvious parent material.

Then, talking of parenting, Robert's car came up the drive with Molly in the passenger seat. He'd picked her up from the bus stop and they'd had a quick spin, driving around the industrial estate.

'Is she getting any better?' Suzy whispered to him, behind Molly's back.

Robert made a face. 'She couldn't get any worse.'

Molly was wearing heavy boots with her version of school uniform. Suzy wasn't sure that baggy cut-off trousers and a huge V-neck sweater over her skirt, shirt and tie, were strictly regulation. But she was in the sixth form now and allowed some leeway.

That night, they actually achieved the pleasant family supper Suzy had hoped for, and they talked about everything but mines and murders.

* * *

On Thursday morning Suzy felt ready to cope with the commute again and set off for Manchester.

It was a busy day on *Living Lies*. She still hankered after the celebrity special, but she didn't want to incite mutiny in the team.

The contributors for the next series were looking good. There were several secret charity workers, a few surreptitious entertainers, including the director of a major bank who was a burlesque artist, and an elderly grandma who had a secret life with a thirty-year-old lover. The skill was in the tone of the films, but after a decade the team had got that right.

At five o'clock Suzy left them looking through more applicants, took a taxi to the Premier Inn where she left her bag, and then walked to St Peter's Square to get the Metro Link to Altrincham.

It was a cool, dark evening, but not wet, and the market town had a welcoming feel. Goose Green was an attractive old area behind the station; the wine bar lights glowed welcomingly. Suzy went in and blinked, getting her bearings. And then she saw Ellie, sitting at the bar. Except of course it wasn't Ellie. It was Carrie. Slightly younger, blonde, slimmer, though of course Ellie had been in thick clothes and a ski jacket, wrapped in a duvet in the chalet basement.

'Carrie? I'm Suzy.'

'Hi, take a seat — a bar stool, anyway.' Carrie's voice sounded familiar, with a Manchester accent she shared with her sister.

Suzy ordered a red wine for herself and another large white for Carrie, who said, 'I'm drinking too much. I have been since Ellie died.'

'It must be very difficult . . .'

'Of course it is!' Carrie sounded scornful, and Suzy knew she had to go carefully. Carrie's tone had changed from the phone call for some reason. Suzy was wondering how to start, when Carrie said, 'It's funny, you know, how some people won't talk about Ellie and some people can't get enough of it.

I've had one girlfriend who seemed to get some sort of thrill going over it in detail, and one male friend who was just a ghoul. It brings them out of the woodwork.'

Suzy nodded. She realized she was being tested herself. 'You look like Ellie.'

'Yes, but I'm not her. You can't recreate Ellie through me. That's what her friends want. Not that she had many friends left, by the time that man had finished with her.'

Suzy said carefully, 'I've no desire to recreate her through you. Yes, I think Ellie and I were friends, though we only met once. At least, the potential was there. She emailed me after the holiday, but it went into my spam folder. I feel terrible about it. I didn't follow it up until I was going to London two weeks ago; I sent her two emails then, but obviously there was no answer.'

'Because she was dead.'

'Exactly.'

'So why are you interested in what happened to her? Material for a TV show?' So that accounted for the change in tone. Suzy realized that Carrie had googled her, and for once she regretted the BATV award.

'As I said, this is absolutely nothing to do with my job, Carrie.'

Carrie looked into her wine glass and pursed her lips but said nothing more. Suzy went on: 'Ellie was in contact with a hostel for women survivors of domestic abuse in Cumbria, near where I live. She was asking for my help. She had confided in me about her relationship. The trouble is, we were evacuated because of possible carbon monoxide poisoning. I think I was affected. My memory of that night is really woozy.'

'And?'

'Ten days ago the woman who ran the hostel we talked about was killed in the same way as Ellie. Falling off a roof. A lot of people think it was murder. It made me think. Two women, connected to each other, killed by falling off roofs. It was too much of a coincidence for me . . .'

'So you decided to do a Miss Marple?' But Carrie's tone had softened. 'Actually, that's really interesting. You think that Ellie's lover killed them both?'

'J? Yes.'

'J?' Carrie sounded scornful again. 'You expect me to believe that Ellie confided in you, and you don't even know his name?' Then she said quietly but forcefully, in a voice like a steelier version of Ellie's, 'I'm sorry. I wanted to discuss my sister, but not with someone who either didn't really talk to her or didn't listen.' The words were shocking, but they jolted Suzy into one of those odd experiences where memory and reality overlap. She was looking at Carrie but seeing and hearing Ellie. '*I've talked to A . . . J went berserk.*'

Without knowing where it came from, she said, 'Jerry. J was for Jerry. I remember now. How could I have forgotten?'

Carrie nodded, looking more like her sister than ever. 'So, she did confide in you. Ellie was so wrapped up in that man and his rules that she hardly ever used his name, but if she told you, it means she must have really warmed to you. Jerry is right.'

Jerry was a nickname for Jermyn, Suzy thought. Of course. Now she could recall more of what she and Ellie had talked about, thanks to Carrie's resemblance to her sister. Suzy remembered slowly, that before Ellie's conversation had gone very deep, Suzy had talked about how she too wanted a change in her life, perhaps taking on more local work. Like being communications officer at St Jane's Hostel. St Jane of Annecy on the edge of the Alps where they were staying . . . what a coincidence . . . Maybe that had encouraged Ellie to confide about her abusive relationship.

'Tell me everything you know about this man, Carrie. Did you ever meet him?'

'No way. He was strictly under wraps. He met Ellie through her work about five years ago. Some church tower was falling down. St George's or something. He was with a company from the North East who specialized in stonework.'

Scott Jermyn. Of course. DecorMetal again.

Carrie went on, 'There's a big company up there which usually does this stuff. But they were booked up, so Jerry's company stepped in. He was a real charmer. He knew his stuff and Ellie was impressed. Ellie's job was a bit weird, and she fell for the fact he was interested in what she did.'

'What did she do? I thought she was in insurance?'

'Yes. But it was insurance for churches and church buildings. Ellie was always interested in churches. She qualified as an accountant. But she worked at quite a high level as an actuary in a small insurance company specializing in church roofs and stuff like that. I can see why she wouldn't have gone into detail about that with you. It's a bit obscure.'

Carrie was speaking more freely now. She had thought at first, when Ellie had talked about Jerry with such enthusiasm, that this was the man to make her sister happy. But as the months and then years went on, and Carrie never got to meet him, she became suspicious. The man seemed to control Ellie more and more. She lent him money, kept her flat available for him whenever he made his surprise visits, and dropped her friends because she never knew who Jerry would approve of or when Jerry would need her. Sometimes she had bruises or winced when Carrie embraced her. Ellie changed from the happy, bubbly person they had all loved, to someone anxious, preoccupied and depressed.

'Did you know his surname?' Suzy asked.

'Which one?' Carrie asked drily. In the end, even Ellie had been unsure about his real name. He used several surnames, Carrie said. It wasn't unusual in men running parallel lives. Suzy knew all about that from *Living Lies*. Jerry's excuse was that he had a few business ventures on the go. Just like Scott Jermyn. Classic stuff.

It was ten o'clock when Suzy left Carrie. Ellie's sister was already on her second bottle of white wine.

* * *

As she was walking to the hotel at the other end of the tram journey, Suzy rang Rachel. She had thought about her next step.

Rachel groaned. 'If it isn't first thing in the morning, it's last thing at night. What is it this time? Finding Lord Lucan?'

'Rache, this is really important. I do need you to find something out for me, and as soon as you can. But it's to do with a local church in Islington — St George's. Do you know it?'

'Not intimately. I'm Jewish, remember? But I like Christmas as a spectator. And I know the administrator.'

'Really?' Rachel's ability to befriend a huge range of unlikely people was staggering, and she was genuinely interested in all of them.

'This lady is really sharp. I met her at the Barnford History Society'.

'So Rache, could you ask her something for me? As soon as you can?'

'Okay, what?'

'They had some work done on the church tower a few years ago . . .'

'Tell me about it! The church is still in a hairnet. Falling masonry. They're always trying to raise funds. The company before last who were supposed to repair it were rubbish, apparently.'

'Rachel, this is important. I need to know the name of that company and the names of the men doing the job. Was it DecorMetal? And Scott Jermyn? I think he was Ellie's killer.'

Rachel went silent. Then she said, 'All right, Suzy. I'll ask. But please, please, be careful. If you are onto him, he could very well be onto you.'

CHAPTER TWENTY-NINE

The Lord made me have dominion over the mighty.
Judges 5:13

Suzy had a restless night. She had called Robert and updated him. He agreed that everything seemed to point to Scott Jermyn. But there was no sign of Jermyn in Tarnfield, and no one had any idea where he had gone.

'Don't do anything else, Suzy,' said Robert. 'Maybe you should stay with Ro tomorrow night?'

'What? In case Jermyn comes back to attack me? He has no idea that we're on his trail. Plus, Ro's going to see her son up in Edinburgh. And I can't foist myself on anyone else.'

'Why not stay on in the Premier Inn in Manchester and come home on Saturday?'

'Robert, the Briars is my home and I want to be there.'

'Okay. But just say the word and I'll cancel my trip to the RRA in Leeds.'

Suzy thought of Robert's face, beaming at the thought of being given his sensitive task by the Bishop of Norbridge. 'No, don't do that. Really. I won't be home till about three in the afternoon. Then *LEE'VE IT TO LEE* is coming back. He's protected me from Jermyn before, remember?

But seriously, the Briars is like Fort Knox when we use all the locks. Totally secure.'

'Well, if you're sure . . .'

'I'm sure.'

The hotel was comfortable, but Suzy wasn't. Her decision to go home the next day was vindicated when, at about three o'clock in the morning, she woke with a terrible headache. It eased after lots of water and paracetamol, but her brain still throbbed. She felt stressed out with conjecture, but she couldn't stop. She and Robert needed to find out where Jermyn had gone. Or better still, she needed to get Jed and Ro to find out. But they were increasingly sure of Geoff Black's guilt — so now she had to convince them about Scott Jermyn. And his connection with Ellie, which Carrie had confirmed. The stoneware company from the north, the smooth charmer who chatted up Ellie, the name Jermyn which could so easily become Jerry.

But DS Jackson wouldn't like that.

Suzy was tired and distracted in the office that morning, finding it hard to be enthusiastic. She left before midday and caught the train to Norbridge. On the train she tried Rachel's number but just got voicemail. The journey took under two hours, but she couldn't concentrate on anything. Her headache had come back with a vengeance. Her mind kept going over her conversation with Carrie Fox. There was one thing Carrie had said which rang a worrying bell with Suzy too.

'But why would my sister have wanted to go to a hostel in Cumbria? Just because she liked the fact that it had an Alpine patron saint? I don't think so. In fact why would she want to go to a hostel? I don't see why she needed to leave her flat at all — she could just change the locks and tell security in the building. Or if she were really scared, she could have come to stay with me. She worked from home most of the time anyway. And you say this hostel was for older women or women who had lost children. Ellie definitely doesn't fit with that!'

'I know. That worries me too. But she definitely contacted the hostel for a place. The trouble is that the other woman who was killed was the director, and she had all the information on potential residents. But her paperwork can't be found. We have no idea why Ellie would have wanted to go to St Jane's.'

Where on earth were Deborah's wretched notes? Suzy thought of what Chelsea had said about the memory stick and felt guilty for dismissing her theory with a trite remark about baby unicorns. Presumably if memory sticks could be disguised as Coke cans, they could be other things too. For the sake of something to do, Suzy googled 'novelty memory sticks' on her computer. Toys. Sausage rolls. Lipsticks. £5.99. Lipsticks!

She called Chelsea, who answered straight away. 'Can you do me a favour? Can you go to Deborah's bedroom and get me her lipstick? The bright-red one? You're right. I think it's a memory stick. If you can get it, call me and I'll come for it this afternoon. It's your afternoon off, isn't it?'

'Okay, but why don't you ask Joanne?'

'Because she'd want to look at it first and I haven't got time for that. I need to see it as soon as possible. Just trust me.'

'All right. I'll call you. Are you on a train?'

'Yes. Coming back from Manchester. I'll be home about three o'clock.'

Suzy went to pick up her car in Norbridge, and realized her headache was getting worse. She needed something stronger than paracetamol, but she wasn't sure what. She went to the big chemist in the town centre where Mandy Lewis, Lee's wife, worked. Mandy was in the pharmacy section. She looked very pale and seemed to be walking awkwardly

'Hi Mandy, still got the cramps?'

'Yep. It's bad this month. What are you after, Suzy?'

'I need something strong. I've got a thumping headache. I've had it all day.'

'Ah, what you want is Sologesic. That's what I take. We're out of shelf stock, but I think a new delivery has just come in. Tell you what, take some Ibuprofen for now and I'll bring them with me when I come over with Lee, later.'

'Oh, you'll be with him?'

'Yes. Friday night. He picks me up and takes me home and then we get our glad rags on and go off to the boogie-woogie night in Hardcastle.'

'Oh yes, I remember you mentioning it. Sounds like fun. Although the sound of any music would make my head fall off today. Good job I'm by myself for once tonight. Robert is in Leeds and Molly's over in Pelliter at a party.'

Mandy giggled. 'So you're home alone. At least you'll be able to go to bed as soon as we've gone.'

'Absolutely! Thanks Mandy.'

Suzy left the chemist and walked out into the Norbridge afternoon, but the clouds were so heavy it almost seemed like twilight. Once again, she noticed how much cooler it was than Manchester. But her head seemed easier. Perhaps that was the effect home had on her. She drove slowly to Tarnfield and, on a whim, drove around the Green and looked at Tarnfield House. It was all locked up. No sign of Scott Jermyn.

At the Briars, she felt the unusual silence. The cat was out on the prowl somewhere. The house was calm and warm, and she started to feel better. Suzy made some tea and toast, eating it with the Ibuprofen, sitting in the wicker armchair. Still no message from Rachel, but her friend's fact-finding mission would take time. A text message pinged through, but it was from Chelsea:

> *No chance to get stick yet. Don't worry. Guess wot got a bike now. Old one of Trace's. Love it. Will bike down with lippy after 5 when I've done my washing. Can't stay having supper with my nan.*

It was warm in the kitchen and to her own surprise Suzy dozed off. When she woke it was nearly five o'clock and someone was knocking at the front door. It was too early for Chelsea. Feeling dopey, Suzy went to answer it. Lee and Mandy were both there.

'Hiya!' Lee grinned. 'Have you remembered we're calling round? I know it's dark, but I can have a look at the leak in the attic from the inside. Then with me torch I can go up yon ladder and have a quick decko outside too. Mandy's with me but she's not feelin' too bright.'

'Come in,' Suzy said. 'Oh, thanks for the painkillers, Mandy. I'm feeling a bit better. I'll get the money and make some tea in a minute. Make yourself at home in the kitchen.'

She indicated to Lee to follow her upstairs; she left him feeling the wet wallpaper in the attic and tutting. Downstairs, Mandy seemed paler and more uncomfortable than ever. Suzy had just poured the tea when her mobile rang.

It was Rachel. Suzy said, 'Mandy, help yourself to sugar if you want it. I'll just answer this call, if you don't mind.' Mandy smiled weakly and spooned sugar into her cup.

Suzy walked into the living room to be polite. 'Hi Rache,' she said. 'I'm keeping my voice down because I've got visitors. The roofer and his wife. More leaks. What did you find out?'

'Well, probably nothing of any real interest, I'm sorry to say. I went round to St George's to see the woman I know. She remembers the company that came to repair the church tower very well, even though it was five years ago, because a few weeks later they had some lead stolen from the roof and she said she was sure it was them, but she couldn't prove it.'

'Sounds just like my dodgy company . . .'

'Well, they were from the north. But I think I'm going to have to disappoint you. They weren't called DecorMetal and there was no one called Scott. There were only two of them. One was called Geoff and the boss was a wide boy called Lee Lewis.'

'What? Lee Lewis and Geoff Black? Working in Islington five years ago? Are you sure? That can't be right. Lee's my roofer. He's here now.'

'Well, he was in Islington then. Quite a charmer, my friend said. Could talk the hind leg of a donkey and really fancied himself.'

'Does she know if he met Ellie Fox?'

'She can't say. She didn't know Ellie. But this guy was doing the rounds of the pubs every night.'

'But Rachel, it can't have been him. We know for a fact that Ellie's lover was called Jerry . . .'

'Oh . . . But hang on, Suzy. It's obvious.'

'What's obvious?'

'Well, it's a nickname, isn't it? Lee Lewis. Jerry Lee Lewis. Singer from the fifties. Boogie-woogie. You must have heard of him. For God's sake, Suzy, get away from him!'

'Of course — Jerry Lee Lewis. Rachel, I need to . . .'

Suzy stopped. Mandy was leaning against the door jamb. She was so pale that her eyes were luminous. But her lips were pulled tight. She could hardly stand upright, but she was blocking the way out. And in her hand was one of Suzy's long, sharp kitchen knives. Mandy was shaking. The blade of the knife whipped up and down uncontrollably in her hand.

'Mandy, what is it? Put that knife down. You could hurt yourself.'

Mandy laughed with her little-girl giggle. 'Jerry!' she shouted. 'Come down here!' Then she turned to Suzy. 'Oh, I hurt myself all the time. Don't I, Jerry?'

Lee had appeared behind her; Suzy had been vaguely aware of his heavy feet on the stairs.

'What it is, darlin'?' he said to Mandy's back; for a moment Suzy thought that Lee would gently take the weapon from Mandy's hand. But then Rachel's words superimposed themselves on her understanding. Lee was Jerry and Jerry was Ellie's killer. It was impossible but it was true.

'She knows about the London slag,' Mandy whispered.

Lee's pleasant face creased and reshaped itself into something vicious. He came up behind Mandy. With his right hand he grabbed the knife, and with his left he pulled Mandy's long blonde pigtails into a twist behind her head and yanked, bringing his knee into her back.

So Lee was a wife beater and a predator, and he'd met Ellie in Islington. Suzy was forming a new theory and somehow that made her less scared. Her brain had more to do than panic. But her theory didn't quite work. Lee could have killed Ellie. But he couldn't have killed Deborah, saviour of bullied and beaten women and Ellie's potential protector. He was working at Tarnfield House all day on the Friday Deborah died. There were witnesses.

'Stupid cow,' he said to his wife. Mandy was crying, little whimpering cries.

'I'm sorry, Jerry. It's my fault that she saw that phone. And now she's been talking to someone in London. I heard her . . .'

Lee gave his wife a smack across the back of her head with the fist holding the knife. It was a neat, practised blow designed to keep her face intact. Suzy wondered how she could have been so stupid. Who else would have a classy, real-leather indigo phone case? It must have belonged to Deborah, but it was in Mandy's bag.

While Lee was holding Mandy by the hair, he couldn't advance on Suzy. She picked up her phone. Rachel was still there. Suzy could hear her friend at the other end.

'Rache!' Suzy screamed.

Then Rachel started shouting, 'For God's sake, Suzy, what's going on?'

Lee flung Mandy onto the hall floor and advanced into the living room with the knife. When he got to Suzy, he snatched Suzy's mobile with his left hand and brought it down on the coffee table, smashing it. He was very strong. Then he pushed behind Suzy, and she felt the coldness of the knife on the back of her neck. She could smell Lee's sweat and feel his spittle on her nape. 'Move!' he spat. 'Mandy, open the back door. Leave it open and follow me with them copper pans. They're heavy, mind.'

Mandy scurried to her feet like a crab and scuttled into the kitchen. Suzy followed her, amazed at how calm she was feeling. Delayed shock. But she also knew Chelsea would be on her way on her bike, as soon as she could, and that Rachel also knew what was happening. Lee's murders were elaborate, made to look like accidents. He wouldn't just knife her, she felt sure. He could already have done that. He prodded her painfully, but she walked calmly through her kitchen as if on a film set, and out into the cold rain. Everything looked unreal but crystal clear. Lee had brought a plain pickup truck this time — no cheery van. He and Mandy had planned this, Suzy thought, after she had been daft enough to tell Mandy she would be home alone. They must have already been worried that Suzy had recognized Deborah's phone in Mandy's bag, but the call from Rachel, which Mandy had just heard, had convinced them Suzy knew too much.

'Get into the back. Lie down,' Lee growled. Suzy did as she was told, and the smell of the truck and the force of his arms as he pressed her down frightened her for the first time. But she didn't struggle. He pushed her into the corner, and she slumped, praying that he wouldn't tie her up. He had a rope in his hands, but then Mandy came struggling out of the kitchen with three of the smaller copper pans.

'I canna carry the big 'uns,' she whimpered. She was wearing Suzy's rubber gloves.

'Oh, for Christ's sake!' Lee gave Mandy the knife. 'Watch her. Don't let her move. I'll get the other pans.' Suzy watched as he pulled on a pair of huge leather workman's gloves and strode back into the kitchen.

'Mandy,' Suzy whispered, 'it doesn't have to be like this. They weren't period pains, were they? He beats you up.'

'So? He needs to keep me under control.' Then she said with pride, 'But he doesn't slap the others nearly as much . . . He loves me best.'

Lee came striding out of the house and left the back door swinging. He hurled the remaining copper pans into the truck, just missing Suzy's curled-up legs. The rain was coming down heavily now.

'Get in the truck!' he snarled at Mandy. He had dropped the rope, and now he was in a hurry. With one hand he forced Suzy down, though she went as floppy as she could, and with the other he pulled out the aging tonneau over the open back of the pickup. He pulled it across and laced the sides. Suzy lay there in the dark, aware she could see light where the canvas didn't quite meet the edges. It had started to rain heavily; water was coming in. Lee's truck set off and bounced up the track from the Briars. Suzy could sense when he stopped with a jolt at the main road.

Lee's window was open, and she heard him swearing. 'Effin cyclist!' he shouted.

Suzy forced her hand through the gap where the canvas didn't meet the side and waved. As the pickup took off again the jolt nearly twisted her wrist, and she pulled her hand back inside.

* * *

On the bike, Chelsea, real name Siobhan, watched the truck kangaroo hop madly over the rim of the track and brake. She had braked too and waited for the truck to take priority. She wondered what that aggressive pickup driver had been doing at Suzy's house, and waited for the vehicle to move away. As the truck turned onto the main road from the track to the Briars, she saw a hand poke out from under the cover. Even in the pelting rain she recognized the square black goth nails she had painted a week ago.

Siobhan wasn't sure what had happened, but she knew Suzy shouldn't be in the back of that truck. She pedalled like fury after it, hidden by the dark and driving rain.

* * *

Robert had left his car at Norbridge Station and taken the train to Leeds. Then he took a cab to the RRA headquarters, which took about thirty minutes. He'd had some difficulty reconciling the Rural Reformation Association with Leeds, a city he didn't know well but which he associated with dark satanic mills rather than rural life. But the RRA HQ was in a beautiful stone building near Horsforth, which he thought was a lovely market town as he passed through it at dusk in the taxi. A quick google revealed it had more church buildings than most places, ranging from a Roman Catholic teacher training college, now part of Leeds University, to a clutch of evangelical chapels.

He remarked on this to the priest who met him and showed him his room, with lovely views over the moors.

'Yes. We like to think that we steer a middle path,' the priest said. 'We're evangelical, of course, but we're not excluding. There's some beautiful stuff in the prayer book.' Robert was delighted and surprised to hear it said. He wondered if perhaps Jim Bentley's views were a little too strong even for the RRA. That was encouraging. His host went on, 'We have evensong said at five o'clock. Yes, I thought that would surprise you. Then drinks before supper. We find everyone likes to turn in at about nine. Time for rest and private prayer.' So far so good.

Robert changed and went down to the chapel, a simple room in what seemed to be an austere but attractive barn conversion. He was pleased that they used the traditional Anglican liturgy, saying the Magnificat and Nunc Dimittis and one of Robert's favourite prayers: 'Lighten our darkness, we beseech thee, O Lord . . .' It timed beautifully with a fading of the light through the large plain windows.

Afterwards, with a glass of wine, Robert made sure he ended up next to Archdeacon Bentley. The quiet, peaceful atmosphere seemed to have mellowed the Ven Jim. He seemed more relaxed here, less aggressive. Perhaps he felt safe.

'That was a nice service,' Robert said neutrally.

'Yes, very pleasant. Of course tomorrow we'll really have to get our teeth into some difficult issues.'

'Absolutely,' Robert agreed.

'We have to ensure we get the right people on our church councils.'

'Of course.'

The archdeacon looked at him, surprised. 'I'm glad you appreciate that.'

'Of course I do. It's so difficult. We are only just quorate at some meetings at All Saints in Tarnfield.'

'Really? Even in Tarnfield?'

'Yes. I expect if we can't get the volunteers, the diocese will have to do more to support us.'

The archdeacon made a face. 'We're very busy, you know . . .'

'Yes. So I think it's terribly important to ensure that the good, capable people we have on our councils feel encouraged to stay. If we lost anyone at Tarnfield we would have to come to the diocese for help.'

'But we mustn't let standards drop — our volunteers do need to comply with biblical principles.'

'But sometimes those are quite hard to evaluate, don't you think?'

'No, I don't. The Bible is the Word of God.'

'But as understood by men, of course. Some things can be tricky to interpret. Or apply. Like the food laws in Leviticus, as we discussed.'

Jim Bentley pursed his lips as if to say something angry, so Robert cut in quickly. 'Of course, I really do understand about biblical principles. Ten years ago I would have agreed with you about same-sex relationships. But things change. The trouble is that the Old Testament is very clear on rules. But the New Testament is much vaguer. It seems to be about applying compassion to the individual rather than having a strict code. Isn't that why we call the Testament new?'

'Theologian, are you?' The Ven Jim said, raising his eyebrows.

'Forgive me. Just an amateur.' The Ven Jim had the graciousness to smile. Robert went on. 'But you know, when you meet good, high-principled church people who give up so much of their time as volunteers, and who are struggling with those rules . . .'

The archdeacon was at least listening. Robert took a risk. 'It's like that hymn. By Frederick Faber. You can't fault Faber on biblical principles. He wrote, "*We make God's love too narrow by strict limits of our own. And we magnify His strictness with a zeal he will not own . . .*"'

'Of course I know that hymn. "There's a Wideness in God's Mercy." You think I'm being stricter than God?'

'A little unkinder, perhaps. But I don't think you're really an unkind man. I suspect you understand more than you choose to show . . .'

The two men looked at each other. 'Interesting, Mr Clark,' the Ven Jim said. 'I'd like to chat more to you.'

Robert said, 'That would be good. There are so many ways of doing things, God knows . . .'

'He certainly does! If that's the right pronoun, to quote the Bishop of Norbridge,' said the Ven Jim, referring to their tetchy meeting. They both laughed. It was a bit of a breakthrough. Jim was sounding almost human.

Then Robert felt his phone, on silent, reverberating in his pocket. He wondered who it could be. Suzy wouldn't try to contact him during the supper unless it was urgent. Anyway, it might be a good moment to leave the archdeacon. Quit while you're ahead. 'Excuse me, Jim. I'd better take this . . .'

He went out into the corridor and saw it was Rachel calling. Odd.

'Robert!' her voice was loud and taut. 'Suzy's in terrible danger . . .'

CHAPTER THIRTY

So let all thine enemies perish, O Lord: but let them that love him be as the sun when he goeth forth in his might.
Judges 5:31

The pickup truck lurched on to the industrial estate. Suzy felt the pitted road surface and the way the truck moved more wildly across the broad, unused concrete. Water was pouring down under the covering now; Suzy was soaked and shivering. The truck stopped and she heard Lee and Mandy talking, his voice angry and growling, hers still with the little-girl tone. Suzy realized she had never seen Mandy without Lee except when she was working in the chemist's shop. It was like the relationship Joanne had described — she was never allowed to be alone or with her own friends or family.

Suzy heard a noise which she thought sounded like rickety wooden doors being scraped back and opened; then Lee started the engine again. She sensed that he was driving the pickup inside. The truck stopped, and a moment later Lee started pulling back the tonneau. He tugged Suzy by one arm.

'I'm coming,' she said.

'Shut your mouth!' said Lee and raised his fist.

'Don't, Lee,' said Mandy. 'If her face's bruised, they might realize it wasn't an accident.'

'Get out,' Lee said. He pushed her out of the truck into the rain, and then through large rickety double doors. Suzy was shaky and her eyes needed to adjust. She saw that she was in one of the larger derelict garages on the outskirts of the industrial estate. It was long and low, and lit with dim light bulbs. Lee kept hold of her, but when she glanced around, she saw him pulling the doors to with his free arm. He slid a large new metal bolt across. Hardly high security, but who was looking?

Lee pushed her roughly in the small of her back. 'There's nothing to see. Get over there.' He prodded her over to a chair against the wall. Next to it was another chair with a doll-like figure on it lolling to one side, tied to the back of the chair. There was a makeshift gag from an old striped towel across her mouth. The figure looked up when Suzy landed on the next chair.

'Leila!'

But then Lee held Suzy down and she felt a filthy, petrol-smelling cloth being tied over her own mouth and rope going around her waist and shoulders. She retched and for the first time felt screaming mindless terror, but she made herself breathe as deeply as she could through her nose. She mustn't lose it. Help would come. Rachel knew what was happening and would have called the police. Siobhan would have found the Briars with the back door open and the pans stolen. Lee's idea must have been that Robert or Molly, returning the next day, would find signs of a burglary, and Suzy gone, victim of the metal gang. But Siobhan would have been there within minutes of the pickup leaving. She would see the open door, the missing pans and that Suzy had disappeared, and she would call the police.

But they wouldn't know where Lee had taken her. Suzy couldn't afford to think about that missing connection. She would be found before too long, she was sure.

Lee was already flinging the copper pans onto a mound of metal. There were three or four separate piles of stuff.

When he'd finished, Lee came up to the two women tied to the chairs and put his face close to theirs. Even in the dimness Suzy could see his bloodshot eyes and the open pores on his weather-beaten face. Before he had seemed almost attractive, she thought, with his cheery grin, tan and muscular body. Now, though, he was repulsive.

'I'm going to load up the big truck,' he said, 'and then I'm going to deal with you two. Like I've told you, you've served your purpose, Leila; you're a liability now. You're going to be found dead in a mineshaft. Suicide. First though, I've got to get you to breathe in this water.' He kicked forward a filthy tub, with murky water inside. 'Then when they find you, if they do, they'll know you threw yourself down the shaft and drowned.'

He looked at Suzy. 'I haven't had time to think about what to do with you. It can't be anything too smart, like the others. But I'll come up with something.' He kicked the leg of the chair so she juddered. 'You know what? I think it's in character for you to have run after those metal thieves who stole your pans, and they'll have mown you down, picked up your body and dumped it.'

Lee stared at her, his face only inches from hers, working maniacally. 'So when the stuff is on board and the truck's really heavy, I'm going to run over you and they'll find your body by the roadside in a ditch up by the mines, maybe in a few days' time.'

'Jerry, we need to get the stuff to DecorMetal,' Mandy said. 'We should get out of here.'

But Lee's tongue was running away with him. He liked seeing the fear and the astonishment in their eyes, Suzy thought. She looked back at him blankly, daring him to go on talking. He couldn't resist it, although it meant wasting precious time. He barked at her: 'You don't get it do you? I had two big consignments coming in and Deborah was onto me and Black. But Black was losing it. That's why I killed him. And her. So don't get any ideas. You and this old cow will be next.' He kicked Leila's chair so it jumped and came down sharply on the concrete floor. Leila's eyes rolled in terror.

Then Lee snapped his head up and listened. He stopped, stock still. 'Don't move, Mand,' he said to his wife.

'No.' A voice came from the back of the building. 'Good idea. Don't move.' Out of the shadows, Scott Jermyn advanced on Lee and his wife. He was carrying a shotgun.

* * *

At the RRA headquarters in Horsforth, Robert raced back into the drinks reception and up to where Jim Bentley and their hosts were sipping their wine. They looked at him, startled and alarmed.

'I need to get to the railway station — now,' Robert said. 'My wife is in trouble with intruders in our house. I must get home as fast as I can.' It would be half an hour to the station, then two hours to Norbridge, then fifteen minutes home. That's if he could get a train straight away. If only he'd brought the car. 'I have to go now,' he said. 'Can someone pack my bag and get it back for me? I must leave.'

Jim Bentley came forward. 'What's happened to Suzy?'

'I think she's been attacked. It's ghastly . . .'

Jim said, 'I'll take you on the Harley. We can do it in two hours. The RRA will look after your belongings. Come with me now. I've got another helmet and set of leathers in the pannier — they're very old but they'll do. Don't ask. Just follow me outside and get into them.'

Within minutes, rider and passenger were making their way north out of Horsforth.

* * *

'Stay there, Lewis,' said Jermyn. His voice was different, deeper, with no Estuary accent. 'You,' he said to Mandy, 'untie these women. Now!'

He waved the gun in a threatening way. For a minute Suzy thought Mandy was going to do as he asked; then suddenly, screaming in pain and rage, she hurtled at Jermyn's long, thin legs. The gun went off. In the dimness Suzy had no idea what was happening till she saw that Jermyn was on the floor and Lee now had the gun. He was breathing in a rasping way and waving the gun at everyone else.

'Get up, you cow!' he said to Mandy, giving her a kick. 'One smart move doesn't mean you can relax. Take hold of this.' He handed her the weapon. 'If Jermyn moves, shoot him in the head. We've gotta get out of here. God knows who he's told. But he's got his fingers in so many dodgy pies no one will be surprised he's dead.' He kicked Jermyn hard in the stomach and growled, 'I'm going to load the stuff. Then we'll shoot these two hinnies, and we'll buzz off. No time for smart thinking now, but that's too bad.'

Lee walked towards the big old double doors of the garage. But he didn't get far. With a splitting crack the flimsy doors smashed open as another pickup, a Subaru complete with bull bars, came through, crashing into the wooded slats, which splintered as the lock gave way. At the wheel, hunched, was Molly. Beside her was Rafi Hossein from the Star of Bengal, black hair flopping in his eyes. And behind them, on a bike, was Siobhan.

The Subaru did a dramatic emergency stop inches away from Lee. 'Be careful, Molly!' screamed Suzy. 'Stay in the car!' But the words were just a guttural screech through the towelling gag.

Then Scott Jermyn managed to get up. Mandy was blinded by the headlights, and Lee waited, for a just a nano-second too long, staring at the car and the kids inside. Scott took the gun from Mandy as if it were a twig and pushed her to one side, then he brought the butt of the gun down on Lee's head. Mandy screamed and Scott knocked her down again.

'Don't worry,' Scott said to Suzy. 'I'm on your side.'

In the melee, Molly and Rafi had climbed out of the vehicle, shaken and wide-eyed. 'Mum!' Molly ran over, grabbed the towel from Suzy's mouth and cradled her mother's head against her chest. 'Oh, Mum . . .' The she started to untie her. 'I drove safely. I really did. I remembered what you said about stopping distances . . .' Suzy laughed and cried at the same time.

Jermyn had the gun pointed at Mandy, who was whimpering on the floor. With the gun, he took control. 'Suzy, take the gag off that other woman. But don't untie her until we know whose side she's on. I can't believe I was blindsided by this one here.' He indicated Mandy with his foot, and she yelped, but he didn't kick her.

Suzy took off Leila's gag. The other woman was crying loudly, a sort of wailing.

'Thank God!' Leila sobbed and choked and kept on sobbing. 'Oh, thank God. Suzy, I swear I didn't kill him. I didn't kill Geoff Black. Lee killed him and put my prints on the mallet. I swear it. And he made me steal the halo.'

The halo? What was she talking about? Suzy shook her head. It was too much to take in. As soon as she could stand without shaking, she left Leila and wobbled over to Molly, and they embraced again. 'What happened?' Suzy asked her shivering daughter. 'Why were you here? Why aren't you in Pelliter, at a party?'

'We were going.' Rafi Hossein had a surprisingly deep, gravelly voice, but still had the slim build of an adolescent. His thick black hair flopped over his face. 'I passed my test in September. I was going to drive Molls to Pelliter, but she asked me if I'd take her driving first, so we were here anyway.' He looked sheepish.

Molly said, surprisingly calmly, 'Then Siobhan called me when she saw the truck come into the old garage. I swapped numbers with her last week. It was lucky we were here.' She looked suddenly embarrassed and, even in the circumstances, Suzy felt a surge of shock that Molly and Rafi might have stopped to kiss and cuddle in the privacy of the deserted industrial estate. 'Siobhan said she was at the estate on her bike, and someone had taken you off in a truck. She was outside this building and told me you were inside. Rafi tried to open the doors but we couldn't. So I just drove into them.' Molly suddenly started to cry. 'I'm sorry about the pickup, Rafi . . .'

'It's just an old banger that my bro got off a farmer,' Rafi said huskily. 'It doesn't look too damaged. I thought you were amazing, Molls.'

'Yes, you were!' Siobhan came to put her arms round Molly.

'If you hadn't done it,' Jermyn said, 'Lee would have shot me and your mother. You saved her life.' That made Molly cry even more.

Crumpled at Scott Jermyn's feet, Mandy moaned. Lee was unconscious just a few feet away.

'I need to call the police,' Jermyn said. 'It will be a while before they get here.'

'I've done it.' Siobhan said.

Suzy felt faint, went back to her chair and collapsed, with Siobhan, Molly and Rafi around her. Next to her, Leila was still crying. Molly asked, 'What happened at home, Mum?'

Suzy explained how Lee and Mandy had taken her off in the pickup.

'But he could have knifed you in our kitchen!' Molly said in horror.

'No, that's not how he operates. It has to be clever stuff. He killed Deborah Arbiter, somehow. He told me so. And he killed Ellie, the woman in Islington.'

'I think the police will find out more from him when he comes round,' said Jermyn. 'I bet he's a squealer. It'll be all about him.' He closed his eyes and leaned back against the wall. He'd had a bad knock himself. He'd tied Mandy up lightly with a rope Rafi fetched from Lee's pickup. But while Lee was unconscious on the floor, she had no will left for fighting. She lay and moaned, muttering to herself.

It seemed to be forever before DS Jackson turned up, with his boss the detective inspector. When the two police cars arrived, Scott Jermyn went forward to shake hands.

'I'm Scott Jermyn, private investigator.'

Jed nodded, and then took in the rest of the scene.

The detective inspector said, 'We'll need statements as soon as possible. Ambulances are on the way. Jed, you know these people. Fill them in.'

'Suzy, we managed to get hold of Ro. She's coming back from Edinburgh and she'll be here very soon to be with you too. And there's been a message from your husband, via the RRA in Leeds.' Jed must be the only policeman in Britain who would know what the RRA was, Suzy thought, feeling strangely lucid and even giggly. Shock, she thought, still delayed but coming quickly over the hill. Jed said, 'Robert's on his way home. On a motorbike, apparently.'

Scott Jermyn looked up sharply and then looked away. An ambulance had arrived. Lee was photographed and taken away on a stretcher. He had started to groan. Mandy howled like a wounded animal until the police let her go with him. Then came more pictures and brief statements. Suzy was cold and wet, and starting to shake again; Leila was so stiff and sore, she couldn't stand. A second ambulance arrived to take them to Norbridge General. As they were being helped inside the roar of a large motorbike came thundering down the concrete stretch to the derelict garage.

Robert got off, unstrapped his motorcycle helmet and ran to Suzy for a long embrace. Eventually she said tearfully, 'How did you know to come here?'

'Texts from Molly.'

'Great. But you look ridiculous in that leather gear,' she said. 'Like Evel Knievel!'

'You're showing your age,' Robert replied. But it was a relief. Suzy was still her old self. Then he watched as Scott Jermyn strode forward.

'Hello, Jim,' he said.

'Hello, Scott,' the archdeacon replied.

'Ah,' said Robert. 'Scott, I think I might be wearing your leathers. They're rather long in the leg for me.'

* * *

It was an endless, fractured night. Suzy was eventually discharged from the hospital and sent home to the Briars, but Leila was kept in with pneumonia. She had been held prisoner by Lee and Mandy at their bungalow, but then Lee had moved her to the freezing-cold garage.

In the early morning, in the kitchen, Robert and Suzy sat hand in hand, and Ro told them what had happened overnight at the police HQ in Norbridge. 'Mandy won't say anything. But when Lee came round, he couldn't stop talking. He cheerfully confessed to killing Ellie when he was asked about the metal thieving. He couldn't resist showing off about how he had befriended her deliberately when he found out what her job was. Then he had hacked into her PC to find out about unprotected churches which had applied to her company for insurance. None of these churches had Tagpaint, so he knew he could get away with it. He robbed dozens of churches that way over the last five years.'

'How did he get away with killing her?'

'Mandy had an endless supply of antidepressant drugs and sedatives from the pharmacy. Lee sedated Ellie, tipped the booze and pills down her throat, left the bottle with the label torn and illegible, and turfed her over the balcony. Then he left her flat via the back stairs wearing his hi-vis jacket and hard hat. People just don't notice workmen.'

'Why did he do it?'

'She was leaving him, and he couldn't take it. She had no right to, he said.'

'And why did he kill Geoff Black?'

'Because he was "losing it", to quote Lewis. Black was terrified of Deborah and he'd become a liability. Lewis forced booze and pills down Black's throat too. Then he made the murder look just like the Gentileschi picture. Lewis had an old tent apparently, with iron tent pegs, which he boasted about planting in the truck. He set up the whole thing to incriminate Leila. That was a prime example of his smart thinking.'

'Why did he want to implicate Leila?'

'So we wouldn't suspect anyone else. And she was a liability. He had been using her, after meeting her in the hostel grounds when he was doing the gutters in September. She went out for a smoke, and he was eating his lunch. She was an obvious dupe. They had a pretty intense thing going, largely on Facetime or over the phone. She walked out of the hostel last Thursday thinking they were going off to a new life together, which Lewis finds very funny as she's so much older than him. He fitted her up for Black's murder, so no one would suspect him, and he planned to kill her so it would look like suicide.'

'Poor Leila. So that was why she kept saying that Black had killed Deborah. To keep Lee in the clear, because she was besotted with him. But how did Lee kill Deborah? He wasn't anywhere near St Jane's when she died.'

'He's boasted about undermining the stucco parapet so the slightest touch would send it crashing down. He scraped out the mortar and replaced the bricks on top of each other but with nothing to hold them together. Then he tempted Deborah up there somehow, knowing that she would brace her foot against the parapet and it would fall apart and she would plunge to her death. That's how he killed her. She wasn't pushed, but he made the roof so dangerous she was bound to fall. Then he made sure he had an alibi. But that's as far as we've got. He's gone quiet now.'

'That's odd, when he boasts about everything else. I wonder if there are any clues on Deborah's phone about how he got her onto the roof? Maybe that's why he stole it and Mandy had it. Perhaps he lured her with a conversation. Or a text . . .'

Ro said sharply, 'Her phone? Deborah's phone? He stole it?'

'Yes. I've only just realized what I saw. A phone in a purple case. Deborah's. In Mandy's bag. That's why they were onto me. Then Rache's phone call made it really urgent to silence me.'

Ro leapt up from the kitchen chair. 'Crikey, Suzy, you should have said! We need to search Mandy's bag and find that phone.'

* * *

After Ro had gone, Suzy went to bed. She kept her filthy jeans from the night before by the bed; when Robert suggested they should go in the washing machine she said 'no' before shutting her eyes again. The previous night in the old garage, before the police came, Siobhan had said, 'You take this' and pressed a bright-red lipstick into Suzy's hand.

As she plunged in and out of consciousness, Suzy kept reminding herself that Deborah's memory stick was in her jeans pocket, and that she wanted to read the files on it before she gave it to the police. But first, she needed to sleep. The sun came up slowly, over high fells white with the very first frost of winter. Robert held her hand until she lost consciousness.

CHAPTER THIRTY-ONE

Ask counsel, we pray thee, of God, that we may know whether our way which we go shall be prosperous.
Judges 18:5

Suzy slept from eight o'clock on Saturday morning until four in the afternoon. She was woken by Robert saying softly, 'Scott's here, Suzy. With a big bunch of flowers.'

Suzy levered herself out of bed. She felt disorientated and stiff. She showered, put on her favourite pyjamas, her thick fleecy dressing gown and furry bootees, and padded down to the kitchen where the two men were drinking tea and eating fresh brownies. Robert pushed a mug of tea over to her. Scott looked different. He had rather nice dark eyes when he wasn't screwing up his face making stupid remarks. And he had saved her life.

He said, 'I owe you an apology, Suzy. About making a pass that night at the party. But what happened was that I needed to get into my office without a confrontation with Lewis. He was trying to get into my computer.'

'So, you weren't overwhelmed with lust for me?'

'Er, no. I have to tell you, making passes at women isn't really my thing.' Robert was smiling knowingly. 'Rob sussed it out. I'm gay. I know you're not going to believe it, but I'm up here in the Workhaven area because Jim Bentley and I were once an item.'

'What?' Suzy looked at Robert in disbelief, but Robert nodded. She was astonished. And miffed. She worked in media. She was supposed to be the one with the gaydar.

'Jim and I were together for a few years. I was never divorced, but when I split from him that's how it felt. Jim was too religious for me. He was already a keen churchman with a great reputation, but our relationship was a big problem for him. I didn't help. I was angry and intolerant. After we parted, he got ordained and fast-tracked up the Church hierarchy. He had tremendous energy and started all these new churches. I'm afraid I went off the rails a bit . . . still am really . . .'

Suzy nodded. 'I reckoned it was coke at the party . . .'

'Yes. I'm quitting that now. And less booze too. The jack-the-lad persona isn't entirely false, I'm sorry to say. And after Jim, I was always getting involved with poor losers I'd push too far and then dump, basically because they weren't Jim. Occasionally Jim and I would meet up, maybe go out on the bike . . . which would cause a crisis for him. But that's why he still has my leathers after all these years.'

'So you came up here after him?'

'Yep. I decided about a year ago that I'd win him back, whatever it took. But he ignored my messages. Then, when a friend in the Met told me that a lawyer in Cumbria was looking for a private investigator with expertise in metal commodities, it was like an answer to a prayer. Or as Jim would say, it *was* an answer to a prayer. So I came up here to work for Deborah. And see Jim.'

'So how did that go?'

'Not well. He really freaked. I guess that caused him to have a bit of a meltdown. He'd rejected me and rejected the truth about himself. We've been talking about it overnight. Mind you, he has a lot of respect for Robert. He thought Robert guessed.'

'Well, not about you, until we got to the industrial estate,' Robert said, 'but I had a hunch about Jim.'

Suzy paused to take this in. Her mind felt surprisingly clear. Still shock, she supposed. 'So, basically, as well as this astonishing relationship with the Ven Jim, you came to Tarnfield to work for Deborah? Like Jarrold.'

'Correct. Jarrold was investigating as a geologist, but Deborah wanted somebody on the inside of the business at DecorMetal. She'd had a tip-off about metal thieving in the north and she reckoned DecorMetal was on the receiving end. It was easy for me to ingratiate myself with the company. I really do know my stuff when it comes to metal theft. Whoever tipped Deborah off had got it right, but that source dried up, Deborah said. She suspected Geoff Black, but I reckoned he wasn't the boss man. Not enough nerve. I was looking for someone who was pulling Black's strings.'

'And how did you get on to Lee Lewis?'

'On the Sunday after Deborah died there was a full moon. I heard a noise, went out and saw Black and Lewis jacking up the Hosseins' Prius and nicking the catalytic converter. Lewis was clearly in charge, but I needed to watch him after that to get proof that he was behind all the thefts. I'd already made sure he would be staying around Tarnfield when I put him onto doing your roof, so I could keep an eye on him. I'm sorry about that too, by the way. He was an awful roofer!'

Suzy laughed. Scott had a sense of humour. Robert said, 'And what about Geoff Black?'

'Black was Deborah's first suspect, like I said. So I hired him to do some building work for me. Then I realized Black didn't have the bottle to be in charge of the metal thieving business and I asked the foreman on my building work to give him the boot. But Lewis had already killed Geoff Black, in that funny way with the tent peg. I gather on the QT that Lewis has confessed to that.'

'Yes,' said Suzy. 'We've heard that too. And what's happening to DecorMetal now?'

'Not much. There's this planning debacle over the Arbiter mines, and when it comes out that they've been dealing knowingly in stolen metal they'll be finished. Lewis must have reckoned he had to get his stash of scrap to them asap, hence all this activity. I've been following him for the last few days.'

'So you were up here all the time. Where did you stay?'

'In a bothy in the fir plantation. I don't recommend it. I'm not really your outdoor type. Talking of which, Deborah told me months ago all about hiring Jarrold. That's how I had his phone number. We were both part of her big picture, which was to expose DecorMetal. After she died, I worried in case Jarrold was implicated in her death. A sort of double agent. I'd never met him, so I invited him to my little soirée. But one chat was enough to convince me he was boringly straight in every respect. Gorgeous though.'

Suzy laughed. 'So what will you do now? About Jim Bentley for a start?'

'That depends on him. I can make any adjustments he wants, including celibacy if it's really necessary. We're both older and wiser. I need to change my crazy lifestyle anyway. I've been way over the top. Time to calm down. I love Jim. And I accept his faith. I might even give it a go myself.'

Suzy smiled. 'One last thing. Who really owns Tarnfield House on the Green?'

Scott smiled. 'Good question. Who do you think? Deborah, of course. Or after probate, I suppose, the hostel.'

Deborah. How many secrets had she had? Suzy needed to read what was on the USB lipstick as soon as she could.

'Anyway,' said Scott, 'I'd better be off. I suppose we'll all be tied up in this for a while. For the moment I'm in the Holiday Inn in Workhaven. Maybe next week I'll see you in church!'

'And come to supper soon,' said Suzy. 'When I'm up to cooking.'

Scott's face lit up and he looked totally different. 'I'd love that,' he said. 'If your brownies are anything to go by!'

Suzy smiled guiltily. She still couldn't bring herself to tell him they'd been baked by her daughter.

* * *

When he'd gone, Suzy went up to the back bedroom office. She had put the lipstick in her dressing gown pocket and fingered it from time to time during Scott's visit. She slotted it into her PC. Suddenly lines and lines of files appeared on her screen. It was true, Deborah had taken copious notes. Many were names Suzy recognized, but there were dozens of other files which meant nothing to Suzy — something called Be Profit Investments, numerous accounts spreadsheets, lists of contacts, dozens of presentations to various funding organizations, and charities, including one for vandalized churches. Masses of material. And many of the files were cross-referenced.

She noticed that Ellie had a separate file in her own name and wasn't under 'Residents' or 'Applicants'. Suzy went straight to this file. In it there was a copy of one email from Ellie, but from a new email account called eltodeb@gmail. It seemed that after the skiing holiday Ellie had opened this account purely to get in touch with Deborah, and had presumably used another device which Jerry couldn't access. The email was very circumspect but crucial.

Dear Ms Arbiter,
I would really appreciate a telephone conversation with you. I came across your name and your work when staying in the Alps earlier this year, where I met someone from Tarnfield.

So Ellie hadn't mentioned Suzy's name. Perhaps she was disappointed and hurt that Suzy hadn't replied to her. Perhaps she was just being very careful. The email went on:

It was a fortuitous meeting. I have of course googled you and seen that, as well as running your unique hostel, you're involved with a Church of England charity dealing with the restitution of damaged or vandalized churches after metal thefts, something I understand all too well through my job. I believe I know something which would be of interest and help to you. I'm an insurance actuary, dealing in church insurance for a small but key insurance company. It's taken me a long time to work this out, but I believe I am involved with a man who is using information obtained from my PC to rob churches in the north. One thing I do know about him is that he's based in North Cumbria. He let that slip when we first met. But he uses aliases. I've just terminated my relationship with him, and he's gone to ground. If I could be given a short-term place at your hostel, in the role of an abused woman (something I know all too much about, sadly) between us we could identify him.

This is all rather complicated, so could we speak? My number is below.

Hoping to hear from you.

Eleanor

There was the date of a phone call between Deborah and Ellie. Ellie must have confided her suspicions about her lover, even if she didn't get very far, and Deborah must have offered her the room at the hostel, as noted in Joanne's file.

And Deborah had saved that room even when the communication ceased at Ellie's end. Deborah was three hundred miles away from the Barnford Estate and knew nothing about Ellie's death. She would have thought, as Joanne had suggested, that Ellie had been intercepted by her abuser, or returned to him, or moved on in a different way. Clearly Deborah hadn't had enough information to identify Lee Lewis as the metal thief. But Ellie had planted the seeds, and Deborah's suspicion fell first on Geoff Black. Ellie's file said *Ref: Geoff Black.*

And *Ref: Scott Jermyn.*

Just as Scott had said, he had been employed by Deborah as a spy with DecorMetal. He had known about everything the company was up to, and he had also been investigating Black. Scott had a huge expense account mainly for refurbishing Tarnfield House. *Ref: DecorMetal.*

Deborah's file on the company was lengthy. It went back to the eighties and their first planning application to reopen mines in South Cumbria. There were numerous scans of press cuttings about the high-profile public enquiry and Deborah's humiliating defeat. Then, a year later, there were more cuttings about the company's disastrous bad practice, leading to the poisoning of the rivers. Every year since losing the case against them, Deborah had made notes of the company's accounts, and anything else she could find, as she tracked them. She had even noted when they started to deal in scrap metal, big time. She had suspected they were getting the metal illegally. So when she got Ellie's tip-off, it all fell into place. But how had she found out so much about DecorMetal, before she employed Scott as her insider spy? The DecorMetal file had a note, *Ref: Be Profit Investments.*

Be Profit was a company with one sole director, Joanne Butcher. Joanne had always been low-profile and anonymous and she must have been a good alias for Deborah. She probably went along with it, with no idea what Deborah was really doing. A decade before, Be Profit had bought shares in DecorMetal. As one of a very small group of DecorMetal shareholders, Joanne alias Deborah at Be Profit had learned all about the tungsten discovery and the interest shown by the big Arctic America multinational in the Arbiter mines. So Deborah had hired Jarrold to try and see them off. *Ref: Tony Warsbrook.*

Suzy clicked on his file. So, Warsbrook was a major shareholder in DecorMetal. What's more, he had bought the shares back in the early eighties. He had set Deborah up to lose the protestors' case against the mining application, not just to destroy her, but to profit from it. *Ref: Deborah Arbiter, memoir.* It was ironic that after they had won the right to mine, DecorMetal had screwed up, polluting the area so badly that they had to give up the project.

Deborah Arbiter's memoir went back a stage. It gave a personal account of her fight against the company when they first applied to mine in South Cumbria, provoking a huge hostile reaction. At the last minute, just a day before the public enquiry hearing, Tony Warsbrook had told her on the quiet that her expert witness had been discredited. Deborah trusted Tony Warsbrook implicitly and stood her chief witness down, as Warsbrook suggested. As a result she lost. The company won the right to mine. Warsbrook told everyone that she had lost the case deliberately to suit her family because her father had mines he wanted to sell. That was how Warsbrook saw her off as a rival, exactly as the woman in the Midland Hotel had said.

Warsbrook then sat tight for over thirty years, keeping his shareholding in DecorMetal. When they discovered tungsten in the Arbiter mines, he must have thought his patience was rewarded. But Deborah's latest investigations torpedoed that hope. And there was enough in Deborah's files to do to Warsbrook's career what he had done to hers — destroy it. Suzy wasn't a political journalist, but she knew someone who was. This memoir had to go to Rachel.

* * *

There were lots of other files that Suzy wanted to look at but, before exhaustion took over again, she looked at *Contingency, in the case of . . .*

To honour St Jane of Annecy, our patron saint, I have had two ugly platinum ingots brought from South Africa by great uncle George Arbiter made into a halo for the saint. Around the edge I have had inscribed St Jane's motto and a quote from her: 'Offer little things with great love.' The halo can be sold immediately and used to tide the hostel over without delay if we ever hit hard times. St Jane had a sense of humour too! She will know the halo has gone to good use. She can have a cheap tin one from then on.

And then she looked in *Email Drafts*. Deborah had obviously cleared her PC, but she still needed it to send emails. It looked as if she would draft them as documents, move them to the stick, delete them from the PC, then copy and paste them into her email account when she was ready, deleting them again after they were sent.

Most were business emails. But the last draft made Suzy's eyes fill with tears.

My dear friend and colleague, Joanne.

I'm drafting this now, and sending this to you the minute I get back from going on the roof. Yes, that's right! I know you'll try and stop me so I'm not telling you first.

I've heard from Lee the roofer that not only is it safe to go up and look at the beautiful view, but he's spotted something large and bright and shiny up there, which MUST be the missing St Jane's halo. I've been waiting for a chance while you are all in the lounge to go up there and get it! Thank God it's turned up. It's a lot more valuable than you realize — in fact, that halo is our slush fund in case of emergencies! I know, I know — you will say it's my mischievousness to keep the money to hand in this way, but that bright halo will see us through any dark times.

I know you think I should have called the police when I started to suspect Leila of stealing the halo, but I couldn't do that. And if we get it back, then we can forgive her, and no more need be said.

I'm writing this in a hurry before the sun goes down. So sorry for all this secrecy. I know you'll forgive me. I've transferred all my files onto this horrible red lipstick memory stick I keep on my dressing table because of security — someone has been hacking the PCs and I don't want them to get this information.

Tonight while we celebrate, I might not get time to say all this — hence having an email prepared to send you. But thank you. You and Jarrold have been a wonderful help in seeing off a terrible threat to our whole way of life, and I have a lot more to tell you when it all calms down.

I couldn't have done any of it without you. Thank you again for being my wonderful strength and support.

See you soon.

Deborah the Judge

CHAPTER THIRTY-TWO

Hear, O ye kings; give ear, O ye princes; I, even I, will sing unto the Lord; I will sing praise to the Lord God of Israel.
Judges 5:3

Suzy had a drowsy evening and with her medication she slept for another twelve hours. When she woke, she was shaky and uncharacteristically weepy. The clear, unnatural state induced by shock had gone, and the medication had worn off. She hadn't dreamt, but she felt shivery and insecure.

Ro popped in to see her again. 'I'm sure I shouldn't be doing this,' Ro said, 'but I thought you'd like to know how Lee lured Deborah onto the roof. Leila has told us everything.'

Suzy smiled weakly. 'I already know.' She told Ro about the memory stick.

'Suzy, you're amazing. Fancy finding that! We'll need that stick . . .'

But I'll give it to Joanne first, to pass on to you, Suzy thought. Joanne needed to know, from Deborah's own mouth, why her friend had gone on the roof. And how much Deborah loved and valued her.

Ro was saying, 'So like Leila told you in Lee's old garage, she nicked the halo. And Lee planted it on the roof. Then he texted Deborah to tell her it was safe to go up there and that he'd seen something like a big shiny plate. Deborah couldn't resist trying to get it back.'

'And the text messages were still on Deborah's phone . . . that's how you know . . .'

'Yep, Lee made Leila nick the phone and hand it over to Mandy when she went up to St Jane's with the prescriptions. We found Deborah's phone in Mandy's bag, thanks to you. Leila has told us that Lee was all excited about the St Jane's halo. He said it was very valuable. But he couldn't steal it straight off, because he could have been seen by someone sitting under that chestnut tree. So he loosened the halo and Leila stole it after dark when she went out for her usual fag. She put it in a giant handbag. Then she kept it until Lee reappeared to do another job at the hostel. It was part of his 'smart thinking' to tempt Deborah onto the roof.'

'Leila must have been absolutely besotted . . .'

'Yep. But Leila also knew she was deceiving Deborah, who had been so kind to her, and she was very troubled. And Deborah was very shrewd. She suspected Leila and kept quizzing her, under that tree. Deborah's Tree they call it. Another biblical reference, apparently.'

Ah, the 'tree time' mentioned by Adelina, Suzy thought. 'But wouldn't Deborah wonder why the halo was up there on the roof?'

Ro said, 'Maybe she thought Leila squirrelled it away up there while she made contact with the metal thieves. And anyway, Deborah would be compelled to retrieve it as soon as possible. She wouldn't waste time asking questions. She just needed to get it back.'

'And what's happened to the halo now?'

'It's gone. Missing. It fell with Deborah and a load of masonry. Lee was pressuring Leila to find it in the grounds, but she couldn't. He was furious about that. Losing the halo was probably Leila's death warrant as far as Lee was concerned.'

'Poor Leila. Joanne would have been much tougher about wanting the halo theft investigated by the police. But Deborah wanted Leila to be redeemed.' *Deborah and her charges*, Suzy thought. Her family. A mother in Israel, as Joanne had said.

Ro paused and smiled. 'Oh, by the way, Lee was also using Mandy to drug Deborah. He was a real chancer. According to Joanne whenever Mandy delivered prescriptions to the hostel, she always had coffee. She and Deborah were the only ones who took sugar. Lee told us Mandy would pop a ground-up beta blocker into the sugar bowl to give Deborah nasty dizzy spells.' Ro laughed. 'Mandy was drinking tea here last Friday, wasn't she? I'd love a coffee, Suzy. But no sugar!'

* * *

When Ro had gone, there was still one other thing bothering Suzy. Ellie Fox was a clever woman. Her first email to Suzy had been a masterpiece of discretion, giving nothing away to identify either Suzy or Deborah to anyone hacking her computer. And later, because she suspected Lee had access to her PC, she had changed her email address to write to Deborah and must have used another device.

So how did Lee know that Ellie was planning to come to St Jane's?

Then Suzy had an astonishing thought. Perhaps he didn't. Perhaps Lee never knew that Ellie and Deborah were in touch with each other! What had Lee said in the garage? '*You don't get it do you? I had two big consignments coming in and Deborah was onto me and Black. Black was losing it. That's why I killed him. And her too*.' No mention of Ellie at that stage. . . but he had definitely killed her too.

So maybe Lee really had murdered Ellie just because she was going to break off with him. Then he had killed Deborah because she had started nosing around Black, his accomplice. He used the same murder method because he had no reason to know the women were connected. But it was Ellie's tip-off to Deborah which was fatal to him. Ellie was the person who put Deborah onto the metal thief in the first place.

And because of that Deborah had employed Scott Jermyn, who hadn't given up, even after Deborah died. He had started to suspect the roofer, and he knew he was right when he saw Lewis stealing the Hosseins' catalytic converter.

But when Deborah had gone onto the roof that Friday afternoon to retrieve the halo, she must have still thought Lee Lewis was a helpful, happily married man, and that Geoff Black was the metal stealer. She was on the brink of getting the halo back and redeeming Leila, getting Black arrested for theft, stopping the reopening of the Arbiter mines, and most of important of all, disgracing DecorMetal and her own nemesis, Tony Warsbrook.

Victory! Like the Old Testament Deborah's victory over the Canaanites. No wonder she had told Joanne they would have something to celebrate that night! But instead she fell to her death through the parapet which Lee had weakened. And she died like Ellie.

Suzy thought of Lee's cheery smile, his pleasant manner, the way he had seemed so considerate to her. His catch phrase, 'All it needs is a little bit of smart thinking', made you believe he really was doing you a favour. Yet his really 'smart thinking' went into his murders.

Then she felt sick. Maybe Lee had been sizing her up too . . . he had heard what Scott had said during his fake pass at her. Poor Suzy Spencer, harassed about the chimney. Stuck in Tarnfield and hankering for an affair. Fed up with her husband and with rural life. Would Lee have tried her next? He would certainly have wanted to stop her looking too deeply into Deborah's death. Thank goodness he had never known that she had met Ellie!

She found she was shivering uncontrollably. She crawled back into bed and slept again.

When she woke, she felt well enough to get up, call Carrie Fox, and tell her that her sister was really a hero.

* * *

Six weeks later Suzy was recovering, and life was back on track. But different. She had accepted the development job at *Living Lies*, on a part-time basis of three days a week. She was also working as press officer at St Jane's, and developing a podcast with Alan Robie and Stevie Nesbit about the realities of living in the country. They were a surprisingly funny double act.

The first Saturday in December was Alan and Stevie's big civil partnership party. The village was overwhelmed with excitement. The Hosseins were doing the catering, and the gorgeous Winston Harris, Stevie Nesbit's co-star from the hit soap *The Medicine*, was the lead singer. After the shock of Lee Lewis's arrest a month earlier, the party was a tonic for everyone. Leila was out of hospital and back at the hostel. She had not been charged with anything. The stolen halo was never mentioned. Jarrold Arbiter the geologist and Paula Stovey the musician were a public item now, and Jarrold was looking at possible professorial posts at Durham and Bristol. 'Bristol's not far away,' Jarrold had said. 'At least not by Texan standards.'

The church hall was buzzing. Winston's version of 'I Will Survive' had them all rocking and rolling, and the Reverend Linda Finch, their much-loved vicar, made a wonderful speech. 'Alan and Stevie are in our hearts and at the heart of our village life,' she said.

Alan spoke in turn. 'And thank you all for coming. We have all been through such a lot. There has been the tragedy of Deborah Arbiter's death. We have boundless respect for her work. And we remember Geoff Black too. There has been so much violence in our midst. But a major disruption to our way of life has been forestalled by the work of Jarrold Arbiter.' There were cheers and a few whistles from the cast of *The Medicine*, who had no idea what Alan was talking about but loved Jarrold's film star looks.

'And we hope this party will help us move on, without ever forgetting. Stevie and I owe heartfelt thanks to so many people. But I'd particularly like to thank my fellow churchwarden, Robert Clark, for his support. Not to mention our vicar, Linda Finch. And talking of the Church hierarchy, I'm so pleased to welcome here the Archdeacon of Workhaven, the Ven Jim Bentley!'

Everyone turned to look. Even those who had no idea of the bridge being built gave a rousing round of applause. Jim wasn't in his formal gear, but dressed in leather trousers, a charcoal grey shirt and a heavy silver cross. Next to him was Scott Jermyn, in his signature narrow jeans, but with an oversized grey linen jacket and a much more relaxed look.

Alan asked everyone to raise a glass to Tarnfield; there was a roar of approval.

Scott was now back in Tarnfield House, which was up for sale. Joanne had raised a loan, based on the potential profit from selling it. Joanne was at the party in a slinky black satin dress; Suzy wondered how many people would even begin to guess at the scars underneath. But Joanne looked good. Having her son nearby as a local eco-champion was the best outcome she could have hoped for.

Siobhan, formerly known as Chelsea, was there too, linking arms with Tracey, her aunt. Her grandmother, Moira, had been persuaded to come. Moira's husband Geoff had been a rogue, but ultimately a victim, and Moira was not to blame. Alan Robie had played it exactly right in his speech. At the mention of Geoff's name Moira had gasped slightly and wiped her eyes. And now despite everything, she had a lot to look forward to. Before Suzy had relinquished Deborah's lipstick USB to Joanne and ultimately the police, she had found plenty of documentary evidence that Deborah had contacted a woman in a hospice in London, who was probably Moira's daughter and Siobhan's mother. But it was only circumstantial.

At the party, Siobhan crept up and whispered, 'He's going to do it.' Her face shone.

'That's great news,' said Suzy.

'Yes! My dad disappeared and my stepdad was crap, but my grandad is going to do this for me! Isn't that wonderful? Some men are all right.' Moira had approached her old boyfriend about taking the DNA test. Although he was terminally ill, he wanted to prove before he died that Siobhan was his granddaughter. With samples from both grandparents, a test would prove well-nigh conclusive.

After Winston finished his first set, Stevie took Suzy to meet him. 'Wow!' said Winston. 'So you're the executive producer of one of the best shows on TV! I love it. I think it's time for me to come out to everyone. Have you ever thought of doing a celebrity version of *Living Lies*?'

'Well, actually I have . . .'

The next day, Winston sang the 'Libera me, Domine' from Fauré's *Requiem* to a packed All Saints Church. The money raised from the party, and that day's congregation, would be enough to pay for the church roof repairs — and for Tagpaint treatment.

* * *

Nine months later, 12 August was the saint's day of St Jane of Annecy, patron of those separated from their children. Suzy suspected that the use of St Jane as the hostel name had been a caprice of Deborah's when she bought the statue. It was true, the Judge did have a mischievous sense of humour. The statue was a statement. It made clear that the hostel had a religious base. It gave Deborah the idea of focusing on older women who had nowhere to go. It cemented Deborah's connection with the Savoy countryside which she loved, and it had also given her a chance to get rid of the ugly platinum ingots and use them as the halo.

The hostel had written off the halo now. It had never turned up. But the potential sale of Tarnfield House, at a much higher price than Deborah would ever have forecast, meant that the hostel was financially secure, and its unique service protected.

On a personal level for Suzy, the celebrity-themed *Living Lies Big Time* had been a major success with Winston Harris as the first star, and she was launching another *Living Truth* podcast, based on the experiences of Ro and Linda, about country crime . . . and redemption.

The weather was glorious, hot and still. But it was a bittersweet day. Joanne, Suzy, Leila, Moira, Adelina and the other residents gathered under the chestnut tree. Joanne had asked Siobhan to bring out glasses of prosecco. But before the toast, she asked everyone to remember that more than a hundred women die every year in England and Wales because of domestic abuse. Femicide was an overlooked crime. They were all silent for a moment.

Then Joanne waved Siobhan over. The glasses were beautiful old crystal from the Arbiter glassware, the wine punctured by tiny popping bubbles which caught the bright sunlight, like the large shiny tray where Siobhan balanced the glasses.

'Siobhan!' Suzy almost shouted. 'That tray . . .'

'I know!' Siobhan beamed. 'Isn't it beautiful! It's a bit thick and heavy for a tray, but it's very shiny now I've polished it. It's got this nice writing on, about small fings mattering. Like what I do. I love it. I found it in the hawthorn hedge last winter. Once the leaves were all down, you could see it. I don't know what it was doing there. It took a lot of cleaning up. I saved it for a special occasion like today.'

Suzy started to laugh, and Joanne suddenly realized and started to laugh too. 'It's the halo, Siobhan. It's St Jane's halo. Oh Leila — now we have it back . . .' Leila started to cry, and Adelina put her arm around her friend's thin shoulders.

'It's Deborah's doing,' Adelina said. 'And, oh, look . . .' The wine had attracted a large bumble bee, which hovered over the halo. 'It's a bee. That's what Deborah means in Hebrew. Deborah, Judge and Prophet. Her name means "The Bee".'

'She's here,' whispered Joanne. The bee hovered for a minute and then, in the way bees have, it suddenly swerved sideways, upwards and into the tree, out of sight.

'Well, that's that. I'm getting whimsical in my old age. Come on,' Joanne said, 'time to go and get some of Siobhan's delicious nibbles in the kitchen. Maybe we can have another ceremony when we reattach the halo.'

'I'd check out how much it's worth first,' Suzy said quietly. 'Deborah meant you to spend the money and give St Jane a tin halo instead! She won't mind!' The platinum would be another boost to the hostel funds. What an investment it was.

An investment.

And then Suzy suddenly realized. What had Adelina said? Deborah, Judge and Prophet. The company Deborah had formed to track DecorMetal was called Be Profit. It had seemed a strange name for a company set up by Deborah. But when you said it out loud it was 'Bee Prophet'. Of course. Nice one, Deborah! And Tony Warsbrook, now disgraced, would never have sussed out who was on his case. It was Deborah's victory in the end.

Suzy drained the last of the bubbles from her glass and followed the smiling, chatting residents from Deborah's Tree back into the hostel.

THE END

HISTORY OF DEBORAH AND THE JUDGES

Judges is the name of the seventh book of the Old Testament, the Hebrew scriptures. The book covers the history of ancient Israel from about 1200 to 1020 BC. Moses had led the children of Israel out of slavery in Egypt; he died just as they were about to enter Canaan, the 'promised land'. So Joshua took over from Moses in about 1250 BC and led the invasion of Canaan. By the time Joshua died in about 1200 BC, the children of Israel had occupied much of the land.

Until Saul became the first king of Israel in about 1020 BC there was no settled political structure or authority. The tribes were united only by their loyalty to the God of the Covenant. The final verse of Judges says, 'In those days there were no kings in Israel; everyone did what was right in his own eyes.' The various tribes which later came to make up Israel were consolidating their settlement in Canaan, especially in the central hill country, but there was still a patchwork of Canaanite city states on the plains. Inevitably, there was conflict.

When threatened, the tribes came together in concerted action — and this needed leadership. The Book of Judges describes how a series of charismatic individuals, endowed with God's spirit, rose up as needed to lead the defence of

God's chosen people, being recognized as having authority beyond the territory of their own tribes. There were six such leaders: Othniel, Ehud, Deborah, Gideon, Jephthah and — perhaps the best known to us — Samson. These were the 'major judges'. There were also 'minor judges' whose role was primarily administering justice, not having a military role. The Hebrew word for 'judge' (*shofet*) applied to both major and minor judges. The role was not hereditary: God chose individuals to endow with his spirit as needed.

The Book of Judges presents the Israelites' failure to occupy the promised land as the result of disobedience, violation of the covenant relationship with God, who was using the Canaanites as an instrument to punish his people. Each major judge's story follows mostly a six-fold form:

Israel did evil in the sight of the Lord.
They were delivered into the hand of an enemy.
They cried out to the Lord.
The Lord raised up a deliverer.
The enemy was subdued.
The land had rest.

Even though in each story it is 'Israel' that did evil in the sight of the Lord, it is clear from the detail that these were local skirmishes involving just a few tribes. The conflicts are presented as holy wars in which the spirit of God enabled people to accomplish feats of victory against the powers threatening his plans.

* * *

The account of Deborah occupies chapters 4 and 5 of Judges. She is the only female judge in the book, and is also described as a 'prophetess' — that is, someone who knew the will of God and passed it on to the people. She held court under a palm tree in the hill country, settling the disputes which people brought to her. The name Deborah means 'bee'.

The story describes Deborah's triumph over Sisera, the commander of a Canaanite army fighting for Jabin, king of Hazor. This was the battle of Megiddo in about 1125 BC. With the help of 900 iron chariots, Jabin had been oppressing the Israelites for twenty years. Megiddo is about eight miles south-west of Nazareth, in the plain of Jezreel. It is also known as Armageddon, which means 'hill of Megiddo'. The plain of Jezreel was on an important trade route linking Egypt with Assyria and Mesopotamia. The area was under Canaanite control, guarded by a fortress at Megiddo.

The action started with a meeting between Deborah and her army commander Barak (which means 'thunderbolt'). She gave him a message from God, that Barak was to go to Mount Tabor with 10,000 men from the tribes of Naphtali and Zebulun. God would lure Sisera and his army to the Kishon river and deliver them to Barak's forces. Barak said, 'I'll go only if you come with me.' Deborah agreed to go, and told Barak that Sisera would be delivered into the hand of a woman.

While Barak's army gathered on the slopes of Mount Tabor, Sisera assembled his forces, with their 900 chariots, by the Kishon river in the valley of Jezreel, where the chariots would have space to manoeuvre. But God sent a huge rainstorm which caused the river to burst its banks. The Canaanite chariots and troops became bogged down in the muddy clay, a sitting target for Barak's forces as they came down the hill. All Sisera's army fell by the sword. (A similar thing happened in AD 1799, when the flooded Kishon river helped Napoleon defeat a Turkish army.)

But Sisera escaped the slaughter on foot and arrived at the tent of a woman called Jael. She was married to 'Heber the Kenite'. The Kenites were a clan of metal-workers, and were allies of king Jabin of Hazor. Perhaps Heber worked on the iron chariots. So Sisera would not have been surprised to get a friendly reception: Jael said, 'Come, my lord, come right in. Don't be afraid.' She gave him some milk to drink, put a covering over him, and he fell asleep exhausted. But Jael was probably an Israelite; she certainly saw Sisera as the enemy.

As he slept, she took a tent peg and a hammer, and killed Sisera by driving the peg through his temple.

* * *

The defeat of Sisera's army marked the end of united Canaanite resistance to the children of Israel, who could now pass freely through the plain of Jezreel. But there was still plenty of opposition from surrounding nations such as Midianites and Philistines. These conflicts, and the champions God raised to deal with them, are described in the rest of Judges.

ACKNOWLEDGEMENTS

There are many threads to this book, and I've imposed on many friends, asking advice. I would like to thank in chronological order Fred Baynes, John Watson, Nicki Cloutman, Thomas Hardin, Pippa Tuckman, David Gibson, Dianne Browning and Kieran Davies. The expertise is theirs. The errors are mine.

I would like to thank Lesley Beames for reading and advising on the manuscript.

Heather Parker, the children's worker at St Andrew's Church, Barnsbury, first alerted me to the wonderful story of Deborah the Judge.

I have lost touch with Victoria Kingston, who encouraged me to resume writing fifteen years ago, but should she read this I would like to thank her again.

It's customary in acknowledgements to say that all the characters are fictional and bear no resemblance to any person, which is true of all but one of the characters in this book. The nicest bits of Robert owe a lot to my husband Richard Parker.

Thank you all very much.

ALSO BY LIS HOWELL

THE SUZY SPENCER MYSTERIES
Book 1: THE FLOWER ARRANGER AT ALL SAINTS
Book 2: THE CHORISTER AT THE ABBEY
Book 3: THE DEATH OF A TEACHER
Book 4: THE JUDGE AT SAINT JANE'S

Thank you for reading this book.

If you enjoyed it please leave feedback on Amazon or Goodreads, and if there is anything we missed or you have a question about, then please get in touch. We appreciate you choosing our book.

Founded in 2014 in Shoreditch, London, we at Joffe Books pride ourselves on our history of innovative publishing. We were thrilled to be shortlisted for Independent Publisher of the Year at the British Book Awards.

www.joffebooks.com

We're very grateful to eagle-eyed readers who take the time to contact us. Please send any errors you find to corrections@joffebooks.com. We'll get them fixed ASAP.

Made in the USA
Columbia, SC
12 June 2025

59312774R00195